# The QUEEN of Sorrow

ALSO BY SARAH BETH DURST

THE QUEENS OF RENTHIA

*The Queen of Blood*
*The Reluctant Queen*

# The Queen of Sorrow

BOOK THREE OF THE QUEENS OF RENTHIA

## SARAH BETH DURST

HARPER Voyager

*An Imprint of HarperCollins Publishers*

THE QUEEN OF SORROW. Copyright © 2018 by Sarah Beth Durst. All rights reserved. Printed in the United States of America. No part of this book may be used or reproduced in any manner whatsoever without written permission except in the case of brief quotations embodied in critical articles and reviews. For information, address HarperCollins Publishers, 195 Broadway, New York, NY 10007.

HarperCollins books may be purchased for educational, business, or sales promotional use. For information, please email the Special Markets Department at SPsales@harpercollins.com.

Harper Voyager and design are trademarks of HarperCollins Publishers LLC.

FIRST EDITION

*Designed by Paula Russell Szafranski*

*Map illustration by Ashley P. Halsey*

Library of Congress Cataloging-in-Publication Data has been applied for.

ISBN 978-0-06-241338-3

18  19  20  21  22   LSC   10  9  8  7  6  5  4  3  2  1

FOR LYNNE AND DAVID

# The
# QUEEN
## of Sorrow

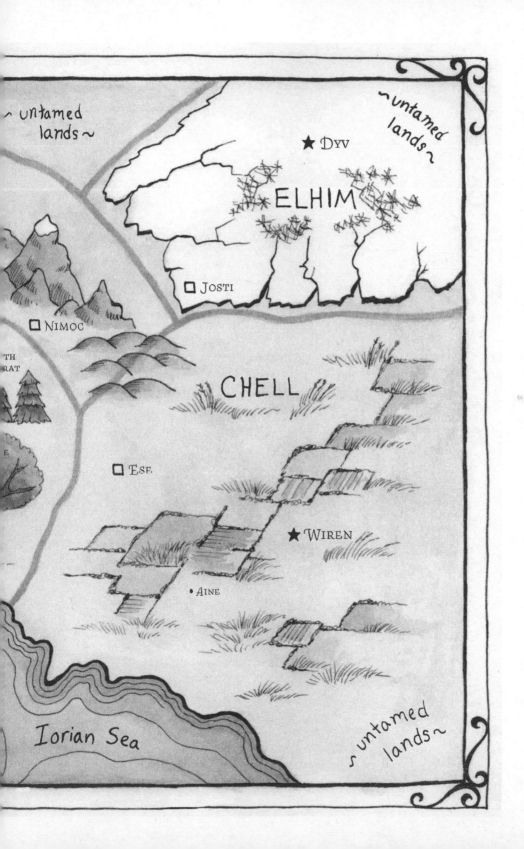

*E*verything will be better soon, Daleina thought.
    She'd climbed to the top of the canopy and was balancing on two slender branches. Spread before her, the forests of Aratay looked magnificent. Red, orange, and yellow leaves blazed like candle flames in the late-afternoon sun.

This high up, she could see across all of western Aratay, even as far as the untamed lands beyond the border. Shrouded by a thick mist, the untamed lands looked as if they were boiling. As she watched, a mountain burst out of the soupy haze, and then it crumbled. Beyond the borders of the world, everything was as ephemeral as a sand castle washed away by waves.

So long as Aratay had a queen, it would never be like that.

*And right now, we have two!*

It was a heady thought, because with two queens . . . *We can fix all that was broken.*

Below her, she heard Naelin—the second queen of Aratay—huffing as she climbed up the tree. Daleina wanted to tell her to call a spirit to fly her up to the canopy, but she didn't bother. She knew how Naelin would feel about that. The other queen despised using spirits for "nonessential purposes." *In truth, she's afraid of them*, Daleina thought.

And honestly, it was a sensible way to feel.

Today, though, Daleina didn't want to be sensible. She closed her eyes and took a deep breath of sweet, fresh air. *Today we begin!*

The branches jiggled as Naelin popped her head up between the leaves. "And why can't"—she puffed—"we do this midforest?"

Daleina tilted her head back to feel the sun on her face. It was as warm as Hamon's caress. She stuffed that lovely thought away, to save for later, when she wasn't with Naelin. "Because it's beautiful up here."

"Beauty." Naelin humphed and heaved herself up. "Sure, it's beautiful. But it's also *reckless*, and we have no heirs."

Daleina flinched—she was the last person who needed to be reminded of *that*—but she refused to let it destroy her mood. Opening her eyes, she pointed to a hole in the canopy. As she'd hoped, from this high up, it was easy to spot the damaged areas. "We'll start with that one."

Once there had been a tree filling that hole, probably a grand one with sprawling branches and dense leaves, but now . . . The barren patch looked like a black island in the sea of green. Merecot had left countless dead zones in the wake of her invasion. *Yet another thing I can't quite forgive her for.* She'd wounded Daleina's beloved Aratay when she'd attacked—killing its spirits killed the land. They'd pushed the queen of Semo out, but her influence was still visible throughout the country.

The time for fighting was over. Now was the time for healing.

"Come on." Dropping down, Daleina scampered over the branch until she found a wire path. She hooked a carabiner over the wire. "The closer we are, the easier it will be."

"Can't we just—"

Kicking off, Daleina sailed through the leaves. She whooped, and whatever the other queen was saying was lost in the rush of wind. She knocked yellow leaves off their branches, and they filled the air, making her feel as if she were flying through a cyclone of gold.

She reached the next tree quickly, landing on a platform. Unhooking herself from the wire, she waited for Naelin to join her.

"You're torturing me on purpose," Naelin said as she landed.

She was sweating, her doelike brown-and-gray hair sticking to her forehead. Her cheeks were flushed.

"Not on purpose." Daleina crouched, peering through the trees. "It's just a happy accident." She flashed her a smile, to show she was only joking. Of course, she wasn't entirely sure that Naelin *had* a sense of humor. They hadn't spent much time together, at least not without either Naelin's children or Ven.

*No matter. I thought it was funny.*

A rope bridge led from the platform toward the barren area—very convenient. She wondered why . . . *Oh. A village must have been there.* Her heart sank. When the tree died, the villagers' homes had been destroyed. Maybe lives lost. Moving more slowly, Daleina led the way from the tree to the bridge. She tried not to imagine how many could have lived there.

*I did the best I could*, she told herself, not for the first time.

Per usual, it didn't make her feel better.

The nation wasn't the only thing that needed healing.

The ropes were mossy and frayed, and the bridge swayed and bounced as she and Naelin crossed to the next platform. From there, they could see the barren area: roughly a circle, the width of one of the massive oak trees that commonly held homes in their branches. Below, very far below, the ground was dry and gray, lifeless. It was ringed by thick underbrush that wouldn't creep even an inch into the dead land—*Not until we fix it*, Daleina thought.

Daleina reached into the pack she carried and pulled out a coil of rope. She selected a sturdy limb and secured the rope. She then swung herself onto it and began rappelling down the trunk of the tree.

"Really?" Naelin said.

"Or we could call a spirit and fly."

With a sigh, the other queen began rappelling too.

Despite the reminder of her losses, it was nice to be out of the palace, away from the courtiers and counselors, away from the minutiae of running Aratay. Only one problem lay before her today: healing the land. *And I can do that.*

She could have done it from a distance—as queen, she had the power. And Naelin certainly had more than enough power at her disposal. The other woman practically radiated strength. But for this first barren patch, Daleina wanted to do it in person, to show Naelin how it was done. "It's a necessary training exercise," she'd told Ven. As champion, he couldn't object to additional training for the new queen, especially since Naelin had jumped from woodswoman to queen with barely any instruction.

He'd seen right through Daleina, of course. "You just want a break from the throne."

"It is an uncomfortable chair," she'd agreed.

"I'll hunt for more pillows while you're gone." And to demonstrate, he'd notched an arrow into his bow and shot it into the nearest couch. Down feathers had puffed into the air.

Halfway down the tree, Daleina and Naelin switched from the rope to a ladder that had been built into the trunk, presumably for the villagers to descend to the forest floor to forage for berries and hunt for deer. It was easier climbing the ladder, and soon they reached the ground and waded through the bushes to the barren area.

It was as lifeless as Daleina had thought. Or, actually, *more* so. She'd seen what drought could do, but even then, there was always a sense of *something* in the soil. Now, though, she felt nothing as dust swirled around their feet while they walked. Kneeling, she scooped up a handful of the dry earth, letting the dead grains fall through her fingers. Sitting on a rock, Naelin drank from her canteen. A few drops landed on the ground and were quickly sucked into the earth.

"When the spirit, or spirits, who belonged to this tree died, the land died," Daleina said. "Bringing it back to life is more than just instructing a water spirit to bring rain or a tree spirit to plant a few seeds. We have to *tie* spirits to the land—otherwise it either stays a dead zone or, worse, the spirits run rampant over it, like in the untamed lands. The trick is that all the nearby spirits are already tied to their own trees or streams or bits of earth, so they'll need to be encouraged to claim more." She caught Naelin's expression out of the corner of her eye. The other queen's lips were curved up in amusement. "What?"

She was definitely laughing. "Nothing."

"This is serious. Homes could have been here. People could have died."

"I know. It's . . . For a minute, you sounded exactly like Headmistress Hanna."

Daleina sighed. "Yet I'm young enough to be your daughter?" She was half Naelin's age and had been queen for only a year longer than Naelin, but she was still more experienced. She'd attended the Northeast Academy, trained for months with Champion Ven, and fought spirits at the Coronation Massacre. It was hard not to wave those credentials in front of the older queen.

Naelin winced. "I wasn't going to say that quite so bluntly, but yes." She put her canteen back in her pack and stood. "I'm sorry, Your Majesty. Teach me how to heal the land."

"Call to the spirits, the nearby ones. Draw them here. And then give them the land. They *want* to be connected to Renthia. They just can't do it without a queen."

"You know, that sounds pretty, but it doesn't actually make sense."

"Look, when you became queen, when the spirits chose you, what did you feel?"

"Besides regret?"

Daleina resisted rolling her eyes. "Yes."

"Power. Lots of it. Like I'd been whispering my whole life and could suddenly shout."

*Good. Yes.* "And . . . ?"

"And I felt the spirits, all of them, across Aratay. I could see their thoughts and feel their feelings. Like they were . . . part of me now." Naelin visibly shuddered.

"Exactly. You're connected to them. Linked to them. We both are. That's the difference between queens and, well, anyone else. So now you have to link them to the land the same way they're linked to us." If Daleina concentrated hard enough, she could feel cobweb-like strands that connected her to the spirits. All a queen had to do to fix the barren area was stretch those strands between a few of those spirits and the barren land. The problem was, she couldn't explain it any better than that. Naelin either felt it or didn't. Daleina was confident in the older woman, though— she was being honest with herself when she noted how powerful the other queen was. Naelin had started out much stronger than Daleina. When she became queen, that impressive power was amplified a hundredfold. "Just try. Do as I do."

"But—"

"Don't be afraid. There's nothing here you can hurt." *All the dying is already done*, she thought. "Come on. We'll do it together."

On her knees, Daleina plunged her hands into the dry dirt. She concentrated, reaching for the closest spirits. She felt them just beyond the circle: a tiny earth spirit burrowing with the worms, a tree spirit hidden between two nearby tree roots, a water spirit skipping through a stream. Gently, she called to them. *Come play? Play here?*

And then she felt a *whoosh*.

*Uh-oh.*

"Daleina?"

"You called too many," Daleina said flatly. It wasn't the first time this had happened. Ven had worked hard with Naelin on her control. Apparently, though, it was still an issue.

"Yes. It appears so."

"Too many" was a bit of an understatement. Spirits *flooded* the barren area: tiny dandelion-fluff air spirits filled the air, massive eagle-winged air spirits blocked the sky, mud-coated earth spirits dug out of the ground, and various tree spirits—some the size of acorns and others the size of a man or a wild boar—ran along the branches toward them. Daleina felt rain spatter her face from the air spirits and a chill wind as a solitary ice spirit zipped past.

"Calm them down!" Daleina shouted.

"But they're bonding with the land! Isn't that what we want?"

She was right—Daleina could feel the dozens of spirits reaching for the air and the soil . . . *No! Stop!* There were too many trying to claim too small a space! They'd—

The spirits attacked one another.

An air spirit with talons shredded a feathered spirit. Snarling, the earth spirits leapt at one another. A bear-shaped spirit made of rocks pounded its boulder fists into a bark-coated tree spirit.

She felt their rage course through her, and for an instant, she was *there*, in the grove again, with her friends dying around her, and Daleina felt herself screaming and she couldn't stop.

*Kill. Hurt. Destroy.*

The spirits screamed inside her head and then turned on her. She felt their white-hot hate sear into her, and she felt pain as they slashed into her skin. Caught in her memory, she couldn't form a clear thought to—

*STOP!*

Coming from outside, from Naelin, the word reverberated through her—Daleina felt it echo through all the spirits and into her, and as one, the spirits halted, as if frozen. She felt arms around her shoulders as Naelin gathered her up and rocked her against her chest as if she were a small child. She didn't resist. She let herself, for a moment, be comforted.

But only for a moment. She was still queen, and she had a duty. Daleina pried open her eyes. She breathed deeply, slowly, as she pushed the memory back down into the tiny box in her mind where she kept it, the day she'd saved her world but failed to save her friends. "Choose a few," she croaked, "and send the rest away."

"How?"

"Reach through your bond to them. Feel it like it's a rope tethering you to them, and then imagine you're tying that rope to the air and the earth. As to the rest, praise their home. Make them *want* to return. Think of the forest, the streams, the rocks, the sky, and make them want to be there." As she spoke, she felt her heart return to its normal thump.

She felt the spirits obeying Naelin and tried to keep her own mind as calm and clear as possible. She let Naelin do it all—keeping her distance, Daleina sensed the spirits struggle and then cave. Naelin had a different style: she ordered more than coaxed. But it worked.

"I'm doing it!" Naelin cried.

"Great. Now fix a picture of the forest in your mind, and tell the spirits to make it grow like that here."

She felt raindrops hit her cheeks. Faster and harder, until it poured down on the dry earth and the two queens. Beneath her, she felt the soil soften, and she sensed the earth spirits swimming through it, drawing life back into it.

An air spirit flitted overhead, dropping seeds into the wet earth, and three tree spirits scurried to the seeds. Green sprouted throughout the barren area. Moss spread and lichen blossomed across the rocks. Vines chased over the forest floor, toward the queens. Daleina felt them curl around her wrists and ankles. "Um, Naelin?"

But Naelin's eyes were closed, her expression blissful.

Daleina elected to stay silent.

She watched as the vines weaved themselves up Naelin's legs. Moving slowly so as not to make a sound, Daleina shook a vine off her arm. Another vine wrapped around her stomach, and flowers bloomed around her waist. She let them stay.

Soon, the grove was draped in color: a cluster of purple flowers, vines filled with yellow and white blooms, and a dancing stream that skipped over green mossy rocks. The luscious scent of honeysuckle filled the air.

Daleina saw Naelin open her eyes and smile, looking all around her.

And then she saw Naelin notice the vines that bound them both.

Daleina felt her lips twitch. *Don't laugh.* She reached out with her mind and caught the attention of a tiny tree spirit with twig arms and a birdlike beaked face. It hopped over to her and began to peck at the vines with its beak as it untangled them with its long stick fingers.

Naelin met her eyes.

And they both burst out laughing.

*I think . . . we can do this*, Daleina thought. With the strength of two queens, they'd heal what was broken, restore the harvest, and bring an era of peace and prosperity to all their people.

*So long as Naelin can avoid destroying everything.*

# CHAPTER 2

I'm home!" Naelin called, and then, bemused, halted beneath an exquisite archway of carved wooden leaves inlaid with polished blue river stones. *Exactly when did I start thinking of the palace as "home"?* She supposed it was close enough these days.

Home was wherever her children were.

And these days, they all lived in the white-tree palace in the heart of the arboreal city of Mittriel, the capital of Aratay—a long way from their tiny cottage tucked in the outer forest. *Life takes strange turns,* Naelin thought. "Erian? Llor? I'm home!"

"They're with their father," Ven said, coming out of the bedroom. He had a towel wrapped around his waist, and droplets of water clung to the scars on his skin before dripping off his muscles. He was drying his hair with a second towel, and clumps of his hair were spiked up, stuck together with water. "Meant to greet you at the gate, but I didn't know when you'd return—sorry."

Crossing the room, she plucked the second towel from his hand and dried water from his neck before smoothing his hair to the side. "We came in through the tower, so you would have missed us anyway." She breathed in the smell of soap as he hooked his arm around her waist and drew her up against him. He was still damp, but she didn't mind. She felt herself smiling—he always seemed to bring a smile to her lips, even without saying or doing anything particularly smile-worthy.

Right now, though, so close to him, she had plenty of reason to smile.

"Everything okay?" He nuzzled her cheek.

*More than okay*, she thought. She kissed his neck below his beard. "Yes." Her fingers slid down to the knot in the towel. "Daleina and I fixed twelve barren areas. By the last few, I was even able to avoid any violence."

"Lovely. Avoiding violence is a plus for any day." He ran his fingers through her hair and kissed her. He tasted like pine tea and mint, and his beard was as soft as moss. She loosened the towel around his waist—and then heard the guard at the door:

"Your Highnesses." *The children were back!* "Master Renet." And her ex-husband. "Queen Naelin has recently returned," the guard told them. "She will be pleased to see you."

Naelin shoved the towel at Ven and shooed him back into the bathroom. "Quickly! Come out when you're presentable." He was smiling at her, silently laughing as she closed the door behind him. She knew she was wearing the same silly smile. She flattened her hair down and smoothed her shirt as she turned to face the door.

It swung open and her children, Erian and Llor, spilled inside. They raced to her—Erian's legs were longer, but Llor was like an arrow. He embedded himself in her waist, wrapping his arms firmly around her with so much force that she let out an "Oof!" Erian, only slightly more dignified at age ten, stretched over Llor to hug her.

Llor's words spilled out like water from a spigot. "Mama, Mama, Mama! Father tried to take us out into Mittriel, but the guards wouldn't let him, not without your permission, so we went to the treasure pavilion instead, but it was boring so we went to the weapons room but the guards wouldn't let me play with any of the swords, even though I promised to be careful, and then we went to the kitchen and ate pie. I don't like cherry pie. It's slimy. Like slugs. Cherry pie is red slug pie."

"Don't be disgusting, Llor," Erian scolded him. "Besides, how do you know what a slug tastes like? Have you ever eaten one?"

"I will if you dare me to."

"I dare you."

"I double-dare you," he said, then cackled with delight. "Now you have to!"

"Do not."

Still in the doorway, Renet lingered with a wistful expression on his face. Naelin knew he wanted her to invite him inside, but she wanted to be alone with Erian and Llor. She got precious little time with them, in between the schedule the palace seneschal set for her and Daleina's requests. "Thank you, Renet," she said, and hoped he understood.

He took a cautious step into the room.

"I'll bring the children by to visit tomorrow. You may go." Inwardly, she winced at herself. That was a terrible way to talk to the man who'd fathered her children. Later, when she had more time, she'd explain . . . *Except there's no good way to say "Thanks, but I don't want you in my life anymore."* Leaving him should have been enough to communicate that. She shouldn't have to keep saying it. *Maybe someday it will be easier.*

*Yes . . . maybe.*

It would be nice if they could be . . . if not friends, then at least two people who didn't conjure up a mess of sadness, guilt, and regret for what could have been but wasn't. That was easier said than done, though. So much history couldn't easily be rewritten. She supposed it would take time.

She left the words unsaid as the guard escorted him out, and he shot one last forlorn look at her, Erian, and Llor. Pushing the issue of Renet aside for now, Naelin hugged her children tighter. "I missed you today!" she told them.

"We don't like when you leave," Erian said seriously.

"You're safe here. All the guards know to watch for you, and if any spirits were to . . . misbehave, Queen Daleina and I would feel it and hurry back. You don't have to worry anymore. Nothing's going to happen to you."

Llor rolled his eyes—he hadn't quite mastered the expression, and his eyes darted back and forth before they went up in an exaggerated way. Naelin schooled her face into bland seriousness so he wouldn't think she was laughing at him. "We aren't *scared*," he said. "We miss you!"

"Then I have good news: how would you like to come with me on a little trip?"

Erian's face lit up like a firemoss lantern. "You'll bring us with you?" She hugged Naelin again. "Yes, please!"

Naelin laughed. "You didn't even ask me where."

Behind her, the bathroom door opened, and she twisted to see Ven emerge, fully dressed, his hair still wet but brushed, sloppily, to the side. Both Ven and Llor paid about the same amount of attention to their hair. "I'll ask, then," Ven said. "Where?"

Llor catapulted himself across the room and into Ven's arms.

Ven caught him neatly and swung him in a circle. "Hey, tiger."

"Roar!" Llor growled.

"To the villages in the outer forest," Naelin said. "It's Queen Daleina's idea. She thinks the people will feel better if they meet me. I can reassure them that the invasion is over, that we're at peace, and that we'll be helping restore the harvest and rebuild their homes before winter. I can also heal any barren areas I come across." Privately, she thought she'd be more useful healing the dead zones than parading in front of people, but she hadn't argued. Well, not much. She *had* insisted on no entourage. Just her, Ven, the children, and Renet (who wasn't an ideal choice, but she'd need someone to watch the children when she and Ven were working). Also the wolf, Bayn (who *was* an ideal choice—the children adored him, and Naelin felt safer when the wolf was near).

Llor tugged on Ven's sleeve. "Ven, Ven, Ven! If you double-dare someone, and they refuse, what do you do?"

"Challenge them to a duel." Ven then flipped Llor horizontal and charged forward at Erian, holding Llor like he was a battering ram. Llor shrieked with delight, roared, and clawed at the air as Erian scampered over a table with gorgeous carvings of flowers and over a couch with golden embroidered edges until she reached the fireplace. She brandished a fire poker like a sword.

Naelin swooped forward and intercepted the poker. "Bad idea." She replaced the poker with a pillow. "Better idea." She then scooped up a pillow of her own, and both she and Erian attacked Ven and Llor with pillows.

"Retreat!" Ven shouted, and then, carrying Llor, raced into the bathroom.

Naelin and Erian collapsed on the couch, laughing. "Nicely done," Naelin told her.

"You'll really take us with you?" Erian asked. "You won't leave us behind, like today?" In her daughter's eyes, Naelin saw a hint of fear—it had been lurking there ever since the invasion and never seemed to go fully away.

Naelin cupped her daughter's face in her hands. "There may be days when I have things I have to do and people I need to help. But I'll never leave you," she told her, trying to make her believe, trying to erase that touch of fear. "Ever."

VEN KNELT BESIDE THE WOLF AND RUFFLED THE FUR ON HIS neck. "Ready for another run, old friend?" He chuckled at Bayn's expression, which said as clearly as words, *More ready than you, old man.*

He stood as Bayn trotted down the bridge away from the palace. Watching him, Ven didn't bother to tell him to be careful—the wolf knew the forest as well as he did. He'd find his own way northwest and most likely be there at the first village on their list, waiting for them, thumping his tail impatiently at the slowness of humans.

Behind him, Ven heard his traveling companions—Erian and Llor teasing each other, Naelin worrying over whether they'd packed enough socks, and Renet bragging about his woodsman skills.

*Maybe I should have told Bayn to let us get a head start.*

Naelin joined him. "I think we have everything."

He surveyed their packs, which were bulging. "Are you sure?" he asked mildly. "Perhaps we could squeeze in a mattress? Or a dozen more gowns?"

She fixed him with a glare. "It wasn't me. The palace caretakers insisted."

He loved that glare. It made him want to wrap her in his arms and kiss her until she smiled again. Turning that glare into one of her smiles was his new favorite pastime. *Later.* "All right then. Let's go. We should reach northwest Aratay in four days."

IT TOOK THEM EIGHT DAYS.

Naelin loved every second of it, even with the overstuffed packs, even with Renet and his sad puppy eyes, even with Erian and Llor daring each other to more ridiculous climbing feats that Ven would have to rescue them from.

For eight days, she was just Naelin, an ordinary woodswoman, traveling through the forest with her family.

And then they reached the first village in northwest Aratay. Bayn was waiting for them just outside the village, looking extra-plump—judging from the chicken feather stuck to his fur, she gathered he'd helped himself to the village's hospitality. She made a mental note to reimburse them for whatever he'd eaten.

"Wear your crown," Renet told her.

"I'm not in the palace," Naelin said. She knew he was right: she was supposed to be introducing herself as their new queen, which meant gowns and crowns. But she hated the way it poked her scalp.

*Admit it,* she told herself. *You hate what it represents.*

She waved off his argument before he could make it, dug the crown out of her pack, and stuck it on her head. Erian arranged her hair beneath it, and Llor solemnly handed her a flower. She tucked it amid the silver filigree on the crown.

"You can do this," Ven told her.

In a low voice so only he could hear, she asked, "What if they don't believe I'm the queen?" Despite living in the palace, despite being able to sense all the spirits in Aratay, despite the incredible (and rather terrifying) boost in power she'd felt ever since the moment the spirits had accepted her as their queen, she still didn't feel royal. She was just a woodswoman, with two children, graying hair, bony elbows, and calluses on her palms from years of mending the shingles on her own roof and scrubbing her own floors. *What if these people sense that?* She was supposed to reassure them that all was well in Aratay, but how could she do that when she didn't feel reassured? In fact, now that she was here, near a village that was not so different from where they used to live in East Everdale, she felt more like an impostor than she ever had.

For decades, she had known full well who she was—had *liked* who she was—and now she was supposed to be someone new. It made her feel like a teenager again, which was not a phase she had any interest in reliving. *It's bad enough that I'll have to relive it through Erian's and Llor's eyes.*

Ven shrugged. "Just instruct the spirits to eat a few of them. They won't doubt you then."

She shot him a withering glare.

He grinned back at her.

"You're impossible," she informed him.

"I think the word you're looking for is 'hilarious.' Or you could go with 'supportive.' 'Ruggedly handsome'? 'Very strong'?"

Llor giggled. "'Very silly'?"

Ven nodded solemnly. "Also 'ticklish.'"

"Really? You?" Llor's mouth dropped open.

Ven poked his elbow. "Right there."

Both Erian and Llor attacked him. He collapsed dramatically, writhing on the ground and howling with laughter.

Naelin watched them for a moment. Out of the corner of her eye, she saw Bayn watching them as well with a long-suffering expression on his lupine face. *Ridiculous humans*, he seemed to be saying. *Playing like pups when there's work to be done.* Her lips twitched, and she and Bayn exchanged glances.

Leaving Ven with the children and Renet, Queen Naelin of Aratay and the great forests of Renthia swept into the village with only a wolf by her side.

No one doubted who she was.

THEY MOVED ON, AND IN EACH VILLAGE THEY WENT TO, THE PEOPLE of Aratay rushed to welcome her. They insisted on housing her and her companions in their finest home, feeding them a feast, and entertaining them with tales and songs. As word spread ahead of them, the villagers would be eagerly anticipating their queen's arrival, ready to fawn over her—and to present all their requests in interminable meetings with the village leaders.

By their eighth stop, a tiny village called Redleaf, she barely had a few seconds alone with Erian and Llor each day before she was whisked away to greet everyone and hear their litany of complaints. "Let me take the kids on a picnic," Renet begged. "They need a break. You can't ask them to sit through another meeting where they can't be near their mother and they're bored to tears."

Naelin refused. She didn't want them out of her sight.

But it was true that Erian and Llor were bored. After sitting through the introduction of half the town's population, Llor began begging and pleading and wheedling and threatening his father's case. "If you don't let us go, I'll sing the alphabet song. Loudly. Over and over. So no grown-up can talk."

She was tempted to let him do just that. Smothering a smile, she glanced over at Ven. If he were to accompany them, then she wouldn't worry. . . .

He shook his head. "I stay with you. It's my job to protect you." He didn't have to say how important Naelin was to Aratay, especially when there were no viable heirs.

"I will guard them with my life," Renet pledged.

"Send Bayn," Ven suggested, ignoring Renet. "He can protect them from all ordinary threats, and with you nearby, no spirit will dare attack them."

"You can make the spirits watch us!" Llor said.

"Absolutely not. That will draw their attention to you." Even as she said it, though, Naelin considered their request for an outing. She looked at Llor's wide eyes and clasped hands. Saw how hopeful Erian looked. Even Renet's expression tugged on her heart. *It's not fair to make all of them suffer through my being queen.* "Very well. Take Bayn, and don't stray too near the border. We're close to Semo in the north and the untamed lands to the west. Be aware of your surroundings. Don't do anything to upset the spirits, and be careful not to step on any weak branches."

Erian kissed her cheek. "You worry too much, Mama. We can take care of ourselves. And we won't let anything happen to Father either."

She forced herself to smile, even though she wanted to say, *I don't like this.*

*No, it's not the picnic that I don't like. It's the fact that I can't be with them. I don't know how to be a good queen and a good mother at the same time.*

Something had to change if she was going to be successful at all this. But for now . . .

"You may go."

# CHAPTER 3

The wolf had never, not once, wanted to eat the queen's children, even on the day when Llor tried to ride him like a pony and Erian (unintentionally) shot the tip of his tail with an arrow. He did, however, want to eat their picnic lunch. Knocking the lid aside with his nose, he delicately lifted the cooked bird out of its basket. Laying it on the branch, he gnawed at it—the bones crunched, and the flesh tasted nutty. He'd grown fond of cooked meat after all his time with humans. Almost as fond as he was of the humans themselves.

Not that all the humans were as fond of him, of course—Renet, for example, showed no love for his children's wolf guardian. On occasion, Bayn liked to amuse himself by startling Renet. But today Bayn left him alone, because the children were so happy to be with their father and the day would be cut short if Renet needed to return to the village to change his pants. The wolf understood enough of human behavior to be sure of that.

He understood rather more than an ordinary wolf should, which seemed to disturb other wolves when they encountered him, but had never bothered him.

What *did* bother him was what he felt from the spirits in the nearby trees. Right now, there were three tree spirits midforest and one in the canopy, plus an earth spirit burrowing beneath the roots of their picnic tree. Spirits were always odd this close to the untamed lands—annoyingly skittish—but this felt . . . *more.* He sensed them like itches in his fur—and they felt increasingly agitated, enough to interrupt his meal and cause him to stare hard at the trees.

The forest was still.

Just a breeze that rustled the crinkled leaves.

Just a squirrel that squawked at the sight of a wolf high in a tree.

The autumn sun was still warm, soaking into the branches and into Bayn's fur, and the air carried the sour smell of overripe berries, rain-soaked moss, and the familiar scent of his humans.

He sniffed the air, alert. Nearby, Erian was showing her father the new knife moves that Champion Ven had taught her. She mimed stabbing a spirit in the eye, a target Bayn approved of. It was always wise to aim for the sensitive parts. He preferred a bite to the throat, but the girl lacked the jaw strength for that. Her father was trying not to look appalled at the sight of his ten-year-old daughter thrusting a knife into the air and talking cheerfully about eyeballs. *I would make a better father for her,* Bayn thought.

Llor, who was nearly seven years old, was competing for Renet's attention by tiptoe walking out onto the narrower part of the branch. "Watch me, Father! Look at this!"

"Llor, come back here!" Renet said. "Erian, that's very nice. You're very fast. Does your mother know Champion Ven is teaching you this?"

"It was her idea," Erian said. "She says even people who are smart and kind and careful sometimes have to stab things."

"Your mother said that?" Renet asked faintly.

Bayn thought he looked a bit wild around the eyes, as if he were a rabbit who wanted to bolt back into a nice, safe hole . . . like the spirits around them were doing.

The spirit in the canopy was swinging away, dangling monkeylike from a branch then leaping to grab the next one. *Something is frightening them,* Bayn thought. He sniffed the air again and let his tongue taste the scents around him. The three spirits at midforest were scattering—one running down the tree, one worming itself inside the tree, and the third fleeing to the next tree. Far below, the earth spirit was burrowing between the roots, its claws scrambling furiously at a mat of dead leaves.

Getting to his feet, Bayn growled.

Shooting the wolf a look, Renet said in a sharper voice, "Llor, come back right now."

"But, Father, I'm fine! I can do this—"

An air spirit dove through the canopy. Its leathery wings hit the branches, knocking off bright red, orange, and yellow leaves that swirled in its wake. Seeing a flash of a long, sharp beak, Bayn bounded across the branch toward Llor.

Llor was screaming when Bayn plowed into him, knocking into his stomach so that the boy tumbled over him onto the wolf's back. He felt wind from above as the spirit hurtled toward them. Launching himself forward, Bayn crashed down hard on the end of the branch.

*Crackle, crackle . . .*

*Crack!*

They fell.

The spirit's talons brushed his fur, just missing them. The boy was screaming, but Bayn landed in a crouch on the branch below and was running a second later.

Above, though, the girl was in danger.

Hoping the boy had the sense to hang on tight—and from the grip around his neck, Bayn thought that yes, he did—the wolf leaped from branch to branch until he was back up to where they'd been having their picnic. Erian was jabbing at the spirit with her knife while her father was pounding on its back with a branch the size of his arm.

The spirit pivoted its head and snapped its bladelike beak at Renet. The man stumbled backward, and then his foot stepped onto open air, beyond the branch. He fell, arms flailing, screaming his daughter's name as the air spirit turned back to Erian.

Bayn had a quick decision: save the girl or save the man.

It was a simple choice.

You save pups.

Always save the pups, for they cannot save themselves.

He barreled toward Erian. As soon as they reached her, Llor slid off Bayn's back into his sister's arms, and the wolf launched himself at the air spirit.

The spirit was twice his size, with that vicious beak and talons. But Bayn was fast, strong, and far more intelligent. He feinted for its neck and then clamped hard on the tendons in its wing, ripping backward as the air spirit pulled away. He tasted its blood—crisp mountain air, the tang of pine, and the acrid bite of soil choked with stone. Not the usual taste of the spirits of Aratay.

There was no time to consider what the odd flavor meant, however. Behind him, Erian cried, "Bayn, watch out!" Turning his head, he saw she was pointing at the sky.

Five more spirits streaked toward them. Alone, he might have fought them, but he couldn't risk Queen Naelin's children. Baring his teeth, he crouched low and jerked his head, hoping the children understood what he wanted.

They did. Llor and Erian climbed onto his back. As the air spirit he'd injured shrieked to the others, Bayn tensed all his muscles and then sprang away from the branch. He sailed through the air in a graceful arc, landing smoothly on a branch of the next tree—if anyone had been watching, they would have been shocked to see a wolf travel through the trees this way, but both Erian and Llor were too young and too scared to question it. He felt them through his back, shaking, tense, and terrified, but he didn't dare pause to comfort them.

He jumped from branch to branch while the spirits streaked through the air after them. Instantly, he knew he'd made a mistake—if he'd fled east toward where Queen Naelin was visiting Queen Daleina's childhood village, Naelin would have known her children were in danger and could have compelled the spirits to stop, but instead he'd run west.

Or more accurately, he'd been driven west.

*Maybe they're not as stupid as I thought.*

And they were proving that. Every time he tried to switch direction, one of the spirits would cut him off. He raced down the trunk of a fallen tree and hit the forest floor. Running faster, he weaved between the bushes and the roots. Crying to one another, the spirits chased him, skimming over the bushes and zigzagging between the trunks. He saw one out of the corner of his eye, pacing him.

No longer screaming, the children were whimpering into his fur. He smelled their fear in their sweat, and it made him run faster. He covered one mile, then two, then three, farther and farther from Naelin and safety.

The spirits, he realized, were trying to trap him against the border of the untamed lands. He'd seen this hunting technique before. In fact, he'd used it himself.

No one *ever* went into the untamed lands. Not even if they faced death. He'd taken down prey within inches of the border, tearing them to shreds when they'd stopped, terrified, their deeply ingrained fear of the untamed lands overwhelming their fear of a predator.

And now *he* was the prey.

He sensed the spirits, flanking him, so he dodged right. The children held on as he veered around the trunk of an oak tree and then plowed through the underbrush. Two spirits darted in front of him. He ran left. Another spirit shot forward, forcing him to swerve again.

*I am not fast enough*, he realized.

Soon, they'd have him corralled.

Ahead, he caught a glimpse of the untamed lands. Through the branches, it looked like the haze above a waterfall. It shimmered and darkened, and Bayn had a brilliant and terrible idea. Switching directions, he did what no ordinary animal would do: he ran *toward* the border.

Caught off-guard, his pursuers faltered for a moment before chasing after him.

Once more, he heard the whimpers of Erian and Llor. He felt the crunch of fallen leaves beneath his paws. *If I can just reach it, the spirits won't dare follow....* Ahead, he saw the haze trembling and shifting as, beyond the borders of the known world, mountains rose and fell, trees sprouted and died, and streams flooded and dried. He heard Erian cry, "Bayn, no!"

But before he could reach the border, two of the spirits broke from the others and attacked from above. He felt Erian and Llor being pulled from his back. He heard them scream. Pivoting, Bayn leapt and snarled, but the other four spirits closed around him.

He was driven back, as the two spirits carried the screaming children up toward the canopy. Fighting, he tried to run after them—but it was impossible. The other spirits cut him off. He retreated, losing inch by inch, backing toward the untamed lands.

As the two spirits carrying Erian and Llor burst through the canopy, he knew he'd lost. *Oh, Great Mother,* he prayed, *I'm sorry my best was not good enough.* And then to the children, he thought, *Stay alive. Until we meet again.*

He broke off fighting and did the unthinkable.

Turning, he ran without stopping, without slowing, without even hesitating. Behind him, he felt the spirits pull up short, watching, as he plunged into the untamed lands.

And the haze closed around him.

# CHAPTER 4

A nother queen would have said yes.

But Queen Naelin had no problem with saying no—not to her children when they asked for something ridiculous (such as "Mama, can we *please* climb to the top of the canopy without safety ropes or adult supervision, where we will imperil our lives by recklessly daring gravity until inevitably we plummet down, breaking all our bones on multiple branches before we crash onto the forest floor to be devoured by wolves, bears, and wolverines? *Please*, Mama?").

And certainly not to the villagers when they asked for her to summon spirits in order to build them a new library.

"You can build one yourselves," she told them. "You have hammers and nails."

Shifting in their seats, the villagers whispered to one another. Naelin raised her eyebrows at them, waiting for them to argue. She did *not* come all the way out to the farthest northwest corner of Aratay to add improvements to their already very nice trees.

"Summoning spirits draws their attention," she said, for what felt like the hundredth time.

"Your Majesty, forgive us," a woman began—she was younger than Naelin, with a baby swaddled against her hip. Judging by her pressed apron and the starched scarf holding back her hair, Naelin guessed she was the village laundress. Redleaf was larger than Naelin's old home village, which wasn't saying much—East Everdale hadn't been more than a few disparate huts tucked into the trees. Redleaf was large enough to *have* a laundress—not to mention a baker and its own schoolteacher—all housed within multiple trees that had been grown and shaped by candidates during the last heir trials, back before nearly all of them had been killed in the Coronation Massacre. Today, nearly a hundred villagers had squeezed themselves into the town meeting hall, a chamber hollowed out of the middle of the largest tree. "The spirits already know we're here. Why not use them for good?" The laundress ducked her head and bobbed in a half curtsy. The baby at her hip gurgled. "Please forgive our presumption for asking."

Naelin waved her hand. "Nothing to forgive." She was never going to get used to people groveling at her. It was ridiculous. Before Champion Ven had plucked her from her quiet, happy life, she'd been no different from them.

Now, though, the crown she wore put distance between them.

As did the power she could wield.

But power came in many different forms, and in this case, it was more important to display restraint rather than give in to these ridiculous demands. She worked out a way to say that more . . . *queenly*.

"It would be irresponsible of me to command the spirits for any reason but dire emergency," Naelin explained patiently. "They're conscious beings, not tools, and using them as tools only fuels their hatred of us. Do you truly want all the nearby spirits to hate you *more*?" Naelin fixed her gaze on the gurgling baby. "To hate your children more?"

The laundress cradled her baby closer.

One of the woodsmen, a grizzled older man with a scar that split his left eyebrow, shrugged. "Begging Your Majesty's pardon, but we already live in constant danger. Be nice to live in constant comfort too. 'Sides, we can't spend the manpower or supplies to build it ourselves. We aren't city folk here. Everyone already does what we can. All we want is a little something special for the children." He waved at the baby too, who cooed, unaware she'd been elevated to be the metaphorical stand-in for all the children of

Redleaf. "You could do it, we heard. You don't have problems like the other queen."

Naelin felt her eyebrows shoot up as she fixed him with the same look she gave her children when their mouths moved without consulting their brains.

He was immediately shushed by the nearest villagers.

"Long live Queen Daleina!" one shouted. And then quickly, "Long live Queen Naelin!"

Naelin felt a headache form between her eyes. "I will consider it."

A few cheered. A few looked worried. Sweeping out of the town meeting hall, Queen Naelin fled as gracefully as she could. Outside the heart of the tree, she inhaled fresh air. Ven was waiting for her—he'd been standing guard outside while she met with the villagers.

"Go well?" he asked mildly.

"Shut up," she told him.

He grinned at her. "You're their queen. In their eyes, you work a dozen miracles before breakfast and eat rogue spirits for lunch, on a crisp bed of lettuce."

"I expect that kind of behavior in the capital, where they can call on the queen anytime, but out here? So far from the palace, where help *can't* come quickly?" She strode away from the hall, passing by the shops and market stalls that clustered on a platform in the center of the village. In a few minutes, she was beyond the town center, out on the thinner branches—homes dangled from them as well, a few built but most budded directly out of the tree itself, but it was blessedly quieter.

"I thought you handled them well." Ven still looked amused, and she wanted to wipe that little smirk off his face. He thought it was *funny* when the villagers treated her like some sort of all-powerful wish granter.

"I didn't stay firm." When she was far enough that she could no longer hear the buzz of voices from the meeting hall, she plopped down on the branch. Her silk dress poofed around her. She flattened the skirts down and wished she'd worn more practical clothes. But the palace caretakers had insisted that she pack ridiculously voluminous dresses—skirts send a message, they said, that the queen is unafraid and will not flee from danger. People needed to see their queen in finery to help them feel safe. *Absurd*, she thought. No one *is truly safe in Renthia.*

Amazingly, the head caretaker was somehow able to veto the queen, and now here she was, feeling like a fool. *Acting* like a fool.

"You heard me. I don't know what possessed me to say I'd think about it. Classic error."

"You could do it, you know," Ven said, sitting beside her.

She glared at him.

He grinned broader.

And Naelin laughed.

She wasn't even sure *why* she felt like laughing. Ven was just capable of making her happier simply by being with her. Leaning closer, she kissed him. He gathered her to him, his arms wrapping tight around her, and she clasped her hands together behind his neck. She felt his heartbeat through his shirt and hers. His mouth roved over her lips and down her neck as her fingers caressed his hair. At last, when they stopped, the air tasted sweeter, the sun felt warmer, and the day seemed better.

Sometimes Naelin thought Ven had a special magic all his own.

"I *could* build them a library," she conceded. "It's at least not a frivolous request."

"The last village wanted a merry-go-round," Ven reminded her.

"Oh, yes, because it's so sensible to make five-year-olds dizzy when they're a hundred feet above the forest floor." She'd said no to that very quickly. *People are ridiculous.* "After Erian and Llor are back, I'll do it. But only a very basic, utilitarian structure. No turrets. No frills." Erian and Llor should return with Renet in another hour or two. That would still give her a couple hours before nightfall to construct the library.

Ven frowned out at the trees, as if he could pierce through the branches to see the children at their picnic. "How far did they go?"

"I don't know," Naelin said. She'd stuck firm to her decision not to have spirits watch over them—that would only draw the spirits' attention to Erian and Llor, and she didn't want that. Besides, with two queens controlling the spirits, the forests of Aratay were safer than they'd ever been. And Bayn could handle all other threats.

Of course, it was hard not to worry about them anyway.

She'd feel better once they were just an arm's reach away again. "I told them to stay close." She'd even drawn them a map, though Renet had claimed to know exactly where they were. She was pretty sure she'd seen Bayn roll his eyes at that.

Ven kissed her forehead. "Stop worrying."

"I can't."

"Your children are lucky."

She patted his cheek. "Oh, I worry about you too."

"You know I can take care of myself."

"That has nothing to do with it." She kissed him again. There were benefits to having her ex-husband and children away for a few hours. It was hard enough trying to balance being queen and mother, let alone lover. She felt pulled in three directions, always disappointing someone. She wished she knew how to be everything all at once. *I used to be one person, needed only by my family.* She'd known how to be that person—mother to her children—but she didn't know how to be mother to them *and* mother to the world. Naelin sank into Ven's arms—

Footsteps pounded behind them.

Sighing as she pulled away, Naelin stood and smoothed her skirt. *Another villager who wants a miracle,* she thought. *I'm getting tired of saying no—*

"Your Majesty!" A woman was running toward them. She was a forest guard, dressed in brown and green with a knife strapped to her waist and a crossbow on her back.

Ven's hand went to his sword hilt as Naelin thrust her senses out, touching the nearby spirits. All seemed calm. She didn't sense any increase in hostility from the local spirits.

Calling over her shoulder, the guardswoman shouted, "She's here! This way! I found the queen!"

"What's wrong—" Ven began.

Then Naelin saw Renet. Held between two woodsmen, Renet was hobbling toward them. His hair was stuck to his forehead with bright-red blood. His pants were ripped, and his leg was gashed, deep enough that the skin had curled back. Naelin cried out. "Erian? Llor?"

"Gone," Renet puffed. "The wolf . . . Spirits attacked . . ."

His words felt like knife thrusts to her stomach. *Gone, missing? Or gone . . . dead?*

"Gone where?" Ven demanded.

"West." Renet pointed. "I don't know—"

Naelin didn't hear anything else. Her mind was already sailing away from the village, westward. She touched the spirits, diving into their minds, rifling through their thoughts, looking for memories of her children. Distorted through their eyes, she saw that Ven had begun running west, leaving the village and leaping through the forest.

A spirit, as small as a songbird, with a wooden body, leaf wings, and only a few thoughts in its mind, gifted her with one vivid image: her children and the wolf on a branch. She seized control of the little spirit and forced it to fly toward Ven, leading him farther west, toward where it had seen her children. Through the eyes of the birdlike air spirit, she saw Ven follow and knew he'd understood.

She widened her mind, reaching out to grab other spirits. There were few nearby but—there! An earth spirit! She felt its terror. She couldn't sense the source of its fear, though. Just . . . *Other.* It repeated that word, "other," over and over in her mind.

Other? Other *what?*

As she touched dozens of minds at once, she pieced the images together: an air spirit with leathery wings and a sword-sharp beak attacking, the wolf saving Llor, Erian trying to defend herself and Renet trying to help her, Bayn saving Erian and Llor as more air spirits attacked; Bayn running away . . . She tracked them, through the fresh memories of tree and earth spirits. The little spirits of Aratay had hidden from the "other" spirits, but they'd watched.

Bayn, carrying Erian and Llor, had run west, and the strange air spirits had chased them . . . *Then what happened?* She sent another one of her spirits to fetch Ven, with orders to bring him faster, and then she pressed harder on the nearby spirits.

She felt them resist, but she was *strong*, and she forced them westward, toward the *other*. And she splintered her mind, trying to touch the spirits that had attacked. If she could find them, stop them, hold them, destroy them—

Her senses brushed up against four air spirits, but she couldn't sink into them. Her thoughts slid across them as if they were made of glass. She battered against them. *Where are my children?* It was as much a question as it was a command, yet she got no response. Through the eyes of her own spirits, she saw the foreign spirits from a half-dozen different directions, fragmented as if she were looking through broken glass. Beyond, the forest seemed to dissolve into a haze.

These weren't her spirits. They weren't from Aratay. She wasn't their queen.

But she bore her will down on them anyway, determined to crack their minds.

In the moments before Naelin found the foreign spirits, while she was pillaging the minds of stray tree and air spirits, Ven was running with no other thought in his mind but *Faster!*

He refused to think about what could have happened to Erian and Llor, or what could be happening right now. Refused to think about what if he was too late. Refused to picture Erian, preening as she mastered another move he taught her. Or Llor, looking at Ven with those wide, hero-worshipping eyes. Refused to remember Naelin tucking her children in at night, or the way they'd started to ask to say good night to him too. He'd told them stories sometimes. Bandaged Llor's knee when he skinned it. Fixed a knife holster for Erian that fit with her new princess dresses. He knew that Llor sometimes snored like a hibernating badger and that Erian squirmed in her sleep. He knew Llor hated nuts, unless they were crushed in a cookie, and that Erian could eat fistfuls of blueberries.

*If I can just reach them soon enough . . .*

He had to believe that Bayn was with them, defending them, buying Ven time to race to the rescue. *Keep them safe, old friend. I'm coming!*

A little birdlike spirit with wooden wings darted ahead of him, flew on, then flew back, as if waiting.

*Naelin sent it*, he thought. "Go!" he yelled at the spirit.

He veered, following it, leaping from tree to tree, running over the branches. After so many years of this, he could gauge every leap in mere seconds. He knew how to cling to the bark, how to use his knives like claws, how to dangle from a slim branch and land on the next one. He used every skill he had to run faster than he'd ever run.

*But not fast enough. I'm . . .*

*I'm too late.*

He knew it in his soul. The fact that Renet had returned to the village, slowed by a leg wound, but not killed, meant the attack was over. Whatever had happened to the children had already happened. It had been too long. *Even Bayn isn't strong enough or clever enough to defend the children from six spirits for this long.*

*Don't think about that.*

It was impossible not to, though.

He drew his sword as his senses alerted him to motion above him. A few autumn leaves swirled down as an air spirit, woman-shaped but with eagle wings and talons instead of feet, broke through the branches above. He crouched, sword ready, but then saw the spirit was falling talons first—

*Another of Naelin's*, he thought.

He lowered his sword and let the spirit pluck him into the air.

With his leather armor bunched in its grip, the spirit carried him through the forest. Branches smacked into his legs, stinging, and he drew his knees up to his chest. The spirit let out a shrill cry that couldn't have come from a human throat. In the distance, he saw the border of Aratay, which was also the border of Renthia itself: beyond it, the haze of the untamed lands curled like a forest fire on the horizon.

They flew closer.

Ahead, only a few yards from the border, Ven saw a clump

of spirits—four air spirits, writhing on a branch as if they were caught in a fire. "There! Take me there!" His air spirit released him, and he crashed down, sword ready.

The four spirits didn't look like the usual Aratayian spirits. Their wings were leathery instead of coated in feathers, and their bodies were bunched with muscles coated in sleek, snake-like skin. Razor-sharp beaks open, they were howling in pain. *Naelin*, he thought. She was trying to force them to obey her and they were resisting.

He leaped in between them and began hacking with his sword.

They sprang to life, focusing on this new threat, and he swirled, kicked, and struck at them, hoping that this distraction was what Naelin needed.

IT WAS.

As Ven engaged the foreign spirits, Naelin sank into their minds. They couldn't fight him and block her at the same time.

She saw images: Erian and Llor, on the back of Bayn, running through the forest. She felt the spirits' hunger, their hate, their *need*. And she saw through their eyes as two spirits—two who had come with the others but weren't with them now—pull Erian and Llor from Bayn's back and then fly north while the other spirits drove Bayn across the western border.

Naelin yanked her mind away from the spirits. And she heard herself in her own body, screaming. "Erian! Llor!"

They'd been taken north.

Toward Semo.

Alive.

Reaching out, Naelin grabbed the mind of a large air spirit and pulled it toward her. Heronlike, it had a sinewy neck, white feathers, and broad wings. She flung herself onto its back and compelled it northward.

As she flew, she flung her mind out like a net, catching every spirit within fifty miles and driving them toward Semo. *SAVE MY CHILDREN!*

*ATTACK!*

Far from the border, in the capital of Aratay, Queen Daleina felt the cry of the spirits in the northwest. Naelin's command shook through her, the other queen's rage hitting her so fast and hard that Daleina sank to the floor.

"Your Majesty!" Her seneschal rushed to her side.

On her other side, her sister, Arin, grabbed for her, touching her arm, her forehead. "Is it happening again? Daleina, can you hear me?" To the seneschal, she snapped, "Get Healer Hamon!"

"Not . . . me," Daleina managed. "Naelin." She felt her spirits race northward, full of bloodlust—toward the border of Semo.

*What was she doing? Naelin!*

They finally had peace! Queen Merecot had been defeated. This was a time of healing! If Naelin attacked Semo . . . She'd start a war!

As the first wave hit the border, the Aratayian spirits crashed into a line of foreign spirits. The Aratayian spirits were a random assortment: a few larger earth spirits made of rocks and moss, mixed with tiny twiglike tree spirits and dandelion fluff-like air spirits, but the Semoian spirits stationed at the border were giants made of granite and dragons made of obsidian. They met the forest spirits as they crossed, and they tore them to shreds.

Daleina felt her spirits die—and with them, bits of Aratay.

Plants withered.

Flames engulfed trees.

Rivers dried.

*No!* What was Naelin thinking?

Daleina forced her mind northward, seizing the spirits before they could plunge over the Semoian border. *No! STOP!*

The minds of the two queens crashed into each other.

# CHAPTER 5

Daleina knew Naelin was stronger. She'd started out stronger than most heirs, and becoming queen had only amplified that strength. Before today, Daleina had considered it a boon to Aratay: two queens, one with training and one with power, to protect their people. Together, they could usher in a new era of peace to their forests and guard their land against threats from within and without. She'd considered Naelin to be a sensible and reliable, even wise, queen.

She'd never considered the possibility that Queen Naelin could lose control.

It felt like a tornado. As Daleina touched the minds of the spirits, she felt their thoughts whipping cyclone-like, caught in a rush of fear and anger. They whooshed northward, swept into the maelstrom of Naelin's fury.

Daleina tried to grab them, but they slipped away from her commands. She felt as if she were shouting into the howling wind, her words swallowed instantly. Jamming her fists into the floor, she concentrated—throwing her full self outward.

*Stop! Do not cross!*

She stretched her mind, imagining her thoughts were a wall that blocked the northern border.

The spirits, propelled by Naelin, battered against her wall. Her body flinched as if she'd been kicked, but she held firm. It didn't hurt that the spirits *wanted* to obey her. They didn't want to leave Aratay, especially once the first few died.

So she fed that. *Stay here, stay safe, stay here*, she repeated. She sent the command flowing into them, undercutting Naelin's pure scream of raw power. Daleina couldn't stop Naelin's push— she didn't have that kind of strength—but she could soften it, and hopefully hold the spirits long enough for someone to reach Naelin.

Distantly, she heard voices shouting at her.

Hamon: "Daleina, can you hear me? Answer me, Daleina!"

Arin: "Is she all right? What's happening to her? Hamon, is she dying? What's wrong with her? Make her wake up!"

And then Hamon's mother, Garnah: "Leave her be. Can't you see she's concentrating? Although how she can with you two hens clucking at her, I don't know." Daleina heard glass shatter as Garnah snapped, "Don't give her that! Idiot."

She blocked them out—Garnah was right, she needed to concentrate. Naelin screamed and flailed—it was like trying to hold back a tidal wave with her arms. Naelin's mind slammed against Daleina's so hard that Daleina cried out. *I can't hold her, not forever.* But that was never her hope . . .

*Ven*, she thought.

She plunged into the minds of the spirits, searching for him.

VEN KNEW SOMETHING WAS WRONG THE SECOND HE SAW SPIRITS streaming north. This was not due to brilliant intuition. It was *very* obvious something was wrong. All around him, the spirits of Aratay were hurling themselves northward in an uncontrolled stream.

"Naelin!" he cried out. "What are you doing? Stop!"

But if she heard him through the ears of the spirits, it didn't make a difference. Screaming, the spirits clawed at the land, trying to cling to the branches, and then they'd suddenly release and hurl themselves full-tilt northward.

He slashed again at the foreign spirits—the only ones immune to whatever Naelin was doing—and then he began running, following the stream of spirits. He spared a moment for regret: he was allowing the foreign spirits to escape. But there was a more immediate danger. All around him, the forest was full of Aratayian spirits, howling and shrieking as they flew and ran and slithered and crawled northward against their will. He weaved among them, ducking and leaping, trying to get ahead of them as they flowed around him. "Naelin! Stop!" he yelled.

Above him, he saw one air spirit break from the stream. It dove toward him—it had an ermine-like body and bat wings, the kind of spirit that Daleina preferred to ride. *You'd better not be attacking me*, he thought. But it was coming at him the same way Naelin's spirit had when it came to carry him, so he jumped, grabbed onto its legs, and instead of fighting him off, it flew upward, bursting through the leaves of the canopy.

Across the forest, he saw trees burst into flame as if struck by lightning, he saw rivers overflow, he saw leaves darken and die, withering to black in mere seconds.

And to the north, at the Semoian border . . . he saw Aratayian spirits dying.

Ever since Queen Merecot's failed invasion, she had kept her most powerful spirits at the border, fearing retaliation. All the border guards had reported on it. And now he was seeing it in person.

*Naelin should know this! What is she thinking?*

Aiming for one of the gaps, the spirits of Aratay were crashing into the Semoian spirits—and dying by the dozens. Even from this distance, he could hear their howls of pain, and he could see the effect on the forest.

"Faster!" he urged the ermine spirit.

He spotted Naelin, on the back of another air spirit, in the thick of the battle. He didn't know what commands she was issuing, but she looked to be lashing out wildly, using the spirits as if they were her fists and swords, trying to cause as much damage as she could.

But the Semoian spirits held their line.

Ven raised his sword and urged his spirit forward, toward the queen. She wasn't blocking herself. She'd given zero thought to defense. It was all attack. *I have to reach her before*—

He was only a few feet away when the stone fist of an earth

spirit slammed into the side of Naelin's head. He lunged for her as she toppled off her spirit. Her body twisted in the air as she fell. Around them, the spirits of Aratay fled south, back across the border, but Ven's mount continued to obey him—he sent a silent thank-you to Daleina as he aimed his spirit into a dive.

He caught Naelin in his arms as a black dragonlike spirit shot toward them. Cradling his queen against his chest, he brought his sword up.

It hit with a *clang* against the dragon's hide.

In Mittriel, Daleina felt the moment that Naelin lost consciousness.

It was as if all the water in a waterfall had suddenly ceased. Daleina gasped for air, suddenly able to breathe again, see again, hear again, feel again. Hamon's arms were around her. Her sister, Arin, was kneeling in front of her, holding her hands.

She felt a faint dimming inside her as her body adjusted to the loss of power that came with the death of her spirits. It was only a slight change—she still felt the strength of the vast numbers of Aratayian spirits, buoying her—but it was becoming a depressingly familiar sensation.

Garnah, Hamon's mother, had plopped herself on top of the banquet table and was helping herself to grapes. "Well now, that was all very exciting. You gave your loved ones quite the scare. Granted, they have the nerves of a chipmunk, but still."

"It wasn't me," Daleina said, mostly to Hamon and Arin. "It was Naelin. Something happened to her children. She lost control. Not of the spirits. Of herself." She shuddered—it was a nightmare scenario, an out-of-control queen. If Ven hadn't been able to stop her . . .

"Oh, how delightful," Garnah said. "A woman with nearly unlimited power is emotionally unstable. Would you like me to kill her?"

"No!" Daleina, Arin, and Hamon said simultaneously.

"Pity," Garnah said, and ate another grape. "Death solves so many problems. Won't you at least entertain the notion? There's a new potion that I've been just *dying* to try, pun intended—"

"Absolutely not," Daleina said. Enough had died. *I have to reach out, try to see how much damage Naelin's ill-conceived attack did.* But first she had to recover. Her mind felt as if it had been shoved through a cheese grater. She also had to conserve strength, in case Naelin woke and decided to rage again. *She's too strong,* Daleina thought. *That power dump probably didn't even leave her winded.*

"Mother, could you please leave us?" Hamon asked.

"Of course." Scooting off the table, Garnah swept toward the door. "Arin, come with me. You haven't mastered today's potion."

Arin didn't move.

Garnah commanded, "Arin, come. The crisis has passed."

Not budging from beside her sister, Arin, squeezed Daleina's hands. "Has it passed?"

Daleina tentatively reached her mind toward the northwest corner of Aratay—*This much I can do without exhausting myself,* she thought. Even still, she felt herself stretch thin as she strained to touch the borders. The spirits had fled, hiding and burrowing as deep and as far south as they could. All was still. Drawing her mind back, Daleina nodded at Arin. "I believe so."

Arin didn't let go. Daleina saw the worry on her sister's face as plain as if it had been painted there, and she felt a stab of guilt—Arin was still so young. Not yet fifteen. She should be in their home village, chasing her dream of someday owning her own bakery, figuring out who she was and what she cared about, maybe finding someone to take the place of Josei, the boy she'd dreamed of someday marrying . . . Instead she was here in the palace, worrying about catastrophes, and Josei was dead, one of the first casualties of Daleina's ascension. Arin's eyes bored into hers. "You'll call for me, if anything changes? If you need me at all?"

"I will," Daleina promised, although she wished she could just send Arin back home. The middle of a crisis was not the time to start an argument with her sister, though. *Later,* she promised herself, *I'll find a way to get her out of danger.* Daleina shot Garnah a look and hoped the woman understood that if anything happened to Arin . . .

Garnah met her eyes without blinking, and Daleina was certain she *did* understand. Hamon's mother had an excellent survival instinct. It was empathy and other ordinary emotions that she lacked. Herding Arin before her, Garnah left the room.

Daleina and Hamon were alone.

"You need to rest," Hamon said.

Daleina shook her head. "I have to stay alert, in case it happens again." But she did lean her head against his shoulder. "It was supposed to be *better* now. Easier." They'd stopped an invasion, thwarted an assassin, and found a second powerful queen to protect their forests. They should have at least bought their country a little more time before the next disaster. *Apparently not*, she thought. "I am going to go down in history as the worst queen in all of Renthia."

He kissed her forehead. "None of this is your fault."

That much was true. "Then the unluckiest."

"Perhaps that." He drew back. "I know it was Queen Naelin, but may I check you anyway?" When she granted permission, he opened his healer's bag, then checked her temperature, blood pressure, heart rate. He had her spit into a vial and tested it by adding a drop of a purple liquid—it turned white when he shook it.

"Not dying today?" she asked.

"Not today," he said with a smile. Hamon's smile was one of the best things in her world. It was as warm as a down blanket in winter and as comforting as an embrace. It made her feel as if she were doing everything right and that everything would turn out fine. Standing, he held out his hand and helped her to her feet. Her knees felt shaky, and she drew a few deep, steadying breaths. If Naelin broke down again anytime soon, Daleina wasn't sure she'd have the strength to face it. She'd end up as a puddle on the floor. *But I may not have any choice*, she thought. Protecting Aratay was her responsibility. *And it should be Naelin's as well.*

"What happened?" Hamon asked as he helped her to her throne. She sank into it gratefully, smoothed her skirts, and straightened her crown. He assisted with her hair, pinning back the loose red-and-gold strands.

"The reports from the spirits are garbled, but from what I can sense, something happened to Queen Naelin's children, and she reacted. Badly. She drove the spirits north, over the border to Semo, forcing them to attack. But it wasn't a controlled attack. This was wild, unplanned. It . . . it makes no sense. I don't know *why* she reacted the way she did, without thought, without care for the consequences." She shook her head. "Ven will send a message when he can—he was there," Daleina said. "Hopefully he can help explain this." She wasn't sure it really mattered, though. Whatever the cause, what she had to focus on was handling the aftermath.

She'd have to reach out to Queen Merecot. Attempt to salvage some kind of diplomacy. They hadn't yet formalized their peace treaty. This would make all of that a thousand times more difficult. Merecot would see it as a breach of trust, if not an all-out act of war. *Why did Naelin do it?* Daleina wondered for the umpteenth time.

Regardless, reports would be coming in soon from across Aratay about the damage. She'd need to assess the level of this crisis and then issue orders to distribute emergency care. Areas near the newly barren lands would have to be prepared to accept refugees—they'd need temporary housing, emergency food, other supplies—and then she'd have to set things in motion for permanent solutions. With winter coming, her people would need both warm homes and stores of food.

The thing was, what she really needed right now was Naelin. But that wasn't an option, and Daleina was still a queen.

"Seneschal!" she called.

The man popped through the door so fast that Daleina was certain he'd had his ear pressed to it. Considering the circumstances, she didn't mind. "Yes, Your Majesty?"

"Summon the chancellors from western Aratay. Do not tell them why—I will explain." As soon as she'd recovered enough, she'd be able to pinpoint the exact spots of the worst damage with greater speed than anyone could report. Help could be in place before the innocent victims even asked for it. *They may need healers*, she thought. "Hamon . . ."

"I'm staying here," he told her firmly. "But I will send messages to my colleagues."

"Good enough." She squeezed his hands. "Don't be specific as to the cause, just be factual with the medical need—we need them focused, not panicked. I'll provide precise locations by morning. Go."

He left, and she waited for the seneschal to return with the chancellors. After the rescue forces were mobilized, she would need to make a speech to her people. She realized as she thought about it that she'd already decided to lie to them, at least for now. They'd been through enough, felt enough fear.

They didn't need to know they couldn't trust one of their queens.

# CHAPTER 6

Naelin woke alone in an unfamiliar bed. She stared up at the ceiling. The quilt smelled like herbs, rosemary and sage. More dried herbs hung from the rafters. *I'm in Redleaf,* she thought. Her head felt fuzzy, and it was hard to remember why she was here, or even where *here* was. Thoughts kept slipping away from her, like wriggling fish in a stream.

*My children are gone,* she thought.

Then: *No, that can't be right.*

Erian and Llor were curled in the beds in the other rooms. If she went to the doorways, she'd hear their breathing—Erian's soft and even, Llor with a slight snore because he'd had a bit of a cold. She'd been making him breathe in the steam from a mug of pinewood tea before bed.

Standing, she walked into Llor's bedroom. She swayed as she walked, her head pounding and her vision tilting with blots of blackness that came and went. And then her mind cleared again for a moment: *They're not here. They're gone. I lost them.* The memory made her gasp as if she'd been stabbed.

Llor's favorite stuffed animal, a squirrel he called Boo-Boo, was propped on his pillow. Erian had made it for him out of old bedsheets and had sewed buttons for the eyes, lopsided. One was cracked. Sitting on the bed, Naelin hugged the squirrel to her chest.

It smelled like him.

Lying on his pillow, she cradled the squirrel against her.

As her mind began to knit itself back together, she was clear on one important detail: she knew whom she must kill.

Of course, killing Queen Merecot of Semo would not be easy. She was powerful, possibly as powerful as Naelin and certainly better trained. She'd been through several years at the same academy as Daleina and had been a queen for longer than either Daleina or Naelin.

But it had to be done. There was no question that those spirits—the air spirits that had kidnapped her children—were foreign. They owed their allegiance to another queen. And the logical answer to the question of *which* queen was Merecot. They'd fled north, after all.

Perhaps she'd taken the children for revenge. Naelin had killed her sister, Alet, albeit in self-defense. Naelin had also been instrumental in thwarting her invasion plans. Or perhaps the attack was part of a broader scheme to invade Aratay again—the problem of too many spirits in Semo still remained. Perhaps Merecot sought to weaken one of Aratay's queens, in preparation for another battle.

Naelin didn't care what the reason was. There was no forgivable reason.

And there was nothing—absolutely nothing—Merecot could do or say that would prevent Naelin from destroying her and taking back her children.

Struggling against the fog in her mind, she tried to think through the logistics: she'd need Queen Daleina's help. The disaster at the border had proven that an all-out attack was useless. Merecot's borders were too well defended. Naelin also wanted Ven's assistance. She'd have better odds with a trained warrior at her side. It might not be easy to convince him to leave the forest, though. He was a sworn champion. His duty was here in Aratay, preparing a new heir.

Well, she had a duty too.

Leaving Boo-Boo, Naelin placed her crown on her head and checked herself in the mirror. Dark circles under her eyes might have been distressing if it hadn't been like she was staring into the eyes of a stranger. She pressed her hand against the mirror, over her own reflection.

Her vision swam again as the black blots popped like bubbles.

On an ordinary morning, Llor would have been calling for help with tying the drawstring on his pants, and Erian would be trying to slip past her without brushing her hair. Erian hated to brush her hair and would avoid it for days if allowed to, at which point it would be more snarled than a bird's nest. Naelin would then have to brush it out strand by strand, joking about how many birds were living on Erian's head.

Consumed by her chaotic thoughts, Naelin didn't realize she was pushing harder and harder against the mirror until she knocked the glass out of its frame. Lunging forward, she tried to catch it, but it hit the wall and shattered in her hands.

She pulled her hands back. A shard had sliced one of her palms. Blood welled up in the cut, and she stared at it fascinated at the brilliant red against her skin. It didn't hurt, not at first, but then it did.

Holding her wounded hand in the air, she walked to the kitchen, turned on the water, and winced as the cold hit the cut. Blood mixed with the water and pooled in the bottom of the sink. She wrapped a towel tight around her hand and tied it off, one-handed. The cut wasn't deep but it was long. She looked back across the kitchen to the bedroom and saw the drops of blood that she'd left in a trail. Getting to her knees, she scrubbed it with another towel.

She again lost track of who she was and why she was here.

That was how the village leader found the queen of Aratay, on her hands and knees, cleaning his floor with one hand while cradling her other bandaged hand against her.

"Your Majesty!"

She heard the shock in his voice. Didn't care.

"Are you injured? Let me send for the doctor—"

Naelin stood as memory and awareness slammed back into her. "I'm well."

That was a lie, though. And not because of the cut.

*I will never be "well" again. I endangered my children. All of this is my fault. If I weren't queen, they'd never have been taken.* "Champion Ven and I will be returning to the capital shortly," she said. "I thank you for your hospitality."

She stared at the towel in her hand, wondering what she'd been doing—cleaning when she should be on her way to Mittriel. She was wasting precious time while Erian and Llor were in danger. But it was so hard to think through the throbbing in her head.

"The villagers . . . That is, we wish to hold a memorial service for your children, if you would like that. We are a small village, and it could not be anything fancy, like in Mittriel, but we wish to show our respect for your loss—"

"No."

He looked lost. "Forgive me, Your Majesty—"

"They aren't dead."

"Of course." She could tell from his voice that he didn't believe her, but he also feared angering her. "Please, we meant no disrespect—"

Naelin brushed past him, unable to summon the strength to be polite. She stepped out of his home and into the village center. Already it was bustling with people going about their daily lives as if it were a mere ordinary day, and she felt as if she'd stepped into a bizarre dream. How could they live their lives like normal when her children were missing? How could the sun shine, the wind blow, life continue? She felt so much anger and fear and guilt and pain churning inside her that she thought it must be radiating out of her, staining everything.

Pausing, the people watched her as she passed. She heard them, distantly, as if they were speaking to her underwater. *Deepest sympathy. Express our condolences. Such a tragedy. We know how you feel. We have lost—*

*Children.*

*Fathers.*

*Mothers.*

*Brothers.*

*Sisters.*

*Friends.*

*We have lost too. Time will help. Time heals all wounds. You must celebrate their lives. You are lucky to have had them for as long as you had. They'll always be a part of you. Be strong. Everything happens for a reason. All things must pass.*

She didn't acknowledge them, not even to tell them they were wrong—her children weren't dead! But she was too focused on the task ahead to care what they thought or said. *First, find Ven, and then we'll leave, return to the capital, and plot out the best way to rescue my children from Semo.* She'd welcome all the help she could get—when she struck at Merecot, she wanted to be certain she would not fail.

*I failed my children when it mattered most; I won't fail them again. I will save them from Merecot, no matter what it takes.*

A man stood in her path.

He looked familiar—one of the villagers she'd spoken to before? "I know why you said no," he said. "You were afraid. Because of your kids. You didn't want to draw spirits to your kids, and so you didn't use your power. Fear made you say no. But you lost them anyway, because life is cruel like that, and no matter how careful we are, sometimes bad things happen. Can't stop the bad things, no matter how much you hide."

"Why are you saying this?" He wasn't spouting the typical sympathetic drivel that all the other villagers had been spewing. In fact, he sounded almost hostile, on the verge of insulting her.

"Because you don't have anything more to lose. So you might as well use your power. We heard—we all heard—what you did. Sending the spirits to their death in Semo, making more barren areas. You clearly aren't afraid of doing harm anymore, so you shouldn't be afraid of doing good. You're supposed to be the Mother of Aratay, you know, not just a mother of two."

Before he could say anything more, other villagers swarmed around them, shushing him, apologizing to her, and bowing deeply as they pulled him away. She stood, staring, as he was shepherded into one of the shops, out of sight.

*How dare he?* she thought.

*He's right,* she also thought.

Not about the library, of course—the callousness of using her emotions to get such a trivial thing made her want to tear the man's eyes out. But about her power in general . . .

*Until Erian and Llor are back with me, I have nothing. And so, I have nothing to lose. No one can hurt me, because I am hurt beyond repair. No one can kill me, for without them, I am already dead.*

Holding on to that concept like Llor held Boo-Boo, she closed her eyes and called to the spirits. She felt . . . not rage . . . but fear, their fear of her, and it tasted like copper on the back of her throat. She swallowed it down, consumed it, and wrapped it in her own fear for her children. The spirits drew closer to her.

They didn't want to be afraid of her, their chosen queen, she sensed, but they'd felt her last command, felt the deaths of their brethren as they clashed with the spirits of Semo. She could feel the spirits straining, torn between the need to hide and the need to fly and run and build and destroy. *Come,* she told them. *Build.* She guided them in, toward the heart of the village, and then she pushed an image into their minds: a library with soaring turrets, spiral stairs with curled railings, shelf after shelf all engraved with images of vines and roses. She picked the most fanciful library she could imagine, a castle of a library, high in the trees, the kind that would have seen Erian squeal with joy and Llor ask to climb to the tippiest-top, and she thrust the command into the minds of the spirits.

She felt a breeze in her face, warm and smelling of spring blossoms, an impossibility this far into fall, but she breathed it in and opened her eyes, lifted her face to see the spirits spiraling above her through the branches of the tree. The tree spirits sank into the trunk of one of Redleaf's trees, and the bark began to pulse and bubble. *Yes, there,* she told them, and directed them as the bubble grew and stretched and split into spires.

Naelin had the spirits hollow the spires and widen holes to be windows. They grew stairs from another branch, and vines wrapped around one another to make the railings. Swirling her finger, she told them to curl the ends into flourishes, and then raised her arms to direct them as they spun banners made of leaves out from the tips of the spires. Around her, she heard the awed murmurs of the villagers, but she didn't let that distract her. She led the spirits like a conductor leads an orchestra, creating her own kind of music.

*Fill it with stories*, she ordered the spirits. She harnessed a dozen for this task—a dozen of the smartest, who could understand a complex command. *Stories that will make the people laugh and cry and feel whole. Stories that break, and stories that heal. Find them stories, to give them hope in the bleakest of times.* She imprinted the image of books. *Cross all of Aratay. Go to the wordsmiths.* The wordsmiths would provide them with books, illustrated and bound. *In exchange for their books, you will strengthen their roofs, fix their doors if they need it, and repair their bridges.*

As she finished issuing her orders, Naelin released them and sank back into her own body. For an instant, she felt as if she had touched something wonderful and beautiful—for an instant, she had forgotten what happened.

She'd forgotten they'd been taken.

She'd forgotten they could be dead, that it was likely they were dead, that spirits didn't kidnap people—they killed them.

She'd forgotten she'd failed to save her children.

And as the knowledge crashed back into her, she felt as if she couldn't breathe. She fell to her knees. Around her, Naelin heard the shouts of joy, the gasps of wonder, all the awe in the voices of the men, women, and children of Redleaf.

She felt arms around her—familiar arms—as the throbbing in her head finally receded and the cloudy chaos of her wriggling thoughts cleared at last. She was herself again, her mind whole and her heart broken.

Ven.

"They took them," Naelin told him. "Erian and Llor. The spirits took them north. And they drove Bayn west, into the untamed lands." She felt his arms tighten as he absorbed her news.

Into her ear, he said, "Just keep breathing. One breath, then another."

"And then it will get better? Then I'll be able to accept that they're gone? Then I'll admit that I failed them and the spirits killed them and rescue is hopeless?" Even she heard the danger note in her voice. With her mind clear, she remembered how Ven had shouted for her to stop, and how Daleina had interfered with her attack. Anger ate at her pain, and she wanted to scream and rage:

*It's not hopeless! The spirits took them into Semo! Alive!*

He was silent a moment, only then admitting, "No. I don't think it will get better."

That was, oddly, the right answer. She hadn't thought there was one. *Keep breathing. It won't get better. Keep breathing anyway.* It wouldn't be better until her children were back in her arms and Merecot was dead.

# CHAPTER 7

Queen Merecot of Semo allowed the spirits to destroy a mountain. She watched from above, through the eyes of an air spirit, as earth spirits gnawed at the granite cliffs and ice spirits froze and thawed the mountain streams, causing the fissures to widen on the face of the mountain. Fire spirits tossed molten rock over the once-dormant crater as if they were children playing catch. She felt their glee, a wild kind of joy that burned in her veins.

Behind her, miles from the destruction but inches from her, she heard the familiar tap of a cane—the former queen of Semo, Queen Jastra. Merecot hadn't summoned her, and the old queen hadn't knocked. She'd simply strode into Merecot's chambers as if she were always welcome. Used to obeying the ex-queen, the guards hadn't thought to stop her.

*I'll to speak to them about that. Sternly, with colorful language and a few choice threats.*

She contemplated requesting a lock, but she knew it wouldn't be wise—her guards had to be able to reach her quickly, in case of any assassination attempts. Given her past experience . . . well, she knew sometimes people tried to kill queens. And if she were asleep when an attack came, she'd need the guards—the spirits wouldn't defend her if she wasn't awake to summon them. Instead they'd happily watch her be murdered. *Probably while eating snacks and cheering as if it were a sporting event.*

Jastra spoke. "I'd thought that, after the demands of the crown were lifted and all my lovely power at last diminished, I'd want nothing more than a peaceful life where I could putter in a rose garden and meddle in the lives of my grandchildren. But it has been so much more satisfying to stay and meddle in yours."

Merecot's lips twitched, but she kept her focus on the faraway spirits. *What is the old woman getting at?* The word "meddle" was at least accurate. Jastra never shied away from expressing an opinion or doling out advice.

"Choosing you was the best decision I've ever made."

*She means it,* Merecot thought with a shock.

The truth and warmth in Jastra's voice was undeniable. Merecot felt a lump in her throat and tears prick her eyes, which was an annoying and embarrassing reaction when she was trying to concentrate. She'd never had anyone appreciate her before. Not her teachers at Northeast Academy—they'd expelled her despite her skills. Certainly not her parents—they'd resented the very fact she'd been born. "Careful," Merecot said. "You'll make me feel emotions that I'm not equipped to process. Like gratitude."

Jastra cackled. "Then I'd best think up an insult."

On the mountain, the fire spirits dove into the crater and then flew up in a billowing cloud of ash and fire. Switching focus, Merecot ordered the air spirits to funnel the toxic smoke upward before it could spread.

She heard Jastra ease into a cushioned chair. It creaked beneath her. "Or I could insult your sister instead. If she hadn't failed, you would be queen of Aratay by now, and there would be no more need to play catch-the-lava with fire spirits."

All the warm, fuzzy feelings fizzled away. She should have known the moment was too nice to last. "Nice" wasn't for Merecot; "nice" was for other people and their lives. *And that's fine. I don't need nice, not from Jastra and not from anyone.*

"Admit it: your sister was foolish. She allowed sentiment to slow her hand."

Lava crept down the side of the mountain. Merecot didn't have to direct the ice spirits to freeze it—they pounced on it with savage joy. Howling, the fire spirits spewed more. Inwardly, she howled with them. Outwardly, she was silent.

Jastra sounded smug. "You're learning control. Good. A year ago, you would have flown into a rage if I'd dared make such a statement. It is gratifying to see you mature. Not many queens have the opportunity to observe their successor grow and blossom. I am blessedly lucky."

*If it weren't for my "control," you'd be dead.* "It would be prudent of you to remember you aren't here because of luck, blessed or otherwise." Merecot delivered a pointed look to the older woman. Queens who abdicated (the very few who did) were always targeted by the spirits they used to command and typically didn't live long before suffering some kind of "accident." Without a queen's additional power, they couldn't defend themselves against all the spirits who hated them. Merecot was protecting Jastra—that had been the agreement when Merecot was crowned, and she'd abided by her promise. So far. "You test my patience. It is not wise."

The old woman laughed again. "Perhaps I'm merely testing to see if you will crack, so that I can take the reins of power back again."

"Unlikely. You've become a coward in your dotage, content only to criticize from the shadows. If you were to become queen again, the people might remember you caused all their problems." As two fire spirits charged down the mountain pulling a river of lava, Merecot sent three air spirits to blast them back into the crater. The lava hardened, and the earth spirits shattered it from beneath.

"Ah, my child, you do make me proud."

Merecot didn't know if the old queen was impressed with her power over the volcano or her ability to insult the weak and elderly. *And the annoying. Don't forget that.* But Merecot couldn't stay angry with Jastra. No one had forced the former queen to abdicate. She'd done it of her own free will for the good of her people and had tapped Merecot as her chosen replacement—in Semo, the queens selected a solitary heir. Only Merecot had been permitted into the hidden grove to claim the power.

The fact that Merecot had maneuvered to be in that position was beside the point.

Jastra had believed in her. *And despite my failure in Aratay, she still does.* Merecot felt the cloying lump in her throat again and chose to ignore it.

"Why exactly are you here?" Merecot asked.

She meant why was Jastra in her chambers, but the former queen chose to interpret the question more broadly. "To make amends for past wrongs, to complete my destiny, to aid you as you complete yours—pick one, Your Majesty. Or perhaps I am here because the palace chefs make a wondrous soufflé." Jastra pushed herself to standing, wobbling as she took a step forward. Quickly, Merecot retrieved the old queen's jewel-encrusted cane and presented it to her. Jastra patted her cheek in a condescending manner—or what Merecot thought of as "Jastra's manner."

"Such a good girl. Don't you worry. Everything will work out." With her cane, she toddled across Merecot's chamber. "Let me know when you're ready for our next step."

"*My* next step," Merecot corrected. "You aren't my puppet master."

"Of course I'm not." Jastra looked aghast at the thought, an expression Merecot thought was a trifle overdone. "I merely offer sage advice. It's a prerogative of cowards in their dotage."

"I know what needs to be done," Merecot replied, but she couldn't help a small smile. *Dotage indeed*, she thought. Jastra may have walked with a cane, but her mind was sharper than most Merecot had met. *Granted, most people are idiots, but still . . .*

"I know you do, my dear," Jastra said. All traces of mockery and condescension were gone from her eyes. Instead her expression was a mix of pride and sadness, and Merecot felt as if she were looking at the true Jastra, not the royal face she showed to others.

Merecot wanted to say something. Such as *Thank you for believing in me.* But she was afraid it would sound sentimental. Or un-queenlike. Jastra could mock her for showing emotion, and Merecot couldn't risk that. *I'm supposed to be the ruthless queen, after all, who puts the needs of Semo—the needs of Renthia—before my own.*

Jastra cupped Merecot's chin in her wrinkled hand. "I meant what I said: I chose well when I chose you. You can do this. You can do what I could not. You can change the world."

Merecot swallowed. "I won't let you down."

"I know." Jastra gave her a gentle smile, the kind that said she meant it. She then thumped on the door with her cane, and the doors were swung open.

The guards bowed as the old queen hobbled past them, and they bowed again to Merecot as they shut the door. For an instant, Merecot wanted to call her back to keep her company, to talk to her, to bolster her confidence some more. But she didn't.

It was enough to know there was one person in Semo who was on Merecot's side.

Sinking onto a pillow-laden couch, Merecot checked on the spirits at the volcano. All seemed well. Half the crater had been eaten down by lava, and the mountain was riddled with fissures. But the lava and smoke seemed to have died down, and tree spirits were scurrying over the cooling earth, causing stubborn little plants to sprout in the crevasses. In a few hours, the mountain would be dormant again, and she'd be able to release the tame spirits she'd forced to guard the wild ones. *I saved thousands of lives, again, and no one knows. I am the unsung hero. Perhaps I should hire a few musicians to record my heroics. And sculptors.* She had yet to employ any artisans to immortalize her reign. Somehow it seemed more appropriate to hire them *after* she'd saved the world.

*But I will do it.*

*Jastra believes I can.*

"THIS IS TOO SLOW," NAELIN DECLARED.

Ven was securing a rope to a tree—the bridge ahead was damaged. He'd already shot an arrow with a rope into the next tree, burying the bolt deep into the trunk.

Grabbing the minds of three nearby tree spirits, Naelin propelled them toward the bridge. *Fix it.* She formed an image of a finished bridge. Obeying, the spirits began to grow branches from the trees and weave them together.

"That isn't necessarily faster," Renet pointed out. "We can just use the rope."

"It needs to be done. Regardless, we aren't taking the bridge. We're going to fly." Closing her eyes, she reached for the three nearest large air spirits.

"Uh-uh, Naelin, you know I'm not comfortable traveling—"

"Then don't come," she cut him off. She didn't understand how he could talk about comfort when their children were missing. *The more time we waste* . . . She chose not to finish that thought. *The faster, the better.*

Lifting up her face, she watched three air spirits slice through the canopy. Sunlight wavered as the leaves shook and fell all around them. The air spirits she'd called looked like jaguars, with orange-and-black markings on their fur, but they had blue-and-purple iridescent wings like peacocks.

Rejoining Naelin and Renet, Ven shielded his eyes as he looked up at the spirits. "Yours?"

"We're going too slow."

"As you wish, Your Majesty."

Renet fidgeted beside her as the three spirits landed. "Naelin, can't we discuss this?"

*There's nothing to discuss.* The longer this took, the longer Erian and Llor were in danger. She strode toward the spirits. "If we stay on foot, it will take us five days to reach Mittriel." She swung herself onto the back of the closest one. It hissed like an angry cat as she settled her weight onto it and grasped its neck fur. "If we fly, we can be there tomorrow."

"Naelin . . ."

Ven clasped Renet on the shoulder. "No shame if you choose to continue on foot. I'll leave you enough supplies." He handed Naelin's ex-husband a coil of rope and an extra knife.

Renet refused them. "I'm not traveling alone. Are you crazy?"

"Your choice." Climbing over the branches, Ven mounted a

second air spirit beside Naelin. He looped a length of rope around the spirit's neck and around his waist. "Secure yourself?" he suggested.

"I won't fall," Naelin said. *And if I do, so what?* She'd make another spirit catch her. Gone were her qualms about drawing the attention of spirits. All her carefulness hadn't protected the two people who mattered the most.

"Do it anyway," Ven said.

Reminding herself she had no rational reason to be angry at him—if he hadn't carried her away from the battle, she'd be dead and her children would still have been taken—Naelin tied herself onto the spirit.

Swearing under his breath, Renet climbed onto the back of the third spirit and tied himself on. The jaguar spirit snarled, flicking its fat tail. "This is a bad idea," Renet said. "Just want to be on the record saying that."

She also had no rational reason to be angry at Renet. He wasn't a warrior. It wasn't his fault he hadn't been strong enough to protect the children.

But logic didn't keep her from wanting to growl at him.

"Duly noted," Naelin bit off, and then she commanded the spirits, *Fly!*

With a roarlike cry, the spirits launched themselves up from the branch. Naelin felt the wind in her face as they soared upward between the branches. Orange and yellow leaves blurred around them until they burst through the canopy into the sun.

Her stomach felt as if it had stayed behind down in the branches. But she just gritted her teeth and held on. The wind yanked on her hair, pulling it into her eyes, and she wiped it back so she could see.

Below, the forest looked like a toddler's painting: reds, oranges, and yellows spattered everywhere, on a backdrop of dark green. The sun bathed it all in light, so bright that it even washed the blue out of the sky. If she'd turned around, she would have seen the haze of the untamed lands, where Bayn might or might not be alive. If she'd looked north, she would have seen the mountains of Semo, where her children might or might not . . .

She didn't look.

They flew until the sun began to sink and the stars began to poke through the darkening blue. Beneath her, Naelin felt the spirit's wingbeats begin to slow. Touching their minds, she felt their exhaustion. It seeped into her bones and muscles.

As much as it annoyed her to stop, she guided them down into the trees. Landing on a broad branch, she slid off the spirit's back and sagged against the trunk of the tree. Her legs felt wobbly, as if they'd forgotten how to stand. Beside her, Ven and Renet both dismounted. Renet dropped immediately into a crouch and hung his head between his knees.

*Leave us*, she told the spirits.

The winged-jaguar spirits obeyed, taking off from the branch and then gliding between the trees. They disappeared into the gathering shadows.

"Decent place to camp," Ven noted.

Lowering his pack, he took out a tangle of rope. Ven strung hammocks, and Renet tied their packs securely to the trunk. "I can start a fire," Renet offered. His voice sounded rough, as if he hadn't used it in days. He wasn't meeting her eyes either, which was fine with Naelin. If he met her eyes, she'd see all the memories they shared together: first steps, first words, the time when Erian first toddled out of her own bed and climbed into theirs, Llor crafting drums out of boxes, crates, pots and pans . . .

"I'll do it," Naelin said, stopping him before he gathered any wood. She tried to make it a kind of peace offering. He had to be going through the same kind of agony she was, clinging to the belief that it wasn't too late, that they could still be saved.

Ven handed her a fire stick, but she rejected it. Instead she reached out with her mind and grabbed control of a nearby fire spirit. Yanking it to their camp, she instructed it to burn in the crook of the tree.

Not far from their camp, a tree spirit cried out.

Naelin silenced the cry, holding the tree spirit still with her mind as if pinning it with her hands. At the same time, she kept the fire spirit pinned in place in the fire pit. This fire spirit looked like a lizard with red, orange, and blue flames for scales.

"Ven, do we have dinner?"

Unstrapping his bow, Ven selected three arrows. "We will." He then bounded off over the branches while his hands fitted the arrow to the bow.

Naelin unpacked a few herbs. She had no appetite but was aware she had to fuel her body to keep it functioning. Which is exactly what she was doing right now: functioning. Soon, though, she'd need to be more—if she was going to attack the queen of another country, she'd need every ounce of strength.

"I can never decide if it's arrogance that he doesn't bring more arrows, or if he just knows he's that good," Renet said, watching Ven leap from branch to branch.

"He's experienced."

"So am I, but I take a quiver."

"Your idea of hunting involves a visit to town and a nap. Besides, I can help him." Turning her attention to where Ven stalked, several branches above them, creeping up on a hole in a branch, Naelin snatched a nearby tree spirit and made it collapse the squirrel's hole.

The squirrel darted out.

Ven shot it between the eyes.

It fell from the branch, and Naelin instructed a hawklike spirit to retrieve it. Winging down from the upper branches, the spirit scooped the carcass up in its talons, then dropped it into her hands. She pulled the arrow out and handed the animal to Renet while she cleaned the tip. "You're scary when you're like this," Renet told her. "You know that, right?"

"You wanted this. Me using my powers. Me wielding a queen's powers."

"Yes, but . . ." He stopped, and she knew what he was going to say: not at the cost of their children. He didn't say it, and she felt her anger toward him soften. "Never mind."

She wanted to apologize for snapping at him, for feeling so much like a volcano about to erupt and destroy everyone around her. He didn't deserve that. No one did. *Except Merecot.*

Bending over the squirrel, he skinned and prepared it. He dropped the remnants down the trunk of the tree, to be scavenged by animals far below their camp. "You don't need to forgive me. I won't forgive myself."

She knew the words she was supposed to speak: *It's not your fault, you couldn't have fought the spirits, you did your best*, but she couldn't make herself say them. Ven shot two more squirrels, one arrow each, and Naelin repeated the process, fetching the bodies via spirit and giving them to Renet to skin. Taking the meat, Naelin skewered it onto a branch and positioned it over the fire spirit. Flames licked the edges.

As Ven climbed back to their camp, he said, "You drove them out, didn't you? Not sporting that way." He took back his arrows, checked to be sure the points were clean, and put them back in his quiver. He stowed the bow as well.

"I want to reach Mittriel as quickly as possible," Naelin said. "We eat, we sleep, we go. Whatever you're going to say, I don't want to hear it." She rubbed herbs onto the squirrel meat, twisted the stick, and instructed the fire spirit on how to hold the flame and how hot to blaze.

They waited in silence while the meat cooked, then ate in silence when it finished. Naelin watched the fire spirit coil and uncoil itself in the crook of the tree, shedding embers as it moved. If she stared at it long enough then closed her eyes, the light twisted behind her eyelids—a dance only visible after she stopped watching. It helped to have the fire spirit instead of a real fire. It didn't remind her of the fire in the hearth at home that had kept Erian and Llor warm on cool autumn nights like this.

"You aren't going to leave it there as we sleep, are you?" Renet asked.

"It won't dare harm you," Naelin said. She climbed into her hammock. The ropes folded around her. *Sleep hard*, she ordered herself. *Please, no dreams.*

"But if you're asleep . . ."

"Scream if it bites you. I'll wake." Closing her eyes, she tried to will herself to sleep. Nearby, she heard Renet and Ven climbing into their hammocks.

She heard Renet whisper, "I can't tell if she's serious or joking."

"Unclear," Ven said.

"Whatever you do, don't ask her," Renet said.

"You do realize she can hear you, right?" Ven asked. Naelin heard him shift and a branch creaked. She heard all the noises in the night forest: the wind rustling the leaves, the owls hooting to one another, the croak of the frogs far below. The forest was unbearably loud.

"Sorry, Naelin," Renet said. "It's just . . . This isn't like you. Keeping a spirit so close."

*I'll never be "like me" again.* She could see that, objectively, like a healer viewing a broken body. *I failed the only task that ever mattered: keeping my children safe. I'm broken.* "It will keep us warm tonight, and no one will have to feed the fire."

"Not such a big deal to toss in another stick," Renet said. "Couldn't you just–"

"Fine." Using her mind, Naelin shoved the fire spirit away from the camp. It squawked, then unfurled blackened wings from its lizardlike back, and flew in a streak up toward the sky to vanish amid the clouds and stars. The embers sputtered in its wake. Clambering out of his hammock, Renet coaxed the fire back to life.

She tried to force her body to relax, compelling it to obey her as if it were a recalcitrant spirit. Each body part she ordered to calm, tensing then releasing each muscle. She'd done this before, when she was a child, after spirits had murdered her family. She remembered lying alone at night, with the forest sounds all around her, and coaxing first her legs then her arms to lie limp until at last she succumbed to sleep. She hadn't thought about that in a long time–those first few nights, when she was so afraid she'd see and hear them again in her nightmares.

She hadn't thought she'd ever have to do this again.

"I don't want to not talk about them," Renet said out of nowhere. "That feels wrong."

Far below, the frogs were calling to one another. Llor had always like the sound of them. *Like an orchestra. But one that hasn't practiced,* he'd say. *Like at school. They're terrible.* "Everything about this feels wrong," Naelin said. "Please, let me sleep. Talk tomorrow." *Or after I save them.* She didn't let herself hear his reply—she sent her mind out, mixing with the spirits, submerging herself in the comforting maelstrom of their anger and hate.

She slept at some point, linked to the spirits, and when she woke, she felt as if she were seeing the forest through a thousand eyes all at once. Her head spun. Lying still, Naelin focused, drawing her mind back bit by bit into her body, feeling her legs, arms, back, face. Ven and Renet were already awake, wrapping up their hammocks and putting out the fire, leaving only a bowl-like divot of char in the crook of the tree. She lay there, not wanting to move, not wanting to think, not wanting to face the world, and then she propelled herself out of the hammock. She wrapped up her ropes and secured them onto her pack.

"Llor used to like to surprise me awake," Renet said, his voice warm with the memory.

She flinched as if smacked across the knuckles.

"He had a feather that he'd stick in my ear and wiggle, but long before he struck, I'd hear him cross the boards—they creaked. I kept promising you I'd fix that. Should have done it. But it wasn't the creaking that woke me, it was the giggling."

She remembered. Llor couldn't help laughing in anticipation. When he was even younger, he'd do that if someone tried to tickle him too—just the sight of his sister wiggling her fingers would send him into a fit of giggles. His laughter had been the brightest, best sound in the world. "Still not ready to talk," Naelin said. She felt a lump in her throat, thick and heavy, hard to swallow around. "But do what you need to do." It was his pain too. She couldn't deny him that. She could, though, not listen.

And not think.

*I won't reminisce about them as if they're gone for good. They're still alive. They have to be.*

Reaching out, she summoned three more air spirits—one was a wispy swirl of feathers and the other two had human bodies, swan wings, and smooth, featureless faces. She climbed on one, and so did Ven and Renet.

As she flew, Naelin plunged her mind into the spirits of Aratay, preparing them for battle. She pulled tree spirits from their homes and sent them northward, toward the border with Semo.

She guided air spirits high above the canopy and had spun them until she had whirlwinds. The earth spirits she fed, drawing them through the soil and rocks, until they grew stronger, full of their connection to the earth. They sucked in her rage, like water into a sponge, but she didn't feel it diminish—instead it grew, spreading and expanding through all the spirits of Aratay, until Naelin felt them like fire inside her veins. It hurt as it burned, but it was a good hurt.

Today they'd reach the capital, and then she'd release all that fire at Semo.

ACROSS THE FOREST, VEN SAW MITTRIEL RISING GLORIOUSLY above the forest. Its trees were white spires piercing the green of the pines and the gold of the autumn leaves. Waterfalls crashed between the trees, and bridges, teeming with people, spanned between the massive trunks.

*We can't fly there*, he thought. *Not without being seen.*

Right now, that was the last thing they wanted. If there were even the faintest chance Erian and Llor were still alive, as Naelin believed . . . and he wanted to believe they were . . . then drawing attention could endanger them. *Until we know who took them and why, we have to be careful.*

He urged the spirit forward as if it were a horse, trying to get close enough to Naelin to shout to her. His spirit flattened its wings and shot forward, knocking him back. Gripping the rope that held him on, he stayed mounted, and his spirit mount finally pulled alongside Naelin.

Focused on the city ahead, she didn't look at him.

"Naelin! We have to land! You can't come into the capital like this—you'll terrify everyone if we come racing in on the backs of spirits. We'll start a panic!"

She frowned at him. Her mouth opened as if she were saying, *"What?"*

He pointed exaggeratedly to the forest underneath them. "Land! Now!"

*That* she seemed to understand. His spirit did as well, and dove, and it was all he could do to cling to its neck as it bashed into the trees below. He saw in a flash the tangle of bridges before the spirit plummeted between them. "Land!" he shouted at it. He thumped its neck. "Land, you stupid thing!"

He saw the forest floor below—closer, closer, closer... The spirit shot upward and then glided onto an empty bridge. Quickly he untangled the rope and jumped off. He glared at it. Given that it was eyeless, he didn't know if the spirit could appreciate the balefulness of his full glare. "You realize I have a sword," Ven told the monster, just in case.

Beside him, Renet got shakily off his spirit. "It realized if you struck it, you'd fall." He untied his safety rope and stepped back from his spirit. "Ugh, I hate these things."

A few yards away, Naelin dismounted, patted the feathery neck of her spirit, and then raised her hands. At her unspoken command, all three spirits flew off into the trees.

"Good riddance," Renet said, and Ven was inclined to agree with him. He'd far rather trust to his own skill and luck when he traveled than to be so dependent on a being that hated him. The only thing that kept the spirit from dumping him a mile up was Naelin's control, and while Ven trusted her, he still didn't like it.

An entire life with spirits as your enemy didn't just go away because the damn things were convenient.

He watched as Naelin frowned at the trees, calculating the distance to the palace, and he wasn't surprised when she turned to him and demanded, "Why stop here?"

"I was trying to tell you in the air, but there are two reasons: one, the people are already on edge. If they saw their queen racing to the palace weeks sooner than expected, they'd think another battle was imminent. We'd panic them. At worst, cause a riot. At best, scare people who have already been scared enough." He scanned the nearby area. They were on the outskirts of the city, a quiet neighborhood. Given the time of day, it was mostly empty—the children were in school, and the adults were working, in one of the shops or in the palace or elsewhere, keeping the city functioning. The key was that no one was around. *Good.* When he turned back to look at Naelin, though, any relief he felt washed away. There was something about her eyes. Then it hit him.

They reminded him too much of a spirit's.

"Second reason," he continued, slightly rattled, "we don't know who took Erian and Llor and what they want. If the children are still alive, we don't know what actions will help and what will endanger them further." He thought of Bayn. At least he could hope that Bayn could take care of himself. He didn't have that kind of confidence about the children, especially in the clutches of spirits.

"They *are* alive, we *do* know what will help, and another battle *is* imminent," Naelin said flatly. "As soon as I inform Queen Daleina, I am going after Queen Merecot of Semo and saving my children."

And *that* was precisely what he was afraid of. Oh, he hadn't known exactly what she was thinking, but he'd recognized that focused, battle-ready air. *So she blames Merecot . . .* He couldn't blame her, given their history, but there was no proof. "Naelin . . ." he began.

"*She* did this?" Renet cut in. "Are you sure?"

"I am. The spirits weren't from Aratay."

"Naelin—" Ven tried again.

"Don't tell me I can't or I shouldn't. I won't hear it. I showed her mercy! And this is how she repays me?" Her face was flushed, and her fists were balled. He shot a glance at the nearby houses and wished they'd had this conversation farther from the capital. One saving grace was that in their traveling clothes, they didn't look like a queen and champion. *Just ordinary travelers in a heated discussion*, Ven thought. *Nothing to see here.*

"I'm not telling you no or yes or anything, my queen," Ven said, keeping his voice calm and soothing. Inside, though, he wanted to shout, *No!* There was no proof they'd been kidnapped by the queen of Semo. Renthia had other countries with other queens. Just because the spirits had fled north, it didn't mean Semo was guilty—all it meant was that north was the closest escape route.

Besides, if she charged into Semo without a plan, she'd be killed. He'd defend her with his dying breath, if he had to. But how could he defend her from herself? "All I'm saying is we don't need to declare our intentions to everyone in Mittriel. Approach the palace as if all is well. Speak with Queen Daleina. And then we decide, *together*, the best way to proceed."

He was rather proud of his little speech. Very measured and rational advice. And hopefully Daleina would be able to slow her down. Together, they could decide on a reasonable, achievable response that wouldn't endanger the children or Aratay or its two queens.

"Fine," she snarled. "We walk. Just three ordinary citizens on an ordinary day."

Shouldering a pack, Naelin marched down a bridge.

He and Renet watched her for a moment. "This isn't good," Renet observed. "I know how she feels—I feel it too. Helpless. Angry. But I've never seen her act like this. Once, maybe, when we had rats in the house. She was this determined."

"I take it things didn't turn out well for the rats."

"Or the house."

They watched her for a moment more, until she shot a look back at them. The look said clearer than words, *Move now*. They hurried after her. "We're going to have to talk sense into her," Ven said. "She's acting on raw emotion. That won't help Erian and Llor."

"No chance she'll listen to me," Renet said. "It's all you. You're the one she trusts. Besides, you're the one who will be there when she meets with Queen Daleina."

Ven studied Renet. *He's right.* Naelin did not have a high opinion of her ex-husband, and even though she hadn't said it out loud, the fact that they'd lost the children on Renet's watch had to have an effect. *She still hasn't forgiven me either, for not being able to protect them. But then, I haven't forgiven myself.* If he'd gone with them . . . If he'd kept them in the village instead of allowing them to go off on that damn picnic . . . If he hadn't placed so much responsibility on Bayn . . . *Oh, old friend, I hope you survived.*

But he knew it was a thin hope. No one survived the untamed lands. They were death, destruction, wild pain. This was the world, and that was *beyond*. No human, no animal, no spirit ever went beyond. To go beyond was to never return. *Still, Bayn's not like other wolves.*

He almost laughed at the ridiculous optimism. "I'm sorry," Ven said to Renet. "For what happened. For Erian and Llor."

"She won't even talk about them," Renet said.

Ven nodded. He got that. She was too full of pain to have any room for Renet's pain.

"Do you . . ." Renet's voice broke. "Do you really think they could be still alive? They were taken by spirits. How could . . . Is it possible . . ."

"Naelin needs me to believe it. So I do." Or at least he'd believe it was possible.

He let Renet talk all the way to the palace, story after story about Erian and Llor. Half-listening, he watched Naelin—back straight, chin high, fists curled—and wondered whether he was going to need to keep her from starting a war, or help her start one.

# CHAPTER 8

Queen Daleina lowered her head onto the exquisite table—crafted out of rare suka wood and inlaid with mother-of-pearl shell mosaic, a coronation gift from the queen of the islands of Belene—and slowly thumped her forehead on the surface.

"Your Majesty?" one of the chancellors asked tentatively.

She didn't lift her head. The shell mosaic was nicely cool. "Exactly how bad will the harvest be? Broad numbers, please."

Another chancellor cleared his throat. "We lost twenty-five acres of mature trees in the northwest, one hundred fifty per acre. The windstorm battered the trees so badly the fruit was knocked off. The harvesters have gathered as much as they could but the vast majority wasn't ripe, and the long-term damage to the trees themselves . . . well, frankly, it's devastating. If you could send spirits to regrow—"

"Seneschal, please add it to the list." She raised her head. "Next?"

The chancellor who represented western Aratay rose. "As you know, we've also seen significant damage in the wake of Queen Naelin's, um, response—"

"Yes, I know. What do you need?"

"Homes. We lost many homes when the spirits died. Your seneschal has our list of requests, but what I wished to speak with you about was the current problem: the last twenty-four hours have seen a marked increase in spirit attacks. The spirits' behavior has been unusually aggressive, and there have been numerous injuries, some quite serious. Forgive my presumption, Your Majesty, but could there, perhaps, be a causal relationship between—"

Daleina cut him off. "I will look into it. Thank you. If that's all . . ." She looked at her seneschal. *Please let that be all.* Her head was throbbing so enthusiastically that she thought her skull would bruise.

The chancellors started to protest, but the seneschal was bobbing his head, effectively ending the session. "If you'll follow me, ladies and gentlemen . . ." He led the chancellors to the door of the council room. She rose. Each of them bowed to her before filing out, and she acknowledged each of them with a solemn nod that she hoped communicated *I am competent and all will be well soon.* Shutting the door behind him, the seneschal left her alone.

She sank back into her throne in front of the mosaic table but didn't let herself rest. Instead she sent her aching mind outward—yet again—to touch the spirits around the capital. While she couldn't directly hear Queen Naelin's thoughts, she could feel the agitation Naelin left in her wake. The woman was a storm sweeping across the land, without any consideration for the damage she was causing.

*There's a reason I don't keep my mind open to the spirits.* And it wasn't lack of power or fear of death, though those were factors. *The spirits don't need to feel my every emotion.* She raised her voice, "Seneschal?"

He popped his head back into the room so fast that she knew he'd been plastered against the door. "Yes, Your Majesty?"

"As soon as Queen Naelin reaches the palace, please see that she's escorted to me." She had an additional thought: it was possible that the older woman wasn't going to listen to a scolding by a younger queen. "Also, could you please ask Headmistress Hanna from Northeast Academy to join us?" Perhaps the headmistress could offer Naelin extra training—Naelin had become queen at a time of emergency and had skipped over all of the lessons in magic theory and history, instead going straight to the practical application of power. *That* part she'd mastered quickly.

*Too quickly*, Daleina thought.

"And please send for Healer Hamon with his medicine bag—but take care not to alarm him. Only a touch of head pain, thanks."

He bowed. "I will have food and drink sent as well, for your guests."

"You think of everything, Belsowik." She deliberately used his given name—he insisted she use his title most of the time, but she wanted him to know she valued him specifically. Not just anyone could be as efficient and thorough as he was. "Your queen is grateful."

She was rewarded by seeing him blush at the praise. Still, that didn't stop him from chiding her. "My queen needs to take better care of herself. Your evening activities will be canceled tonight, and you will rest after you meet with Queen Naelin."

*If I can*, she thought. "I will," she promised him.

"Rest now."

Obediently, she laid her head on the table with her arms curled beneath her cheek. She closed her eyes. What seemed like only a moment later, she felt a warm hand on her shoulder, and she blinked her eyes open—her eyelids felt crusty, and her mouth tasted like it was stuffed with spider webs. Hamon was beside her, crushing herbs into a goblet. "This will keep your head clear, but then you'll need to sleep."

"My seneschal tells me that's on my schedule." Daleina ran her tongue over her teeth and patted at her hair. Accepting the goblet from Hamon, she drank. It tasted like pine tree with a hint of apple cider and cinnamon, not at all like medicine. "Nice."

"My mother's concoction." He held up one hand to forestall any comment. "I tested it myself, and there are no unusual side effects. All it should do is clear your head, and perhaps slightly improve your eyesight and bone density—it has a few vitamins."

She drank the rest of it. "How is she?" What she really wanted to ask was: how are *you* with her? Hamon had a strained relationship with his mother. *And that's putting it mildly. If she hadn't saved my life and Arin's . . .*

He smiled, though it was a bittersweet kind of smile. "She hasn't killed anyone lately. Or if she has, she's become more skilled at hiding the bodies."

"You don't believe her promises that she's reformed."

"No more than I believe a spirit will become my best friend." He took back the empty goblet and then, after a hesitation, leaned over and kissed her cheek.

She laughed. "*That* was a kiss?"

"You're on the throne. More seemed inappropriate."

Grabbing a wad of his shirt in her fist, Daleina pulled him closer so fast that he dropped to his knees, and kissed him thoroughly. He slid his hands around her and over her, until both of them were breathing fast and she didn't feel the least bit tired anymore.

She heard the seneschal clear his throat from the entrance, and Hamon jumped to his feet. He straightened Daleina's skirt and smoothed her hair, tucking loose strands behind her ears. She grinned at him, drinking in his handsomeness. "Thank you for your ministrations, Healer Hamon. I feel better already."

He kissed her lightly again. "You said the seneschal cleared your schedule tonight?"

Her smile widened. "Yes, isn't that lovely?"

He lifted her hand to his lips and kissed her knuckles. "*You* are lovely."

"Charmer," she murmured. And then her good mood drained away as she thought of what had to happen before she was free to be with Hamon again.

He saw her shift in mood. "Daleina, what is it?"

She reached out with her mind briefly and touched the thoughts of the spirits in the palace. She felt them churning, like water in a waterfall. "I have a meeting."

"About what?" She heard the concern in his voice.

She judged the other queen to be only a staircase away. She felt, rather than saw, the candles in the hall blaze as the fire spirits reacted to Naelin. "I have to tell a mother not to care so much about her missing children."

*Missing, and nearly certainly dead*, she thought.

He left her with one more kiss, and Daleina waited on her throne. She was aware of the second throne beside her, one that Naelin had sat in only a handful of times, since their unusual co-rule began. There was no known protocol for how to deal with such a situation. According to all records, such a situation had never occurred before, and before recent events, Daleina had thought they were handling it well—double the queens should have meant double the protection for Aratay.

Now she wished Naelin were merely a powerful heir that Daleina could order to stand down, rather than a queen. She was going to have to rely on Naelin's willingness to cooperate, and she couldn't count on that. "Seneschal, could you please help me display the damage reports, as well as the requests for assistance?"

"Of course, Your Majesty." He scurried forward and placed the stack of papers in front of her. Standing, she began to lay them out side by side on the wood and mother-of-pearl table. Homes, schools, shops, libraries, fields, orchards, bridges, marketplaces . . . Outside the door, she felt Naelin arrive—tree spirits crawled over the door as if they wanted to tear it apart. She heard their claws scrabble at the wood.

Ready to rush to the door, the seneschal hopped away from the table, but Daleina laid a hand on his shoulder to stop him. "I suspect she'll make a dramatic entrance. I'd rather you weren't harmed, Belsowik."

He waited beside her, tense.

The door, a heavy oak door, blew open and slammed against the wall. Chittering like squirrels, spirits ran across the walls and onto the ceiling. Daleina let them—she had no fear they'd harm her; they were her spirits too, no matter how strong the other queen was, and she could stop them if she had to.

*I'm almost certain I can. . . .*

Lizardlike fire spirits scorched the wood ceiling and then dove into the cold fireplace. Embers smoldered as the lizard spirits writhed in the grate. An ice spirit, lithe and tall, slipped along the ceiling. Shaped like a human, it ran its long fingers over the edge of the table, causing frost to spread in flower patterns, then drifted to the window. It curled its body onto the sill, bending into itself in a tighter coil than any human body could bend. Dozens of tree spirits, each no larger than Daleina's hand, skittered around her feet.

"Go," she told Belsowik.

He scurried out the door. She knew he'd stand just outside with the guards until she called for him again. Gathering her inner strength, she faced the new arrivals.

Ven first: he looked weathered, as if he were an old shirt that had been scrubbed in the wash too many times. She wondered if he'd slept in days. *Probably not.*

Daleina crossed to him first and embraced him warmly. "Champion Ven." She then turned to Naelin. Usually, the other queen was unremarkable. Usually, she looked like the motherly woodswoman she used to be—sturdy, steady, rational. But now she looked wild, almost feral. Her eyes flickered around the room, at the spirits, at the papers on the desk, at the fire that now, suddenly, roared in the hearth, fed by the fire spirits. Her uncombed hair floated in a halo around her head, and she had a streak of soot on her cheek. She still wore one of the voluminous gowns from the palace courtiers, but the skirt was ripped— *intentionally*, Daleina thought, *so it won't impede her movement.* She'd clearly come straight here from the village without another thought.

*I hope the people didn't see her. She'd cause a panic.* It wasn't that Daleina cared about the gown or Naelin's hair. *It's just that sometimes the role of queen is reassuring people that they aren't going to die today.*

Right now, nothing about Naelin was reassuring.

"Queen Naelin, I am deeply sorry for what you have endured. Please know that we will do all in our power to determine the fate of your children."

Naelin began to bow, then stopped as if suddenly remembering she wasn't required to bow anymore. "Thank you, Your Majesty. I am counting on that."

Daleina wasn't precisely certain what to say next. She didn't know the other woman well enough to guess what she wanted to hear, though she could guess what *not* to say. "All of Aratay sorrows with you. Indeed, all of Aratay has felt your pain." She took a breath—Naelin's expression was as blank as stone. If it weren't for the agitation of the spirits, Daleina wouldn't have been able to tell she felt anything at all. "I know you have suffered a tremen-dous loss—"

"I'm not in mourning," Naelin snapped. "There's no 'loss.' They were kidnapped."

Daleina had witnessed enough spirit attacks to know they didn't kidnap children. They killed. But if she needed to be in denial, that was fine. After all, the message Ven had sent de-scribed the children as "missing," and she intended to respect that. "If the situation were any different, I wouldn't dream of asking you to—"

From the doorway, Headmistress Hanna said in her clipped no-nonsense voice, "What our polite queen is attempting to say is: you must knock it off."

*Perfect timing,* Daleina thought.

Naelin looked startled.

Daleina shot a grateful look at the headmistress as the sen-eschal wheeled her in, then retreated again. The headmistress had lost use of her legs in the battle with Merecot and now trav-eled in a special chair. It was designed to clip onto ziplines and pulleys for travel between trees and had wheels that unfolded to traverse floors and bridges. In it, Headmistress Hanna looked as if she could crush several dozen spirits beneath the wheels while calmly lopping off the heads of multiple others. Daleina knew for a fact that Ven had insisted on several hidden blades in the armrests. *Times are difficult,* was all he'd said.

The elderly woman was dressed seriously, with a black robe that clasped at her throat. Her white hair was pinned into a bun. She looked every inch the strict schoolteacher-warrior that she was. "Even in your dreams, you have left yourself open to the spirits," Hanna continued, "and your emotions have leached into the spirits. All of Aratay is suffering with you. As queen, you are connected to the spirits in a way unlike any heir—the spirits fuel you, giving you a queen's special strength, but you also influence them. You must close yourself off from them before you cause more harm. I will show you how."

Straightening her shoulders, Naelin seemed to be steeling herself, and Daleina wondered if she was going to refuse. *She can't*, Daleina thought, *and she won't—not once she's seen what's happened*. To ensure that, though, Daleina gestured to the table before the other queen could speak. "I have collected reports from across Aratay, Naelin. There have been spirit attacks. Lives lost. Homes lost. Harvests damaged." She tapped her finger on the list, indicating the areas worst hit. "If we work together, we can repair much of it, but we have limited time before winter. I know you didn't intend for these consequences—"

Naelin interrupted her. "I intended to save my children, and I might have done so, if you hadn't interfered." Every word was clipped, as if she were holding back a landslide worth of anger.

Daleina flinched. She hadn't looked at it that way—she'd been trying to prevent a disaster, not keep Naelin from saving her children. She glanced at Ven. He looked worried, which wasn't good.

"You know as well as I do that those spirits were from Semo," Naelin continued—if she noticed the glance between her champion and Daleina, she didn't acknowledge it. "Six air spirits from Semo—they'd have no reason to cross into Aratay without orders. Spirits stay with their queen. Which means Merecot forced them to attack . . ." Her voice faltered, and she swallowed and continued on. "They acted under her orders, which means that she has Erian and Llor."

That . . . was possible, she supposed. "All I could glean from our spirits was that they felt 'other,'" Daleina said, bemused. She had assumed they were rogue spirits—it happened sometimes, albeit rarely, that a spirit was able to throw off the will of its queen for a brief period of time and cause deaths. Rogue spirits often had to be eliminated, regardless of the damage it caused to the land. And she might have done just that if Naelin had been here to help her, and she said as much. "I've searched for them without success." The fact was, she hadn't had as much time or energy to devote to the search as she might like, given all the other crises she'd been presented with—crises that Naelin had, however inadvertently, caused. "The thing is, we don't know they're from Semo. In fact, I very much doubt—"

Naelin shook her head. "They don't matter. They're puppets with teeth. Only the one pulling the strings matters. And if we work together, we can bring her down and save Erian and Llor, but I need your help to—"

"No," Daleina said, as gently as she could.

Naelin reeled back as if Daleina had struck her.

Daleina reached out toward her, then let her hand fall. "Naelin . . . Queen Naelin . . ." She searched for the right words. *I have to make her understand!* "I know you're in pain, but we have to think of the *whole* of Aratay. To wage a war against Semo—"

"Only its queen."

Shaking her head, Daleina tried to sound as firm as she could. "You can't attack a queen without attacking her country. Innocents will suffer, and you don't have any proof that she was responsible." And, as she'd said, Daleina very much doubted there *was* such proof. If Merecot had sent spirits to attack the queen's children, it was a stupid move—and Merecot was many things, but "stupid" wasn't one of them. She was subtle and devious and ruthlessly ambitious but never stupid.

She hated to say it, but the only one being stupid right now—

"Of course she was responsible!" Naelin shouted. "She had motive! Plenty of it. Revenge and ambition." With each outburst, the spirits on the ceiling gnawed through the wood with gusto. Vines shot out of the moldings and twisted around the sconces. Fire spirits whipped in circles within their flames, tossing sparks onto the floor.

Sending soothing thoughts, Daleina tried to calm them. It wasn't easy, though, as she had to keep her thoughts quiet and unobtrusive, not wanting to agitate Naelin any further. "Motive isn't proof, and I can't condone an attack—"

"You cannot prevent it," Naelin warned. Or, rather, *threatened.*

Daleina stood up straight at that, chin up, posture as regal as she knew how to make it. She may not be as powerful as Naelin, but she knew what it meant to be threatened, and she was not about to let *anyone* presume such a tone with her.

Sensing the tension, Ven laid his hand on Naelin's arm. "Naelin, don't do this. You'd throw Aratay into civil war. Innocent people will die."

Stepping back from him, Naelin pulled away. "You too?" she

whispered. "You'd abandon all hope of saving them? Just because you fear the consequences?"

Daleina wished she could comfort her. *This must feel like betrayal, all of us against her.* But she couldn't let the other queen start a war. *We haven't even recovered from the last battle.* The forest bore the scars.

And, because of Naelin, they now bore even more.

Headmistress Hanna clicked her tongue in disapproval. "You'd kill other people's children in a doomed quest to save your own. You have no proof your children are even alive, much less with the queen of Semo."

"They *are* alive! And we can keep our people safe if we work together," Naelin said, her voice shrill. Daleina shot a worried look at the spirits on the roof, who were still agitated. "You can defend Aratay while I attack Merecot."

"Say you attack, and say you win . . ." Ven said. "What if Merecot wasn't responsible? What if you kill her, and she doesn't have—never had—Erian and Llor? What if attacking her distracts you from finding whoever was truly responsible?"

Continuing to send soothing thoughts toward the spirits, Daleina pressed on. "You need to stop, assess, and *then*—when the immediate crises are over and when we're sure who's to blame—then we'll act. Together. I swear it. Your children will not be forgotten. But we have a responsibility to *all* the children of Aratay first."

Ven took Naelin's hands. "If this wasn't a random attack or a rogue spirit, we'll find out and we'll catch whoever was behind this. I swear it too."

Headmistress Hanna rolled forward, halting in front of the two thrones. Her back was straight, her chin lifted, and Daleina felt, for a moment, the same way she had years ago, before she entered the academy—as if the headmistress had all the answers. "After I've given Queen Naelin the training she needs, I will go to Semo, as ambassador. It's past time for a healthy dialogue between Semo and Aratay to be opened. While I'm there, I will search for any evidence that Queen Merecot was involved in the attack on Bayn and the children."

That was *not* what Daleina had expected her to say. She stared at the headmistress, the woman who had devoted her entire life to her students, to training future heirs—the woman who had been wounded permanently while defending them. "You'd do this? Leave Aratay? But the academy—"

"Will function fine without me," Hanna said. "And I would appreciate a change. Add to that the fact that I knew Merecot as a student, and I believe I am the ideal person to go."

Considering it, Daleina ran quickly through the pros and cons—Hanna was valuable here, both for her experience at the academy and for her always-wise advice. She was one of the few allies who knew everything that Daleina had done, both the good and the bad, and Daleina trusted her absolutely. She'd miss having such a trustworthy friend so close. In addition, if Merecot did mean to hurt Aratay, Daleina would be sending the headmistress directly into harm's way. On the other hand, Merecot knew and respected the headmistress, at least as much as she respected anyone, and Headmistress Hanna had no illusions about the flaws in Merecot's character. Hanna knew the history of the countries, was even-tempered and diplomatic, and, in short, would make an ideal ambassador.

*This might be just the thing to begin a peaceful dialogue between—*

Leaving the hearth, the fire spirits crackled as Naelin cried, "*My children are* alive! And in danger! And you talk about ambassadors and harvests and—don't you understand? We must act now, before it's too late!"

Daleina felt the pain radiate out and pour into the spirits. She tried to stem the flood, thrusting her mind into the spirits' swirling thoughts. *Calm! Stay calm! Don't—*

But they howled, from deep within the bowels of the earth.

She felt them shift, reach, claw, scream.

And the earthquake struck.

*Stop!*

Naelin heard the word well up inside her—but she couldn't say it. Once the power began to flow out of her, it gushed faster and faster until it was a flood that shuddered through her body. She felt it ram into the nearby spirits, felt their screams, and felt the earth shift as every earth spirit beneath the city bucked and writhed at once.

Only then did she cry out to them, *No! Stop!*

But it had no effect.

She pulled at her power, trying to draw it back inside her, as the throne room around her shook. She dropped to her knees. Dimly, she was aware of the others, crying out, falling. Tiles fell from the walls and shattered. A chandelier plummeted from the ceiling and hit the wood and shell table in the center—the table cracked in half.

*I can't stop. I don't know how to stop!*

She was hurting people. Badly. People could be dying. Innocent people. She pictured the papers that Daleina had shown her, lists she'd barely looked at. *I'm attacking my own people!*

*I am worse than Merecot.*

She felt the waves of rage inside her turn inward.

She didn't deserve . . . Didn't . . . Couldn't . . . Before the thought could even be completed, she felt arms around her, warm and familiar. She felt Ven's breath in her hair as he whispered her name, felt him stroke her back, felt him rock her side to side, as if she were a child who'd had a nightmare—the way she'd rocked Erian and Llor late at night, when they'd woken in a sweat, screaming out for her.

Just his arms and the whisper of her name, over and over.

With a shuddering gasp, Naelin pulled herself together enough to look around.

"What have I done?"

"Order them to stop!" Daleina snapped. "Help me!"

Beside her, she heard Headmistress Hanna, calm and no-nonsense: "You must construct a wall within you. Picture it as clearly as if it were in front of you. Every brick. Every chink. Pour the mortar. Smooth it."

She did as the headmistress said.

"Think only of the wall. Feel the divots in the bricks. Smell the clay. Row by row, lay your wall around your mind. All your thoughts and feelings reside within. Allow no gap, no sunlight, no hint of wind—build it higher, as high as it takes."

Naelin built, brick by brick, in her mind. It wasn't difficult for her—she *had* the power—but it was still taxing, as hard as if she were doing it for real. She labored, and sweat poured down her face.

Ven was murmuring, but she didn't hear him. Only saw the bricks. Only felt them beneath her fingers. She poured the mortar in her mind, thick so nothing would get through. She walled off the sunlight, she dammed up the flood, she sealed herself inside.

And then she opened her eyes.

"I'm sorry," she said quietly.

Ven kissed her forehead, which was damp with sweat. "If they're alive, we'll find them. Somehow. I promise. But you need to make sure there's a home to bring them back to."

THREE MINUTES BEFORE THE EARTHQUAKE, IN ANOTHER BRANCH of the palace, Queen Daleina's sister, Arin, was measuring one teaspoon of ervo juice. She poured it into the test tube and then exhaled. *Now for the tricky part.* She had to add precisely three drops, no more and no less, with five-second intervals between each drop to allow the potion to mix at the correct rate. All the ingredients needed to be combined in a particular order with the proper timing, or else its potency would be reduced. She'd already mixed one subpar potion earlier, and now there was a frog in the palace garden hopping around with yellow and purple fur.

Done correctly, this potion should strip the skin off a spirit.

Incorrectly, and the results were . . . less impressive. And furrier. The potion was her own concoction, guided by Master Garnah. Arin had progressed quickly past the basics and was developing her own course of study. She had no interest in becoming a poisoner like Master Garnah, but she *was* interested in potions that could affect spirits.

"Slow and steady," Master Garnah advised. "Consider it a dance, with a partner who might or might not kill you if you step on his feet."

"Sounds like a sensible dance to decline." Dipping the eye-dropper into the distilled water, Arin prepared to add the first ingredient—water, harmless on its own but host to all the other more volatile components.

"Ah, but it's the most exciting, beautiful dance there is! If you don't dance it, you haven't lived." Positioning her arms as if she had an invisible partner, Master Garnah swirled around the room. She bypassed the other tables, the pile of supplies, and the stack of dead frogs. They'd started with rats as their subjects, but Master Garnah wanted the potions tested on non-mammals as well. "The dance with destiny! Or death. Or immortality. What-ever. Take your pick of something poetic." Swishing past Arin, Garnah called out, "Three drops, my dear!"

Arin held the dropper over the test tube and added three drops. She then went for the next ingredient, which was known for its explosive qualities. Five drops. *Almost done.*

Last ingredient.

She felt the tremor through her feet, and then the table be-gan to shake. Her hand, with the final ingredient in the dropper, shook.

Glass tubes and bottles rattled together. A bowl slid off the table, and the liquid spattered across the expensive carpet. Arin felt a yank on her arm as Master Garnah pulled her back. She turned and ran as the floor rocked and shook.

Master Garnah shoved another table over and pulled Arin with her behind it. "Down!"

Arin obeyed, crouching down as the world shook and shud-dered. Cracks ran down the walls and sounded as if the whole palace were breaking apart—

*Boom!*

The potion exploded, and shards of glass shot into the walls. She saw them embed in the wood, above where they hid.

And as suddenly as it had begun, the earthquake ended. Everything was still.

Arin stared at the shards of glass stuck into the wall.

Standing, Master Garnah dusted off her knees. "Invigorating," she commented. "Come, you must learn faster. There are many more potions you need to know."

"But the quake . . ." She had to see if Daleina was okay. Had spirits caused it? What happened? Had there been an attack? Semo again?

"Potions," Master Garnah said, climbing over a fallen chair. Glass crunched under her shoes. "There's no time to waste. Don't you understand?"

"Understand what?" Climbing out from behind the table, Arin began to clean up the broken bottles. Powders had spilled on the floor—they'd be useless now. *I need a broom.*

"A queen is supposed to keep us safe," Master Garnah said. "And a content, stable queen will do exactly that. But with a queen of sorrow . . . You must learn quickly, girl. Sooner rather than later, you will need to be able to keep yourself safe"—she plucked a bit of glass from the wall and shook it at Arin—"or you will find yourself in pieces.

"Now—leave the mess, and learn!"

# CHAPTER 9

"Y ou must be drenched in diamonds, my queen, per tradi-tion," the courtier said. Merecot hadn't bothered to learn her name, but the lady wore a row of jewels in the curve of her ear and gold strands laced in her hair. "If you will permit me . . ."

Merecot waved her hand. "Drench as you please."

Cautiously, the lady approached her, and Merecot wanted to bare her teeth and growl to see if she'd flinch. But she resisted the urge, because she wasn't five years old. *Oh, but it's tempting!* Suppressing a grin, Merecot held herself still in front of the mir-ror as the courtier draped necklaces around her neck, fastened bracelets all the way up her arms, and wove jewels into her black hair. As she decorated her queen, the courtier began to prattle about the jewels with increasing confidence. "The Crown was given this necklace by the town of Erodale, during the reign of Queen Eri of Semo. It was carved by the master jeweler Hoile, in his final year of life. It is said that his blindness cleared, and he regained the strength in his hands for the length of time it took him to carve the thirty-six petals into the shape of a perfect rose. When he finished, he carried his masterpiece to the queen and presented it to her. As she clasped it around her neck, his blind-ness returned, his hands shook again, and his heart gave out. He died at her feet."

She had a story like that for every single bauble.

Merecot would have demanded silence, except that she had a more effective way to skip the history lesson. So instead of listening to the courtier's prattle, she sent her mind sailing out of her chambers, out of the palace, and across the mountains, skipping from spirit to spirit like a rock across the surface of a pond.

She pushed her mind farther, beyond the border, into Aratay. Most queens wouldn't even have had the strength to reach this distance. *But then most queens are not even close to me.* There was something strangely soothing about the unpleasant sensation of spreading herself so thin and wide that she could brush against the forests of Aratay.

*Not that I miss the forests.* She didn't. *Shadows everywhere. Always having to worry about the stupid bridges breaking.* She'd climbed enough ladders and swung on enough ridiculous ropes to last her several lifetimes. Besides, she'd left behind her worst memories between those branches, and she didn't regret that for one second. But she had spent the majority of her life above the forest floor, with leaves overhead, and sometimes it felt strange to feel her feet on the ground and see the open sky with nothing brown or green to obscure the sun. And the mountains—oh, the glorious mountains! They were why she had chosen Semo, as opposed to the flat farmlands of Chell or the icy glaciers of Elhim or the ever-present salty stickiness of Belene.

The mountains were fists punched at the sky, fabulous "you don't own me" gestures at the world. Her favorites were in the west, with their sharp ridgelines and sheer cliffs, but she also admired the southern mountains, with their boulders that could crush a town. And she admired the people who lived in them, carving out lives on the stone faces, eking out their existence from the plants and animals that were hardy enough to live there.

*I fit well here,* she thought.

*If only there were no spirits trying to destroy everything that's beautiful and good.*

Merecot rode with the wind above a snowcapped peak and then soared down the other side. She was only dimly aware of her body, back in her chambers, as the courtier rebraided her hair to hold even more diamonds, plumbed from the depths of the mountains.

Shivering, Merecot strained harder, sweeping her awareness over the strange *other* feel of the spirits of Aratay. They moved like bugs through her consciousness, making her itch, until at last she brushed against the minds of spirits that felt familiar, hidden in the shadows where the Aratayian spirits wouldn't see them—touching them felt like breathing in fresh mountain air.

Her spirits, the ones she had sent into the forest.

The ones she'd sent with a purpose.

She touched their thoughts. *Did you succeed?*

Images were blurred—golden trees, blue sky . . . and then a wolf, running with the queen's children . . . and then a wolf, running alone . . .

*Did you catch them?*

*Did you kill him?*

From across the border, it was difficult to sort through the tangle of the spirits' memories. But then she saw an image, as crisp as if it had happened in front of her: the wolf running alone into the untamed lands.

Merecot laughed out loud. Distantly, she heard the startled courtier speak, but her mind was too far away to hear words. She felt the spirits' confusion, then disappointment, then fear. Fear of her anger at their failure.

She consoled them. *But you didn't fail!* Granted, the Protector of Queens wasn't dead, as she'd ordered, but he might as well be. Given what he was, he couldn't return from the untamed lands, not on his own. *He's as good as dead. But what of the children?*

The spirits milled in confusion. They didn't know . . . They . . . She suddenly realized she was touching only *four* minds. *Where are the other two?*

*North* was the answer.

Merecot issued a command to her four spirits to return home, secretly and carefully, and then she drew her mind back across the border, across the mountains of Semo, toward the castle. Casting her mind out wide, she found the two missing spirits.

They, along with their prizes, were not only in her land, but they were drawing rapidly close.

*Nearly here!*

Yanking her mind back, she crashed into her body. She swatted away the hands of the courtier. "That's enough," she snarled at her. Merecot's eyes fixed on the mirror. Glittering, she looked as if she'd fallen into a vat of glass shards.

"Go. And send Jastra to me."

She paced, which was not an easy feat in the layers of formal skirts. The voluminous fabric swooshed and swished as she paced in a tight circle in the center of her chambers. *Am I ready? I must be ready!*

Moments later, the guards swung open her doors, and Jastra entered. She too had dressed for the Harvest Festival, festooned with rubies, emeralds, and sapphires—precious stones were considered fruits of the earth, appropriate to the celebration of the literal fruits of the earth. She wore no fewer than six necklaces, as well as a sapphire the size of Merecot's fist nestled on top of her head. It was brilliantly blue against the thin white of Jastra's hair.

"My dear, you look lovely," Jastra said. "You honor our people."

"Leave us," Merecot ordered the courtiers and the guards.

Bowing, the courtiers scurried out, and the guards shut the doors behind them. Jastra clucked her tongue. "You seem nervous. Don't be. You'll have one of the court historians on each side of you, and they will feed you all the ritual lines. They know it backwards, forwards, and upside down. Sometimes I think they're born knowing—"

Shaking her head, Merecot beamed at Jastra. She wasn't nervous. She felt like dancing! Seizing her mentor's hands, she squeezed them in excitement. "The Protector is gone, and our guests are nearly here!"

"Splendid!" Jastra said, beaming at her with a beloved parent's pride. "You do realize they'll most likely cry. Or even scream. Children often do."

"I'll make sure they're happy here," Merecot promised. "Semo is the most beautiful land in all of Renthia. Full of delight. They'll enjoy their stay."

Jastra patted her hand.

And Merecot added, "And if they're lucky and both queens of Aratay see reason, I may not even have to kill their mother."

"I do admire your optimism," Jastra said fondly.

ERIAN WAS TERRIFIED.

Or, at least, she had been at first, when the spirits with vicious beaks attacked her and Llor, chasing them as they fled on Bayn. When they'd plucked her away from the wolf, she thought she'd die from fear. She'd screamed so hard that she'd scraped her throat and lost her voice. She was left merely whimpering as the spirits carried them north.

But she couldn't stay terrified forever. Oh, she was still scared. She wasn't stupid. She knew what rogue spirits did to people they caught.

Except that the spirits *didn't* tear her and Llor limb from limb.

Or eat them.

Or skin them.

Or squeeze them.

Or drop them.

And after a few hours, being afraid became...well, *boring*. She began to notice they were flying between mountains, extraordinary mountains, with peaks so high they vanished between clouds and cliffs so steep and sheer they looked like petrified waterfalls. And the colors! The stone wasn't just grayish, like on the forest floor. It was shimmery black or as red as the sunset or streaked with glittering white sparkles.

Snow clung to the ridges and peaks, and far below, she saw rivers—great, gushing, white foam rivers—battering the walls of canyons.

The two spirits carried them between the canyon walls, and the only sound was the rush of wind. But that sound was so loud that it was like a steady scream. Erian wondered if, when the flight ended, she'd be able to hear anything else.

Eventually, the flight did end.

As the sun sank, so did the spirits, gliding down into one of the canyons. She saw a dark blotch on a canyon wall, which grew as they flew closer—a cave. And her terror returned as they flew inside, into the darkness.

*Now they'll kill us!*

She was dropped a few inches above the rock floor and landed with a thump. It hurt for an instant, but she hadn't fallen far. She scrambled, trying to get her feet underneath her to run away—she didn't know where to. The cave was halfway up a cliff. But everything inside her screamed, *Away, away, away!*

She smacked into a cool leathery body—the spirit!

Screaming, she ran in the other direction and then tripped over something soft. She sprawled forward, scraping her hands on the rocks as she tried to catch herself.

"Erian?"

She'd tripped over Llor. Crawling to him, she wrapped her arms around him tight. He was crying, big heaving sobs that shook his body. "Shh," she said into his hair. "You're okay. We're okay."

"Are we going to die?"

"No," she said instantly.

"I don't want to die. It'll hurt. And I'll miss you."

She agreed with that with all her heart.

"Is Bayn all right?"

*I don't know*, she thought. But what she said was: "I'm sure he is."

They held each other in the dark cave for hours. A few times, Erian tried to crawl toward what she thought was the mouth of the cave, but the two spirits blocked the way. Eventually, the children slept, curled around each other.

At dawn, the spirits pried them apart, lifted them in the air, and flew on. After the initial burst of fear, Erian began to feel numb. And hungry. And thirsty. And she had to pee.

She cried when she couldn't hold it any longer, as the pee dripped down her leg. But by sunset, she didn't care anymore, and all she could think about was how thirsty she was. She barely looked at the mountains as she hung from the spirit's talons.

The two spirits cawed to each other, and at last she raised her head.

And saw the castle.

It was beautiful: all white stone, carved into the side of the mountain, with turrets and towers and bridges and fantastic waterfalls. It sparkled in the setting sun. Erian blinked at it, unsure if she was imagining it. *I could be seeing things. That could be what happens before you die of thirst.*

But the two spirits flew toward a balcony and then in through a broad, open window. They deposited Erian and Llor onto a soft white carpet, thicker than grass. Erian lay there for a moment, trying to remind her arms and legs how to move.

She heard a woman's voice. "Welcome to Semo."

"You're her," Llor said. "The mean queen."

Erian lifted her head and saw jewels, glittering brighter than the night sky. The queen of Semo was covered in strands of diamonds that draped down her huge skirts. More diamonds were woven into her black hair so that they glittered like stars in the night sky. She had a white streak in her hair, like Alet had had. *They were sisters*, Erian remembered. Beside the queen, an old woman was dripping with just as many sapphires and rubies. Her wrinkled cheeks had been rouged red to match the rubies, as if she were trying to transform into a jewel. It was a sight that didn't make any sense to her tired brain.

But she knew Llor shouldn't have called the queen "mean."

The old woman wrinkled her nose. "You should have them bathed."

"Immediately," Queen Merecot agreed. She bent her lips into a smile—it didn't look normal on her. It looked as if someone was squishing her cheeks so her lips turned upward. "And how would you like some food and drink? Cake, perhaps? All children love cake."

Erian picked herself up off the floor. She straightened her shoulders and lifted her chin, aware how filthy and smelly she was but deciding not to care. She didn't like how the queen said "children," where she didn't look that all old herself. Certainly not as old as Mama. "We'd like to go home, Your Majesty. Please send us there."

Queen Merecot turned to the wrinkled woman. "She did say 'please.'"

The old, wrinkled woman pressed her lips together and fixed Merecot with a disapproving look that reminded Erian of Mama. "Don't taunt them."

Chastened, Queen Merecot gave Erian and Llor another over-bright smile. "Please don't be afraid, children. I mean you no harm, and your stay here will be temporary. I will ensure you're comfortable and happy during your visit."

Nodding at Queen Merecot, the old woman clapped her hands as if this were all very exciting. "You'll have your very own room and play areas. Games, clothes, food, desserts, everything you want, you may have!"

*I want to go home*, Erian thought, but didn't bother saying it again.

"You're not victims," Queen Merecot said, as if she wanted to reassure them. "You're pawns."

Erian did not feel reassured.

"You're a bad person," Llor informed her. Sliding closer to him, Erian elbowed him in the stomach. *Don't make her mad,* she wanted to say.

But Queen Merecot merely smiled—a real smile this time. "Yes, I am," she agreed, without any trace of anger in her voice. "But I am a very good queen."

THE DIFFICULTY WITH THINKING ABOUT MERECOT AS HER ENEMY was that Daleina still thought of her as her friend.

Even after the invasion.

Even after the poisoning.

In a way, she understood those things, and so she still saw Merecot as the girl in the room next to hers at the academy, who helped her with her summoning lessons and who flooded her bedroom when Daleina accidentally set it on fire. *I can't hate her. Maybe I can't forgive her, but I can't hate her either.*

Standing on her balcony, Daleina let the vines in the railing grow and twist around her hands. A tree spirit scurried over her fingers, and she ignored it—she had to conserve her energy. Her first task was to soothe the spirits and stop the random attacks, and then she could figure out how to fix the homes and the orchards. Reaching out with her mind, she sent soft thoughts as far as she could:

*Calm. Calm. Calm.*

"Our people will starve if the harvests fail," Champion Havtru said behind her.

She broke her thought, took a deep breath, and reminded herself he was here to help. "We have emergency stores. We'll open them if we need to."

"Won't be enough. It'll be a lean winter."

"Lean is not the same as starving, though." The tree spirit, which looked like a knot of brambles the size of a chipmunk, nibbled at Daleina's fingers. Glaring at it, she sent it scrambling away. "I will do the best I can. And when she's ready, I'm certain Queen Naelin will assist as well." *If she's ever ready.* According to Ven, after Daleina had sent a nicely worded diplomatic latter to Queen Merecot—apologizing for the "incursion" and inquiring about any knowledge of the children—Naelin had shut herself in her room and, with the assistance of Headmistress Hanna, was consumed with trying not to cause another earthquake.

Daleina didn't want to be insensitive, but a little help would have been nice. Responsibilities didn't end when tragedies struck. *I'd thought she was so strong.* And then Daleina immediately felt guilty for thinking that—in truth it had only been a few days, and Naelin still believed her children were alive. *There's as little proof of that as there is that Merecot's the cause.*

"Oh, of course, Your Majesty! I didn't mean to criticize. Just was thinking that Queen Naelin picked the worst time of year to agitate the spirits."

Daleina didn't disagree with that. But she couldn't say it out loud. So she decided to switch tack. "Havtru, tell me, how would you prioritize the requests for assistance?" Coming back inside, she waved at the sheath of papers that the seneschal had left for her. So far, she hadn't touched them. Keeping people from dying today had taken priority over keeping people from dying in the future. She glanced at him and noticed he was twisting his hat in his hands as if it were a wet dishrag and shooting glances at the door as if he wanted to be anywhere but here. She knew he wouldn't leave—Ven had insisted that a champion guard her in addition to the usual palace guards, at least until the spirits were calmed, and he'd assigned Champion Havtru—but it was clear he felt out of his element.

*Let me tell you about being queen sometime.*

He swallowed a few times. "Your Majesty, I don't feel qualified—"

"You lived in the outer forest. A berry picker? That was your former occupation?"

"Yes, Your Majesty, but surely there are chancellors—"

"The chancellors prioritize their own regions, and the courtiers overvalue the cities. I want the opinion of someone who will look out for those who have no voice."

He bowed and picked up the sheath of papers, though he didn't look happy about it. *I can't care if he's happy or not,* she thought. *I need help!* It was too much—the amount of damage that Naelin had done was overwhelming, and the country was still recovering from what Merecot had inflicted on them when she swept down with her spirits from the north. Rubbing her tired eyes, Daleina wondered if she'd ever stop feeling like she was making things up as she went along. She couldn't imagine Queen Fara had ever felt this way. *Maybe she just hid it better.*

One of the guards by her door called, "Champion Ven, Your Majesty!"

"Allow him in," she answered.

She heard Ven's familiar footsteps—the soft, measured steps of someone who was always alert—as he entered her chambers and then came out on the balcony. He nodded to Champion Havtru, then bowed to her. "Your Majesty, a message has arrived from the queen of Semo. She sent it with a spirit bearing an ambassador's colors."

"Since when are champions in charge of delivering the mail?" But that flippant question was mostly to cover the fact that her heart was thumping faster—this was the first they'd heard from Merecot since the attack on Naelin's children, and what the queen of Semo said would determine the fate of many.

Ven flopped into a chair and ran his fingers through his hair. He looked, Daleina thought, more like an unkempt scarecrow than a crisp soldier. She wondered when the last time he'd slept was. "Ever since paranoia became a required personality trait." He laced his hands together, as if to force himself to sit still. "I came to counsel caution."

"I'm always cautious."

"It's with the guards right now. You should ask Hamon's mother to check it before you open it." He held up a hand to forestall any objections. "I know she is not the most trustworthy person, but she is the most knowledgeable. Queen Merecot has already resorted to poison once. I know you want to trust that your mercy transformed her, but humor me."

In theory, it was sound. But she didn't want to owe more favors to the Queen's Poisoner than she already did. It was bad enough that the woman had been instrumental in saving her life. "My guards always examine—"

"Please, Daleina."

He so rarely called her just Daleina anymore, especially in front of other people. Havtru flinched at the familiarity, then buried himself again in reading through the requests.

Daleina raised her voice. "Seneschal? Please ask Queen Naelin to join us in the Master Poisoner's laboratory and have the missive from the queen of Semo transported there as well. Carefully. As if it contains a nest of venomous snakes."

"Because it might," Ven put in.

Daleina shot him a look. "She needs diplomacy to work. Her people require it."

"Only while you're alive."

Without dignifying that with a response—because he was right; she may have a co-ruler but she still had no heirs—Daleina swept out of her chambers. The palace guards folded around her in tight formation, flanking her as she strode through the halls. Fire spirits flitted from sconce to sconce, following her, watching her, hating her. As they touched each candle, it flamed up and scorched the ceiling. *Calm*, she thought at them. *Calm*.

She wished it would work on herself.

*Calm*.

Outside of Garnah's room, Daleina waited while the palace guards checked for threats. From within, she heard Garnah say in a mild voice, "You may not want to touch that."

And then Daleina's sister, Arin, chirped, "Definitely don't touch that! Or that. Or . . . no, not that either, unless you want to itch. And spit up blood . . . You can touch that one. It just smells nice."

Another familiar voice—Hamon: "I can vouch for them. For now. But we thank you for your conscientious thoroughness."

"We do *not* thank them," Garnah said. "Oafs."

That was enough. Daleina swept into the room. She knew she looked regal—she wore her tiara of curled vines and her silver gown, the one she'd picked because it made her look older and she'd wanted to impress the chancellors with her seriousness—and she was rewarded with Garnah, Hamon, and Arin all falling silent, bowing and curtsying. She thought about telling her sister not to curtsy to her, but it was important right now that Garnah see her as the queen of Aratay, not a piece in whatever game she was currently playing. "We require your assistance," Daleina declared.

Garnah cleared her throat. "Is that plural, or the royal 'we'?"

*Depends on how royal Naelin is feeling*, Daleina thought.

Ven stepped forward. "The queen of Semo has sent Their Majesties a message. We wish for you to examine it before the queens read it."

"Ah, you think poison?" Garnah asked. "Unlikely, since that approach already failed once. Granted, it's a classic for a reason, and I can't help but be flattered that you would come to me, Your Majesty. Unless you chose me for my expendability, rather than my expertise."

"Queen Daleina isn't like that, Mother," Hamon said.

"She's a queen," Garnah countered. "She *should* be like that. Have no fear, Your Majesty, I would be delighted to be of service in any way I can. I am anxious to prove my loyalty, though some would say I already have."

"Those people just haven't met you yet," Hamon muttered.

Garnah laughed. "Delightful boy." Reaching over, she patted his cheek, and Hamon flinched. Looking from one to the other, Daleina wondered what they'd been talking about before she'd entered. Hamon didn't visit his mother willingly.

The guest room had been converted into a laboratory with long tables running against the walls, and dozens of beakers and test tubes and other glassware. Containers of powders labeled in Arin's neat handwriting were stacked beneath one table, and all the rugs had been rolled up and taken away. Even the curtains had been removed. Except for one divan, the furniture in the room was practical: tables, benches, stools, and one gurney. Thankfully, it did not hold a body. Or worse, a live "patient." Hamon had told her plenty about his mother's old experiments. Garnah had sworn up and down that she didn't engage in that sort of "basic research" anymore, and Daleina had made Arin promise to tell if she encountered anything of questionable morality. But still . . . *I've become just as paranoid as Ven.*

It was no more than a few awkward minutes before Queen Naelin arrived, which did nothing to diminish the awkwardness. In fact, the presence of the Queen of Sorrow (as Daleina had heard a few courtiers call her) increased the tension in the room to such a level that Daleina thought she could taste it: thick and sour.

Queen Naelin pushed the wheelchair that held Headmistress Hanna, who had been attempting to teach the older queen more techniques to control her thoughts and emotions. Hanna had reported privately that it was like trying to teach a rock–she listened but she was so set in her ways, you didn't know if she absorbed any of it. Still, Hanna was trying to squeeze in as many lessons as possible, in case Daleina agreed to send her to Semo. *But I haven't agreed yet*, Daleina thought. *It depends on what Merecot says.*

"I am sorry for your loss, Your Majesty," the Queen's Poisoner said with a bow. "Know that I and my skills are at your disposal, should you require it."

"*Mother*," Hamon growled.

Garnah blinked. "What? What did I say?"

"It's not certain they're dead," Ven said. There was a hardness in his voice that Daleina hadn't heard before, as if he wanted to hit something or someone.

Naelin growled, "They are *not*."

"We are pursuing diplomatic answers," Daleina said firmly.

"Ahh," Garnah said. "So that's why you're having me check her letter? Because 'diplomacy' involves possible death?"

"A precaution," Daleina said, and wished the letter would arrive already. She looked at Naelin and thought she'd never seen a person look so hollow. She wondered if it would help to have Havtru talk to her—he'd lost his wife in a spirit attack, before he became a champion—or if there were something in Garnah's repertoire of potions that would ease Naelin's pain. Even with Hanna's impromptu lesson during the earthquake, she could feel the despair and anger leaking through to the spirits.

Queen Naelin didn't speak again.

"Your Majesty . . ." Arin hesitated, opened her mouth, and then shut it and shrank back as if she'd changed her mind.

"Go on," Hamon encouraged her, always kind. Daleina spared a smile for him.

Daleina also smiled at her sister, and Arin said in a rush, "Erian and Llor were two of the bravest kids I've ever met. Two of the bravest people. And I just . . . I mean, I can't help thinking if they could have survived . . ." She swallowed. "I just wanted to say I believe you. I believe they're alive."

"That makes three of us, then," Naelin said. "You, me, and Ven. The rest of Aratay seems to have already condemned them."

Tentatively, Daleina reached out to touch the nearby spirits, to make certain they weren't going to explode into violence again, but they felt subdued, as if they were absorbing more sadness than anger. She met Ven's eyes and saw pain in them. The silence in the room was oppressive.

At last, two palace caretakers and more guards arrived, thankfully breaking the somber spell. Escorted by the guards, the caretakers carried a thin lacquered black box that appeared to be shaped from a single piece of wood. Smooth, it had no joints, only a lid. They placed it on one of the worktables, bowed, and retreated.

*This must be the letter. And . . . a gift?*

Garnah stepped forward. Reaching into the pockets on her skirt, she withdrew a variety of powders and began to sprinkle them on the box. She muttered to herself as she examined it from every angle, and Daleina watched as fingerprints appeared in the dust—Garnah then tossed a few drops of liquid, and the powder puffed into a cloud above the box. It dissipated in the air. "Outside is fine," she announced.

"Did you test for—" Hamon began.

"Obviously."

"But what about—"

"Don't be an idiot."

"You can't know—"

"It's safe." She opened the lid and lifted a parchment out. "The gift itself is wrapped in velvet, and here is the letter." She sniffed it and then applied an assortment of different powders, which turned purple then white. She knocked them to the floor. "Nothing alarming about the letter. You may read it." She held it out.

Hamon took it and then passed it to Daleina, who read. "It's addressed to Queen Naelin, not to me." *Curious,* she thought.

"Read it aloud," Naelin said without turning around. Her eyes were fixed on the fireplace, where two fire spirits curled between the logs.

"'To Queen Naelin of the forests of Aratay, long may you reign in Renthia.'"

Garnah murmured, "A pleasant beginning."

"Quiet," Hamon said.

"Merely expressing an opinion."

"Read on," Naelin said.

Daleina saw two lizardlike fire spirits spit flames onto the hearth. Headmistress Hanna clearly noticed too, because she began whispering in Queen Naelin's ear. The fire spirits withdrew to the logs, smoldering, their ember-black eyes glaring at the humans as if they wanted to flay them all alive. *Which they do, of course,* she thought. *Fly and burn and bite and claw.*

Daleina read, "'Please accept my most profound apology for...'" Her voice trailed off as she scanned ahead. *Oh.*

*Oh no.*

She raised her head to look at Naelin.

"It seems *I* owe you an apology," Daleina said, trying to keep her voice calm. She forced herself to steady her hands so no one would see they'd begun shaking. "Your children are alive. This is, in essence, a ransom note."

Across the room, Naelin made a strangled kind of sound.

"I believe it's written by Merecot herself, not a scribe." Daleina held the parchment out so Headmistress Hanna could see.

"Yes," Hanna confirmed. "I remember her script. She always scrawled like that. Lousy penmanship."

Continuing, Daleina read out loud, "'Please accept my most profound apology for the inconvenience and pain I have caused you through my actions.'"

Naelin hissed. "'Inconvenience'?"

The fire spirits crackled.

"Control your emotions," Hanna cautioned.

Naelin glared at the headmistress, but she did, in fact, seem to calm—or, at least, the spirits did.

"'The fact that I have had to resort to such methods horrifies me, but I must put the needs of my people before my own personal views. Let me lay bare to you the truth: I sent six air spirits into Aratay with two purposes: one, to eliminate the Protector of Queens, the wolf known as Bayn, who would have surely stood in the way of my ultimate goal.'"

"*Bayn?*" Ven said.

Daleina lowered the letter. "Does anyone know what she means by 'Protector of Queens'?" She'd never heard the term before, least of all applied to her wolf, whom she hadn't even allowed herself to truly mourn. *He was my friend, but "Protector"?*

"What of my children?" Naelin said.

Daleina read on. "'And two, to secure your children, to be used as leverage against your good behavior. I have taken this action to ensure that you fulfill what you have already promised. It was *never* my intent to harm a single human of Aratay, least of all your children. And I have not harmed but a single hair on their heads.'"

Hamon frowned. "Isn't the expression '*not* a single hair'?"

"Apparently, the queen of Semo has a delightful sense of humor," Garnah said. She lifted a clump of hair from the box. "She's not much for subtlety, though, is she?" Daleina guessed it was snipped from one of Naelin's children.

Naelin let out a noise, half like a growl and half a moan. She looked as if she wanted to tear the world apart with her bare hands. Ven clamped his hands down on her shoulder and whispered furiously in her ear. Headmistress Hanna also wheeled closer to her, talking rapidly.

Daleina waited for the next earthquake.

It didn't come.

*She's learning control.* Daleina was impressed. *This letter makes me want to cause an earthquake.* How could she have misjudged Merecot so badly? She'd been so convinced that Merecot couldn't be responsible, that she wouldn't be so stupid.

She'd been wrong.

Daleina quickly summarized the rest of the letter. "She demands one of us come to Semo and assist her with the 'overabundance of spirits' in her lands. She claims she only took the children to provide incentive and that she had to take dramatic action in order to catch our attention. She goes on to promise they'll be treated like honored guests and will be returned as soon as negotiations are concluded."

"It's a trap," Ven said.

Garnah snorted. "Obviously."

"Not so obviously," Hanna argued. "She's desperate. She was desperate enough to try to kill Queen Daleina, desperate enough to invade, and now desperate enough to kidnap Naelin's children. She wants to save Semo, and since we haven't helped her do that yet—"

"We've been healing Aratay! Healing it from *her* actions!" Daleina had planned on sending an ambassador sooner, but with winter coming and the harvest in danger . . . "There were other priorities."

"Not for her," Hanna pointed out.

Closing her eyes, Daleina crumpled the letter in her hand. She knew she should be done feeling betrayed by Merecot—after all, her former friend had had her poisoned—but this was a fresh surprise. *I shouldn't have stopped Naelin from attacking.* She should have joined in, thrown all the spirits of Aratay against the border and broken through. "If you want that invasion, Naelin, you have it."

Naelin didn't respond.

Daleina opened her eyes.

She saw Naelin had crossed the room to the box that held the locks of her children's hair. She'd taken a curled strand away from Garnah and was stroking it. "Attacking would endanger Erian and Llor. Ven, you were right. We needed to know who and why."

"Now that we do, how do you want to proceed?" Daleina asked. "This isn't merely a move against your children—an attack on our soil is a direct challenge to our sovereignty. It must be answered." She wondered if Naelin understood that. This wasn't just about Naelin's children; it was about all the children of Aratay. If Merecot thought she could simply take the queen's children . . .

*It can't be allowed. It's an act of war.*

"I go to Semo," Naelin said, as if it were the most obvious thing in the world. "I help her with the spirits, and then I bring back my children."

Garnah heaved a dramatic sigh. "Did you miss the part where this is a *trap*? You step foot in Semo, and she will kill you. She's already confessed to trying to kill your wolf 'protector' . . . which, I might add, is a bit unhinged."

Hanna rolled forward. "Accept my offer to be ambassador. Let me assess the situation and determine whether or not this is actually a trap or if the children are in fact there and alive. Merecot won't refuse an ambassador—it's a clear indication that we're taking her seriously and a logical precaution. I'll make my assessment as quickly as possible, and if she seems sincere, I will send word for Queen Naelin to come."

"You'd be placing yourself in danger," Ven objected.

"I work with spirits," Hanna said. "I've always been in danger. Besides, those children are worth the risk to me."

*It's not a terrible idea.* Not only would Hanna be able to determine whether Merecot was sincere in her plea for help, but she might be able to gather information that would lead to a successful rescue. "If Merecot truly wants our assistance, she won't hurt our ambassador." Daleina looked to Naelin.

"If," Ven emphasized.

"I should go now," Naelin said. "I'm their mother."

*You're also a queen*, Daleina wanted to say, but she didn't because she didn't think it would help. Naelin hadn't forgotten she was queen, or that they had no heirs. *She simply doesn't care. Her children come first.* "This is the safest way to proceed, for them and for Aratay."

NAELIN HAD NEVER HATED BEFORE.

Not like this.

This . . . felt like the hatred of the spirits. She wanted to rip the very mountains from the ground and bury Merecot beneath them. But she knew Daleina was right. And Headmistress Hanna was right. Even Garnah was right.

It could be a trap.

And if she went, without any plan or preparation, she could be killed and her children doomed. But if she were to be patient and agree to send an ambassador . . . she might learn a way to rescue Erian and Llor without springing whatever trap the northern queen had planned.

And yet everything inside her screamed, *Save them now!*

She desperately wanted to. Wanted to find the person who thought it was okay to take her children, to take their hair, and show that person just exactly what it felt like to have something taken from them.

Quite simply, their blood.

But she had to be smart and careful. She had proof they were alive, or at least almost proof, and it would be foolish to rush in and jeopardize the chance of keeping them alive.

How she was tempted, though . . .

"We send Headmistress Hanna," Naelin ultimately agreed. "She confirms they're there and sends us a report as quickly as possible—the second she knows they're alive. Then I go in and save them, either by helping with the excess spirits in Semo if this is not a trap or by force and guile if it is one."

Garnah clapped her hands like a gleeful child. "And then you kill Queen Merecot?"

"Yes," Naelin said and met Daleina's eyes. *She has to see we can't show mercy this time. What Merecot did wasn't just against me; it was against all of Aratay. It was an act of war, and as Daleina said herself, it must be answered.*

She saw the younger queen's shoulders sag and then straighten. Naelin waited, not breaking eye contact. At last, Daleina said, "Yes, then we kill her."

# CHAPTER 10

The air was still. No breeze.

The rain didn't fall. It misted in a weak drizzle that only dampened the canopy and didn't reach the forest floor. Grayness obscured the sky.

Fires wouldn't light quickly. Even the most skilled woodsmen had to strike multiple sparks before anything would catch, which shouldn't have been the case, given the lack of a proper rain.

Fruit rotted before it ripened, or failed to ripen at all.

Across Aratay, the people counted their canned fruit, preserved meat, and sacks of flour—and then counted again, hoping they had missed something that would help when the cold struck so that they'd be able to feed their families through the winter, but knowing it wouldn't be enough and that counting wasn't changing the fact that the harvest had failed.

That the queens had failed.

As she traveled north as the new ambassador to Semo, Hanna could feel the anguish coating the land in a musty gauze that dampened all joy and darkened all colors. She had coached Queen Naelin as much as she could before she left, but the new queen was too powerful and already too set in her ways on how she used her power. It was why heirs were always found as girls, to be trained while their minds were still malleable. With half a life already in hand, Naelin couldn't just shake the foundations she

had built that informed who she was. And yet that very founda-
tion *had* been shaken—her belief in her ability to keep her children safe—and now her emotions leaked through every time she
wasn't consciously blocking them, even in her sleep.

While she fretted, the land fretted too.

In all honesty, it matched Hanna's mood as well. She *wanted* to
believe this wasn't a trap, that Merecot was merely desperate on
behalf of her people, that the children were alive and unharmed
and would be returned safely to their mother . . . but after all
she'd seen and everyone who had died, it was hard to believe that
everything would be all right. That it even mattered what Merecot's intentions were. She felt as if she'd used up the last vestige of
her optimism during the queen of Semo's invasion. *It died while I
watched children die.* Over the years, she had watched too many
die, and yet this somehow felt worse.

*Because betrayal always hurts more than random violence.*

Wrapped in her thoughts, Hanna traveled north without talking to the four guards who accompanied her about much more
than practicalities: would she be more comfortable sleeping in a
hammock or on a platform, did she feel she could wheel across
this bridge, would she wait while they attached the safety harnesses to her chair, could she be patient while they fetched the
basket for her to ride in. She was aware it was not simple to travel
through the trees with an old woman who couldn't walk, even
with a chair adapted to the forest, and she prided herself on keeping any complaints about her own discomfort to herself and handling her aches and pains as best she could.

Champion Ven would have told her not to be a martyr. *But I
am so very good at martyrdom*, Hanna would have replied.

She noticed when the forest began to change, switching from
hearty oaks to spindly, stark-white birches. With their golden fall
leaves, they looked like bright candles against the dark pines. After another day of traveling, the guards called a halt to ask her,
with respectful bows, how she would prefer to continue: on the
forest floor—which would be easier to wheel over, since it lacked
the vast roots of the deeper woods but would leave them more
vulnerable to bears, wolves, and other predators who hunted

below—or the bridges, which ran nearly all the way to the border but were often rudimentary at best. The chair was well suited for the capital, but this far out . . . "I leave the decision in your capable hands," Hanna told them. "This is not my area of expertise."

The truth was, even when she didn't need the chair, she hadn't left the capital in many years and rarely even left the academy—and then, usually only when she was summoned to the palace. She found, as they continued on via the bridges, that she was beginning to look forward to seeing Semo. She'd never imagined she'd have the chance to travel beyond the forests. "I very much hope the experience is not the death of me," she said.

"Your pardon, Ambassador?" one of the guards asked as he carried her across a swaying rope bridge. Another guard carried her chair.

"Talking to myself," Hanna said with a wave. "It's one of the joys you'll discover as you get older: the amusement of your own company."

"I see, Ambassador."

She patted his weathered cheek as he lowered her back into her chair. "No, you don't. But you're polite, which is important for our new role." She looked at each of her guards. Queen Daleina had spared four of her personal guards, two men and two women. When Hanna had objected that it was too many, Daleina had said, *Possible trap, remember? I don't want to receive a message that you've been assassinated and have to listen to anyone say "I told you so."* Hanna pursed her lips and hoped that they were all worrying too much and that Merecot's letter had been truthful. "So that we're clear, I do not expect any of you to take a knife in the gut for me. It would be far better to deflect the blade in the first place. Be alert. We don't know what we will find when we arrive."

All of them agreed, because it was sensible, obvious advice, but she felt better for having said it. She had to trust that they were trained enough to avoid obvious mistakes. *And I have to hope that I don't make any either.*

She made a point to memorize their names, scolding herself

for being so self-absorbed that she hadn't done it earlier: Evenna, Serk, Tipi, and Coren.

Evenna, the head guard, had a husband back in Mittriel, a scar on her left cheek, and skin as black as Healer Hamon's. She was middle-aged and had been a palace guard for twenty-four years. Serk, the oldest, was bald except for a blue ponytail. He used to be a border guard before he moved to the capital to take care of his aged parents. Tipi was young, energetic, and had a twitch in her right hand that she controlled when she climbed. Coren, the youngest guard at nineteen, fidgeted a lot, mostly because he was nineteen. All of them were much younger and more fit than Hanna and seemed to take their roles as her guards very seriously. *That bodes well for their survival*, Hanna thought. *Or at least for mine.*

As they journeyed closer to the border, she found herself thinking more about what was to come than what she'd left behind. She also felt the sun on her face more often as the forest began to thin. The canopy above was no longer a thick snarl but instead a lacework of leaves that allowed light to filter through in golden shafts. But what was amazing was she could still hear canopy singers high above, even though the upper branches were as thin as a child's arm.

While the guards made their camp on a platform that straddled three trees, Hanna listened to the canopy singers. There were two: a baritone and a soprano, one to the east and one to the west, singing back and forth to each other.

It was an old song, about the Great Mother, who died to save humans from spirits. Some stories referred to her as a baby or a young girl, but this ballad treated her as if she had been a grown woman. The soprano sang her verses. Hanna let the melody soak into her as it soared with the breeze in between the leaves and up toward the night sky.

"What's she saying?" Serk asked.

"She's singing her sadness, knowing she must sacrifice herself if humans are to survive," Hanna answered. "In the beginning, all of Renthia was like the untamed lands, with wild spirits making and unmaking the earth we stand on and air we breathe. It took the death of the Great Mother to give us the power to defend ourselves. Before that, there were no queens. Listen—the next bit is the Great Mother singing to the first queen."

The baritone chimed in, taking the part of the Great Mother:

*You alone within the storm*
*of hunger and unfinished pain*
*must touch the minds unfettered*
*and be the spirits' bane.*

The soprano answered back, a cry of loneliness that pierced higher than the sounds of the crickets and evening birds:

*I cannot breathe another breath,*
*without you.*
*I cannot see the sky*
*with evening stars and golden moon,*
*their beauty is a lie;*
*do not let me walk alone—*

And the baritone harmonized with her, telling the first queen that while she must touch the spirits alone, she has not been forsaken. The Great Mother has sent a protector to stay by her side and guard her from harm while her mind tames the wildness all around.

Hanna wondered aloud at the word "protector."

"The first champion," Evenna responded.

That was the most likely interpretation, Hanna agreed. It made more sense than having a wolf as some kind of special protector. She wondered what Merecot had been thinking, though. She must have had a strong reason to go after Bayn. *I suppose I'll find out soon enough.*

It was an appropriate song for the canopy singers to sing, while the forests were gripped in the queen's sadness. It held sorrow but also hope. Hanna wished that Naelin were here to hear it, but since she wasn't, Hanna was determined to wring as much meaning from it as she could.

*Even when we feel the most alone, we are not. Even when things are the most bleak, they will get better. There is* always *hope.* A lovely, if simplistic, sentiment. Listening to the glorious vocals, Hanna almost believed it.

# CHAPTER 11

Ven claimed the practice area at the palace. It wasn't that he forbade others from using it—it was merely that by using it, he dominated it, and that meant he got it to himself.

Squirreled behind the ornate palace trees, the training area held an obstacle course of vines, ropes, nets, ladders, and beams built to mimic the toughest of forest terrain.

Ven began with the vines, leaping off a branch and swinging one-handed to the next vine. Grabbing it, he swung to the next and then the next, and then up straight onto a wall with two-inch handholds six feet apart from one another. He climbed, swinging his body like a pendulum to reach up to the next handhold until he reached the waterfall.

Gallons of water were dumped continuously, using a waterwheel and pulley system to create a gushing waterfall down the side of the tree. The handholds were within the waterfall—you had to reach into the pouring water, let it hammer your face, and reach by blind feel up through the water to climb.

Ven climbed it in less than thirty seconds.

He then leapt off the top of the waterfall onto another vine and swung across to a platform. He was breathing hard but felt good. Champion Havtru, who was waiting on the platform, passed him a cup of water, and Ven chugged it in one gulp.

"No safety harness?" Havtru asked.

"Done this course hundreds of times." He refilled the water from a pitcher and drank it again. "Besides, I stay sharper if there's no harness."

"You're making the rest of us look bad."

Ven reached for the pitcher to refill his glass, changed his mind, and drank directly from the pitcher instead. Water spilled down his cheeks, but his shirt was already soaked from the waterfall. "Just need to stay ready."

"Ready for what?"

*Anything*, he thought. *Everything*. "Tomorrow. Or maybe the next day. Who knows."

"You expect the worst."

"Always. It's how I'm still alive."

Havtru nodded, but then shook his head. "Can't do that. Gotta keep thinking it'll be better, you know? But that's not why I'm here—I wanted to ask you about the girl I'm thinking of picking to be my new candidate. I think she shows real potential, but she's as meek as a baby bunny. Scared of every shadow."

Grabbing a towel, Ven dried his neck and hair. "She's right to be scared."

"Yeah, that's not helpful."

Ven smiled ruefully and then shrugged.

"Anyway, I was hoping you could talk to her—"

"No."

Havtru opened and shut his mouth like a fish. Finally, a "What?" escaped his lips.

"Does anyone know you've decided to choose her? I assume she's at an academy—have you told her headmistress? Has she met the queen yet? Either queen?"

"Um, no. Only decided to choose her a few days ago."

"It could be I'm being paranoid." *Eh, who am I kidding? Of course I'm being paranoid.* Question was: Was it unwarranted? He didn't think so. Aratay had two queens but no heirs—and if the attack by Merecot's spirits proved anything, it was a reminder of how precarious their situation was. They needed heirs. *Specifically ones not in danger of being murdered.* "But my advice is don't tell anyone about her," he continued. "Don't bring her to the palace. Don't introduce her to the queen or talk about her to the other champions. Train her in secret. That way, if an assassin begins targeting candidates, he or she won't know to target her."

Havtru shook his head. "But the assassin was stopped. Killed. And Queen Merecot of Semo has asked for peace—I heard that Headmistress Hanna is traveling north to serve as ambassador."

"You heard right," Ven said. "And I'm saying it changes nothing."

Havtru tugged on the royal champion insignia on his jacket. He obviously didn't like Ven's advice, and Ven felt bad about that—but he'd feel worse if he was right, hadn't acted, and the candidates all died, again. "You think the queen of Semo—" Havtru began.

"Or the spirits themselves. Some of them are smart enough to target known candidates. And if the queens lose control . . ."

"Surely they won't. We have two! And the death of Queen Naelin's children—it was a shock, but it was also a one-time event. She'll recover. She won't be the same—you can't be after something like that—but the shock of the moment has passed."

Ven tried not to flinch at the mention of death. They had all agreed not to let it leak that Queen Merecot had kidnapped the children. Or that she was involved at all. "Just a precaution, Havtru. Humor a paranoid old man."

The other man almost smiled. "If you're old, I'm ancient. But yes, I'll do it. She can tell her headmistress she's going home to visit family, and I'll take her to—"

"Don't say it out loud. Not here. Not even to me." He hadn't noticed any spirits in the practice area, but the palace was crawling with them. Better not to take the risk. He didn't need to know where Havtru would be training his candidate.

"Are you doing the same with your candidate?" Havtru asked.

Ven eyed the course and wondered if he should go again. He hated the way he felt helpless to support Naelin, and he kept thinking how he'd failed Bayn and the children—not only had he not been able to keep Erian and Llor from being kidnapped, but the air spirits who'd attacked them had escaped and Bayn had been lost. Everything about that day had been the stuff of his worst nightmares. He'd been late, like he'd been on the day Greytree, Daleina's childhood home, was destroyed. *I'll never be too late again,* he vowed. "Haven't taken another candidate," he said.

Hadn't even thought about it.

Didn't want to.

Havtru seemed surprised, even shocked. "But you're the best! You need to train another candidate—the queens need an heir, a good one."

*Naelin needs me now. And Daleina. I failed the last three queens in one way or another. I don't know if I can go through that again. What I can do, though, is give you all the time to find the next one.* "Train your candidate. But keep her secret, to keep her safe," Ven said.

"I will," Havtru promised.

Rather than continue the conversation, Ven jumped off the platform and onto a vine. He started the course again and tried to block out every doubt, every fear, and every emotion he felt.

He tried to move faster than ever.

So he'd never be late again.

AFTER AN HOUR, VEN FINISHED HIS WORKOUT, WIPED THE SWEAT from his face and armpits with a towel, and then trudged back into the palace. He bypassed the blue-robed caretakers who fluttered around him, trying to steer him to the baths, and he climbed the spiral stairs toward Naelin's quarters.

*She won't care if I'm clean or dirty.* Her practicality was one of her best qualities. She knew people sometimes sweat and smelled and bled and cried and basically acted human. He didn't have to be anything other than who he was with her. *And if she wants to rage and cry and be human, I'll be there for her.*

That was all he could do right now.

Not that he didn't wish he could do more. *Like march into Semo and steal away Erian and Llor.* He hated waiting for someone else to act.

But that wasn't his call.

In this branch of the palace, the walls were white wood, like the pulpy heart of a tree but polished until it gleamed. Fire spirits kept the sconces burning by dancing from wick to wick, and their shadows writhed on the walls. There were cracks like knife-cut scars that ran through the wood. *Probably from Naelin's earthquake.* In more peaceful times, Daleina would have sent tree spirits to heal the hallways. *Not exactly a priority now.* If anything, they were important reminders that Aratay was far from safe.

Especially while Aratay was still without heirs.

Guards were posted outside of Queen Naelin's chambers. He nodded to them, but before he could ask them to announce him, a man spoke from down the hall. "She ate one pear and a slice of bread." It was Renet, slumped against the wall. "At least she's not starving herself."

"How long have you been here?"

"I only want to make sure she's okay."

Ven turned to one of her guards. "Is she okay?"

The guard nodded crisply. "Yes, Champion. Healer Hamon visited this morning and checked her vitals. She has taken nourishment, and she has slept. But she has requested privacy."

Ven considered leaving without announcing his presence—if she wanted to be left alone, then she should be, but he also wanted her to know he'd come by. *If she decides she doesn't want to be alone, I want her to know I'm near. We can be impatient together.* "She doesn't have to see me if she doesn't want to, but could you please tell her I came by to see if she's all right?"

The guard knocked on the door and relayed the message.

Ven heard Naelin's voice from within, too muffled for him to parse the words, but the guard had his ear pressed against the door. "She said to tell you she's occupied and to ask you to take Master Renet elsewhere."

NAELIN PACED FROM ONE END OF THE OVERLY ORNATE BEDROOM to the other. She knew she'd made the right decision, both for her children and for Aratay. *But it should still be me, traveling to Semo, taking the risks, searching for Erian and Llor.*

She'd reconsidered her decision to remain here six times every hour, beginning the moment Headmistress Hanna started north. She wasn't used to second-guessing herself. *Much less third-, fourth-, or fifth-guessing.*

Out of the corner of her eye, she saw a flicker in the fireplace. She glared at it, and the fire spirit shriveled. It was a tiny one, the shape of a lizard, its scales stained with soot. Its tongue was fire, and a white-hot stripe burned along its back, ending in a blue flame on the tip of its tail. "Come to mock my pain, spirit? Your kind must be enjoying this." They lived to see humans suffer, after all.

To her surprise, it spoke. She hadn't thought a spirit so small would be able to talk. Its voice was a crackling hiss. "I want to burn for you."

She was about to send it away, but then she stopped. "You do? And what do you want to burn?" She felt its eagerness, an itch inside her mind.

"Anyone. Everyone."

Naelin studied the little spirit. It was writhing on a cold log, boring a circle of char into the bark. *Maybe I can't do anything to help Erian and Llor right now . . . but maybe I can be ready when it's time.* "How would you like to play a game?"

The fire lizard wiggled in excitement.

Throwing open the wardrobe, she pulled out one of the more ridiculous dresses, a poofy concoction that reminded her of an overstuffed peach pie, and then hung it from the bed canopy. She made a mental note to apologize to the caretakers later—she'd find a way to make it up to them. "Let's pretend this is an enemy spirit."

Silently, she issued the order:

*Burn it.*

*Hurt it.*

With glee, the lizard bounded out of the fireplace. Leaping up onto the bed, it danced across the hem of the dress, licking it with its fiery tongue. The fabric began to smoke.

*Higher,* Naelin ordered, sending the lizard running up the skirt and bodice of the dress. She didn't want to torture the Semoian spirits; she wanted to defeat them. It would be useful to know which orders were most effective.

Soon, she sensed other fire spirits had crept down through the chimney and were clustered on her hearth—some were like the lizard, others were more like tiny dragons, still others looked like little people made of flame. She reached out to them, commanding them to act in concert, attacking the poor innocent dress.

Smoke thickened in the bedroom, and Naelin summoned air spirits to whisk it away out the window and up the flume. And once she had the air spirits around her, she set them to destroying a finely crafted table.

She was standing in the middle of a cyclone of destruction, feeling better than she had in days, when a guard knocked on her door. "Your Majesty," he called through the door. "Champion Ven has come to inquire as to your well-being. Also, Master Renet remains in the hallway, awaiting your pleasure."

She'd forgotten that Renet was outside—she'd told the guard she didn't want to see him right now. Looking around the room, she thought she was still not ready for visitors, albeit for entirely different reasons. "Please tell Champion Ven I am . . . occupied." Beside her, a tree spirit pierced a cushion with needle-like spears that it grew from its knuckles. "And please ask him to take Renet elsewhere."

*I've found my own way to cope with waiting. He needs to too.*

Turning her attention back to the spirits, she practiced splitting them into groups and guiding them to attack a couch cushion from multiple directions.

The cushion did not survive.

He wasn't offended. He knew the need for time alone. And she deserved to have whatever time she wanted without either her lover or her ex-lover lurking nearby. "If she asks for me, please send word," Ven told the guard. To Renet, he said, "Come with me."

"Where to?" Renet asked. He didn't budge.

One of the guards scowled at him. "When the Queen's Champion issues an order, you don't question it." The other leveled a kick at Renet's knees. A light kick, but it still sent Renet scrambling to his feet.

Truthfully, Ven didn't have an answer—he didn't think Naelin cared where in the palace Renet went, as long as it wasn't near her. Ven headed for the stairs. Behind him, he heard Renet follow, albeit slowly.

"I loved her before she was queen," Renet said, following Ven down the stairs.

"I know." What he didn't know was why Renet was bringing it up now.

"I saw the potential in her before you even knew she existed. She was the queen of my heart before she was queen of this land. Someday I'll win her back."

Ven tried to summon some sympathy and failed. This wasn't the time for either of them to feel jealousy—Naelin needed all the support they both could give her. He made a noncommittal sort of grunt.

More plaintively, Renet asked, "Do you think she will ever allow me to win her back?"

Ven suppressed a sigh. "I don't know that I'm the best person to answer that."

"I don't deserve her. Probably never did. But a person can change. Can't they?"

Ven was grateful when his feet led him to where he hadn't even realized he was going: to the eastern throne room, where Queen Daleina was. Because if he couldn't serve one queen, then he would be useful to the other. He didn't pause as the guards threw the doors open in front of him but strode inside without slowing.

Daleina and the seneschal looked up from the stacks of papers they had spread across the council table. He saw the dark shadows under her eyes and the wisps of hair that had escaped her crown. Behind him, he heard Renet halt abruptly.

"Your Majesty," Ven said, inclining his head. "Apologies for the interruption. This is Renet, father to Erian and Llor. He needs something useful to do. A distraction from his . . . current situation."

Daleina looked startled for only an instant, then masked it. "Welcome, Renet, and please accept our sympathy for the current situation. We would be delighted for your assistance, if that's your wish." *She's had too much experience with surprises lately,* Ven thought.

Renet's jaw hung open. "Uh . . . ." Belatedly, he dropped into a bow so low he nearly toppled over. Recovering, he straightened. "Your Majesty, I . . . That is . . . Ahh . . ."

"Champion Havtru had been assisting us in sorting through requests for help." Daleina waved her hand at the papers. "But he pleaded champion duties today. You could take his place. The requests must be organized by priority. Imminent death takes top priority; aesthetics are last. I'll review them when you're finished. Seneschal, would you please show Renet what needs to be done?"

The seneschal bowed to her. He was a thin, tall man, taller than most, with a hawklike nose that had been broken once and white eyebrows that obscured half his eyes. His uniform was, as always, crisp and pressed. Ven remembered his name was Belsowik, though like his predecessors, he insisted on being known only by his title. He valued his duty above his personal needs. Ven approved of that. "Of course, Your Majesty."

Queen Daleina swept around the table and placed a hand on Renet's shoulder. "Thank you." The words were heartfelt, and Ven knew he'd at least done something right today.

Renet looked as if he were going to faint. Ven suppressed a grin and managed to look the stern warrior while the young queen swept past the overwhelmed man and then looped her hand through Ven's arm. He guided her out of the throne room. Under her breath, Daleina said, "If I see one more paper, I will shred it into flakes."

"I think I know a cure for that."

"Hamon isn't—"

"No medicine involved." He led her up the palace stairs, higher and higher.

Spirits flitted around them, more than usual. A tiny air spirit with dragonfly wings and a humanlike face hovered by Daleina's shoulder and stroked her hair before darting away. Tree spirits poked their heads out of cracks and knots in the wood to watch her pass.

A fire spirit curled up in a sconce leapt to its feet and writhed as if it wanted to catch her attention. Ven saw her pause, focus on it, and the spirit curled back around its wick and seemed to purr like a cat that had been stroked.

"You want to tell me what's going on with them?" Ven asked. He'd never seen spirits act so . . . non-homicidal before. *It's almost as if they like her.*

"I think what happened with Naelin upset them," Daleina said. "They're making nice so that I don't hurl them across a hostile border like she did. Or so I'll protect them if she tries again." She held out her hand as they walked out onto a balcony, and a spirit shaped out of wisps of cotton landed on her index finger. "I didn't know they could even *be* scared." She cradled the spirit in her hands as if comforting it and then released it. It circled around her head once before flying up toward the clouds.

"Don't feel so sorry for them that you trust them," Ven cautioned.

"I'll never do that. Remember who trained me." She smiled, but there was sadness there too.

He knew she was remembering her friends who had died in the Coronation Massacre. He could read the shadows on her face—he knew he wore those same shadows on his own. So many had died over so many generations at the claws and teeth of spirits. Still, though, even he saw that there was beauty to them.

Leaning against the balcony rail, he watched two tree spirits race over a branch. They looked like squirrels that had been dipped in vats of paint. Both had autumn-colored leaves sprouting from their bodies. Chittering, they disappeared into a hole in the tree.

"So what is this cure?" Daleina asked.

Ven jumped onto the balcony railing and reached up to unhook a clip from a wire. The wire path connected this part of the palace to a tree in the heart of Mittriel. It wasn't used often because queens typically traveled with a retinue of guards. He wiggled the clip at her. "You need to soar."

He saw her try to glare at him and then she gave up and

grinned. Squatting on the railing, he held out his hand. Daleina scooped up her skirts with one hand and took his hand with the other. Up on the railing, she hooked herself onto the wire path. He secured himself onto the wire as well.

Pushing off together, they sailed above their city.

# CHAPTER 12

Near the northern border of Aratay, Hanna and her guards descended from the trees to cross the final miles to Semo on the ground—the trees were too thin and spaced too far apart, and the population was so scattered that there were not enough bridges for Hanna and her entourage to be able to travel at mid-forest level. She rather liked approaching from so low, however. It made the moment feel, well, momentous.

*Certainly the view is glorious.* Ahead, between the last few trees, were the mountains.

Snowcapped peaks broke the horizon into a serrated line. It looked as if enormous claws had scraped away the blue of the sky. The faces of the mountains were a mix of gray and black, and Hanna had the urge to paint pictures of them, even though she had never painted before in her life. Like the forests of Aratay, the mountains of Semo were breathtaking in their extreme beauty.

"Most impressive," she declared.

The nearest guard, Serk, snorted—politely, but she heard it and raised her eyebrows at him. Ducking his head, he mumbled, "I miss the forest already."

"Semo has trees too." She pointed ahead to a patch of fir trees, a swatch of beautiful dark green framed by severe mountains. A vast waterfall tumbled beside the trees into a lake that glittered like a thousand jewels in sunlight.

"It's not the same."

It certainly wasn't. Whereas Aratay was an unbroken sea of forest, the trees in Semo were scattered and seemed spindly, overwhelmed by the grandeur of the mountains. Yet there was beauty there too. "Come now, mountains are invigorating!" Hanna rolled herself forward, out of the forest, until she felt it: the border. She was surprised she could sense it, since she wasn't a queen, but her skin prickled and her nose twitched with a nascent sneeze. The air even tasted different, as if an additional spice had been dropped into it.

It was, she was certain, the change in spirits. Within the trees, the spirits were tied to Daleina and Naelin, as well as Aratay itself, but here all of Nature was linked to Queen Merecot. Hanna was surprised that it was a profound enough difference that she, who was not sensitive to all kinds of spirits, could feel it.

In response, she felt, oddly, excited, which was not an emotion she'd expected to experience again. "It will be a new adventure!" Hanna turned her chair's wheels and kept rolling forward, toward a wildflower field that was dotted with rock piles.

Hand on her sword hilt, Evenna jogged by her side. "Alert, everyone! Watch for spirits."

The guards tensed, and even Hanna looked about intently for Semo's border protectors. *So... where are they?* Hanna wondered.

She'd only just completed the thought when the rock piles in the wildflower field began to shift and move—and she saw they weren't random piles at all.

They were earth spirits, stone giants.

One after another, they rose to their full height, towering over Hanna and her guards. Each was at least twenty feet high, with arms and fists of stone.

Two of her guards drew swords and stepped in front of her, while the other two notched arrows in their bows. Hanna laid her hands on the knives tucked into the armrests of her chair, though she didn't know what good arrow and steel would do against stone.

She wondered how quickly she and her guards could flee. Surely the Semoian spirits wouldn't follow them back into Aratay. *But I can't flee—I didn't come all this way to be turned back at the border.* "Don't retreat unless they attack," Hanna ordered her guards.

"Madame Ambassador . . ." Evenna began.

"Lower your weapons and identify yourselves!" a voice boomed—it came from a pile of rocks that hadn't moved. Hanna squinted at the rocks. Could that be a person?

*If there's a human guard here . . . maybe this won't be a disaster.*

Not lowering her bow, Evenna called back, "Identify *yourself*!"

Hanna held up a hand to quiet her, then raised her voice. "I am Ambassador Hanna of Aratay, en route to parlay with Queen Merecot of Semo. These men and women are my escort." As she spoke, she reached for an air spirit—while she didn't have the broad power of a queen or even an heir, she did have some finesse with the spirits of the air—and found one nearby, darting between the wildflowers. *Reveal him*, Hanna told it.

It was a tiny, mischievous spirit—a slip of air that looked like a translucent butterfly—and it didn't fight her. Giggling softly, it flitted behind the rock formation.

Leaning toward her, Evenna advised, "We should retreat. No Semoian spirit would dare harm you within the trees."

"They won't harm me here either," Hanna said with more confidence than she felt. Just because the stone giants hadn't attacked, it didn't mean they were safe. It could be they were under orders to attack only those who came a certain distance across the border. "Diplomatic protection. I travel under a flag of peace, at least metaphorically . . . though perhaps we should have brought a literal flag." Queen Daleina had sent word to Semo to expect an ambassador, but if that news hadn't spread to the border guards . . .

Hanna heard a squawk from behind the rocks as, surprised by the spirit, the speaker jumped up. She saw a flash of gold and black, and that was enough. She relaxed a minute amount. "It's a human guard. Good." A human could be reasoned with. To the Semoian guard, she called, "I have a letter from my queen. Perhaps you wish to examine it?"

Coming forward, the border guard examined her papers. He

was a young man with a sparse mustache and a gold-and-black uniform that looked dusty up close. His sword sheath, hanging from his belt, was battered and worn, as if he used it daily. Finally he seemed to accept the letter as legit. "Keep to the roads," he cautioned. "Not all of the mountains are as stable as they once were."

"Oh?" Hanna used her favorite tone for encouraging students to talk.

"You might say that Semo has experienced its fair share of change in recent years."

"And why might I say that?"

The border guard's gaze shifted to the stone giants, who still waited motionless in the field. Hanna wondered if they'd been ordered to obey his commands—and she wondered how this young man felt about that.

But he returned her papers without answering her question. "Stay on the roads. And do not camp in areas with minimal vegetation. Bare rocks often signify an avalanche-prone area."

"Sounds alarming," Hanna said, keeping her voice light and friendly. "We lack such exciting features in Aratay."

"Small price to pay for not living in a tangle of weeds." The Semoian guard nodded at the border of Aratay. "Begging your pardon, Madame Ambassador."

Beside her, one of her guards, Tipi, began to reply, and the headmistress laid a hand on her arm to caution her into silence. "We thank you for the warning," Hanna said.

As soon as the Semoian waved them on, her own guards wheeled her down a gravel path, away from the border. "'Tangle of weeds,'" Tipi muttered. She was from the Southern Citadel, known for its tangle of magnificent magnolia trees. "Better than this rock pile." She glared balefully at the *living* rock piles—the gigantic earth spirits—who watched them pass with flat eyes made of shale.

"Hush," Hanna said. "Every land has its beauty. Besides, let's not offend our hosts." She was certain that the stone giants were spies as well as guards and would be reporting to Queen Merecot on their arrival, so she plastered a reassuring smile on her face and beamed at the scenery.

Soon, though, they left the border, and the earth spirits, behind.

Yellow and white flowers clumped together between the tall grasses, creating a lovely quiltlike blanket at the foot of the mountains. *I don't see any cause for alarm yet*, Hanna thought. *This is very nice.*

As the path climbed upward, Hanna saw blueberry bushes and requested a pause to gather some. These bushes were stuffed with clusters of deep last-season berries—in Aratay, the berries hadn't ripened like this. *More proof that the bad harvest in Aratay was the result of unhappy spirits, rather than natural weather*, she thought. Not that she required proof. Right now, Semo seemed to be a safer place to be than Aratay.

As they passed a bush, Hanna wormed her fingers in between the leaves to pluck a few berries. She popped one in her mouth. Soaked in sunlight, it tasted like the last vestiges of summer. "Delicious," she proclaimed. "Stop here."

Serk produced a sack, and all of them turned to the task of stripping the bushes of as many berries as possible, taking care not to alarm any nearby tree spirits by damaging any branches or leaves. Hanna was delighted—she hadn't had a picnic in years. *I might as well enjoy myself before—*

"Alert to the sky!" Tipi called.

All four guards aimed their bows upward, arrows notched. It was impressive, considering they'd just been picking berries.

Hanna tilted her head back, shielded her eyes, and watched as six spirits with leathery wings flew toward them, carrying a chariot between them.

*—before Merecot finds us*, she finished.

Encrusted in jewels, the chariot glistened in the sunlight. Hanna watched the spirits circle once and then fly down onto the path. At Hanna's command, her guards lowered their bows but didn't relax. She didn't expect them to.

One of the spirits paced forward. Its body was shaped like a horse, but it bore leather-textured bat wings. It spoke with a mouth that looked as if it could grind rocks. "Queen Merecot welcomes you to the glorious land of Semo and invites you to complete your journey in comfort and see our beauty from above."

Hanna's youngest guard, nineteen-year-old Coren, fidgeted beside her. His hand clutched his sword hilt. "I am *not* traveling by spirit."

"You will do as the ambassador says," Evenna barked at him. "If she wishes to travel by spirit, we travel by spirit. If she wishes to travel by dancing bear, then dancing bear it is." Turning to Hanna, she said, "Ambassador, how would you like to proceed?"

Hanna considered it. There was a reason no one traveled via spirit except in dire emergency. You were placing yourself at the mercy of their temperament and trusting in the control of their queen. And these were foreign spirits under the control of a queen whose motives were . . . self-serving, at best. Hanna knew she didn't have anywhere near the kind of power to wrest control from Merecot if the queen intended them ill. She'd be trusting in Merecot's desire for diplomacy. Yet that was okay.

*I did come here to determine precisely that.*

"It is a three-day journey by foot across the mountains," Serk said. "Treacherous terrain, with all the dangers that go with it. If these spirits are to be trusted—"

"You can't trust spirits," Coren objected.

Hanna agreed. But it wasn't about trusting the spirits. It was about trusting Merecot . . . Frankly, she wasn't sure which was more deadly.

The spirits waited. One of them pawed the ground with its hoof. The chariot was wide enough for all of them, with velvet-cushioned seats. To reject it would be to insult Merecot, which may have been why she'd sent it—to see what they'd do. "It's a test," Hanna said. *She's testing to see if we truly want peace. Or to see how gullible we are.* "If any of you wish to return to Aratay, I will send a message with you absolving you of any responsibility. But I will ride."

Evenna snorted. "Our job is to guard you." Without hesitation, she lifted Hanna out of her chair and into the chariot, then shot pointed looks at the other guards. Bringing Hanna's wheelchair and their supplies, the others joined her, cramming together on the cushioned seats. They positioned their packs on the floor between them but kept their weapons accessible, though once they were airborne, there would be little they could do.

Hanna hoped she was making the right decision, for all their sakes.

Running up the path, the spirits stretched their wings out, then kicked off the gravel and soared into the air. Hanna gripped the sides of the chariot as it tilted. Wind rushed in her face, stinging her eyes and battering her cheeks, but she kept looking straight ahead as they flew toward the mountains.

They flew high, bursting through the clouds, until around them was a field of whiteness, broken only by mountain peaks, and then they swooped down, flying between the mountains. Outwardly calm, Hanna kept a firm grip on the side of the chariot as she watched the scenery zip past.

On the side of one mountain, she saw an avalanche: earth spirits tossing rocks back and forth, like children playing catch. As the rocks tumbled down the mountain they sounded like thunder. She watched tree spirits rip apart a boulder by penetrating it with roots that thickened and split the solid stone. Air spirits swirled with storm clouds over another mountain.

Semo, she noted, was thick with spirits. Very active spirits.

*Perhaps it's not so safe after all.*

Below in the valleys, she saw towns nestled beside rivers. Strips of bare rocks surrounded them, as if avalanches had fallen again and again toward them but had always been diverted. Their fields were dotted with boulders.

She filed all of this away, cataloguing it in preparation for her first report back to Daleina.

They flew for hours as the sun trekked across the sky from one mountain range to another, until at last Hanna spotted a city carved into the side of a white stone mountain. In the late-afternoon light, it gleamed, its turrets sparkling as if embedded with flecks of diamonds—which it probably was. Waterfalls, brilliant blue, chased down the many levels of the city, and gold flags flew from the peaks of the spires. It was a most impressive sight, and Hanna made sure to be properly impressed. Merecot would certainly expect that. In fact, she had most likely instructed the spirits to bring them in from a direction that would best show off the capital city.

It's what Hanna would have done.

Flying up, the spirits brought the chariot to the peak of the mountain, where a platform of stone extended in a circle around the snowcapped tip. Hanna felt the chill in the air, and felt the jostle to her bones as the air spirits clattered down on the paving stones.

The horse spirits folded their wings and waited as Hanna's guards climbed out and then helped Hanna into her chair. For one brief moment, she permitted herself the luxury of anger.

*I should be walking out of this chariot, and it's Merecot's fault that I'm not.*

However, she buried these thoughts away as she always did. Others had lost their lives. She'd lost only her mobility. Still, that word "only" gnawed at her.

After the guards had removed all the packs from the chariot, they fanned out on either side of her, at attention, as if they were honor guards. She wished she'd had the opportunity to freshen her clothes. After all the travel, she imagined she looked rather like a crumpled scrap from the bottom of a pocket.

Again, probably exactly as Merecot intended.

The chariot with its spirit steeds ran toward the end of the platform and off it, sailing into the empty air and then soaring up toward the clouds. Hanna watched them as they disappeared.

"Pleasant way to travel, wouldn't you say, Ambassador?" a woman's voice said behind her, and Hanna pivoted her chair to see that Merecot—*Excuse me, Queen Merecot*, she corrected herself; she'd best remember that here—had joined them on the platform.

She looked . . . well, not quite the same as Hanna remembered. She still pictured her as the gawky, arrogant child who had cheated on her exams. Now that gawkiness had stretched to regally tall, and Merecot wore her jeweled gown as if she'd been born to it. Her throat was encased in gold rings, and bracelets worth more than half the houses in Mittriel covered her upper arms. Her dress was black with a single white stripe down the center, to match her hair, and it was studded with diamonds. An entourage of her guards, clad in steel armor, flanked her.

The Semoian and Aratayian guards sized one another up, and Hanna briefly imagined them as dogs sniffing one another. They stopped short of that, though.

"Headmistress," Merecot said, a note of surprise in her voice. And then she laughed lightly, though the sound didn't have much humor in it. "Daleina didn't share her choice of ambassador with me, only your expected arrival date. I wonder if she thinks you'll grade me. Do I pass or fail?"

Hanna bowed her head politely. "Your Majesty." She wondered if Merecot would be foolish enough to mention the wheelchair, or if she'd have the presence of mind to guess the probable cause. No, she wouldn't bring it up—Merecot had always been shrewd. Not subtle, but shrewd. She wouldn't begin negotiations by placing herself in a situation that warranted an apology.

Instead, Merecot laughed again, warmer this time. "You know, I hadn't expected my old headmistress to ever bow her head to me. If I'd known that would be a perk of this job, I would have jumped at it sooner."

"Queen Daleina and Queen Naelin wish for me to recite various pleasantries to you," Hanna said. "Do you need to hear them, or can we pretend that I said them and proceed to the rest-and-refreshments stage of the welcome?"

"They didn't really send pleasantries, did they? Just told you to make some up."

*Like I said—shrewd.* "True."

"Then let's save us both the hassle. I have much to show you, and we have much to discuss, and you have already had a long journey. Really, I don't want you falling asleep on me while we're solving the fate of our nations."

*No wonder Merecot failed diplomacy class*, Hanna thought. "Before I trust a single word you say, I will need to see Queen Naelin's children."

"Of course," Merecot said. To one of the guards, she said, "Fetch the children. We will be conducting our discussion in my audience chamber."

Hanna swallowed back myriad other questions—were the children well, how soon could they be returned, and what had

Merecot been thinking by doing something so idiotic. Instead, she schooled her expression into polite interest and, pushed by her guards, followed Queen Merecot of Semo into the castle.

DALEINA HAS A VICIOUS SENSE OF HUMOR, MERECOT THOUGHT. *That's a surprise.* She plastered a welcoming smile on her face—which felt as fake as the smile on a mask—as she ushered Head-mistress Hanna into the castle.

Ambassador *Hanna,* she corrected herself.

Honestly, she didn't think Daleina could have picked anyone who would have irritated Merecot more, or set her more on edge. She felt the flesh between her shoulder blades itch as if it were being prodded by the tip of a knife, but it was only the ambassador's gaze. *Full of disapproval, undoubtedly.* Merecot half expected to be confronted by a stack of exams and report cards and then lectured about all her academic failings.

*I would have passed if I'd tried,* she thought. She simply hadn't deemed it worth her time to bother. *Clever of Daleina not to tell me whom she was sending.* The missive had stated only that an ambassador would be arriving within the week. So when the headmistress of her old academy had been lifted out of the chariot, looking about one hundred and fifty years old with her startlingly white hair and thousand wrinkles, Merecot was . . . surprised. Even shocked. Perhaps displeased. *Pissed off,* Merecot thought.

And guilty.

It was hard not to feel that as she walked alongside the head-mistress's wheeled contraption. She didn't let it show, of course—she was determined to be the perfect hostess and the consummate queen—but it needled her nevertheless as she regally escorted her guests through the jewel-encrusted mirrored halls to the audience chamber, a beautifully ornate room filled with red velvet couches, black basalt statues, and crystal chandeliers. She instructed her servants to bring an assortment of their finest wines and Semoian delicacies, and then she called for several musicians to play a few of the less grating mountain tunes.

"The children will arrive soon," she told her guest. "Until they do, I'd be honored if you'd agree to begin our discussion. I know you've had a long journey, but the situation in Semo is urgent. If you could delay your rest until after I've presented the problem to you, I would appreciate it." *See, I can be as delightful and gracious as Daleina.*

Hanna gave her a narrow, condescending look—the same one Merecot had seen so many times at the academy. "You aren't happy to see me."

Merecot kept her smile. "Of course I am thrilled and honored. I asked for an ambassador, and the queens of Aratay sent one of their favorite pets."

Ambassador Hanna's eyebrows shot up, and Merecot again felt fifteen years old, standing in the headmistress's office after the entrance exam and listening while this woman berated her for her so-called-selfish ambition and questioned her commitment.

"Poor word choice?" Merecot offered.

Two servants wheeled a tray of pastries, including a cake with steam rising from its center, as well as crystal glasses, each with a different wine in shades from pearl to blood-red. They parked it in front of the headmistress's chair. Hanna selected one of the smaller pastries, stuffed with lamb and herbs, but didn't eat it. "I'm sure it was exactly the word you wanted to use. But to be clear: I volunteered for this. If we are being honest with each other, I thought diplomacy would be best served by an ambassador who could see you as the child you once were, rather than the murderer you've become. How's that for word choice?"

Around them, the servants and guards, despite their training, let out shocked gasps. Merecot folded her hands and tried to decide if she was offended or impressed. "Beautifully phrased."

"It's a gift," Hanna said modestly.

*It's something.*

But if Hanna was willing to be that blunt . . . then perhaps this wouldn't be a disaster after all. Merecot narrowed her eyes as she studied her old headmistress. Perhaps Daleina *hadn't* sent her as an insult. Hanna had ruled the Northeast Academy for twice as many years as Merecot had been alive. She'd seen queens rise and fall, survived events that should have killed her off many times over. Perhaps, just perhaps, there was still a chance this would work. . . .

"Leave us," Merecot barked at the servants and guards.

Of course, Hanna's guards didn't leave, and Merecot's own guards objected to leaving their queen alone with a foreign national and her soldiers, but Merecot overruled them.

Hanna placed her uneaten pastry on a plate and crossed her hands, waiting politely.

Silence fell over the audience chamber. Merecot felt the twisted metal crown scratch against her scalp and was aware she'd picked a gown of too-heavy material. She was sweating beneath it and hoped that wasn't noticeable. "Come with me," Merecot said. "Alone. You must see if you are to understand. We won't be gone long, and the children will be here by the time we return, so no time will be wasted."

She saw Hanna hesitate and shoot looks at her guards. Her guards would not like this, but Merecot did not care. It was essential for the ambassador to see what she faced, and that couldn't happen in the ornate safety of the castle.

*This better work,* Merecot thought, *or I'll be humiliating myself for nothing.* In order to prove that all she claimed was true, she'd have to show weakness to her former headmistress. *She has to see that Semo can't continue like this, that I can't continue.*

"You ask too much—"

"You know I have killed before for what I want, so trust me when I say I would kill to protect you," Merecot said. "Not because I like you. But because I need you."

STRANGELY, IT WAS MERECOT'S BLUNT ADMISSION OF GUILT THAT made Hanna want to trust her. At least, within reason. Addressing her guards, Hanna ordered, "Test the food for poisons. I'd like to eat when I return."

"There's no poison in the food," Merecot said dismissively.

"Of course there isn't," Hanna said with a smile. "Merely a precaution. You'll have to pardon an old lady for her paranoia. After all, it's not as if you've poisoned anyone before." Before

Hanna had left Mittriel, the Queen's Poisoner had given her and her guards packets of powders to use to test for poisons—they couldn't identify all poisons, but Merecot wouldn't know that. They could at least weed out any obvious ones and hopefully serve as a deterrent for any more imaginative concoctions.

"Aren't ambassadors supposed to be more diplomatic?" Merecot asked.

"How would you know? As I recall, you cheated on those exams." For a brief moment, Hanna wondered if she was taking the wrong tack, baiting a queen. Ultimately, though, she found it wasn't as important as not conceding anything at this point. *It's crucial for Merecot to know she doesn't frighten me, even with her crown and all her queenly power. Especially since I have something she needs: Daleina's trust.*

"You came here determined to see the worst in me," Merecot said. "I hope you'll feel differently after our venture."

Behind her, Hanna heard her guards mutter to one another. Stepping forward, into Hanna's line of sight, Evenna spoke for all of them. "Madam Ambassador, I must object. It's our duty to accompany you." She was glaring at Merecot as if she did *see* the worst in her and had no intention of stopping. Her fingertips were drumming on her sword hilt, and she looked as tense as a jackrabbit. *If I said "attack," she'd be mid-leap before I finished the word.*

"Peace can only thrive in an atmosphere of trust, which is what we are trying to build here." Hanna leveled her most stern, no-nonsense headmistress look at Merecot. "Am I correct in assuming your motives are honorable?"

Merecot's lips twitched. "I'm always honorable, though the code I abide by is my own."

Hanna snorted but didn't argue with her. She'd already put her life in Merecot's hands once, when she'd chosen to ride in her chariots. To balk now would be foolish. *I didn't come to Semo because it was the safe thing to do.* "Let's go." She pivoted her chair and headed for the hallway, but Merecot stopped her.

"I have a better way," Merecot said with an obnoxiously arrogant smile. Crossing the room, the queen threw open the windows. Mountain air swirled into the room, stirring the curtains.

Hanna suppressed a sigh. *Merecot always did like to show off.* Keeping a pleasant expression on her face, she wheeled herself back as Merecot summoned an air spirit. It swooped down, hovering just outside the open window. Like the ones who had pulled the chariot, this one had the shape of a winged horse. Its wings were closer to a bat's than a bird's, it had the sharp teeth of a wolf, and it wore a saddle that was, like everything here, dotted with jewels. *Jewels must be as common as leaves here*, Hanna thought.

With a flourish, Merecot turned back to them, as if expecting applause.

"You have your spirits well trained," Hanna observed politely.

Merecot let out a laugh that was more of a bark. "Some of them." And with that cryptically bitter statement, she climbed out the window and mounted the air spirit.

At Hanna's command, her guards lifted her out of her chair and onto the spirit. Evenna whispered a steady stream of words of caution, and Serk grunted his agreement, but she had to ignore them as she settled into the saddle. She was sorry this was upsetting her guards. In truth, it was upsetting *her*—she wished this could have waited until tomorrow so she'd have a chance to rest. *Not likely to—*

The spirit launched itself into the air before she could even complete the thought. They flew northwest, wind in their faces and other air spirits all around them, flitting and diving and chattering on the wind.

As they flew farther, Hanna saw a red smear in the distance. It looked like an ember against the clouds. And then she lost sight of it as the spirit plunged into a cloud. They flew for what felt like hours, shrouded in murkiness whiteness. She lost track of time. The chill from the air settled into her bones, making them ache, and the roar of the wind in her ears became a steady hum.

When they at last emerged, the red smear was no longer distant. Hanna saw it clearly: a volcano, mid-eruption. *A live volcano! In Semo! This can't be!*

Yet clearly it could.

Fire spirits danced in the center of the flame, and around the eruption, air spirits flew in circles rapidly enough to create a cyclone, the wind containing the fire and ash and funneling it upward. *It looks,* Hanna thought with a shudder, *like what you'd see across the borders of Renthia, in the untamed lands. But that's impossible—*

"Look and witness!" Merecot called over the wind. "You see before you our bane! You know we have too many spirits. But what you and Queen Daleina don't grasp is what that means. These 'excess spirits' chose me as their queen, the same as every other spirit in Semo. They're linked to me. But unlike the others, they are *not* linked to the land. They *can't* join with it, even though they want to; there simply isn't enough land to go around. And so they seek to destroy it, to unmake it."

Hanna reached out with her mind. She didn't have much range, but it didn't take much to touch the spirits in the wind. A fierce hunger slammed into her, and she recoiled. The spirits' minds swallowed hers, and she couldn't feel her own body, couldn't tell if she was holding on to the saddle—and then her grip loosened, and she slid to the side, off the saddle.

She fell.

Spirits surrounded Hanna, and she was swept into the cyclone. She lost every sense of what was up, down, and sideways as she tumbled through the sky. The heat from the volcano pounded against the circle of wind, and the sound was a roar that penetrated into her bones.

*If I die here, she will be blamed ... but I'll still be dead.*

Hanna reached out with her mind and tried to control the nearest air spirits—but they were too wild, and she wasn't strong enough. She felt herself slipping, blackness crawling into her vision and across her mind, until she lost consciousness.

WHEN SHE CAME TO, HANNA WAS LYING AWKWARDLY ACROSS Merecot's lap, on the back of the air spirit. Raising her head, she saw mountains—they were nowhere near the volcano and cyclone. *I'm alive. That's a surprise.*

"Not dead?" Merecot asked, and then exhaled an enormous

sigh. "Thank the spirits. Or more accurately, thank *me*. Couldn't you have strapped yourself on if you knew you were prone to fainting?"

"I am *not* prone to fainting," Hanna said indignantly. "You have an active volcano in your land! Not to mention unchecked tornadoes." She would have been satisfied with a more distant view. An up-close tour hadn't been necessary. *Merecot's flair for the dramatic nearly got me killed.* If Hanna weren't positioned like a saddlebag, she would have delivered a scathing glare.

"What I was about to say, before you had your moment of melodrama, was that the excess spirits are the reason that I invaded Aratay. There's plenty of room in your forests for them— look at all the barren areas! If I had been able to spread my spirits across both Semo and Aratay, then there would be enough land for all of them, and my people wouldn't have to live in constant fear of an eruption or avalanche wiping out everything and everyone they hold dear."

Hanna mentally checked her body. It all ached. She felt as if she were one massive bruise. It hurt to breathe. Even her legs twinged, though she knew that was false pain. And yet what bothered her the most was the nonsense penetrating her ears. "So this is why you tried to kill Daleina? You wanted to rule both Semo and Aratay, in order to save Semo?"

"Yes. Exactly so."

"It never occurred to you to simply *talk* to her first? Ask for help? She might have been able to offer help with controlling them."

"Frankly, no. But now that I know she's amenable to negotiations, I'd appreciate it if you would present her with my request: send Queen Naelin to Semo to help me with the excess spirits. Our combined power may be enough to tame the excess spirits and save this land."

Hanna shook her head. "Why would they possibly help you? Both queens have ample reason to distrust you. You attacked our country, and you poisoned Daleina. You took Queen Naelin's children, and attacked the wolf Bayn."

"I had to get her attention! Daleina promised in the grove that she would assist me, but that help hasn't materialized. And Semo can't wait much longer. You saw the volcano! Even I can't contain forces like that forever, and when my strength fails . . ."

Hanna was surprised to hear frustration in her voice. And fear.

"Let me show you what's at stake."

At Merecot's command, the air spirit soared eastward. While Hanna's position across the saddle was not the most comfortable, it did afford her an excellent view of Semo. It was quite a populous land, with pockets of houses tucked onto the sides of mountains and in the valleys between them. Most of the lower slopes were farmed, with terraces and plateaus, and the houses themselves were either within the mountain, cavelike, or jutting out at dizzying heights. Hanna could see why they'd be afraid of out-of-control spirits—their lives were precarious enough as it was.

*It's responsible of Merecot to care about them,* Hanna thought. Regardless of whether Merecot cared because she didn't want to be a failure or whether she truly felt empathy, the result was the same—Merecot believed she was acting in her people's best interests. That much was clear. Her passion was well placed.

It was only her choice of actions that was flawed.

*Very, very flawed.*

When they reached the palace in Arkon, the air spirits flew through the open window and servants and guards swarmed over Hanna and Merecot. Hanna's guards fussed over her until she shooed them back. Sinking into one of the velvet couches, Hanna stuffed herself with pastries and sipped at the sweet wines, trying to corral her mind into thinking coherently.

Merecot hadn't overstated the problem. Now that Hanna had seen it for herself, she understood better the desperation that had driven her to act so recklessly.

But that didn't excuse all the harm she had done.

"You said I would see the children when we returned," Hanna said. If she had treated the children well, if she intended to bargain with them in good faith . . . *Or as "good faith" as possible for a kidnapper and murderer . . .* if she was acting with the best interests of her people in mind, then perhaps this could still all be resolved happily.

*"Perhaps" being the key word*, she thought. But still . . . if there was even a chance at a peaceful resolution . . . *We don't have to forgive her for all she's done, but we do have to find a way to co-exist with her.*

Merecot crossed to the door and flung it open. "Send them in!"

Hanna heard them before she saw them: laughing and shouting, their feet pounding on the stone corridor, and then two richly dressed children tumbled into the room.

Erian and Llor.

Their faces were flushed. They were smiling. They were alive.

Seeing Hanna, Llor's face lit up. "I know you! Erian, Erian! Look! We know her!" Both of them rushed to her side.

"Headmistress Hanna!" Erian said. "We're so happy to see you! Queen Jastra told us we'd be seeing a familiar face soon."

"I'd hoped it would be Mama," Llor said.

Erian quickly added, "But it's nice to see you too."

Llor nodded in agreement. "You have a very nice face."

Hanna felt herself smiling. No one had ever said she had a nice face. Usually students were too busy worrying over whether they'd pass or fail to think about whether their headmistress seemed "nice" or not. "Are you well? How has Queen Merecot treated you?"

"She gives us chocolate," Llor said.

"She hasn't hurt us," Erian said, her eyes serious—Llor might not understand exactly what was going on or why he was here, but from Erian's expression, Hanna was certain that Erian did. "But she hasn't let us go home. Are you here to take us home, Headmistress?"

Hanna hesitated, unsure how to answer the question. She didn't want to give her false hope, except would it be false? So far, all that Hanna had seen matched what Merecot claimed.

Queen Merecot swept forward. "It is all in your hands, Ambassador. Will you ask Queen Naelin to come to Semo and help me save *my* children, the people of this land?"

Hanna studied Erian and Llor for a moment more. Both were

unharmed, well fed, and seemed to be—with the exception of missing their mother—happy. And Semo was exactly as Queen Merecot had described, overrun and in danger.

It could still be a trap, of course. But she'd seen enough to feel certain of one thing: Queen Naelin needed to come. Her children were here and alive, and there was a chance—a thin chance, true, but still a chance—to establish real, lasting peace. "You will keep your word? You will return the children if Queen Naelin negotiates in good faith?"

"If Queen Naelin comes to Semo and agrees to help me find a solution to our problem, then yes, her children will be free to go." Queen Merecot made a shooing motion with her hand, as if the children were an irritation she wanted to be free of.

*She probably* does *find them irritating,* Hanna thought, suppressing a smile. Merecot didn't strike her as the maternal type. Oddly, it was that little human reaction that made Hanna believe her, if not precisely trust her.

"Very well," Hanna said. "I will send word to my queens. You'll have help saving your people. But if you play us false . . . If you harm these children . . . If you fail to return them . . ."

Queen Merecot raised her eyebrows. "Ah, so this is the part of 'diplomacy' where we make cryptic threats? Believe me, Ambassador, I am well aware of the stakes and what will happen if I fail."

Before Hanna could respond, Erian piped up. "Mama will kill you, that's what will happen." Her brother nodded stoutly beside her. "Yes," Hanna said mildly. "I believe the children are correct."

Queen Merecot was silent for a moment. "Send your message, Ambassador."

# CHAPTER 13

Naelin knew that Ambassador Hanna would send her report soon. She'd promised—as soon as she'd assessed the level of threat, as soon as she'd seen the children, as soon as she had any information, she'd send word.

"Soon" wasn't soon enough.

After Naelin had the spirits demolish her chambers and then repair and rebuild them, she left her room and wandered through the halls of the palace. Courtiers and caretakers bowed to her, offering their condolences for her children's supposed death.

She smiled brittlely at them and thanked them without correcting them.

It was safer if they didn't know the truth. Or what she hoped was the truth.

*Where is that message, Hanna?*

Most regarded Naelin as if she were a fragile teacup that would shatter if they even went close to it or a wild animal who could snap at any moment. *I can't blame them,* she thought. *I am dangerous.*

Fleeing from all the sympathetic and nervous glances, she ended up in the palace kitchen, which was empty except for Arin, Daleina's younger sister. She was braiding dough to make a knotted pastry. Naelin stood in the archway silently for a moment, wondering if she should leave. Arin looked perfectly content, stretching and twisting the dough in peace, and Naelin didn't want to shatter that peace with her own anxiousness.

Naelin's eyes drifted to the winch for the dumbwaiter, and she remembered Erian and Llor telling her how Arin had turned the crank and lifted them up to the Queen's Tower with the precious antidote. Their words had tumbled out of their mouths so fast that she could barely piece together what they were saying, but she knew that Arin had trusted them to save the queen—and they'd done it. Naelin had been bursting with pride when she'd heard.

*No more remembering! No more thinking! Enough!*

"May I join you?" Naelin asked.

Startled, Arin jumped. "Your Majesty! Yes, of course. Please. Can I get you anything?"

"Not unless you can bake me some patience."

Arin looked sympathetic. "No word from Ambassador Hanna yet?"

Naelin sighed and shook her head. She sank onto a stool next to Arin. At least she was with someone who knew the truth—Arin had been in the room when Daleina read the ransom letter. Here, she didn't have to fend off unwanted sympathy.

"You need a distraction," Arin said. "A hobby. Like this." She dipped a thick paintbrush into a cup and began painting butter onto the surface of the dough. It gleamed in the firelight from the kitchen hearth.

"I used to make charms," Naelin offered. She'd been good at it, back when she'd believed that was all she needed to protect her family.

"Then make some." Arin nodded at the pantry and at the dried herbs that hung from the rafters. "You're in the best-stocked kitchen in Mittriel, and it's not like you need to ask anyone's permission, being queen and all."

It was strange, but sometimes it still took a little reminding that as queen, all of this was technically hers (hers and Daleina's, anyway). As that seeped in, so did Arin's suggestion, and it was registering as a fairly good idea. Everyone could use more spirit-protection charms, and thanks to her power, hers always had

SARAH BETH DURST

been potent. The more she thought about it, the more she found herself without a reason *not* to do it. It was late, well after cleanup had been completed from the evening meal, and no one was going to disturb them.

With a confidence she hadn't felt in days, Naelin busied herself with choosing ingredients from the myriad shelves. She pushed aside a stack of bowls to clear room to work, opposite Arin. For a while, both were silent—Arin with her bread and Naelin with her herbs. She wove a simple earth-spirit protection charm made of forest-floor herbs and laced with dried peppers. The secret was the combination of herbs, to create a scent that seemed both natural in its components and unnatural in its combination, that would repel the spirits.

"You could add more oomph to that," Arin said. "A few sprigs of basilwort, combined with this powder that I've been working on—it won't just repel them; it will burn them."

"You've been learning that?" Naelin asked. "I thought you were apprenticed to the Queen's Poisoner. Aren't you learning about poisons?"

"Only against spirits. Every apprentice choses a specialty—though I think Master Garnah may be disappointed in mine. She likes human targets." Arin shook her head in disgust, then looked at Naelin. "It doesn't matter—here, I can show you what I've been working on, if you like," Arin said, wiping off her hands. She had a smudge of flour on her cheek. "Can you call a fire spirit?"

Naelin called to one as if whistling for a dog. It darted down the chimney and landed in the fire in the kitchen fireplace. Embers popped out onto the hearth, and the wood crackled. The tiny spirit was humanlike with a child's eyes and metallic red scales over its body.

"Better stand back," Arin warned.

Naelin retreated to an alcove that held a table and stools, where the kitchen staff took turns resting on busy days. She watched as Arin drew a vial out of her pocket and shook it. Arin pursed her lips and steadied her aim—then threw.

The glass shattered on the bricks in the fireplace, and purple powder exploded into a cloud over the fire. Naelin jumped as it *boomed*.

She heard shouts from above, then footsteps.

"Oops," Arin said.

"Everything's all right!" Naelin shouted up at the palace guards.

They didn't believe her, of course, and came pouring into the kitchen. But as the purple smoke cleared, it was clear there was no danger. Only one tiny fire spirit knocked out on the hearth. Naelin crossed to it. Picked up its arm and dropped it. The thin charred arm flopped back onto the brick. She touched the spirit with her mind—it was alive, but it was . . . asleep?

The guards, reassured that their queen was neither in danger nor causing danger, retreated to the stairwell, and Naelin faced Arin. "Let's *definitely* put that into charms."

Arin grinned, and Naelin found herself grinning back.

Side by side, they worked late through the night, until the pre-dawn hours, when the kitchen workers began to drift in, to begin their morning preparations. Gray light was warming the windows when the two finally ceded the kitchen to its staff. Swarming around them, the staff helped them put away the leftover herbs and ingredients, despite Naelin's protests that she could very well clean up herself—she'd made the mess; she should clean it. The staff, though, was far more efficient, and Naelin and Arin found themselves scooted over to an alcove, along with Arin's bread and a stack of powder-laced charms.

"If you weren't queen, I'd say we should open up the best hedgewitch shop in the city," Arin said, hugging the charms.

"It would have been a thriving business," Naelin agreed.

"I'd planned to open my own bakery—that was my dream, with Josei. He was the baker's boy in the town where my family lived. He was my best friend. We'd even talked about marrying when we were older."

Naelin heard the past tense. "Spirits?" she guessed.

"Yes, when Queen Fara died."

"I'm sorry."

"After he died, people kept saying that: 'I'm sorry.'"

Naelin thought of the people in the palace and the villagers in Redleaf and their endless, empty sympathy. She supposed it was the only thing they knew to say.

And she'd just done it to Arin.

"At first it didn't help," the girl continued. "I kept wanting to scream at them, 'If you're so sorry, why didn't you save him?' But it's not as if anyone could have saved him. It just happened. And suddenly every dream I had, every plan we'd made, were all dead too." She looked at Naelin. "I'm not saying it's the same as for you. I know Erian and Llor aren't dead, and maybe Bayn isn't either, but . . ." She trailed off, as if she wanted to say more but didn't know what words to use.

Reaching across the table, Naelin squeezed Arin's hand. Arin squeezed back, and then she broke apart one of the loaves she'd baked, sharing it with Naelin.

Naelin bit into a piece. Sweet, soft, and flaky, it was one of the best breads she'd ever eaten. Despite her apprenticeship to a poisoner, Arin clearly had a gift for baking. She should've had the chance to open that bakery with her boy. *Strange, the twists that come while we make other plans*, Naelin thought.

"Guess we should probably sleep," Arin said, watching the kitchen staff scurry through, preparing to make breakfast for the courtiers, guards, and everyone.

"I think we may have missed that chance," Naelin said, nodding to the stairwell. The seneschal had just poked his head into the kitchen and was looking around. His eyes lit up beneath his fluffed eyebrows when he spotted Naelin, and he trotted across the kitchen to the alcove.

With full formality, despite this being a kitchen not a throne room, the seneschal bowed. "Queen Naelin, a spirit has arrived, bearing a report from Ambassador Hanna. Queen Daleina was in the middle of meeting with the champions when it came. She insists on waiting for you before sharing it."

Naelin sprang to her feet. "Keep the charms," she told Arin. "And . . . thank you."

Naelin followed the seneschal up the winding stairs. She

wanted to run like an impatient child. *Please let it be good news! Please!*

He led her up—and up and up—to the Chamber of the Queen's Champions, at the top of the easternmost tree. "Couldn't some queen have installed a lift?" Naelin puffed. She was used to climbing through the trees, but this was a ridiculous number of stairs. *Aren't we there yet?*

"Your predecessors have expressed similar sentiments," the seneschal said blandly—he didn't *seem* to be laughing at her. He wasn't panting at all, though, she noticed. "Some used spirits to convey them to the chamber."

"I won't use spirits for my convenience. Only when it's necessary." And there was only one scenario she currently hoped would make it necessary: rescuing her very-much-alive children.

She climbed the stairs faster.

Guards greeted her at the top of the steps, and she barely nodded to them as she passed. All the champions, including Ven, were seated in a ring around the edges of the chamber.

She'd been up here only once, after she was first crowned, to meet the champions. Since then, the vines that circled the arches had withered, with only a few golden leaves still clinging to them. A second throne had been added, this one not grown from the tree itself but still just as beautiful, made of a deep cherry wood and decorated with curls of white pine. Still panting from the climb, Naelin plopped into the throne. She felt the eyes of all the champions on her.

Naelin studied them right back. She didn't know many of them, but most appeared . . . the kindest word was "grizzled." Most looked as if a bear had chomped on them, then spat them out because they were too tough.

Then came back for seconds.

It was an amusing thought, but then she noted the empty chairs too. Champions who had died and hadn't yet been replaced.

She could see their assessment of her in those experienced faces, some curious, others openly hostile—she hadn't won any friends lately, with the spirit deaths and the earthquake and every other disaster she'd caused. She felt a touch of guilt at that, but also dared them to have their reason for living torn away from them and see how they—

An air spirit grew agitated in the corner, and Naelin quickly retreated behind the wall Hanna had taught her to construct.

Once more in control, she sat up straight, composed.

Queen Daleina nodded regally at her, and Naelin wondered how many times she'd practiced that nod before she'd perfected it. The red, gold, and brown streaks in her hair were artfully arranged in coils beneath her crown. This young girl couldn't come close to commanding the spirits like Naelin could, and yet every time they were near each other, Naelin always felt like the lesser queen. Maybe it was Daleina's training. Or her experience. Or maybe she was just born wiser than her years. But being with her made Naelin feel as if she were a child, desperately hoping that Daleina could somehow make everything all right. Naelin glanced away only to meet Ven's eyes, and she saw her own anxious hope mirrored in them.

"Are they alive?" Naelin demanded.

"Yes," Daleina said.

Naelin closed her eyes for a moment as a wave of relief crashed through her, as strong as a storm. Then she opened her eyes and asked, "Are they unharmed?"

"Yes."

She lowered her face into her hands. Her body was shaking, and she tried to control it . . . and failed. She didn't sob, but the tears came nevertheless. *Alive and unharmed!* Daleina couldn't have given her any better gift than those yeses.

Queen Daleina raised her voice to address the array of champions, catching their attention before they could ask any questions. "I apologize for the secrecy, and I thank you for your patience." Briefly, she summarized the situation: Queen Naelin's children were alive, Queen Merecot had used Semoian air spirits to kidnap them, and Headmistress Hanna from Northeast Academy has been deployed as an ambassador to assess the situation.

As she spoke, she tapped a roll of parchment against her palm—

Ambassador Hanna's report. Naelin, composed once more, stared at it as if she could read through the back of the paper, if only she looked hard enough. She wanted to know more! What had her children said? What were they doing? Were they scared? Did they miss home? Did they know how much she missed them?

She wasn't the only one who wanted to know more—the champions burst into talking all at once.

Naelin wanted to yell at them to shut their mouths and let Daleina finish, but Daleina merely waited while they chattered louder and louder like excitable birds whose nests had been invaded. Fidgeting in her throne, Naelin felt as if their voices were pecking inside her head:

*Outrageous!*

*Kidnapping the queen's children!*

*It's an act of war! Unconscionable!*

*We must retaliate!*

*We must mount a rescue mission!*

Finally, Ven's voice cut through the others. "Your Majesty, what is Ambassador Hanna's report?" Naelin shot him a grateful look.

"Ambassador Hanna reports that the children are alive and well. They appear to be treated as guests and have suffered no injuries. She believes that Queen Merecot acted out of desperation, on behalf of her people."

There was another outburst at that:

*No excuse!*

*They're only children!*

*Unforgivable.*

"In exchange for their safe return," Daleina said, her hands folded across the parchment. Naelin noticed she wasn't as calm as she looked—bits of the paper crumbled under her fingers as she clenched and unclenched her hands. "Queen Merecot requests that Queen Naelin visit Semo and use her power to assist in the taming of the excess spirits of Semo."

"It's a trap, of course," one of the champions said, surging to his feet.

"That was our belief at first as well," Daleina said. "We deployed Ambassador Hanna to determine whether or not it was. She deems it safe enough for Queen Naelin to accept Queen Merecot's invitation, and I trust her judgment."

Another champion rose to her feet. "Your Majesty, with all due respect, Ambassador Hanna does not possess the power of Queen Merecot. If she were misled—"

"She is not the kind to be easily misled."

"—or manipulated."

Another spoke. "Or if Queen Merecot merely changes her mind. She's asking us to relinquish our safety net! Aratay has no heirs! If Queen Naelin leaves Aratay and cannot return, for whatever reason, we will again be vulnerable."

Again, the champions squabbled like a flock of chickens.

Naelin lost track of who was speaking. Reaching across, she extracted the message from Daleina's grasp and read it. The ambassador's report was concise, and she outlined her suggestion in clear terms, as well as her certainty that this would solve both Aratay's problems and Semo's. "I will, of course, go," Naelin said.

The champions fell silent.

Lowering the letter, Naelin looked at them. She didn't see why this was even open to debate, but she tried to formulate her thoughts to explain her reasoning. It was very tempting to say, *Because I said so.* "First and foremost, I *will* reclaim my children. But second, this is best for Aratay. If I can help solve the problem of Semo, we will be safe from any further invasions. Our people will be safe."

"But . . ." one began.

"Do you know I have a nickname already in the outer forest?" Naelin said. "They call me the Mother of Aratay. And I say I will go, for the sake of *all* my children."

Her words were met with silence—the kind of silence that feels full of unspoken arguments. The champions shifted uncomfortably in their living wood seats. A few of them glanced at the sky, at the ever-present air spirits that circled above the chamber, like buzzards over a soon-to-be corpse.

"I will leave immediately," Naelin said to Daleina.

At that, the champions began to argue again.

She waited, letting their voices rise to shouting, her eyes only on Daleina. *She agrees*, Naelin thought. *She knew as soon as she read the report, I'd go.*

When a moment of quiet descended on the chamber, while the champions drew breaths to argue again, Naelin rose from her throne. "You may debate it all you wish, but in the end, it is not your decision to make. *We*," she said, pointing to Daleina and herself, "are the queens of Aratay. Not you."

She left the council while the champions continued to argue in her wake, like children who won't admit the game is lost.

IGNORING THE ARGUMENTS SWIRLING AROUND HIM, VEN CROSSED to Daleina and knelt in front of her. "My Queen, with your permission, I will accompany Queen Naelin to Semo."

Behind him, Champion Sevrin grunted. "You want to make the situation worse, Ven? By the spirits, I thought you had more sense than that."

Rising, he pivoted. His hands clenched, and he deliberately unclenched them. "She'll need a guard."

"Send a palace guard." Sevrin waved in the direction of the stairs. "Better yet, send a squadron of soldiers. Don't send a champion."

"Champion Sevrin is correct," Champion Jalsia said. "Your skills are needed here, now more than ever. Aratay needs heirs! If this is another ploy by Queen Merecot . . ." She didn't need to finish her sentence. Nods were echoed all around the council chamber.

It hadn't occurred to Ven that his fellow champions would object. "Queen Naelin needs—"

"She needs a soldier, not a lover," Sevrin said, and Ven seriously considered smashing his balled-up fist into the man's face. If Daleina hadn't lightly and subtly touched his arm at that very moment, he might have done just that. "And Aratay needs its hero champion," Sevrin continued. "You've heard the songs, I assume? You're the finest champion who has ever lived, trainer of two queens, warrior extraordinaire, and other drivel. We in this room may know better, but if you abandon Aratay in its hour of need, the *people* will panic. The people are counting on *you* to find the next queen-to-be."

Despite Daleina's hint, Ven's hand strayed toward his sword hilt. He'd never draw on another champion, but his fingers were now brushing the pommel. Through clenched teeth he said, "I'm not abandoning the people of Aratay; I'm serving its queen." That any champion would be so shortsighted as to fail to see that—

"You're serving yourself," Sevrin said, "as you always do."

"And what's that supposed to mean?" Now he *did* put his hand on his sword hilt, but he made himself remove it. A fight here wouldn't help anyone.

"First Queen Fara, now Queen Naelin," Sevrin drawled. "Some say you serve yourself when you serve your queens." He pushed himself off his seat and crossed to Ven. Stopped only inches from him. "Some say you think with the wrong sword."

Ven did not draw his weapon at that. He looked back at Daleina, and tried to apologize without words. One of her eyebrows shot up, but she said nothing.

He turned back around . . . and punched Sevrin in the face.

With a howl, Sevrin staggered back. Blood poured from his nose, but he wasn't stunned—he *was* a champion himself. With a roar, he launched himself at Ven, fists flying. Ven kicked back, hitting the larger man square in the gut and sending him crashing into the seats. Other champions sprang out of the way.

Daleina's voice cracked across the chamber. "Enough!"

Ven, muscles still coiled, watched Sevrin as he pushed to his feet. Scowling at Ven, he wiped the blood from his upper lip with the back of his hand. It smeared onto his cheek. "They speak of you with such respect." Sevrin spat onto the council floor, at Ven's feet. "They don't know how weak you truly are, confusing duty for 'love' and queens for toys."

Queen Daleina rose to her feet, and above her, the air spirits shrieked. All the champions reacted—drawing swords, kicking aside the chairs, crouching at the ready—but Daleina stood straight and tall, motionless while the spirits circled. "And what of *this* queen, Champion Sevrin?"

Sevrin blanched, seeming to realize the implication he had made concerning her.

"Champion Ven will accompany Queen Naelin to Semo. His so-called weakness *is* his strength. He would die to protect her. Isn't that correct, Champion Ven?"

He knelt on one knee. "It is, Your Majesty."

"Then not sending you would be stupid," Daleina said. "And I strive to avoid stupidity. Champions, return to your chosen candidates. Continue to train them. And pray they will not be needed anytime soon."

The spirits cried once more and then flew higher, into the clouds.

The champions bowed and filed out of the chamber, except for Ven. He stayed kneeling before Queen Daleina, his head bent, though he watched Sevrin and the other champions tromp past and down the spiral stairs, until at last they were alone.

Daleina sank into her throne. "Did you have to hit him?"

Ven considered that. "Yes, I believe I did." He didn't plan to make a habit of it, especially while Sevrin carried that wicked ax of his, but the situation had warranted it. "There is nothing dishonorable or selfish about what I've done." It demeaned both women to suggest it, implying they didn't choose him as freely as he chose them.

"He was goading you," Daleina said, tapping the parchment against the armrests of her throne. "He wanted to prove you're ruled by emotions, not logic. He was angling for me to remove you as a champion—subtlety is not his strength."

Rising to his feet, Ven said, "I've noticed."

"Nor is it yours," she snapped.

Ven winced. That was fair. He supposed he should have waited until after the champions had left to announce his intention to accompany Naelin. The champions were right to worry—without heirs, Aratay remained vulnerable, and Ven had sworn the same oath they had.

But there was another oath he'd made in his heart . . .

Daleina looked toward the north, over the canopy of trees.

Ven followed her gaze. The mountains were too distant to be seen from Mittriel, but the damage from the invasion was still visible—new trees had been grown to replace the damaged ones, and they formed a river of golden leaves against the dark green of the old pine and the red and orange and brown. "Do you think it's a trap?"

"Yes. I don't know. It could be." Ven hesitated, weighing the various risks. "It doesn't really matter, though, does it? And it's why I'm going, to protect Naelin against any attacks with blades, fists, or claws. But if Queen Merecot was to attempt poison . . ."

"I'll order Poison-Master Garnah to accompany you."

"She won't be willing to leave her son." That wasn't his only objection, though. Truthfully, Garnah was the last person he would trust on a diplomatic mission. She was more likely to cause disaster than prevent it. But he could appreciate Daleina wanting Garnah out of the country, as far from Arin as possible.

She rose again. "I will speak to her. You wish to leave at dawn, I presume?"

He bowed. "Yes, Your Majesty. I officially request a leave of absence from my champion duties, until the completion of this mission."

"Granted," Daleina said. "But Ven . . ."

"Yes?"

"You will always be my champion."

# CHAPTER 14

Flanked by Ven and Hamon, Daleina strode through the palace and tried to ignore the tree spirit that was nestling into her crown. It was muttering to itself in unintelligible words that sounded like wood splintering while it wound her hair into a nest and cuddled with the jewels on her head. Out of the corner of her eye, she saw Hamon shooting glances at her crown.

"Daleina . . ." Hamon began.

"Yes, I know."

"But it's staying."

"I know."

Ven looked amused. "You might start a new fashion."

Hamon did *not* look amused. "If it should panic or turn on you, its claws could—"

Daleina interrupted him again. "I *know*." She swept down the hallway. Up ahead, two guards stood at attention on either side of Poison-Master Garnah's door, ostensibly protecting the dangerous concoctions inside but also monitoring Garnah's movements. They inclined their heads as she approached but otherwise remained vigilant. One of them spotted the tree spirit in Daleina's hair—she saw his eyes widen. "The Queen's Poisoner is dangerous. It's important she be reminded that I'm *more* dangerous."

*Let them all think about that.*

She wasn't certain she believed it, but it sounded good, and she needed all her self-confidence wrapped around her like armor if she was going to convince Garnah to cooperate.

Stepping forward, Ven swung open the door for her, and she entered the room.

Arin scurried forward. "Daleina!" She wore a thick leather apron and a falconer's gloves. Her hair was pulled back into a bun that didn't allow for any strand to slip out, and she had protective glasses on her face.

"Please don't hug me if you've been playing with poison," Daleina said.

Her little sister skidded to a stop.

"Why is that even a thing I have to say?" Daleina asked.

Across the room, Garnah chuckled. She was not dressed in any protective gear. Instead she wore layers of flouncy lace that billowed around her like a child's drawing of a cloud. Three peacock feathers stuck out of her elaborately braided hair. *She looked like she's been playing dress-up in a courtier's closet*, Daleina thought, and wondered if Garnah was deliberately mocking the court ladies or if that was merely an accidental bonus. With Garnah, it could be either. "Your Majesty," Garnah said, rising then curtsying. Her skirts pooled around her. "My beloved son." Crossing to Hamon, she embraced him. He stiffened, and Daleina thought he'd rather bolt than endure her touch. But he was here to help, not cause a scene, and so he didn't move. Garnah then turned to Ven. "And the gruff, muscly man." She pinched Ven's bicep.

"You insisted on coming," Daleina told him.

Garnah glanced at Daleina's crown. "Nice hat."

The spirit hissed. Garnah stuck her tongue out at it.

*So much for impressing her*, Daleina thought.

"To what do I owe the pleasure of this visit? Or are you here to visit my protégée?" Garnah frowned at one of the workbenches. "Arin, don't let the wormtongue bathe in the hazel brine for more than three minutes."

"Oh!" Arin hurried back across the laboratory, secured her glasses, and then used tongs to lift a gnarled root out of a container of algae-green water.

Hamon shook his head. "Mother, tell me you aren't teaching

her how to make beetle bane." Daleina recognized the name of the poison—it was a common one for eliminating vermin from crops of berries, but mishandled it could be toxic. It was one reason why every cook washed berries before cooking with them.

"She's not making beetle bane," Garnah said.

"I'm making breath-choker juice," Arin said cheerfully.

Daleina sighed. If their parents ever learned about half the things that Arin was meddling with, they'd yank Arin out of Mittriel so fast that she wouldn't even have time to pack. *I should tell them. Even if they blame me.* At least at home her sister would be safe. "Is that as ominous as it sounds?"

"Certainly hope so," Garnah said. "Otherwise she'll have to start over. But you didn't come to talk about mundane things like death. What do you need, Your Majesty?"

Daleina debated several ways to frame the request and then opted for the direct approach. "Queen Merecot has Queen Naelin's two children, and has requested Queen Naelin's assistance in exchange for their safe return. I need you to accompany Queen Naelin to Semo and do what you can to keep her alive until the problem of excess spirits is solved."

"And after it's solved," Ven put in. "Keeping her alive in general would be good. We like her living." He was fingering the hilt of his sword, and Daleina wasn't certain if it was Garnah or the spirit on the crown that was making him uneasy. *Or maybe it's the deadly poison that my baby sister is brewing . . .*

"We don't trust Queen Merecot for obvious reasons," Daleina said, "and I believe that your expertise and experience would make you the ideal choice—"

Garnah smiled sweetly. "You're so kind to think of me, but no, thank you."

Daleina tried again. "Your service would be greatly appreciated. And well rewarded. In fact, if this mission is successful, you and all those who accompany Naelin would be considered heroes. Songs would be sung about you by canopy singers for generations."

"While all that fame sounds lovely, I cannot leave my beloved son now that I have at last found him." Garnah patted Hamon's cheek, and he flinched. "I assume you won't be going to Semo on this joyful jaunt?"

"I'm needed here, with Queen Daleina, as her personal healer," Hamon said.

"Very personal, I know." Garnah winked. "But don't think I disapprove! I think it's delightful! What more could a mother hope for, than for her son to find happiness in the arms of—"

Ven growled, "Enough."

Garnah clapped her hands together. "I've embarrassed the unflappable champion! Shall we discuss your love life next? It's all very romantic. Many forest girls fall asleep each night by imagining a champion will choose them above all others and elevate them to a life of importance and meaning."

His hands were clenched into fists. "Queen Naelin's life had meaning before me."

"Oh, that's right, it did!" Garnah's voice was filled with mock surprise. Daleina knew she should say something, stop this before . . . before what? What was Garnah aiming at? What did she want? "She had her children, the center of her world, the reason for her reluctance to claim power. They were her meaning in life. And because of you taking her unwillingly out of the life she'd chosen for herself . . . she lost them."

She heard Ven's breath hiss as if he'd been punched in the stomach, and Daleina stepped between Garnah and Ven, using the breadth of her skirts as a barrier between them. "Poison-Master Garnah—"

"I lost my son once," Garnah said, all amusement gone from her voice. "He was the center of my world, my meaning in life, and I won't lose him again, no matter the cost. You may command me to leave, but I will resist. You cannot force me to leave my reason for being. I'm quite certain Queen Naelin will feel the same way, once she has reclaimed her lost children."

Hamon sighed. "Mother, there's a vast difference between you and Queen Naelin. You didn't lose me. *I* left *you* because you're an immoral serial killer."

Garnah was silent for a moment, then said, "I prefer 'amoral.'"

Daleina didn't know whether she wanted to laugh or scream.

Instead she crossed to the nearest workbench and studied the array of scribbled-on parchment, bottles of herbs and other ingredients, and beakers of oddly colored liquids. Maybe she shouldn't push Garnah to go to Semo. It had seemed like such a perfect solution: the poison maker could protect Naelin (and as a bonus quit tormenting Hamon and corrupting Arin), but even if she issued an order and even if Garnah obeyed, Daleina didn't know if she could trust her. *Maybe I'm being selfish, wanting her to go. If I send enough protection, it feels less as if I'm sending Naelin to her death.*

Beside her, Arin had taken off her glasses and the thick leather gloves. She neatened a stack of papers. "I'll go," she said quietly.

Daleina flinched. "Don't be absurd."

"I may not be training as a poisoner, but I think my skills may be even more useful," Arin said. "I have been working with Master Garnah to develop defensive potions, effective against spirits. I can help defend Queen Naelin and her children against Queen Merecot's spirits."

"Absolutely not." Arin was barely more than a child! It was one thing to apprentice her to a confessed killer—that was bad enough—but to send her into known danger in a foreign land . . . Merecot could blame Daleina for the death of her sister, Alet. *I'd have to be foolish to give Merecot such an easy way for revenge.* "I need you here."

"Actually, you don't. You have Healer Hamon and Master Garnah. Let me go, Daleina. I can be useful. I know I can. And unlike anyone else you send, no one will think that I'm there to guard the queen—they'll look at me and see a young girl. I'll be like a secret weapon."

Daleina wanted to shake her by the shoulders. "You *are* a young girl."

"So were you not too long ago. I may be young, but I know how to defend myself."

"Against a queen? Against her spirits?"

Pressing her lips together, Arin reached up to the tiny spirit that had nested in Daleina's hair. *Do no harm*, Daleina reminded the spirit. Gently, Arin untangled the hair around it and lifted it over the crown. Cooing to it, she held the spirit cupped in her hands.

Daleina held her breath. She knew exactly how much courage it took for Arin to stand there, holding something that had the capacity to maim or kill her when Arin had no power to—

Shifting the spirit to one hand, Arin drew out a powder with another and blew it into the face of the spirit. And the spirit stiffened as if it had been frozen.

Arin set it down on the workbench and flicked it with her finger.

The spirit fell over.

"I know potions that can flay the flesh off them," Arin said. "Potions that cause them to sleep. Potions that confuse them. I can set them on fire with one vial of the right powders. I can cause them to drown in their own breath. I can stop them from harming me or Queen Naelin. Let me go, Daleina. I will make you proud."

Daleina stared at her.

Arin stared back.

Laughing, Garnah applauded.

"Absolutely not," Daleina said, storming out of the room as regally as she could.

EVERYONE HAD AN OPINION ON WHO SHOULD ACCOMPANY QUEEN Naelin, what route they should take, when they should leave, and what supplies and weapons and gifts they should bring with them. Ensconced in a throne room, Queen Daleina listened to the string of chancellors, champions, and others who all knew best until her head throbbed.

She nodded politely at each one and instructed her seneschal to take a note, which he diligently did. She agreed to putting together an entourage of courtiers, diplomats, and guards. She agreed to task tailors and seamstresses with crafting royal gowns that would impress the Semoians. She even entertained the suggestion of designing a new flag for Aratay, which a standard-bearer—who would of course be part of the entourage—would carry. And she accepted offers from historians who wished to record this historic trip, singers who wanted to immortalize it, and an artist who wanted to paint the grand journey.

All told, if she followed the advice, preparations would take two months.

Her cheeks began to ache from smiling so much as she listened and nodded to the final opinionated visitor of the day. She kept smiling as the seneschal led him out the throne room door and closed it firmly behind him.

She massaged her cheeks. "They're under way, yes?"

The seneschal nodded. "Queen Naelin left with Champion Ven several hours ago. They should be well beyond Mittriel by now."

Daleina sagged back into the throne. "Excellent."

Neither of them mentioned Arin, though she knew her seneschal knew everything she knew. *She'll be safe, that's what's important*, Daleina thought. *Someday she'll forgive me.*

"Pardon me for asking, Your Majesty, but won't your advisers and the chancellors be irate when they discovered you deceived them?"

She waved her hand nonchalantly. "*I* will be irate when I discover that Queen Naelin deceived *me* and left of her own volition. But then I will accept that one queen can't command another, and Queen Naelin has an independent streak."

The seneschal collected the papers. She watched him as he sorted them, piled them, and then straightened the edges. *I would have just tossed them in the fire*, she thought, but she said nothing.

"You disapprove?" she asked.

"Never, Your Majesty," he said instantly. "It's not my place."

"It's everyone's place to have an opinion. What's yours?"

"On the contrary, it is my job to *not* pass judgment on the decisions of Her Majesty, only to ensure the smooth execution of her wishes." He hesitated. "I do, however, worry."

Daleina felt herself smile, in spite of everything. "As do I, Belsowik. But Naelin and Ven will be safer and faster on their own than in a group waving a flag that says 'Target here!'" She trusted Champion Ven and Queen Naelin to reach Semo without an army at their side. Ven could defend against all physical dangers, and Naelin could handle anything magical thrown at them. *They'll be perfectly safe,* she thought.

*At least until they reach Merecot.*

My turn for an adventure! Arin thought, and she stifled her grin. She didn't want Champion Ven and Queen Naelin to see how excited—and nervous—she was. In truth, she hadn't expected Champion Ven to invite her along after Daleina had said no so adamantly. He'd told her why he'd wanted her: in addition to requiring her skills with potions, he wanted an excuse to stop at her parents' house on the way. He didn't want Queen Naelin to have to camp outside any more than strictly necessary, but he didn't want anyone to guess where she was.

Champion Ven had insisted they leave stealthily. She'd never done much sneaking, but she liked it. They'd exited the palace through the kitchen, carrying sacks of nut flour out to the food-storage tree—Arin hadn't even known there *was* a food-storage tree. Apparently, it held extra food for the people of Aratay in case of emergency, as well as for the palace. Daleina had insisted on canceling all feasts until the harvest crisis was over, so, dressed in kitchen aprons, Arin, Ven, and Naelin had helped shift sacks from the palace to storage. From there, they'd lurked in the shadows until the guard shift changed, and left the palace grounds when no one was watching.

Ven had grumbled about that for a while—it shouldn't have been possible to slip out.

Arin had pointed out that the guards were supposed to keep people from slipping *in*, so technically they weren't failing in their jobs by letting the three of them *out*.

He'd just grunted.

"Keep your head down and shuffle your feet more," Ven advised her now. "You're bouncing too much. General idea is *not* to draw attention."

"Sorry." Arin tried to shuffle more as she followed Ven and Queen Naelin across a few sparsely populated bridges until they reached the capital library.

The Great Library of Mittriel was a sight that Arin had meant to see while she was in the capital, but somehow between the in-vasion and all the potion making, she hadn't had time. Accord-ing to legend, it had been grown a century ago from a solitary redwood by a queen with a flair for the dramatic. She had coaxed the spirits into twisting the trunk so that it formed a spiral like a conch shell. "Whoa," Arin breathed as it came into view.

Brilliant orange, the leaves of the Great Library blazed as if they were on fire. They crowned a tree of deep russet red that curved in a vast spiral. It was so grand that Arin thought there should be trumpets playing and canopy singers singing above it. Beside her, Queen Naelin murmured, "Erian and Llor would have loved this."

"Maybe you can bring them to see it, once we get them back," Arin said, and was rewarded with a startled almost-smile from Queen Naelin.

"You brought me here on purpose," the queen said to Ven.

He pointed toward the highest branches. "There's a wire path—"

"This is a place of hope. Like the library I made in Redleaf." Queen Naelin waved her hand at the glorious tree, with its en-trance draped in elegant vines. "You want me to have hope."

Champion Ven met her eyes, and Arin had the sense that a thousand unspoken words were passing between them before Ven said one single word: "Yes."

Ven led the way into the library, and Arin continued to gawk as she climbed the wide staircase. Shelves had been carved into, or grown out of, the curved walls, with vines cradling the books, and decorated with wooden sculptures of birds and deer and bears and foxes. The books themselves were works of art too, with spines of carved wood or intricately decorated leather. All of it was lit by sunlight filtered through stained-glass windows so that reds and blues danced across all of the surfaces. There were no candles, just the slivers of colored sunlight and the soft glow of firemoss to chase away the shadows. As they climbed higher, more light streamed through the stained glass until Arin felt as if they were swimming in jewels.

Hand in hand, the queen and champion climbed higher through the library while Arin followed behind them, feeling as if she'd been entangled in an old ballad, a classic one with lots of adventure between queens and spirits. The sight of all the beautiful books only added to that feeling. She reached out and ran her fingertips over the spines. She wondered who would be adding Naelin and Daleina's stories.

She wondered if any would mention her.

*Queen Naelin was right—this is a place of hope. And dreams.*

At the top of the spiral, as promised, was a wire path. It was tucked into a bower of roses and flowering vines with cushioned chairs, ideal for curling up with books, with a view of the forest canopy and the glorious blue sky. Ven stopped, and Arin saw he was looking at Naelin, not at the view. The queen faced north.

"We'll bring them home," Ven promised.

"I can't help feeling, despite Ambassador Hanna's reassurances, that it's still a trap."

"Of course it's a trap." Ven shrugged. "We'll still bring them home." He turned to Arin and held out a harness. To her surprise, he was smiling—it was the kind of smile that Daleina used to give her, right before dumping a bucket of cold water on her head because Mama said to give her a bath. "Have you ever ridden the wire paths?" he asked her.

"No." She took the harness and puzzled at the clips.

He helped her attach it. "Listen to my commands so you don't crash into a tree."

Her heart was thumping fast. She'd been wanting to try this ever since Daleina had first told her about riding the wire paths, but now that she was here, her stomach was flopping back and forth like a fish on a riverbank. "What if I get sick?"

"Aim downwind" was his advice.

"Very helpful," she grumbled as she stepped up onto a bench. "How do I—"

He gave her a push.

Arin shrieked as she plummeted off the top of the tree, then an instant later, the harness caught her and she was sailing through the canopy, skimming over leaves and between branches, and her shriek turned into a laugh.

*This is amazing!*

They switched wire paths twice on their way out of Mittriel and didn't stop until they'd reached the village of Threefork, Arin's home. It was near sundown. Birds called to one another as they settled into their nests for the night, and the branches rustled with squirrels and chipmunks hurrying home.

Looking down at Threefork, Arin felt a little like one of the chipmunks.

Like nearly all the other villages in Aratay, Threefork was nestled in the arms of trees so massive you couldn't see them in one glance. Shops and businesses were clustered on platforms around the fattest tree, with bridges connecting all the houses that either budded from or were built onto the various branches. Firemoss lanterns were strung everywhere to light the village at night, and colorful scarves were strung along the bridges to brighten the village during the day. It wasn't unique or special. *But it's home*, Arin thought.

After they'd unhooked from the wires and climbed the ladder down to midforest, Arin led the way. Ven was a step behind her, alert as if they walked through a pack of wolves, and Queen Naelin walked beside him, her hood drawn up around her face.

"Put your hood back, Your Majesty," Arin whispered. "If you look like you're hiding, you'll make people even more curious."

Queen Naelin obeyed but didn't speak.

Smiling and waving at her old neighbors, Arin greeted people as they passed. Leaning out their windows, many waved back. Others hurried to join her on the platforms. Everyone seemed to have a question for her: What was the palace like? How was dear Daleina doing as queen? How wondrous that Ingara and Eaden's girl should be queen! Had Arin met the second queen? What's she like? Did Arin have fancy dresses now? Had she been to any banquets? Were there festivals every night? Did she see fighting during the invasion? Did she kill any spirits? Had she seen anyone die? Had it been as bad as people said? What were the queens going to do about the harvest? The winter stores weren't what they should be . . .

Arin answered everything as best she could, except the death questions, as her friends clustered around her. She introduced

Champion Ven, whom they were all in awe of, and she introduced Queen Naelin as "Caretaker Neena," a name they all immediately accepted. No one in Threefork knew what the second queen looked like, though many of them had an opinion about her. Most popular was: "I heard she went stark raving mad when spirits killed her kids, and she tried to destroy the whole country!"

"It wasn't exactly like that," Arin told them.

"Then what *was* it like?" It was Eira, Josei's sister and Arin's friend. Squealing, Arin hugged her friend, and Eira squeezed her back. Eira beamed at her, dimples deepening in both her cheeks. She then looped her arm through Arin's as they walked. "You must tell me everything. You've been in the palace so long! Everyone thought you weren't coming back."

"Of course I was coming back! I only went to make sure Daleina was all right." *That's true*, Arin thought. Everything else . . . Well, it had just sort of happened. She hadn't planned any of it. *Except I chose to learn potions. And I chose this trip.*

Eira yipped like an excited puppy. "So you're back to stay? I knew it! Oh, Arin, I have the best news to tell you! But your parents should be the ones to tell you. They arranged everything. They're going to be so excited to see you! I think they were afraid you were never coming home again."

Arin winced. She avoided looking at either Naelin or Ven. She hoped they wouldn't be the ones to break the news that she wasn't here to stay.

But Eira didn't seem to notice Arin's discomfort. Forging ahead and dragging Arin with her, Eira parted the crowd. "Let the girl through! She's been traveling! You can gossip later."

Arin thought it was funny that Eira, who was younger and shorter, was able to part the crowd, whereas the Queen's Champion and an actual queen had been stuck in the swarm of curious townspeople, but it did work. Everyone scooted back, and Arin, Ven, and Naelin were able to cross the platform that was the town square and onto the bridge that led to Arin's house.

Home!

She'd been so busy with Master Garnah that she'd barely

paused to picture it, and now home was right in front of her, nestled in the tree branches. It was a green cottage with orange-brown tiles, draped in flowers and stuffed with charms. Exactly like it had been when she left it.

Ven nudged her forward. "Enjoy your homecoming," he murmured in her ear. "You earned this."

Giving Eira one more hug and waving at everyone else, Arin held on to the straps of her pack and ran toward home. "Mama! Daddy!"

The door flew open. "My baby!"

"Mama!" Arin plowed into her and threw her arms around her mother.

Laughing, Mama hugged her back just as hard. "You're here! It's really you! Daleina sent word, but I didn't think you'd be here so quickly. Come in, come in." She bustled them inside.

*Wait,* Arin wanted to say. *How did Daleina know to send word? I snuck away—*

But then she saw Daddy standing by the sink, a dish in one hand and a cloth in the other, and all thoughts left her mind. He beamed at her, and Arin ran into his arms. "I missed you so much!" Arin cried.

Behind her, Mama was saying, "Champion Ven, welcome again to our home." She heard him murmur thanks and introduce Caretaker Neena. Her mother greeted her warmly, inquiring about her journey, offering their hospitality.

Patting Arin's hair, Daddy said, "Sweet pea, you have no idea how happy we are to see you. The house has felt so empty without you!"

Quickly and loudly, Arin said, "We can't stay long. We're on a trip to introduce Caretaker Neena to Ven's family. She's his chosen love."

Ven did not react to this lie. He merely creased his lips into a smile within his beard. "My mother and sister live near the northern border. Your home is on the way." For all Arin knew, that was true. She'd never thought about Ven having a family, though of course he must. He hadn't sprung out of a tree in full leather armor, with a quiver on his back and sword at his side—even if that's what some of the songs said. She tried to picture him as a child and failed.

Mama turned to Naelin and said, "We're delighted to meet the one who has captured the heart of the Queen's Champion. He's grumpy sometimes, but he's a good one."

"He is," Naelin agreed.

And Arin could have sworn she saw Champion Ven actually blush.

Mama shooed them all inside, bustling around them and offering them chairs and rockers and telling them to make themselves at home. Arin dropped her pack, and Ven stacked all their supplies in a corner.

Soon, Mama and Daddy were piling the table with food—the nut bread that Arin always loved, the leaf-wrapped spiced boar meat, and the little triangles of berries in puff pastry that melted in your mouth.

*Dinner's ready—they must have known we were coming*, Arin thought, once more unsure what that meant. *More proof that Daleina knew and told them. Does this mean she approves of my going? But she'd said no . . .* And if Daleina knew, did that mean her parents knew? But they hadn't recognized Queen Naelin . . .

Mama interrupted Arin's thoughts. "Arin, could you get the plates, please?"

Arin jumped up to carry plates to the table. She poured berry juice for everyone. Ven tried to help with getting utensils, and Naelin began folding napkins, until Mama shooed the two of them back into their seats, saying they were guests.

In minutes, everything was ready.

Standing at the head of the table, Mama sliced the nut bread. Using the knife as a server, she laid a piece on each plate as she said in her storytelling voice, "In the beginning, there was only light and darkness, and we were alone, floating in the light and dark for uncounted time, until at last a child was born, a baby girl. It was the first birth."

Sitting in her old chair with the creaky seat, Arin felt like she hadn't ever left. Their meals always started like this, with a story to say thanks. Mama and Daddy liked the old traditions—they never skimped on charms in the roof, they left the first cut of wood outside for the fire spirits to claim, they planted acorns to appease the tree spirits every spring, and they always told a gratitude story before eating.

*I'd missed this in the palace*, Arin thought. She hadn't even realized she'd missed it. Everything had happened so quickly: Daleina's poisoning, the invasion, her apprenticeship. *As soon as we're done in Semo, I'll come back.*

". . . the newborn child spoke one word, 'Earth,' and the spirits of the earth were born from her command. They fashioned earth beneath our feet so we could stand. She spoke again: 'Air,' and we breathed freely for the first time. 'Water,' and we drank. 'Fire,' and we were warm. 'Wood,' and we had trees for homes and plants for food. 'Ice,' and we had seasons to grow and seasons to rest. And so we multiplied, until we were too many for the world. And she spoke again, one more time, 'Die,' and the spirits who had made our home became our scourge and sought our deaths. And so we cried out to the baby, 'Save us!'"

Daddy took up the old familiar tale in his deep, soothing voice that made Arin think of lullabies: "So she laid her body in front of the spirits. Ice froze her skin. Fire burned her. Water drowned her. Air tore her limbs. Earth buried the pieces. And then Wood caused her to grow. From the pieces of her body grew stalks that blossomed, turned to fruit, and ripened. When the seed fell it was in the shape of little girls, and the spirits listened to what they said. The place where she sacrificed herself became the first sacred grove, and the first to fall from the fruit of their mother became our first queen. It is she we thank for this meal, for our home, and for our lives. Her blessing on us."

"Her blessing on us," Arin echoed, and she bit into her mother's nut bread and sighed happily. She'd tried to bake this bread in the palace ovens, and it hadn't tasted the same. Maybe it was the kind of wood Mama burned in their oven, or maybe it was the type of nuts they harvested. Or maybe it was some other kind of magic, unknown to queens and champions and other fancy folk. But this . . . it tasted like home.

"We tell another version of the tale up north," Ven said. "In ours, the baby is a woman called the Great Mother of Spirits. And her body split apart to form the different groves—one for Aratay, one in Semo, one in Chell, one for Elhim, and one for Belene."

Mama poured pine-needle tea into mugs, and Arin got up to help hand them out to everyone. Even though she hadn't been home in months, she didn't think to act like a guest. Naelin and Ven were the guests, not Arin. This was home, even if she knew she wasn't staying. She loved the way it smelled: the spice of the tea, the warm sharpness of the wood-stoked oven, the fresh baked bread. The palace always smelled like flowers. *And sometimes like blood*, she thought.

"Would you like to tell us the tale?" Mama asked Ven politely.

"It's supposed to be sung, and you don't want to hear me sing it, trust me," Ven said. "My sister is the one with the beautiful voice. She's a canopy singer." He helped himself to a pile of leaf-wrapped boar meat and then stuffed one in his mouth.

Arin wished for a moment that they were actually traveling to Ven's family, not to the foreign land of Semo, and that this were only a short, simple trip. *For now, I'll pretend it is.*

They all ate for a moment in contented silence.

"I saw Eira when we arrived," Arin said to her parents. "She said you had a surprise?" Perhaps they'd sold the house and were going to move to Mittriel to be closer to her and Daleina! *It would be nice if the four of us could be together again, wherever we are. Maybe it would make Daleina happy.* Her sister looked perpetually tired and worried. But Arin would miss Threefork. They'd moved here when she was four years old. *I didn't even realize how much I missed it here.* Lately, she'd been too busy to even think or feel.

Both her parents grinned as if they were little kids about to open a present, and then they began speaking at the same time: "You'll never guess—" And "It was extraordinary luck—" Then they stopped, laughed, and Daddy said, "You go first."

"Honey, do you remember the old bakery that you and Josei planned to buy and fix up? The one in Fawnbrook? You two were saving up enough money on your own, and we were so proud of you. It was so grown-up of you to have a plan and pursue it."

Arin felt a lump in her throat. Of course she remembered. It had been her and Josei's dream. As soon as they'd saved enough and as soon as they could, that's what they were going to do: buy the old shop, fix it up, and start a bakery. She'd do fancy cakes for weddings and festivals, and he'd run the front of the shop and deal with the customers. They planned to marry too, when they were old enough, and live together in a home behind the shop. They'd talked about it all the time.

Mama beamed at Daddy. "You tell her. You were the one who did it."

"We both did," Daddy said. Reaching across the table, he squeezed Mama's hand. "Arin, we bought the bakery. It's yours! Your mother and I have been working on fixing it up, according to your plans."

Arin felt as if bees were swarming inside her head. She opened her mouth but no words came out. Their bakery. It was a dream from what felt like years ago. Her and Josei's dream. But he was gone, and she'd thought the dream had died with him. But now . . . Now . . . She looked from Mama to Daddy and back again. Both of them were beaming at her. "Really?"

"Really truly," Mama said.

Arin felt tears on her cheeks. "That's the most . . ." Words failed her. She couldn't think of any that went far enough. Jumping from her seat, she ran around the table and threw her arms around her parents. "Thank you!"

Her parents beamed at her.

And then the memory of why she was here and where she was going crashed into her. "But I can't. I have to . . . Please understand, it's not that I don't appreciate it or want it. I do! It's just that . . . I can't right now. It will have to wait until I come back." *If I come back.* "I'm sorry, Mama, Daddy."

Calmly, Mama picked up the ladle. "Don't you worry, baby. I have faith everything will work out. Would you like some soup, Your Majesty?"

Arin jumped, but neither Queen Naelin nor Ven seemed at all surprised. "You know? You've known all along? I was right! Daleina told you!"

"Of course," Mama said, patting her hand.

Arin felt a burst of love for her sister and her parents, for believing in her.

As the girl Arin babbled happily to her parents about her plans for after Semo, Naelin chewed on a sweet slice of nut bread and tried to keep herself from thinking, *I shouldn't be here. I should be in Semo already.*

Suddenly, the room felt stifling. "Excuse me. I just need a little air."

Arin's mother nodded, understanding in her eyes. "Your family will be together soon."

The sentiment didn't help.

Naelin burst out the door and drew in a breath of night air. It tasted sour as she breathed in the smoke from the chimneys of the village all around. The sun had set, and dusk shrouded the trees in shadows. Lights from the other houses glowed warm amber. Firemoss twinkled from the bridges and ladders.

Naelin heard the door open and shut behind her. "I know I was rude. It's just . . . They're waiting for me. I want to be there already."

"I promised Daleina I'd bring Arin home," Ven said. "Given all that's going on, she felt it was the safest place for her sister."

"She'll be angry at being left behind." She thought of how gleefully Arin had made the potion-laced charms—this felt like a betrayal after how kind the girl had been to Naelin.

"Angry is better than dead," Ven said. "Young people should have their childhoods and not be asked to save the world. We should at least be able to spare them that." He was frowning, and she wondered if he was thinking of the heirs who'd died over the years. He'd been a part of training those young people to risk themselves—she hadn't realized he ever felt guilt over that. "Besides, her parents will keep her from noticing when we leave. I'm planning on being miles away when she figures out we're gone."

Naelin snorted. "The big, strong champion afraid of a child's temper tantrum?"

"Terrified," he agreed. "But more terrified of what would happen to her if Merecot decided to use her for revenge or leverage. Here she'll be protected against anything Merecot tries to do. In Semo . . . It's not right to take a child into such obvious danger."

"Like I took mine," Naelin said.

"That's not what I meant!" Ven said. "It's not your fault."

*Of course it is!* "I became queen. I made them targets. If I hadn't done that, Merecot never would have taken them. We'd all be safe at home."

"You might as well blame me, then. If I hadn't found you and forced you to use your powers, you'd still be in East Everdale with Erian and Llor and Renet."

She felt the spirits around her, feeling her guilt and impatience, and walled her thoughts off as the headmistress had taught her. The last thing she wanted to do was draw spirits to Arin's home. That would be the worst way to repay this family for their hospitality.

"I think my mother and sister will like you," Ven said.

Naelin glanced at him. The warm light from the house was behind him, and his face was shadowed. She couldn't read his expression. "I thought that was a ruse. We aren't visiting your family. Didn't you hear me? I want to reach Semo quickly."

"My mother and sister, Sira, live due north of here. It would make sense, strategically, to stop at their home, both to rest and to gain any knowledge about activity on the border. My mother's a border guard. She should have insight into the mood of the people of Semo. Any knowledge of what we're walking into could be useful, especially if this is a trap. We'll cross the border at dawn, at peak strength, ready for whatever Merecot has planned."

She studied him. "That's the only reason? Strategy?"

"I'd also like you to meet my family," he said simply.

She frowned. *Why does it matter so much to him?* Then she saw the look in his eyes, the warmth that had first drawn her to him.

And for the first time in what felt like a very long time, Naelin smiled.

# CHAPTER 15

Once Naelin and Ven were beyond Threefork, with Arin safe and still asleep in her parents' house, Naelin summoned two nearby spirits: earth spirits who clawed their way out of the dirt between the roots of the vast trees. One looked like a wolverine carved from rotted wood and another was bear-shaped but made of moss and mud.

"They'll carry us."

"Or we could take the wire paths," Ven suggested.

Naelin climbed onto the back of the bear-shaped spirit. She wound her fists in the moss that clumped at its neck. "The wire paths are dangerous."

"Spirits are more dangerous."

"They know I'll destroy them if they fail us."

"You'll destroy part of the forest if you do too," Ven said.

"Then they had better not disobey me."

Ven shot her a grin, and then climbed down the tree and mounted the wolverine. *He trusts me*, she thought. *Even after all I've done.* She grinned back at him. Beneath her, the spirit sniffed and snorted, pawing at the dried leaves on the ground. They crunched beneath its paws.

"Let's go," he said.

*North*, Naelin instructed their mounts.

Both spirits bounded forward.

Above them, the wind blew strong and the trees swayed, caus-ing the light that hit the floor to shift like waves. Autumn leaves swirled as they fell, raindrops of red and amber, filling the forest with each gust of wind.

Behind her, Ven shouted directions: north, then east. Naelin passed it along to the spirits.

As they traveled, Naelin found herself wondering about Ven's family. Ven never talked about them much, so Naelin had as-sumed the memories were painful and hadn't pried. But he'd seemed so eager to introduce her that she thought maybe she'd been wrong. What kind of childhood shaped a champion? What kind of people had raised him? He'd mentioned a mother and siblings, but she had no feel for what they were like or what they meant to him. *I suppose I'll find out soon*, she thought.

As the day waned, the forest floor dipped into shadows. Above, the canopy still caught the low light of the sun, but it no longer filtered deep in between the trees. It brushed the surface of the leaves high above them. She sensed the energy of their spirit mounts beginning to flag—these two were used to resting at night, and with the growing shadows, they began to slow. "I think we've reached the limit for these mounts."

"There's a wire path above us, but it's a ways up," Ven said. "Unless there are winged spirits nearby large enough to carry us, we'll need to free-climb." He dismounted from the stone bear and began to rummage through his pack for ropes, clips, and other climbing gear.

She reached out with her mind and touched several air spirits, but all of the nearby ones were tiny, like puffs of dandelion fluff, drifting with the falling leaves. She also sensed an abundance of tiny tree spirits in this region of the forest, skittering with the squirrels at dusk. Sliding off the back of the earth spirit, she landed on the ground, knelt, and felt through the leaves until she found what she was looking for: an acorn. "Come stand here and hold on to me," she told Ven.

"Exactly what do you have in mind?" Ven asked.

Naelin showed him the acorn and then planted it in the soil. She'd never tried this before, but it *should* work. *If not, I can handle looking stupid in front of Ven.* Concentrating, she called to the tree spirits. *Come. Grow. Tall and straight, up to the sky. Come and grow!*

The spirits poured down from the trees. A few at first, then dozens swarmed over the branches and the trunks, pulled by her call. She stretched her arms out as if welcoming them into an embrace. Chittering to one another in raspy voices, the squirrel-like spirits came first, burrowing into the earth in a circle around them, and she saw a sprout unfurl between her feet. Its leaf was a pale translucent green that almost seemed to pulse with its own light, and then it pushed its way out of the earth, thickening as it grew. She straddled it as more tree spirits filled the forest floor around them: green tangles of leaves with lithe little bodies, gnarled bits of wood with humanlike faces and spiderlike legs, and larger stumplike spirits with faces made of bark.

She saw the sprout split into branches, and she carefully positioned her feet on one tender shoot. "Hang on tight," she told Ven. "This might fail spectacularly."

"It won't," Ven said as he wrapped his arms around her waist. She glowed at both his confidence and his touch.

*Grow faster,* she told the tree spirits, and they whipped around her ankles.

The tiny tree spurted higher, and Naelin grabbed on to the center stalk. It thickened in her hands until she was hugging it. Ven squeezed her, his arms a comforting warmth, holding her steady. Her heart was thumping so fast it felt like fluttering wings within her rib cage. The branches beneath their feet widened until they were standing on them firmly as the tree grew faster and faster, shooting toward the sky.

Branches spread and leaves popped to life: first, pale spring green, then deep summer emerald, then fall yellow, crinkling as they browned. The new tree blended with the canopy all around them.

"Very nice," Ven said in her ear.

She giggled—a sound she hadn't made in years, but it felt good. *I'm getting better at this.* She'd learned a lot since her last encounter with Merecot. *I'm ready for her.*

"Right there." Ven nodded at the next tree.

She saw the delicate line running past them. He pulled out harnesses with clips for each of them and helped attach hers.

"I'll lead," Ven said. "Follow me."

Hooking onto the wire, Naelin and Ven attached themselves to the path and pushed away from the new tree. Naelin glanced back to see the tree spirits scampering over the branches and up and down the trunk. She heard them babbling to one another, and she felt—*joy*. It infused them and leaked inside of her, the joy they felt in growing that tree. It was the kind of joy a child feels when she's fully in the moment, separated from any regrets or worries or anything that isn't the splendor of the *now*. It was the joy of a sunrise, the first moment of an unstained day, in the breath after a dream faded but before memories returned. It was the joy of an awaited kiss. The joy of light after rain.

They sailed across the top of the forest as the sky deepened to a darker blue and the stars began to gleam. The moon was a pale crescent, barely visible and translucent, as if it were shy about joining the stars in the sky.

Ven called out instructions as they reached junctions in the wires, and they switched from path to path. "One more mile!"

As they flew closer, Naelin saw firemoss light glowing in the branches. "Be ready to release," Ven barked. "The path ends just ahead." He put his hand on his clip, and she did the same.

"Now!" Ven released the clip and plummeted down to land in a tarp that had been stretched between the branches—a landing pad. Behind him, Naelin released her clip and fell. She felt the breath pushed out of her as she landed on the tarp beside him and bounced twice.

Near the tarp was a bridge that had seen better days. Frayed, it creaked under their weight. Around and below them, the forest was dark, the floor impossibly far down and sheathed in so many shadows that it was all a morass of gray. Light came from the stars above and the firemoss lights ahead. As the wind blew through the trees, the firemoss seemed to twinkle.

Belatedly, she realized Ven was talking, telling her a story about him and his sister and the first time they'd visited the forest floor. ". . . she'd heard so many stories about wolves and bears and boars that she was convinced she was going to die if her feet touched the soil," Ven was saying. "So you know what my mother did? She brought me down to the forest floor and said to my sister, 'If you're right and the floor is death, then you'd better save your brother before he's gored. And if you're wrong and he doesn't die, then you can admit it and go down without any more fussing. Either way, you're going down to the forest floor.'"

"How old were you?" Naelin asked.

"Three. It took all night, but by dawn my sister had decided she'd better save me. So she came down to the forest floor and carried me back up. I was too small to climb on my own. Don't know how she did it either. She was only five, and I was a big three."

"You weren't eaten by wild beasts or mauled by earth spirits, so she must have found a way. Did your sister stop being afraid of the forest floor?"

A woman's voice said, "Backfired, unfortunately. Can't get her out of the treetops. She hasn't been to the floor in over thirty years." Ahead of them, a woman dropped onto the rope bridge. She had a bow and a quiver of arrows on her back, and was dressed in all green leather, with the pin of a border guard of Aratay affixed to her collar. She had moonlight-silver hair and dark eyes. "This is a surprise, Ven."

"Hello, Mother," Ven said. "It's nice to see you. You're looking well."

She snorted. "You look old, flabby, and soft. Have all the champions abandoned strength for sentiment, or is that only you?"

*Well, this explains a few things*, Naelin thought.

"Mother, we have a journey ahead of us and were hoping to take advantage of your hospitality for the night."

Naelin had never heard him sound so polite or so formal. She studied him carefully. He was as tense as he'd been in the Queen's Grove when they'd been waiting for Queen Merecot and her army. His fingers twitched as if he wished he could close them around the hilt of his sword.

"I'm not hospitable," his mother said. "You know that. Is this your new candidate?" She walked in a circle around Naelin, examining her. Naelin thought about introducing herself, but was curious what Ven's mother was going to say, and if Ven hadn't introduced her . . . *I'll follow his lead.* "Bad choice," Ven's mother proclaimed. "She looks as if she's better suited to picking herbs. She'll face one difficult spirit then she'll crumble. Honestly, Ven, I know you believe yourself infallible since you chose Queen Daleina, but her ascension was a fluke. You can't afford to be complacent when your role is so vital to all of Aratay."

He sighed and shot Naelin a look that was so full of apology that Naelin nearly laughed. "I take it you're still angry at me," Ven said to his mother.

"You left without even a goodbye. And you sent no word. For years, I have to hear news about my youngest child only through stories and songs. Your sister knows more about you than I do, and all she knows is in verse."

He raked a hand through his hair. "I was busy."

"You were hiding from me." She gave another snort. "You knew I'd disapprove. What were you thinking, involving yourself with a queen?"

Naelin flinched. His mother knew about them already? And disapproved? That wasn't anything she thought she'd have to contend with. She was a grown woman, for goodness' sake. Parental approval hadn't been a concern in decades, and it hadn't occurred to her that it would be an issue now. After all, she wasn't even certain that they were still in a relationship—they had barely touched since Redleaf.

"You should have been focused on your duty," his mother continued. "Queen Fara should have been untouchable."

*Oh.*

*Not me.*

Naelin didn't know whether to be irritated or amused. Clearly, Ven's mother was a woman with strong opinions who didn't hesitate to express them. Naelin didn't blame Ven for keeping his distance. The only surprise was that he'd offered to come here now.

"I don't want to talk about her, Mother."

"Bah, you never did want to talk about anything important.

I'd expected that by now, you'd have learned to face straightforward honesty." His mother tapped her foot on the branch. "You'd better come inside. Your sister won't forgive me if she doesn't get to see you. Brace yourself for tears. She's liable to get emotional." Without another word, she pivoted and then leapt across the thin branches of the upper canopy, as nimble as a squirrel. She barely disturbed the leaves in her wake.

"She hasn't mellowed," Ven said. "I thought she might have." He turned to Naelin, and she noticed the shadows under his eyes, exaggerated by the angle of the firemoss light. He looked as if he hadn't slept in weeks.

*This has all been hard on him too*, Naelin thought. *He cared about Erian and Llor. And he cares about me.* She laid a hand on his cheek, against his beard. His expression softened, and he took her hand. She thought about Queen Fara and the heir Sata and the losses he'd already suffered. He didn't talk much about them, but knowing his kind heart, they must have cut him deeply.

"Coming here may have been a mistake. We can camp in the woods. Certainly done it before. I'd thought . . . I don't know what I thought, but it was a bad idea." He made a face. "Sorry to subject you to this."

"If you want to stay, I can handle it," Naelin said gently. Hanna had confirmed her children were being treated well. She could set aside her own impatience for one night, for Ven. "You can see your sister at least." Besides, she was curious to learn more: who were these people who had shaped Ven? What had his childhood been like? She found herself wanting to meet his sister and see his home, which was surprising since all her thoughts lately had been consumed with Erian and Llor. *I haven't been fair to him. I haven't been thinking of anyone else at all.* For all her fine words about being the Mother of Aratay, everything she'd done had been for her children, to the exclusion of all else.

"Please don't hold me responsible for whatever she says," he said. "It's not aimed at you; I'm the disappointment."

"You're the epitome of a hero. How can she be disappointed in you?" The longer she knew him, the more impressed she was. *The more in love.* She smiled to herself. After Renet, she never thought she'd feel this way about anyone again—*and in truth, I never felt like* this *about Renet.*

"She probably keeps a list," he said, pulling out a length of rope and a clip. "Which she's probably going to recite to you. Attach yourself to me. The upper branches can be precarious."

Reaching out with her mind, Naelin brushed against the presence of a few spirits, mostly small and none close. "If you're willing to wait a few minutes, I could summon an air spirit. There aren't any close by."

"Not many spirits would dare be near my mother," Ven said. "Best leave them be. No sense upsetting her any more than I already have." He drew out an arrow with a ring at its end and tied on a rope. Notching it, he aimed into the darkness and shot. She heard the *thunk* as it embedded itself into tree. He looped one arm around her waist, and Naelin wrapped her arms around him. Ven kicked off and swung on the rope through the upper branches. Dry autumn leaves brushed against her arms, and she heard them rustle and crackle as they swung through the shadows. She felt Ven raise his knees, and then they impacted on a platform. He tied off the end of the rope to one of the branches and unhooked the clips that held Naelin. "There should be a ladder . . ." He felt around the trunk. "Here. Follow me."

Ven climbed first, followed by Naelin. She couldn't imagine going *higher* than they already were—soon, they'd be among the very tops of the trees. "Did you grow up in a bird's nest?"

"Nearly," he said. "Mother's not a people person."

Ven stopped, and that made Naelin stop as well. She heard a melody carried on the breeze: a light, wordless tune in harmony with the birds, dipping low to match the owls and then high to imitate a songbird in her nest for the night.

"That's my sister," Ven said, and this time there was real warmth in his voice.

"I look forward to meeting her," Naelin said, and she meant it.

Ven hadn't thought about home in a while, and he *certainly* hadn't planned to return. It wasn't until Arin planted the idea and he had the thought that the distraction would be good for Naelin—a way to slow her down, to keep her from doing anything rash—that he warmed to it. He hadn't bothered to think about whether it would be good for him.

*I've had worse ideas,* he supposed. *Not many, but a few.*

At least no one was likely to die from this mistake. He'd just have to suffer through a night of belittling parental disapproval in front of the one woman he wanted to think well of him. *Yeah, definitely on the list of bad ideas.*

He saw home from the top of the ladder. It looked the same as he remembered: platforms that straddled the upper branches, evenly distributing their weight so they stayed balanced, with bridges between them and tarps on top of them. It was more a collection of tents than a house like you'd find midforest. "It's nicer than it looks," he told Naelin. "There are real beds inside."

"It looks very nice," Naelin reassured him.

He knew she was lying. Mother didn't believe in fancy decorations—their home looked like it belonged to a soldier, because it did. Mother had been a champion for years, until she became border patrol. He'd learned from her to consider all of Aratay his home, not one nook of it. She used to say every tree was their bed, every rock their table, every stream their sink. Still, this didn't feel like just another tree.

*I am getting sentimental in my old age,* he thought.

"You should know that my sister is . . . She's gentle." He didn't know how else to describe her. He wondered what Naelin would think of her—and what Sira would think of Naelin. He toyed with lying to Sira about who Naelin was, to put his sister at ease, but he'd never lied to her. He couldn't. Not to Sira.

"I'm sure she's wonderful. I can't wait to meet her." Naelin's smile was genuine, and no matter what, he felt like he was giving his heart to the right woman.

He just hoped that smile remained when she went inside the house.

He climbed up, swinging onto the platform in front of the door—or, rather, a tarp that bore the seal of a border guard, embroidered badly. He lifted it and ducked inside, holding it up behind him for Naelin.

Naelin entered—he was relieved when she looked around, interested. *Maybe this won't be a total disaster,* he thought. As he'd told her, it was nicer than it looked from the outside. Lots of wood furniture. Lots of quilts. And not a speck of dirt. *Even dirt fears disappointing Mother,* Ven thought.

Mother marched through the kitchen, plucked a kettle off a hook, and shoved it onto a rod that spanned the fireplace. "If you're expecting a victory feast to celebrate your triumphant return home, you're going to be sorely disappointed. Rations are in the barrels. Serve your friend whatever you like."

*Nope, definite disaster.* His mother was determined to be unpleasant. Really, he shouldn't have expected anything less. He did leave without saying goodbye, and he hadn't sent word or tried to visit, unlike his sister, who'd never left, and his brother, who visited on every holiday and undoubtedly sent bushels of flowers on random occasions, purely to make Ven look bad.

"You've eggs," Naelin said, with a nod toward a basket of blue bird eggs on the counter. "I can cook for all of us."

"Suit yourself. You travel with my son, so you're welcome here." Mother plopped onto a chair and put her feet up on a worn table. "All right, Ven, explain yourself."

"Believe it or not, Mother, I'm not here to see you. This is Queen Naelin. We are traveling north to Arkon, to retrieve her children from Queen Merecot of Semo. Naelin, this is my mother, Zenda." He crossed to the kitchen—he still knew where the skillet was. He set it over the fire for Naelin. She'd already located a bowl and begun to whisk eggs together.

"Herbs?" Naelin prompted.

Mother, meanwhile, had snapped to her feet. "Your Majesty!"

Ven checked a cabinet and pulled out a smattering of cooking herbs, which Naelin proceeded to sniff, then crush into a second bowl. An onion and a potato were hanging in a net over the sink. She handed them to Ven. "Dice them," Naelin ordered. He pulled out his knife. "Clean it first, then dice them."

Behind them, Mother said, "A queen, cooking in my kitchen... Your Majesty... I... *Ven!*" She turned on him, and he instinctively sidled beside a stool so it was between him and his mother. Mother did *not* like surprises. *I probably should have taken that into account. And yet . . . it was* almost *worth it, seeing her expression.* "You're not going to say anything further about the fact you're traveling alone with a queen?" Mother demanded. "Where are the palace guards? Where's her escort? Are you crossing the border with the queen? This is unprecedented. And didn't the stories say her children were dead? How did they end up with Queen Merecot? Forgive my frankness, Your Majesty."

A soft voice, sweet as spring wind, whisper-sang from the doorway. "Oh, but it's not unprecedented. Queen Renna the Delighted enjoyed surprising tiny villages with visits. She'd tuck in the little children with a lullaby." Sira stood just inside, her wild hair even wilder than Ven remembered, in a cloud around her petite face, as if it wanted to swallow all her features. She looked smaller than he remembered too, her bird-thin arms and legs like the stick limbs of a tree spirit. But she was smiling at him, and that was all that mattered. "Ven, you came home!"

He crossed the house in two strides, scooped her up, and swung in her in a circle. She laughed like she did when she was a little kid, a peal of bells escaping her grinning lips.

"Silly bear, put me down. You'll break me!"

He put her down and growled like a bear before he remembered that his beloved queen was standing only a few feet behind him watching this entire exchange. He felt his face heat up beneath his beard, which only made Sira laugh louder. "Naelin, this is my sister, Sira."

"We heard you singing," Naelin said. "You've a beautiful voice."

"I sing to the birds," Sira said. "They're the beautiful ones."

"You sing just as beautifully," Ven told her firmly. She'd always downplayed her gifts. He never let her, though, not while he was around. "The birds are envious of you."

Mother interrupted. "Sira, this is *Queen* Naelin, joint queen with Queen Daleina. She's on her way north to bring her children home—apparently, the rumors were wrong. They're alive."

Sira dropped into a curtsy as gracefully as if she'd spent her life in a palace. She was naturally graceful. *A fact that Mother never noticed,* Ven thought. Mother had always focused on Sira's limitations, but she had many strengths. "I know your songs, Your Majesty. I'm so pleased to meet you, and even more pleased to hear your children are well."

Naelin looked startled. "I have songs?"

"Oh, yes. My favorite is 'The Ballad of the Reluctant Queen,'" Sira said, beaming at her. "The descent into minor during the bridge to the second verse is lovely." She sang the melody wordlessly, holding out the last note for an instant, then fading it. "It's for sunset after a particularly beautiful day, when you don't want it to be night yet." Ven was watching Naelin's expression closely and saw it tighten, the instant before she turned back to add herbs into the bowl of eggs. *She's thinking she should have stayed reluctant.* It was easy to guess her thoughts these days. *Too easy.* But his sister couldn't know that, and went on. "I sing it to the dawn and the night, to the wind and the rain, and they come to listen."

"You know they'd come anyway," Mother said.

"Maybe. Maybe not." Sira was as patient as ever, with her secret little smile. She'd always known how to let Mother's words roll off her. He wondered how she did it—they stuck like burrs into Ven.

"Your singing is important," Ven told Sira. "Gives the rest of us a reason to keep fighting." He felt Naelin studying at him, and he focused on the potato, skimming off the skin with his blade and slicing it into chunks. He hadn't directed those words at her, but he didn't regret that she'd heard them. She'd probably accuse him of lacking subtlety, which Daleina had so recently commented on.

*I carry at least five weapons at all times. Subtlety isn't what I do.*

They fell into silence as Naelin prepared the rest of the meal, issuing the occasional order. Sira set out plates, even scrounged up napkins, which she folded into flower shapes.

Mother watched it all from her seat, feet firmly on the table, crushed leaves stuck to the soles of her boots. All of them sat when the eggs were ready, and the kitchen was filled with the smoky, oniony, thick scent of an ordinary midforest home—a smell that he didn't associate with this eagle roost of a place.

"Thank you for your hospitality," Naelin said as she spread her napkin on her lap.

"You cooked, Your Majesty," Mother said.

"With your food," Naelin pointed out. "I like to cook." To Ven's surprise, she sounded cheerful. *Could she actually be enjoying this visit?*

"Food serves a purpose: keeping a body strong," Mother proclaimed. "Never saw much point in fancying it up. People who waste their time on that are fools."

Ven put his fork down. Didn't slam it. He was proud of that. "You're insulting your guest, Mother."

"*Your* guest," she snapped. "Told you, I don't do hospitality." Then her eyes widened. He crossed his arms and leaned back as Mother ducked her head in a bow. "Beg pardon, Your Majesty. Of course you are welcome here. These are your woods. Ven will tell you—I'm a woman with strong opinions who speaks her mind."

"Except when you don't," Sira said, still sweet and gentle.

"Always," Mother said.

"Not always. You haven't told Ven that you missed him yet."

Ven reached across the table and covered his sister's hand with his. *That's Sira*, he thought, *always seeing good, even where there wasn't any.* He shouldn't have stayed away for so long. As long as she was here, he could weather whatever Mother said. Sira beamed back at him with the same wide, guileless eyes she'd always had. Changing the subject, he asked Mother, "How's the border?"

"Tense."

"Any hint what's going on beyond it?"

"Been tense over there for years. Worse now. There was some hope when the new queen took over, but then after the invasion failed . . . Yeah, they don't like us much. Your Majesty, speaking from my professional opinion, if you're planning a visit, you should bring a squadron with you. Or at least more than just my son." Mother fixed her eyes on Ven, and he felt like squirming as if he were thirteen and caught borrowing her longbow without permission. "Why didn't you bring your candidate?"

"I don't have one at present," Ven said. "Queen Daleina has released me from my duties as champion in order to escort Queen Naelin on her mission."

"I see."

He braced himself as she stared him, an inscrutable look on her face—he couldn't decide if it was better or worse than her usual look of profound disappointment.

"After dinner, spar with me, Ven."

Her words surprised him . . . and yet didn't.

"Of course, Mother."

VEN STRIPPED OFF HIS ARMOR, LEAVING HIM IN JUST A SHIRT AND pants. He laid his knives in a pile, joined by his bow and arrows—when Mother said "spar," she meant swords and only swords. He then climbed down onto one of the platforms, where she was waiting, just below Mother's house. "Live steel or wood?" he asked.

"Live," Mother said.

"Wood," Naelin said, coming out onto the platform behind him. He turned to face her, but he couldn't read her expression. Her eyes looked hollow, as if she hadn't slept in days, though he knew she had. Or thought she had.

"Your Majesty, with all due respect . . ." Mother began.

"I need him whole," Naelin said.

*Ouch.* "I can handle myself," Ven said. He'd sparred with the best champions in Aratay, trained for years, kept himself at peak readiness. His mother was seventy years old. Surely she must have slowed by now.

*Surely . . .*

"Of course you can," Naelin said. "Use wood anyway."

He saw Mother smirk, but she picked up two practice swords. He knew they didn't have bladed edges, but they were vicious things: hardened oak with weights shot through them. Looking at them made his arms and legs ache—he knew the kind of bruises they could leave. Mother tossed him one as if it weighed nothing. Catching it, he rocked back a step, and she smirked again. She was going to enjoy this.

*I shouldn't have said yes. What am I trying to prove?*

At the same time, though, how could I say no?

*No was never an option here.*

Sira approached him with a jar of ointment. He smelled mint and the acrid stench of redberries—a bruise-soothing mixture. Wiggling the jar, she smiled at him. "I'm ready. Would you like me to sing while you fight?"

"Oh, Sira." Mother sighed.

"Yes," Ven said firmly. "I'd love that."

Sira asked Naelin, "Can you provide a rhythm? Beat that hide with the stick, an even rhythm. *Bah, bah-bah, bah, bah-bah . . .*" A tanned squirrel skin was stretched across a frame in one corner. Ven stretched out his arms, getting used to the weight of the wooden sword as Naelin began the beat.

Sira began to sing, deep and low, an old battle hymn, and Mother leapt off the platform and landed in a crouch on a lower branch. "Come on, boy!" she called.

Seventy years old.

*She hasn't slowed a bit.*

He jumped down, and she was charging at him before he'd even landed. He sprang up to block her blade. The force shook through his muscles, but he held steady. She pulled back and was swinging again, a swift strike toward his side. He dodged and danced backward, noticing as he did that the limb she'd chosen was narrow, with the thickest part behind her. It bent beneath him, bouncing him up a quarter of an inch. He added that into his calculations as he dodged and struck.

She was as nimble as he'd remembered. More so.

From above them on the platform, Sira's voice soared. His body absorbed the rhythm of the drumbeats, which he knew was one of Mother's tricks: her enemy would move subconsciously with the beat, while she would remain unpredictable. He concentrated on making his strikes staccato, out of sync with the song, but she adjusted quickly, blocking and striking back with all the ferocity of . . . *of a mother whose son has wronged her.*

"I am sorry for not sending word," Ven said.

"You should be." She wasn't winded. But then, neither was Ven. "You raised me to face what battles came my way, and so I did." Strike, block, spin.

Balance.

Adjust for the bounce in the branch.

Position the feet, and lunge. Strike, punch, kick. And duck.

*Thwack.* He felt the flat of the wooden blade hit his side. Breath hissed through his teeth. Mother didn't let him recover. She was on him again, strikes and jabs that he parried back. He shot one look at Naelin, to be certain she was still safe while his attention was diverted—he wouldn't put it past his mother to use her against him. Sure enough, Mother saw the glance and used it, racing up the branch to swing hard at the support that held the platform level.

*She wouldn't . . .*

She did.

With the wood sword, she hit the support so hard that it was knocked out of position. The platform jerked down, and Sira's song cut off in a shriek. The drum stopped, and Ven immediately raced toward them—to where Mother waited.

He saw her but didn't slow. He let the blow hit him, bending so that it impacted his back instead of his neck, and he bashed into the support until it wedged into position. The platform jerked again, steady. He saw Naelin help pull Sira back—both of them safe.

Grabbing a branch, he swung to land in the crook of another tree's branches.

Mother did not pursue. "Still thinking with your heart instead of your mind. You will never be a truly great champion until you conquer that."

He'd heard all of this before. "I am not choosing love over duty, Mother. I am choosing both." Out of the corner of his eye, he caught a glimpse of a spirit: a large air spirit, with translucent wings and a body that blended into the leaves, and he made the calculation. Then he leaped the one direction Mother wouldn't suspect: backward against the same weakened support, knocking it out completely. The wood slammed into Mother, sending her flying onto her back.

As the platform fell, the air spirit swooped in with a cry, catching Naelin and Sira on its back with its translucent wings spread wide. Below them, the platform tumbled down, hitting against the branches below.

He watched Sira and Naelin be delivered safely back to the house, and then he laid down his practice sword and offered his hand to his mother, hoping she wasn't bruised too badly. "Do you concede?"

She didn't take his hand. "No."

Ven scooped up his sword again just in time.

CHAPTER 16

From a platform with drying laundry, Naelin watched Ven and his mother continue whacking at each other as if nothing would give them greater joy than to decapitate the other. Keeping a safe distance, Naelin sipped at a mug of willowbark tea. Beside her, Sira hummed and swayed side to side.

"It's nice to have Ven home," Sira said serenely. "Mother's happy."

Zenda landed a vicious strike on his thigh. Yelping, he flinched, but then lunged only an instant later to hit her shoulder. The impact sounded like a branch cracking. His mother didn't slow. "She is?" Naelin asked.

Sira waved her hand at the two fighters. "This is how she and Ven talk."

Taking another sip of tea, Naelin watched them for another moment. "They should try nouns and verbs."

Sira giggled.

Naelin put down her tea. Maybe they'd stayed long enough. Especially if Ven's mother was this angry. "We should keep traveling." If she summoned a few nocturnal flying spirits, they could fly through the night and be at the capital of Semo well before dawn.

"You shouldn't cross the border in the dark—the Semoian spirits won't like it. Stay here tonight, and cross at dawn. Please, Your

Majesty." She was smiling at Naelin with a hopeful, childlike expression. "Let them have their reunion."

Looking at her, Naelin couldn't say no. She couldn't crush the light in those eyes. *Now I see why Ven has his hero complex.* His sister was exactly the kind of person he'd be drawn to defend. She may have been his older sister, but there was an innocence to her that made you want to protect her. Naelin thought that Ven's decision to become a champion might have had as much to do with wanting to protect Sira and make the world safe for her as it did with his mother's training and expectations.

"The first stars are about to appear, and it's time for me to welcome the night. Would you like to come with me to sing them into shining?" Sira asked shyly, as if she'd asked and been denied a hundred times. Naelin would rather have kicked a kitten than say no. She glanced once back at Ven and his mother, who were dodging between shadows as they leapt from branch to branch.

"I'd love to come with you," Naelin said.

With a happy chirp, Sira scrambled up the side of the tree, swinging from rope to rope as she climbed even higher up. Naelin hesitated for only a second, then climbed after her.

Sira was as nimble as a squirrel with apparently zero fear of plummeting to her death. Reaching out with her mind, Naelin reassured herself that there were ample air spirits to catch them both if they fell again, and then she sharply withdrew her mind. *I'm doing it again. Depending on them, as if they were trustworthy.* She climbed higher, not as nimbly as Sira but equally without fear. *If I fall, I fall, and that will be my fate.*

They rose higher into the canopy than Naelin thought possible, or wise. The branches that held them bent and swayed, and Naelin clung to them, trying to convince herself they weren't going to snap, that Sira wouldn't lead her too high for humans to climb.

"You're afraid of the forest floor, but not of *this*?" Naelin asked.

From above her, she heard Sira's tinkling laugh. "Ven told you that story, did he? I'll happily walk on the ground, but only when it holds an interesting story to sing. Right now, the best stories are up in the trees."

Naelin climbed higher until she was above the canopy. Her hands and feet splayed wide on four different branches to keep her balance.

She felt the sun on her back before she saw it.

"Look, it's nearly set." Sira's voice was filled with reverence, and then she lifted her face toward the soft rose light and began to sing. From across the canopy, other distant voices melded with hers—her melody wrapped around another's, at first discordant then blending together, the notes dancing around one another, touching and breaking apart.

Naelin heard a touch of sadness inside the sweet melody, and at first she thought she'd imagined it, but then the minor notes began to pile on top of one another, sung in Sira's sweet voice and echoed by the countless other canopy singers across the roof of Aratay. The dying sun hit the yellows and reds of the autumn leaves, and fire spirits danced in the light, and then the sun sank and spread into the west.

A single note, low and vibrating, sang out as the final drop of gold disappeared. Naelin felt the note deep in her bones. And then the note soared up and up, higher, and Sira pointed to the east, where a single star shone, bright against the deep blue. "I call the first star Hope," Sira said. She then pointed to a faint dot in the northeast, a hand's spread away from the first star. "And the second star Courage."

"That's lovely," Naelin said.

"It's from the Song of the First, about the first queen of Renthia, who looked to the sky for hope and courage in the days when the land was only wildness." She looked shyly at Naelin. "Can I ask you a question?"

"Of course." Naelin wondered if it was going to be about her and Ven.

"All the rumors said that when your children were attacked, the wolf Bayn was driven into the untamed lands. How could that be? I know the creatures of the forest, and no animal would willingly cross into the untamed lands."

"He ran into the untamed lands to escape." Naelin sighed, thinking of the wolf who had been a guardian and friend to her children—*and to me.* "He probably died soon after he crossed. At least, I've never heard of anyone surviving the untamed lands." Still . . . she *wanted* to hope. After all, he wasn't like other ordinary animals. Crossing into the untamed lands wasn't the first unusual thing he'd done. He always seemed to know exactly what they were saying and what they needed. "Have you ever heard of any animals coming out of the untamed lands?"

"No." And then she brightened. "But I do know songs about the untamed lands."

"Could you sing one for me?"

"They're mostly sad. You might prefer a happier song. I know lots about the night sky, and travelers who found their way home. Or I could sing you one about Ven, if you'd like. It embarrasses him, but I like it. I wrote it."

Naelin was sure it did embarrass him, but she was equally sure he'd never stop his sister from singing it. Not if it made her happy. "What was he like as a child?"

"Always serious. Always trying so hard. I think he believes that if he's strong enough and fights hard enough and runs fast enough and leaps high enough, death won't catch him. Mother believes that too. She taught it to him."

"But not to you?"

Sira lifted her arms up, letting go of the thin branch she'd held. "I know we're all stardust, shining in the darkness for a while then winking out. I'm not afraid of dying." She said it so matter-of-factly, and she looked so fey, a blue shadow against the even darker blue sky, that Naelin believed her.

Naelin looked to the north. "I used to be afraid of so many things. But everything changed when Erian and Llor were taken."

"I felt the world change when they were lost," Sira said.

"Thank you." It seemed the right thing to say. But she couldn't stop thinking about Bayn. "You said the songs you knew about the untamed lands were 'mostly' sad. Are there any that aren't?" It would be nice if she could think the wolf was all right. He had tried so hard to protect Erian and Llor.

Opening her mouth, Sira began to sing again, this time with words that flowed out of her like a waterfall:

*Beginning—*
*We are here in the darkness, unfolding.*
*Opening—*
*We are waking in the wildness, molding*
*Ourselves into shapes with names.*
*Speaking—*
*Not alone, we answer, echo, echo,*
*We tell the nothingness we came,*
*And it embraces us, unfolds us, molds us, names us.*

And then her voice shifted, becoming a tone that did not sound human, and Naelin shivered at how closely she echoed the odd cadence of a spirit:

*You, who have come where you do not belong,*
*You, who have come before your time,*
*You, who were formed from the formless,*
*You, who have called out your name,*
*When you should have been nameless,*
*We will rip you, rend you, tear you from our world,*
*Heal what you have sickened—*

"I thought this one wasn't a sad song," Naelin murmured.

Sira looked startled, as if Naelin had poured water on her head. She broke off her song. "Oh! I'm sorry! I didn't think! It has hope at the end—the First, our first queen, wasn't alone. When all seemed lost and the few people who were left alive were surrounded by spirits bent on their deaths, the First went back into the untamed lands, where we were formed, to pray to the Great Mother, and when the First came out again, she was accompanied by a Protector."

"She went into the untamed lands and came out again?" Naelin repeated. She'd never heard a tale like that. "But that's not possible. No one's ever done that."

"It's a very old song. It wouldn't surprise me if only canopy singers know it."

"And who was the 'Protector'?" *I've heard that term before . . .*

Queen Merecot's letter, she remembered, the ransom note. She'd called Bayn the "Protector of Queens." No one had known what that meant, and Naelin hadn't thought about it much at the time. She'd been too caught up absorbing the implications of Queen Merecot's letter to think about the wolf. *Odd that the word is associated both with Bayn and this tale of the untamed lands.* "What do you know about the 'Protector'? Who was he or she?"

Sira thought, tapping her lips with her forefinger. "A few songs mention him—always a him—at the side of the First. Other singers have told me he was the first champion, and that the title simply changed over the years. Except there was only ever one Protector in the songs, and there are many champions. There are those who believe he was a kind of enlightened spirit—or an uncorrupted one, a spirit the way the spirits were supposed to be if the Great Mother had completed her work, devoted to humans instead of despising them, at one with Nature."

That didn't make sense, Naelin thought, at least when it came to Bayn. She'd never heard of an "enlightened spirit." And the wolf was obviously not a champion.

"There are also songs that hint the Protector is some kind of immortal, or that he bears an immortal destiny, but those singers were known for being caught up in the beauty of their own poetry, so that could be exaggeration. Do you want to know what I think?" She leaned closer as if she wanted to impart a secret. Her eyes were sparkling and her lips were smiling.

"Yes, I do. Tell me."

"I think the Protector was the First's lover."

"Oh?"

"Yes. I think he wasn't protecting Aratay; I think he was protecting the queen. I think he was more than the first champion. And do you know what else I think?" She lowered her voice even further. "I think Ven is *your* Protector. He loves you. I can see it. Feel it. He would set aside his fear of death for you. He would follow you into death."

Naelin felt herself blush.

Laughing, Sira wiggled down the branch, descending fast from the canopy. The peal of her laughter lingering behind. Naelin hung on as the thin branches shook. The crisp autumn leaves clicked and crackled as they smacked together from the movement. Only when it steadied enough did Naelin feel safe enough to climb down too.

As she descended, the branches closed above her, blocking off the starlight and moonlight until she was climbing into shadows. Naelin thought about reaching out to a spirit to help her—but no, she would *not* depend on them. She reached with her foot down for the next branch. Soon, she'd switch to ropes, but she couldn't remember exactly how far until the ropes began—

She felt hands on her waist, steadying her. "Rope ladder is to your left. Reach out and you'll have it," a familiar voice said in her ear. Ven.

He held her as she reached, stretching her fingers and pawing at the empty air, until the tips of her fingers touched the rough dryness of a rope. Her hand closed around it.

With Ven, she climbed the ladder onto a platform. Below was the warm light of his mother's house. She heard voices rising up from it—the cascading light laugh of his sister, Sira, and the knife-sharp voice of his mother, Zenda.

Ven's arms were still around her waist.

The shadows felt like a blanket around her, and she leaned her head back against Ven's chest and listened to him breathe. She supposed this meant he'd survived his "talk" with his mother. She thought about asking how he was, but instead just let the silence wrap around both of them.

*The First went into the untamed lands and came out.*

It was just a bit of a nearly forgotten legend.

But that title "Protector" . . . Merecot had used that title to refer to Bayn. Why? What did it mean? It was a tenuous thing, a single word in common between a song and a letter. Yet it felt like there was a connection between the two, and she was determined to find out what it was. *After we save Erian and Llor, maybe there's a chance we can also save Bayn!* All this hope was a heady thing—it made her feel like anything was possible. "Tomorrow we'll reach Queen Merecot," Naelin said.

"Yes."

*Then maybe we'll have answers, including why she targeted Bayn. And what she wants from me.* "Good. I'm ready."

"Naelin . . . I need to know . . ."

She waited, thinking about what Sira had told her, about how he loved her. *I love him.* But she couldn't remember if she'd ever told him. *If he says the words, I will. I won't even hesitate.*

"Are you still planning to kill her?"

She startled and then nearly laughed at herself for thinking that Ven was thinking about romance when he was busy plotting how to keep his queen from committing murder. "I don't know. Rescue first, then I'll think about revenge."

"Just don't . . . I don't want to lose you to revenge. If you lose control again . . ."

Naelin *did* laugh then, though it wasn't anything to laugh about. He was afraid of her, of what she'd do, of the harm she could bring to the people of Semo and the people of Aratay . . . people like his sister, Sira, who didn't deserve to suffer because of Naelin's rage and despair.

"I'm going to see this through, as I promised," Naelin said. "I'm not going to harm Queen Merecot unless she tries to hurt us first." *I am, though, going to ask her a few questions,* after *she returns my children.* Naelin turned then, within the circle of Ven's arms. Reaching up, she touched his face, felt the stiffness of his beard and the weathered softness of his cheek, and before she could remind herself that she had no feelings anymore, she kissed him.

He kissed her back, tentatively at first but then more desperately, as if he were a drowning man and she could save him.

She wasn't certain she could save anyone.

But she didn't stop kissing him.

IN THE PALACE IN MITTRIEL, DALEINA WOKE, STRETCHED, AND felt the silken sheets slip over her naked body. She then curled against a sleeping Hamon and worried about whether she'd sent Queen Naelin to her death—and by extension, Ven.

"Did I make a mistake?" she whispered into the darkness.

Hamon shifted and mumbled, "Of course you didn't."

She laughed, despite herself. "You don't even know what I'm referring to."

He flopped one arm across her stomach. "Don't need to. You're alive. That's proof enough." Snuggling closer, he burrowed his face into her neck. She felt his breath hot against her skin.

It was sweet that he was so supportive, but his statement was ridiculous. "There's a lot of space between no mistakes and death."

He lifted his head and sounded more awake and serious. "Not for you."

*Hard to argue with that.* "But what if—"

He placed a finger over her lips. "No."

"'No' what? You don't know what I'm going to say." She kissed his finger.

"You're going to second-guess yourself." Moving his finger, he kissed her, his lips soft on hers. "Nothing good comes from that. All you can do is move forward. Make the next decision. When I've a patient, I can't take back the medicine I've given her, even if it doesn't work. All I can do is treat the next set of symptoms, even if my medicine caused them."

"If Queen Naelin dies, there's only me. Aratay still has no heirs."

"The champions are training more."

She noticed he didn't say Naelin would be fine. "Not quickly enough." Wrapping a sheet around herself, she extracted herself from the bed and crossed to the balcony. She pushed open the door and stepped outside. The cool night air danced around her, and she wondered what time it was. It was impossible to tell looking out into the forest, but it was still late enough that the city of Mittriel was a black tangle, with the few scattered lights looking like distant stars caught in its branches. She should try to go back to sleep. She wasn't sure she could, though. *They should be near the edge of the forest now,* she thought. *One more day, and they'll be beyond where I can keep them safe.*

"What if it's all part of her plan?" Daleina asked.

"Queen Merecot's?"

She heard sheets rustle and then footsteps. Hamon's arms wrapped around her waist, and she leaned back against him. He smelled like mint and cinnamon and faintly of exotic flowers she couldn't name—he'd been mixing new medicines earlier in the day. Some of his ingredients came from as far away as the islands of Belene or the farmlands of Chell. He'd told her once that he even used a lichen that grew only in the crevasses of glaciers in Elhim. As she mused on what made Hamon's profession, she felt an idea begin to form, so faint that she didn't dare call it an idea yet. Quietly, she said, "You use ingredients from other lands in your medicines."

"Mm-hmm, definite perk of being a palace healer. Access to resources beyond our borders." His hands caressed her stomach, and he kissed her neck. "Did I tell you about the lichen from El-him? Grows only in—"

*Resources beyond our borders. Yes.* She stepped out of Hamon's embrace and raised her voice. "Guards, summon the seneschal!" She hurried to her desk and tried to light the firemoss in the lantern. Her hands shook as she fumbled with the fire stick, and Hamon gently took it from her and lit it.

"You may wish for clothes if your seneschal is coming," he said mildly.

She waved him off. "He's unshockable." Sitting with her bedsheet wrapped around her, she shuffled through her papers until she found unblemished parchment. She'd need three copies—the seneschal would neaten her thoughts and prepare the copies. Across the room, she heard Hamon putting on his own clothes and neatening the blankets on the bed. He then was behind her again, brushing her hair back behind her neck and away from the ink as she wrote.

She heard a knock on the door and one of her guards said, "The seneschal, Your Majesty."

"Allow him in," she ordered without looking up.

Footsteps. "Your Majesty. Healer Hamon."

"Seneschal," Hamon said politely.

She kept writing. "I wish to send messages to the queens of Belene, Chell, and Elhim, privately, if possible *secretly*, and I will need to receive their messages equally discreetly."

"Green and black ribbons, Your Majesty," the seneschal responded promptly—she knew he'd have an answer. "Green will alert the queens that the spirit bears a message from the forest queen. Black will signal its sensitivity."

"Good. I will locate spirits who can carry the messages." She'd need ones that were willing to fly a distance, into lands that they weren't tied to, but were calm enough to continue to obey her commands even when they were out of reach of her mind, since even with a queen's power, she wasn't strong enough to send her thoughts beyond her borders. Standing, she handed the paper to the seneschal. "Three copies, by your hand only. Let no one else know the contents. I won't raise hopes when there's a high chance they will be dashed."

Accepting the paper, the seneschal bowed and then backed out of the bedchamber.

Hamon was watching her but he hadn't asked. She loved that about him: he trusted her completely. If she kept secrets, he trusted those secrets wouldn't hurt him. But there was no reason to keep this from him. "As you said, other lands send herbs, food, supplies we don't have here, right?"

"Right."

"So why can't they also send heirs?"

He paused, thinking it over. Then, "You'll be admitting weakness to the other queens. What if they have the desire to expand their land, like Queen Merecot? It's a risk."

"More than leaving Aratay without a viable heir?" Now that things were set in motion, she felt some of the tension leave her shoulders. Keeping the bedsheet around her, she walked out onto the balcony once more. The blackness was fading to a pale gray. *Nearly dawn*, she thought. *I wonder if Ven is watching the sunrise from the northern border.* "I don't mind saving the world—it's what I swore to do. I just don't like worrying about who is going to save the world when I can't."

"You think they'll spare one of their heirs?"

"I think there's a chance, and I can't deny our people that chance." If she were queen of a country with multiple heirs and received a plea for help, she would have spared one. Truly, hadn't Semo done just that to Aratay? Although they more *stole* Merecot than asked for her, or more accurately, Merecot had left, but still . . .

*I have to try.*

"I value our people's lives over my sovereignty."

"Fine. But we don't even know what the other queens are like."

"True. But we do know what the spirits are like, and what they'll do if I die without an heir. Hamon, why are you arguing with me about this?" It was the first solid idea she'd had about how to keep Aratay safe.

He wrapped his arms around her again. "I'm sorry, Daleina. It's only . . . I don't like any plan that presumes you're going to die."

*Oh. I see.* She never really ever thought of it like that, but of course he was right—it was only a problem *if* she died. "This is plan B. Or even C. I don't plan to die."

"Then make plan A: you don't die."

She smiled. "All right. It's official. Plan A is no dying."

"Dying can be plan Z," he said.

"Guess I'm going to need a lot more plans."

He smiled back at her, his special smile that made her feel as if hot liquid were pouring through her. "Do you have any plans for right now?" he asked, and then kissed her neck and shoulders.

"Yes, I believe I do."

She led the bedsheet slip off her, falling into a pile at her bare feet.

# CHAPTER 17

At dawn, Naelin called to two air spirits to carry them into Semo. She'd said goodbye to Ven's mother and sister already, and Sira had climbed monkeylike up to the tips of the trees. The slight shiver of the leaves betrayed that she was high up at the top of the canopy, on branches that Naelin wouldn't trust, and she was singing to the sunrise. "Don't you worry about her?" Naelin asked Ven.

He didn't look up from his pack as he loaded supplies into it. "Always."

"I mean right now, when she's so high up."

He glanced up at the canopy above. The crinkled brown leaves were edged with a lemon-yellow glow, and the bits of sky were pale. "I don't worry about that. She knows how to climb."

"But a branch could snap."

"She'd feel it."

"What do you worry about then?"

"I worry that one day she'll realize the sun will rise whether she sings to it or not, and she'll quit springing out of bed as if the day were made just for her. I worry that she'll realize her little brother sometimes makes mistakes, and that just because she trusts me and Mother, it doesn't mean she'll always be safe or that everything will work out for the best. I worry that she'll stop believing in the power of good over evil, and that she'll learn that sometimes bad things happen no matter how hard you fight."

It was a lengthy speech for Ven. Fighting with his mother must have made him contemplative. She studied him—he had depths it was easy to overlook when he was busy being his competent, in-control self. "And do you worry about me too?"

"Obviously."

"Don't."

He paused his packing and looked at her. "Are you promising you won't do anything to endanger yourself while we're in Semo?"

*I'll do whatever's necessary to save Erian and Llor, so . . . no, I'm not promising that.* "I'm saying that maybe your mother is right. Maybe you should return to Mittriel, be a champion, and I will be a queen." *And a mother.*

He studied her a moment longer. "You think it's a trap."

"I think Queen Merecot was desperate enough to invade Aratay, so who knows what she's capable of? She could have tricked Headmistress Hanna into sending that message."

"You're right. And if it *is* a trap, then it's even more important that I come with you."

Naelin felt a little of the tension seep out of her shoulders. She wanted him to come, desperately. She might need his help to save Erian and Llor. But she didn't want to force him. *I'd never forgive myself if I ordered him to come and something happened.* She was only starting to realize that, for him, there was no place he'd rather be than by her side. It was . . . a strange feeling, to have someone so selflessly give themselves to her when for so long it had been her who'd always been the one who gave and gave. "Thank you." She tried to put every bit of what she felt into those two words. She nearly added, *I love you*, but didn't. It didn't seem right, to tie that love to gratitude.

But she felt it anyway.

His smile warmed her heart even more, and she was pretty sure he heard those unsaid words. "Let's go," he said.

Outside, she mounted an air spirit that looked like a deer with wings. Its antlers were coated in down-soft feathers, and its fur was white. Ven's spirit was shaped like a serpent with golden scales. It had wings like an eagle, which it spread wide until its wingtips brushed the bark of the nearby trees. Naelin had chosen these spirits because they could fly great distances, and she intended to ride them all the way to the capital, bypassing the border guards and arriving on her own terms. She'd heard how Queen Merecot had sent a spirit-pulled chariot for Ambassador Hanna—Hanna had included that in her report—but Naelin had no intention of trusting Merecot with her or Ven's safety.

"Let's fly," she said when Ven had mounted, and the two air spirits pushed off the platform and burst up through the canopy of leaves. She glanced back to see Sira waving at them. She was still singing, her voice rising up with the wind, and for a moment, they flew buoyed by the rising notes, but then her song faded and all Naelin could hear was the wind rushing past her.

From this high above the canopy, she could see it: Semo. Birches marked the border, sentinels with yellow leaves that gleamed in the morning light. Beyond the border were rocks—heaps of granite boulders, fields of stone, and great slabs that looked as if they'd stabbed their way out of the earth. She felt, like itches on her skin, the presence of spirits within those fields, but she couldn't see them. *They're beneath the boulders,* she thought. *Or they* are *the boulders.* She saw wildflowers growing in the cracks, clumps of purples and blues, as well as bushes with so many berries that they looked like bright-red decorations left behind after a celebration.

And then there were the mountains.

At first Naelin thought she was looking at clouds. Surely no mountain was ever so enormous! But as the images resolved before her, she could see they were indeed the various ranges of Semo. Their peaks looked as if they wanted to claw the sky. Her mind tried to wrap around the tremendous size—and then she felt the sudden shift in the world as they crossed the border.

She hadn't expected to be able to sense it. Land was land. But it was as if the air had been pushed out of her lungs, and she was suddenly breathing something else: air too, but with an unfamiliar taste that tickled the back of her throat. *Lemons,* she decided.

*It tastes like lemons and snow ... Maybe pine, but a different kind of pine than at home.*

The air felt colder too, as if she'd stripped off all her layers. And hollow. Or maybe that was how she felt inside—the sense of thousands of spirits around her, linked to her, had faded, muffled, and it was as if those thousands of spirits were instead watching her from a distance.

*It feels like I don't belong.*

She decided this was an accurate feeling, since she *didn't* belong. She wondered if Ven felt the same way, but the wind was too loud for her to ask him, even if she'd wanted to have a conversation about it.

She braced herself, expecting to be challenged by border spirits. But no challenge came. *Perhaps because they know we're coming?* Still, she didn't relax as they flew deeper into Semo.

Naelin had seen enough maps to know the direction they needed to head in: northwest, toward Arkon. But seeing the land on a flat drawing and seeing it beneath them with all its peaks and undulations was entirely different. As the spirit flew to the capital, Naelin drank in the view with all its differentness while trying to make sure they were headed in the right direction.

Just as Aratay had more tree spirits than any other kind, Semo was dominated by earth spirits, and the results were the spectacular mountains with impossibly high peaks wreathed in snow, sheer walls of granite that had burst up from a field, and clusters of red rock towers and arches. Naelin and Ven flew above the rock towers, through the arches, and over canyons so vast that you could have inverted a mountain inside them. But more unsettling than the sheer size of Semo was the way it felt, as if it were all about to collapse in on itself. The spirits of Semo, restless within the earth, brushed against Naelin's consciousness, and it made her want to fly back to Aratay, into the familiar trees, where the ground didn't look as if it were ready to swallow you.

She didn't know how anyone lived here, in the shadow of all this enormity, but proof was everywhere: houses built into the crevasses in the granite fields, clinging to the sides of steep mountains, tucked beneath the arches, built beside rivers at the bottom of canyons ... *A lot of innocent people for Queen Merecot to protect,* she thought.

*If that's what Merecot truly wants to do, then I'll help her do it.*

Because all these people had children too. And if she could protect them ... *I couldn't keep spirits from taking Erian and Llor, but the children of Semo ...* If spirits came for them, it wouldn't be to merely kidnap them. *Maybe there is good I can do here.*

*If Merecot lets me.*

It was a big *if.* Because Merecot had already proven time and time again that she didn't care about innocent lives, not if they stood in the way of what she wanted. But even though Naelin didn't trust her, she trusted what she could see: Semo needed help.

*And I'm strong enough to give it to them.*

Naelin saw the capital before she realized what it was. At first, from a distance, it seemed like yet another natural wonder, but as they flew closer, she saw it in all its glory. Built into a mountain, the marble city gleamed in the morning light with a brightness that made her eyes tear. Walls, towers, and turrets seemed to burst from the rock, and as they flew closer, even the people seemed like they were a part of the mountain—they dressed in the same sparkling white as the city walls, going about their lives in the steep, spiraling streets.

"Naelin!" Ven called. "Welcoming party!"

He pointed and then put his hand on his bow, positioning it, clearly concerned it was *not* a welcoming party. Naelin saw five air spirits shoot out from the window of one of the turrets. Small and streamlined, they looked like arrows.

*Ah, there's the challenge.*

Naelin ordered their two mounts to split and circle the city, keeping a distance from the palace at its peak. She reached out with her mind toward the five foreign spirits—and met a wall. Their minds felt like a slick surface. Her thoughts glided off it.

*Just like the ones that took Erian and Llor.*

That almost unmoored her, but the fact that she was going to see them soon—*I am going to see them soon*—kept her focused.

One of the foreign spirits let out a shrill cry and then dove at

Naelin. Ven shouted, urging his spirit down to defend her. He drew an arrow out of his quiver and had it strung. Rising up, with only his knees holding on to his spirit, he aimed.

Naelin shoved her mind hard at the blankness. *Do not attack!*

But the spirit didn't seem to hear her.

It stayed on course, shooting toward her. Out of the corner of her eye, she saw Ven fire his arrow. It hit the spirit in the right eye, and the spirit howled.

The other four spirits targeted Ven.

"Ven, watch out!" Naelin cried.

He was firing arrows fast, but there were too many. As one swiped at his head, he swung his bow and hit it hard, knocking it aside. The others tore at the wings of his air spirit, trying to claw their way to him.

Naelin tried to force the Semoian spirits to obey her, but her commands bashed into the slick blankness and slid away, so she switched directions and rammed her mind into a spirit in the palace—a tiny, weak fire spirit who was tending to a candle. She forced it to open its mouth and speak:

*Queen Merecot! We come in peace!*

She then grabbed the mind of every other weak spirit on the mountain until they were all shouting the same: *Queen Merecot! We come in peace!*

It echoed through the castle.

*We come in peace!*

Abruptly, the five spirits broke off their attack. They sped back into the turret and disappeared through the window. Ven steadied himself on the back of his spirit. His green armor was ripped at the shoulder, and his air spirit was dripping golden blood from the tip of one wing. It drooped to the side as it struggled to stay aloft.

Naelin scanned the palace, looking for a safe place to land. Pointing at one of the towers, Ven shouted, "There!"

Like the Chamber of the Queen's Champions in the palace of Mittriel, the white castle of Arkon had a broad balcony balanced on top of one of the pinnacles. Flying underneath Ven's spirit, Naelin guided them all toward it and landed. His serpent spirit pitched forward as it touched down and then collapsed on the ground. She dismounted and hurried to it and Ven.

Groaning, he slid off its back, then waved her off. "Just a scratch."

"Let me look," Naelin demanded.

He laid a hand over his wound. She saw his shirt was speckled with blood. "I'm fine. Let's not show weakness in front of Queen Merecot's people." He nodded significantly at something—or someone—over Naelin's shoulder.

She turned to see castle guards dressed in marble-white armor, pouring out of an archway. Ven drew his sword and stood ready by Naelin as she straightened to face them.

*What am I doing here? I'm just a woodswoman.* She'd never imagined she'd leave the forest to stand on the pinnacle of the capital of Semo, on the side of a mountain. *But here I am.*

*I am a not just a woodswoman.*

*I am a woman of the woods.*

*I am the* queen.

Ven spoke in a booming voice: "This is Queen Naelin of Aratay, answering the request of Queen Merecot of Semo. Stand down, or face the wrath of your queen and ours."

The guards did not stand down. Shoulder to shoulder, they held their swords ready, their faces implacable and unreadable through their helmets.

Projecting the confidence of Queen Daleina and the arrogance of Poison-Master Garnah, Naelin walked toward the guards with her shoulders back and head held high, as if she intended to walk straight through them.

Wavering, the guards looked at one another.

"Call for your queen," Ven suggested. "Let her tell you what to do."

One guard whispered to another, who nodded, and then a third guard bolted back through the archway. Naelin halted, waited, outwardly calm, the way she used to wait for Erian and Llor to settle down after chasing each other around the room. *Don't let them see they have any power.* They'd have power only if she gave it to them.

One of the guards began, "If you will lay down your weapons—"

"We will not," Naelin cut him off. She felt a stirring in the air that prickled the skin on her arms. Spirits. Lots of them, close by.

"You cannot be permitted before the queen armed—"

Out of the corner of her eye she saw Ven switch his grip on his sword, still ready. "As I recall," she said, "the last time your queen visited our land, she came with an army. Be grateful we didn't come with one as well."

The guards tightened their grips on their weapons.

Softly, Ven said, "Maybe we should have waited for that escort at the border."

"Nonsense," Naelin said. "Queen Merecot wants us here. That's the whole reason she took my children." She raised her voice louder so it would carry on the wind. "Isn't that right, Your Majesty?"

With a whoosh of wind, Queen Merecot rose beyond the balcony, standing on the backs of air spirits, one foot on each. "Yes indeed. Welcome, Queen Naelin. You disappointed the escort I sent for you and ruined the elaborate welcome I'd planned."

Naelin studied her face, searching for a hint of whether this was a trap, or whether she was sorry for what she did and the pain and fear she put Naelin, Erian, and Llor through. But Queen Merecot neither looked filled with remorse nor did she launch into any kind of confession. *If that's how you want it to go, so be it.*

"You can save your theatrics for another audience," Naelin said. "I'm here for my children, and to discuss the future of Semo."

MERECOT TWISTED HER LIPS INTO A SMILE, EVEN THOUGH WHAT she really wanted to do was snarl at Naelin like a wolf. This was the woman who had killed her sister, Alet. *And I'm not going to forget that.* But she knew she had to make nice. Especially since Ven still had his sword out and was looking exceptionally grumpy, even for the famed champion.

Stepping lightly off the two spirits, Merecot dismissed them and nodded to the guards. "Notify Headmistress . . . excuse me, *Ambassador* Hanna that we will be meeting in the West Room, and arrange for refreshments to be sent there as well." To her visitors, she said, "You'll be pleasantly surprised to discover that Semo has a variety of delicious traditional dishes. Despite the surroundings, we don't eat rocks and gravel."

Ugh, she hated being polite.

"I'm sure it's wonderful," Queen Naelin said in a dry voice. "But before anything, I want to see my children."

"Of course." She'd let Queen Naelin see them. But only see, for now. That was Queen Jastra's advice—keep them apart as long as possible. Once Naelin and Ven had the kids, then Merecot would have no more leverage. And she didn't believe the queen and her champion were here with peaceful intent. Daleina had to be using this opportunity to further one of her own plots, some kind of revenge or power play, and once they'd secured the children, Naelin and Ven would serve as part of her larger plan. *They've already humiliated me in front of my nation and murdered my sister. What's next? Deposing me?* But she kept a pleasant smile on her face, even though it made her cheeks feel like they were going to crack, and led her guests through the archway to the stone stairs that spiraled down into the heart of the palace.

Their steel armor clanking, her guards marched ahead of her. The stairs felt too narrow, with her visitors, her guards, and the heavy stone walls on either side. She'd rather have flown down on the backs of the spirits, but she was sure Naelin and Ven would have objected to that—certainly they didn't trust her. *I wouldn't trust me*, she thought.

*I* don't *trust me.*

She smirked at herself. Maybe this would be entertaining. Maybe she could keep them off-balance enough that they wouldn't enact whatever they were plotting. She needed to hold the cards in this game, and she wasn't sure she did at the moment. But she was going to pretend as if she had every advantage until she figured out if that was true . . . or until she made it true.

For now, though, thanks to her air spirits, she did have one enormous advantage.

She halted at a window overlooking one of the many castle courtyards. Below, ringed by guards, were Erian and Llor. She'd given them marbles to play with. But not just any marbles—these were tiny earth spirits, on orders to both entertain and watch the children.

Erian and Llor were laughing as they chased the "marbles" around the courtyard. The marbles bashed into one another as they rolled haphazardly over the flagstones. "You see? They're happy and unharmed." She shot a smug smile at Naelin—and then her smile faltered.

The look on Queen Naelin's face was enough to shred your heart.

She seemed to be feeling every emotion at once: joy, pain, relief, longing. And Merecot had to look away. *I didn't mean . . .* But no, she *had* meant to cause this. She'd intended to use these children, and she was going to continue using them and using Naelin's emotions for as long as she had to. *For the sake of Semo.*

*For the sake of all Renthia.*

"Once our negotiations are concluded, you may, of course, reclaim them." Under extremely heavy guard, and only if negotiations went well.

"I'll go to them now," Naelin said. "They should know their mother is here."

Merecot sighed dramatically. "I hate having to threaten people." Then she paused. "Oh wait, no. I don't."

She flicked her mind at the "marbles." Each earth spirit stopped, and then they began to roll toward Erian and Llor, coming at them from all directions. The children abruptly quit laughing. They stood back to back in the center of the courtyard.

She felt Naelin's mind poking at the edges of Merecot's control. But these were Merecot's spirits, bound to her, and she was focusing her will on them. She didn't let that control waver. "Discussion first, then you may join your children."

Naelin's mind retreated—it felt like a cloud moving away from the sun—and Merecot switched her order to the tiny earth spirits. *Play*, she told them. *Play nice.* And they resumed chaotically bouncing around the courtyard.

The children watched them warily, aware now of their nature. Merecot was a bit sorry for that. It was easier if one's prisoners forgot they were in a prison. At the same time, though, she really didn't care if two stupid children were happy.

"Follow me," Merecot said crisply, ignoring the death glare that Naelin was shooting her. She led the way, which meant exposing her back to the queen and the champion, but Merecot kept her thoughts flitting from spirit to spirit, using them to watch behind her. Fire spirits lurked in each of the sconces along the corridor, and Merecot was able to see her visitors through their eyes.

For now, she couldn't see a threat from either Naelin or Ven.

Soon enough, they reached their destination. She nodded at the two soldiers on either side of the massive oak doors, which they then pushed open, straining against the weight. Whatever queen had built this castle had liked impressively large things: large turrets, large doors, and large rooms. *It suits a queen's large ego*, she thought ruefully. With the guards standing at attention on either side, Merecot swept into the West Room.

Judged as the most ostentatious room in the castle (*which said a lot, given the competition,* Merecot thought), the West Room looked like a vast cavern, boasting an enormous arched ceiling, a polished marble floor, and huge windows that overlooked the western mountains. The western mountains were themselves ostentatious, their peaks rivaling the clouds, and it added to the overall feel of this chamber. It was a room designed to host large parties, impress visitors, and make them feel small. Merecot felt a little ridiculous using it for so few people, but it would be nice if they understood her problem:

Semo was big and yet it still wasn't big enough.

Her gown swooshed across the stone floor, loud in the silent vast room, and she climbed the steps up to the throne. She sat. "Too obnoxious?"

"A little," Ven agreed. "Your Majesties are equals."

"I'm told that Queen Naelin did not have any intention of being crowned," Merecot said, "whereas I've worked for this my entire life. I don't know that we are equals."

An old yet still strong voice carried across the room. "You'll have to excuse Queen Merecot. She failed her diplomacy classes."

Merecot rolled her eyes as Ambassador Hanna entered the

room. *Oh, yay, she's here.* She conveniently ignored the fact that she herself had called for her. "I didn't fail. All my marks were high."

"True enough. You simply cheated to get them," Hanna said as one of the guards pushed her chair across the room. "Over there." She pointed to the window. "We'll need a table and chairs set around it. Comfortable chairs. This conversation could take a while."

"It will be short," Naelin said. "I won't be kept from my children."

"It will take as long as it takes," Hanna said with that headmistress "charm" that Merecot hadn't missed in the slightest— though it was satisfying to see it directed at someone else—"until all parties are satisfied. Your children are well. Now, we need that table." She beckoned to one of Merecot's guards.

The guard glanced at Merecot, and she nodded. *Let the old woman play at being in charge.* Once the conversation started, then they'd see who really pulled the strings. Merecot doubted it was Queen Naelin. Ven, maybe? Or were they all just a mouthpiece for Daleina?

She wished she could have made Daleina see that the poisoning hadn't been personal. She hadn't *wanted* Daleina to die. Or, at least, she would have cried for her once the deed was done.

They waited while several servants scurried in and out of the room, delivering an overly heavy stone table, chairs plump with pillows, crystal vases with various juices, and an assortment of meat pies, the kind she'd grown fond of. "I recommend the pies. They're mutton, but don't let the word 'mutton' fool you. They actually taste good."

She sat first, since her guests hadn't moved yet, picked up one of the mutton pies, and bit into it. Gooey sauce dribbled from the side, and she caught it on a napkin. She laid it on the plate. "Come on. Don't insult my hospitality. It's not as if they're poisoned."

*That* joke fell like an anchor into the ocean, and all of them stared at her in hostile silence.

Inwardly, Merecot sighed. She knew she was an excellent queen—extremely powerful, confident, and decisive—but this part of being royal was not her strong point. "Ambassador Hanna, since *you* did not fail diplomacy, how would you counsel us to begin?"

Hanna wheeled herself up to the table and selected a meat pie. A servant poured her a mug of hot milk. Hanna dusted each with a powder before drinking and eating, and only then did Naelin and Ven eat.

Merecot supposed it was her own fault they were so paranoid. It would have been funny if it hadn't all failed and left Alet dead.

Hanna spoke. "The situation is as I laid it out and as Queen Merecot had claimed: Semo has more spirits than the land can support. They're warring with one another, and if left as is, they'll tear the land apart. Judging from what I have seen . . . this could happen at any time."

"Can't you control them?" Ven asked bluntly. He was practically bristling with hostility. *I've met friendlier wild boars*, Merecot thought. "You're supposed to be some kind of all-powerful prodigy."

Merecot gritted her teeth, then made herself relax. She needed these people. Maybe. Jastra had advocated for simply . . . *disposing* of Queen Naelin—it was efficient, effective, and would permanently remove one more hurdle on the way to ruling both countries—but Merecot maintained it would be best for everyone if she could convince the queens of Aratay to do what she wished. Especially since she'd already failed to kill Daleina once. "I *am* controlling them. That's the only reason that the country hasn't erupted in endless earthquakes, avalanches, and volcanoes."

"But this isn't a permanent solution," Hanna said, "which is what we are here to discuss."

"It can be a short discussion, per your request, Queen Naelin," Merecot said. *Here we go. Say it with confidence.* "The solution to Semo's problem is a simple one. You and Queen Daleina must abdicate and allow me to rule both Aratay and Semo." She sat back and waited for them to react.

They gaped at her for a moment, then exploded:

"Absolutely not!"

That was Ambassador Hanna.

"That's insane!"

That was Ven.

He continued. "Abdicate to the woman who tried to kill Daleina and invade Aratay? Are you out of your mind?" Merecot wondered if he'd failed his diplomacy class too. "How about *you* abdicate?"

"Yes," Hanna said. "Give Daleina and Naelin control of both Aratay and Semo."

Ven nodded. "Allow them to redistribute your spirits. Your people would be safe then too."

Merecot dismissed this immediately. "Daleina lacks the power and Naelin lacks the experience to control this many across such distances."

"Naelin could be taught."

"There's not enough time. You felt how close the excess spirits are to ripping this land apart and making it as uninhabitable as the untamed lands."

Naelin finally spoke up. "There would have been time if you had come to us, instead of wasting precious days with your plot to kidnap my children."

"But I didn't . . . and I did," Merecot said, wondering if she should sound a bit more sorry. *I'm not, though. I did what I had to do.* She was certain Queen Naelin wouldn't even be here if her children weren't here. "And those are facts now, not hypotheticals. Think about it and you'll realize I am the only logical choice to rule both lands."

"There must be another solution," Ven said.

"None that I can see," Merecot said. And none that Queen Jastra could see either. The former queen had been studying the problem of spirits for years, and she'd come to the conclusion that this was the start of the solution: one queen for both Semo and Aratay. "Your barren lands provide land for my excess spirits. But only I can send them there and tie them to the land, and I can only accomplish that if I am queen of both."

"And I suppose *this* is why you kidnapped the children," Ven said, arms folded across his chest, eyebrows lowered. He looked formidable.

*Good thing I'm not easily intimidated*, Merecot thought. "Obviously. If I wanted you to visit, I would have sent an invitation. But I want you to *abdicate*. It seemed to me that required more incentive."

Hanna and Ven both began to shout again, but Merecot ignored them. She fixed her eyes on Queen Naelin. Naelin was the one she had to convince. And Naelin was quite clearly considering it.

"You don't want to be queen anyway," Merecot said directly to her. "Do this, and I can guarantee you the life you wanted, safe with your family in whatever home you want. I will keep you safe for the rest of my days. Daleina as well. And I will sign whatever treaty you want to bind my successors to keep you all safe as well."

"Don't listen to her," Ven said to Naelin. "If you abdicate, you give up all the power the spirits gave you when you were crowned. You'll have no more power than you had before—and that may have seemed like a lot then, but now the spirits know who you are. They'll all hunt you. Queen Merecot can't keep you safe from all the spirits of Aratay. No queen is powerful enough to keep a former queen alive for long."

"Except me," Merecot said. This she could say with easy confidence. "Would you like proof? I can introduce you to the former queen of Semo, who is alive and well and here in the castle." She signaled to one of her guards.

Rising, she signaled to her guards, who escorted Jastra inside. The old queen had been waiting in the next room. *Most likely with her ear pressed against the wall, eavesdropping.* But Merecot was grateful for her nosiness now, because it allowed her to prove her point.

Bent over her cane, Queen Jastra hobbled into the room. She clasped Ambassador Hanna's hand. "I've long wished to meet you. The reputation of your academy has spread far and wide. You're an inspiration to all."

"An honor to meet you as well," Hanna said, and bowed.

Jastra greeted Ven and then Naelin. "Please believe Queen Merecot. She has the power to protect me, as you can see. These days, I can scarcely summon a fire spirit to warm my cold toes. Yet Merecot is able to defend me from their wrath."

Merecot knew that wasn't precisely true—Jastra had just as much power as she did prior to claiming the crown—but a little exaggeration wouldn't hurt here. And it *was* true that only Merecot's protection kept her alive. A queen gained many spirit enemies during her lifetime, and Jastra had lived a long lifetime.

"You could have a life of peace and quiet," Jastra told Naelin, "if that's what you wish."

"That's all I ever wished," Naelin said. "And if it were only me, I would abdicate in a heartbeat. You're right—I never wanted this. All I want is my family, together and safe."

Merecot could hear the unspoken "but." She waited.

"But Daleina will never agree," Naelin said.

And that was it. With that one simple statement, Naelin doomed Merecot's plan. Merecot tried not to let the depth of her disappointment show on her face. She'd known intellectually that it had been a long shot, but in her heart, she'd been hoping that Naelin would say yes, of course, she'd convince Daleina and all would be well.

But if Naelin wouldn't even *try* to convince her . . .

"Are you certain?" Merecot pressed. "If you went back to her, knowing the scope and urgency of the situation, knowing that your children *and* the children of Semo need this to happen, and you tried to convince her . . . Surely she would listen to her co-queen?"

"Unlikely," Ven said. "Daleina considers ruling Aratay to be her duty, her purpose."

Merecot knew that. Still, she'd allowed herself to hope. "Ambassador Hanna . . ."

"I must agree with them," Hanna said. "Abdication is not an option."

Merecot glanced at Jastra, who gave her a small nod. At least the old queen avoided saying, "I told you so." It had been worth a try. *I suppose I'll need Jastra's plan after all. Pity.*

*It would have been nice to avoid murdering anyone.*

# CHAPTER 18

Ambassador Hanna drank the tea, which despite Queen Merecot's assurances that food in Semo wasn't made with rocks still tasted like rocks. She wished she were in her roost at the academy, where students were in awe and a bit afraid of her. Instead she was playing mediator to two very different and equally headstrong queens.

*I should be retired,* she thought, *soaking in my golden years in a quiet midforest village, far from politics, responsibility, and risk of violent death.* Queen Merecot always seemed a few seconds away from a toddler's tantrum, and Queen Naelin had already destroyed part of Aratay with her emotional needs. *I'm too old for this.*

She leaned forward as Naelin and Merecot launched into another argument about abdication and said, "Perhaps we should break here for the day. Now that the topic has been broached, the prudent choice is to retire, rest, and consider the matter before continuing. Queen Naelin has had a long journey, and I admit that my stamina is not what it used to be." She gave a rueful chuckle, entirely faked—she wasn't tired, but she was getting a headache from the tension in the room.

Both queens scowled at her for the interruption.

"Rest, reconsider, and meet again tonight, perhaps over dinner, *with* the children," Hanna pressed. "Queen Naelin can use the time to familiarize herself with Semo, and Queen Merecot . . . I'm sure you have much that needs your attention."

Slowly, Merecot nodded. Her shoulders sagged—only minutely, but Hanna saw it. *She's tired. Worried, perhaps. Even afraid.* Hanna couldn't imagine Merecot ever admitting fear, but she must feel it. Even from what little Hanna could sense with her limited power, she could tell the spirits in Semo were a breath away from disaster. The land felt like a pot about to boil over and scald anyone close enough to be burned, which was just about everyone in its borders, and possibly some beyond.

Ven pushed back from the table. "The ambassador is right. If you keep at it now, you'll just piss each other off."

"That too," Hanna agreed, wincing slightly at the champion's lack of tact.

"Very well." In a swirl of jewel-laden skirts, Merecot rose and swept across the throne room. "You'll be escorted to your rooms," she said over her shoulder. "Anything you need, simply ask the guards—I'll be assigning them for your own protection, of course, as well as to make sure you don't run around murdering people or stealing from the royal treasury or whatever."

"Your hospitality is extraordinary," Naelin said dryly.

"It is," Merecot said, "as is the trust I'm demonstrating by allowing you here. Don't abuse that trust."

Ven was fingering his sword hilt. *He just can't help himself,* Hanna thought with a sigh. Champions always thought every problem could be solved with a blade. "So we're to be treated like prisoners," Ven said.

"Nonsense," Merecot said. "Go where you want. Do what you want. Just remember you'll be watched, and don't do anything stupid. If you're tempted, simply remember your children are under my *protection.*" She exited with that threat hanging there, and her guards swooped in to drag open the massive door in front of her before just as swiftly shutting it behind her.

Naelin let out a small, humorless laugh. "If she'd left any faster, I'd think she didn't like me." She stood beside Ven as a man in red and gold hurried through the doorway and across the vast room to them.

The man bowed twice. "Your Majesty, I'd be honored to escort you to your rooms. We've prepared the baths for you and your companions, and we are at your service."

"You can escort us to my children," Naelin ordered.

More bows. "Our deepest apologies, but we are not permitted—"

Hanna wheeled forward. "Actually, I'd like to show Queen Naelin the gardens. I think she'd find them soothing after her journey. Could you please escort us there instead? Feel free to send word to Queen Merecot as to where we are, but I don't think she'll have any objections. And if she does . . . she is welcome to come join us for a stroll."

Naelin opened her mouth to object, but Hanna quelled her with a frown.

The servant looked troubled for a moment but smoothed his expression quickly enough. Bowing, he led them—with guards, of course, both Hanna's own and Merecot's castle guards—out of the West Room and down the sloping, spiraled hall.

The castle was shaped, Hanna had discovered, like a conch shell, with curves and spirals, vastly easier to navigate in a chair than the ladders, stairs, and ropes of Mittriel. It also gave the impression of immense distances within the structure, helped by the high ceilings and tall, narrow windows that allowed slits of light to pattern the floor. *A clever design*, Hanna thought. Everything about this castle was designed to impress and intimidate. "You've heard Merecot's assessment of the situation," Hanna said. "I'd like to give you mine."

"Good idea," Ven said.

"My children . . ." Naelin began.

"Your children's safety depends on our cooperation," Hanna said. "You've come this far. Be patient a little longer, Your Majesty."

Hanna said nothing further until their escort had delivered them to the gardens. She was certain that Merecot would have spies, even spirits as spies, following them, but there was no point in making it easy for her. She thanked the servant and wheeled forward in between two stone statues of soldiers with raised swords.

The famed Gardens of Arkon were, like much of Semo, made of stone. The works of spirits, guided by queens of the past, lined the walkways. Hanna's favorites were the ones of people: children carved out of black basalt tossing a ball, an elderly woman carrying a bucket of water all carved out of a blue stone flecked with gold, two men playing a game with round white and black stones, a gardener carved so long ago that the rain had worn away his expression . . .

She rolled down the paths, her wheels crunching over the pebbles. "You can see here what beauty a queen with control over her spirits can create." She waved her hand to gesture at an exquisite sculpture of a mother with a child on one hip and a sword on the other—the sun hit her face just right, to highlight the fierceness of her expression. Hanna was partial to that one.

"Lots of places for an ambush," Ven murmured, checking behind the statue of the mother and baby and keeping his eye on the other shadows. Hanna supposed paranoia went with his job description.

"We're safe enough for now," Hanna said. "Merecot won't dispose of us while there's a chance we'll do what she wants. You're safest when your enemy wants to use you."

"Rather cynical for words of wisdom," Ven said.

Electing to ignore that, Hanna said to Naelin, "Reach out and feel the spirits of Semo."

Naelin nodded, then her face went blank—the peculiar focused-absent look of someone who was pushing their mind out of their body. Hanna wondered how far Naelin's range was outside of Aratay. *Undoubtedly impressive.* Naelin had been able to summon an earth kraken before she was linked to the spirits of Aratay, Hanna remembered. Her powers should still be intense here, even though the local spirits were linked to Merecot. She wondered what Naelin would make of the spirits of Semo.

Hanna didn't have to wonder long.

Naelin's eyes snapped back into focus. "They're wild."

"Some of them, yes. But not all."

Her eyes lost focus again. "You're right. Not all. There are two kinds of spirits here. One feels frightened. They're hiding. The other ... rage, hate, chaos, wildness." She fixed her gaze on Hanna. "I don't understand. In Aratay, there's variation, but not this kind of split. Are the spirits here warring against themselves?"

"In a manner of speaking, yes." Hanna rolled farther into the garden, stopping in front of a twenty-foot marble statue of Queen Jastra in her prime, wearing the steel armor of the guards and holding the head of an earth spirit. Snakes sprouted from the spirit's head instead of hair, and the spirit's eyes were filled with fist-size rubies. "I have been asking questions, mostly of colleagues, scholars of spirits at the University of Arkon, as well as of several long-time chancellors who served the prior queen, and I've unearthed a consensus on what—or rather, *who*—caused Semo's current problem. It seems that Queen Jastra, the prior queen of Semo whom you met, had grand designs on the future of her country. She was ambitious, not unlike her successor, and had plans of uniting all of Renthia under a single queen. Her, obviously. But to do that, she required greater strength."

Ven snorted. "I see where this is going."

"I don't think you do," Hanna said.

"Queen Merecot is intent on carrying out her predecessor's dream," Ven said. "Simple enough. She wants to control the world."

"Right now she's struggling to control Semo," Hanna said. *And "struggling" is an understatement.* She thought of the active volcano she'd seen.

Naelin nodded. "She's holding these spirits by constant vigilance—I can feel it. It has to be exhausting. I don't know how she even sleeps. They're like wolves who've caught the scent of prey."

"When she sleeps, people die," Hanna said flatly. "As powerful as she is, the spirits are strong too. If they were all linked to the land, it would be different ... but a few hundred of them are not. They all want to be—instinct pulls them to bond with Semo as well as their queen—but there are too many spirits for the land to accommodate, which is where the warring that you sensed comes in—they're competing for the land. The question is: Why?"

"The question is," Ven corrected, "What do we do about it?"

Hanna glared at him. "Well, you can't just whack them with

your sword. So hush, Champion, and let me finish. This is important." She turned back to Queen Naelin, ignoring Ven's look of indignation at being shushed. "The wild spirits you're sensing, My Queen—the ones who are connected to Queen Merecot but not to the land—are not native to Semo. In order to increase her power, Queen Jastra ventured into the untamed lands and brought back an army of spirits to her country. It was a clever idea. You felt for yourself how your power increased when the spirits of Aratay chose you. And you've felt how you are diminished when one dies. A queen's power comes from her spirits. Queen Jastra understood this—and she concluded that the more spirits she had, the more powerful she'd be. She thought she could tie them to her and then use them to invade neighboring lands. Except there were too many—and without a link to the land, the spirits are much more erratic. Queen Jastra wasn't strong enough to control them all, which was why she abdicated in favor of the more powerful Queen Merecot."

Naelin's eyes had gone wide. Ven too looked as if he'd seen an apparition. "She went into the untamed lands and *survived*? Naelin, do you think Bayn . . ." His voice trailed off, as if he were afraid to finish the question.

Hanna gawked at the two of them. She'd just revealed the fact that Queen Jastra had definitively proven (and disproven) multiple theories on the nature of queens and spirits that had been the subject of debate at the academies for years . . . and they were focusing instead on a *wolf*?

"It's possible," Naelin said. "If a queen could go into the untamed lands and come out again alive, maybe a 'Protector of Queens' could too." She laid her hand over Ven's. "When this is over, we'll do what we can to find him," she promised. "We'll search every inch of the border, and I'll probe the mind of every spirit within a mile of it."

"Thank you. I—" Ven pulled back from her. "Queen Merecot."

All of them turned to see Merecot march through the garden. She was flanked by her armored guards, as well as three spirits. These spirits were all earth spirits, and they looked like they were pottery come to life. Shaped like dogs, their hides were hardened clay, and their eyes were hollowed-out holes. "So happy to see you're enjoying my gardens."

"We're not," Ven said blandly. "We're just plotting against you."

That caused Merecot to halt in her tracks. Hanna wished she were close enough to elbow Ven in the stomach and was happy to see Naelin do it for her. *Don't bait her*, she thought at him. There was a time and a place for humor, and she was not certain Merecot possessed any of it whatsoever.

"Can you tell us why you targeted Bayn?" Ven asked, his voice still pleasant, as if he were asking about the layout of the gardens. "You called him the Protector of Queens. What did you mean by that? What is he?"

Hanna watched Merecot's face with amusement—*She wants to lash out, but she knows she shouldn't.* She clearly didn't like that Hanna had brought them to the gardens, rather than allowing them to be escorted to the baths as planned, and she just as clearly didn't like to be questioned. *She's still both insecure and arrogant.* Perhaps she even regretted some of her choices. *Not that she'll ever admit it . . . and not that I'd believe her anyway.*

Merecot settled on a benign half-smile. "According to Queen Jastra, he was some kind of 'evolved spirit,' tasked with protecting you or Daleina or whomever bore the crown. She's studied the nature of spirits very closely and believed he could have caused trouble. She recommended he be removed." She waved her hand as if dismissing the entire episode as inconsequential. "This was back when I was targeting your queens, of course. Now that we're negotiating, the situation has changed."

"Of course it has," Ven murmured.

"Removing him was just a precaution," Merecot said. "You weren't supposed to ever discover how he died."

Ven made a sound very close to a growl. "You could show *some* remorse."

"Very sorry about your pet," Merecot said, then she frowned and held up a hand. "No, I *am* sorry. If he was just an ordinary wolf, he didn't deserve his fate. But it is the fate of all of Semo that concerns me."

It concerned Hanna as well.

Semo had too many spirits.

Aratay had too many queens.

*There is another obvious answer,* Hanna thought, *one that isn't Merecot's plan of abdication . . . but I don't know if any of the queens will like it.* "Our land has its problems as well, but I believe these problems share a common solution," Hanna said in her most definitive I-know-best headmistress voice. "You have too many spirits; we have too many queens. One of our queens must release her hold on our spirits and take control of your excess spirits. She can then bring them into Aratay under her command, and tie to them to the barren regions in our land."

*It's the perfect solution,* Hanna thought. *Poetic even.* Merecot was smart—she'd see the logic in the idea, wouldn't she? If she truly means what she says about saving her people . . .

"I'm not giving up my power—" Merecot began.

"You would keep Semo, with as many spirits as needed to keep the land alive, but only as many as you can handle to keep it stable. All you'd lose would be the excess spirits, and they cost you too much energy to control." Hanna kept her voice pleasant and smooth, the voice of a reasonable teacher, even though she wanted to shake the queen and say, *Listen to me, you foolish child!*

"Not practical," Merecot dismissed the idea. "Naelin would have to relinquish control of the spirits of Aratay. I won't have such a powerful queen lurking on my border."

"Fine," Naelin said.

Merecot blinked at her. "Excuse me? You'd really give up power that easily?"

"I said I'd *abdicate* to save my children. How is this different?"

"Yes, but . . . I didn't think you were serious!"

Pleased, Hanna leaned back in her chair. Given Naelin's past performance, Hanna hadn't expected her to be reasonable, but she was satisfied nonetheless.

"But . . . But you can't . . . I don't . . . It's not that simple," Merecot sputtered. "At the same time as you release your spirits, I will need to relinquish power over a segment of my spirits—they'll immediately target me. I will need assurances that you will gain control of them quickly. If you don't . . . I can and will defend myself, but the number of deaths that could occur in the meantime could be catastrophic. I won't have that on my conscience."

"What conscience?" Naelin asked, and Hanna gasped as Merecot sneered, ready to reply. But the queen of Aratay waved away her own comment. "I will take control quickly—that's also fine."

It was kind of entertaining to see Merecot so surprised. She clearly hadn't expected anyone to come up with a viable alternative—let alone one that could work

*One that* will *work. I'm sure of it.*

And if they did agree, then Daleina would keep her throne, Merecot would save her country, and there would be no reason for abdications, assassinations, or invasions. Keeping quiet, Hanna watched the queens and champion with amused interest.

Ven was shaking his head. "To take control of another land's spirits . . ."

"Queen Merecot would have to relinquish them, and I would have to accept them," Queen Naelin said. Her voice was neutral—Hanna couldn't tell what she was thinking. She *seemed* to be in favor of the idea. *Maybe she's willing to cling to anything that will end this. She wants her children back and this ordeal over.* If so, that was good enough.

"It's too dangerous," Ven said. "In the moment you release your spirits before you claim Queen Merecot's, you'd be vulnerable."

He wasn't wrong, but frankly, it was a lot less of a ridiculous request than asking both queens to abdicate in favor of Merecot. And less horrific than poisoning them. "The key part is that these spirits *don't* belong to any land. They're linked to the queen only, and only barely, which should make the transfer smooth. It would have to be done in the grove, of course."

"But it can be done?" Naelin asked.

"Yes," Hanna said. And then amended: "Theoretically, at least."

Ven clasped Naelin's hands in his. "It's too great a risk—"

"To save my children, Aratay, *and* Semo? I don't think it is." Naelin turned to Merecot. "I'll do it."

Merecot opened and shut her mouth twice before finding the words she wanted to say. "You should want assurances from me as well, before you so blithely agree," Merecot said at last. "Once you abdicate, you will be vulnerable. You'll need to rely on me to protect you." She still looked dazed. *She's a planner*, Hanna thought, *and this idea wasn't in any of her calculations.*

Ven spoke up. "I'll be there to protect her as well—and terminate you, if you violate the agreement." Out of the corner of her eye, Merecot saw her guards tense. She held up a hand to calm them. Hanna wished she could do the same to Ven.

"You won't be permitted into the grove," Merecot said as if he were an idiot. *He's not*, Hanna thought. Nothing like this had ever been attempted before, at least as far as she knew. He was right to worry. Just wrong to try to stop this. *It's our best chance to help everyone.* "The Semoian spirits, at least the older ones, are protective of their grove and fond of their traditions," Merecot continued. "Only the worthy can enter. The spirits, not to mention the people of Semo, would . . . object if the sacred ground were violated. Really wouldn't be a good idea to rile them up right before we attempt such a dangerous transition."

Ven was shaking his head, but Queen Naelin laid her hand over his. "It's in her interest to protect me. If this works, she'll save her land. And that's what she wants."

"*Is* it?" Ven asked without bothering to lower her voice. "We don't know her true motives. She's deceived us before."

Hanna winced. Couldn't he at least *try* to be diplomatic? "She's not deceiving you as to the danger to this land. And I should point out that this plan is *my* idea. You trust me, don't you?" She looked first at Ven, then at Naelin, then at Merecot.

*All of them, in their own way, do trust me.*

*And by trusting me, they'll save everyone.*

Hanna couldn't help feeling a bit smug.

NAELIN DIDN'T CARE IF IT WAS A GOOD PLAN OR NOT. SHE ONLY cared that Merecot had said yes. Yes to Hanna's solution. And yes to Naelin being reunited with her children.

Not permanently. Not yet. Not until the transfer was complete and Naelin had released the Aratayian spirits and claimed the excess Semoian spirits.

But it was a start.

She felt spirits watching her: two stone giants that lurked between statues, fire spirits that smoldered on the stone rafters above, an ice spirit in the window frosting the glass. She knew that Merecot had positioned another line of earth spirits just beyond them. The air quivered with them and made Naelin's head feel thick, but she didn't care.

All her attention was focused on one innocuous door, the one Erian and Llor would be coming through.

Ven was talking to her. She didn't hear him. Reaching out with her mind, she tried to see through the eyes of the foreign spirits, to see if they were approaching, but it was like pushing through muck.

A hand touched her elbow lightly, and she jumped.

"I'm here for you," Ven said quietly. "Whatever you need. I love you."

That was the only thing he could have said that had the power to distract her from staring at the door. Even a hurricane would have been a mere nuisance, pushed away with an order to a few spirits. But at Ven's words, she turned to him. "I love you too."

It was surprisingly easy to say. She'd expected it to be a trumpets-blaring kind of moment, but instead it simply felt *right*. Like putting on a warm coat on a cold day.

Glancing over her shoulder, Ven nodded at the door. "They're coming."

As if his words summoned them, the door flew open, and Erian and Llor tumbled inside. "Mama!" And Naelin was running toward them, arms outstretched. She dropped to her knees, and they barreled into her, throwing their arms around her.

Both of them were babbling at once, and she heard only snippets: "So happy you're here!" "Thought you wouldn't come!" "Missed you so much!" And she was talking too: "I missed you both so very, very much."

She pulled back so she could see them.

Erian, her cheeks rosy from playing outside in the courtyard, her hair braided too expertly for her to have done it herself, and a smudge of sugar in the corner of her smile from whatever pastry she ate for breakfast.

Llor, with a smile so wide that he looked like he had chipmunk cheeks. He smelled faintly of warm cinnamon and that odor little boys seemed to acquire from a bit too long between baths.

They were perfect.

"I lost a tooth!" Llor declared.

"Really? That's excellent," Naelin said.

"And I didn't even cry!"

"He didn't," Erian affirmed. "He was very brave."

"You've both been amazingly brave," Naelin told them.

Erian squeezed her hand. "Really, you don't know that for sure. We could have been hiding under our beds sobbing this whole time. But we haven't been. We *have* been brave. We wanted you to be proud of us."

"Oh, my girl, I am. I so very much am." Naelin felt as if her throat were clogged with cotton. "You have no idea how much I missed you."

"We missed you too," Erian said. "So much! And Father too."

"Where *is* Father?" Llor asked.

"He's in Mittriel," Naelin told him. "He'll be so happy and surprised to see you." She half wished she'd brought him with her so he could have this moment too. But the other half was grateful she didn't have to share it with anyone except Ven.

She glanced over her shoulder and saw Ven had drawn back, giving her space, letting her have her moment. She *had* her moment, though, and she wanted him to join in it—to be part of the family he was already so much a part of. She waved him closer, and Llor squealed, seeing him.

"Champion Ven!" Erian cried. Llor echoed her: "Ven! Ven!" And the children pulled away from Naelin and piled onto Ven, bringing him to his knees too. His face cracked into a grin, and Naelin realized it had been a while since she'd seen him smile.

Her own smile mirrored his, and she tasted her tears as they slid down her cheeks and into her smiling mouth.

Llor flopped out his arm, pulling Naelin into the embrace, all four of them jumbled together. *This moment*, Naelin thought. *This is what joy is.*

# CHAPTER 19

The first spirit sent by Queen Daleina left Aratay for the eastern land of Chell. It was a tree spirit, lithe and fast, shaped like a red fox but with scales of emerald green. It ran out of Mittriel along the limbs of the trees, leaping from branch to branch, sailing through the empty spaces between the trees, until it was out of forest. It kept running, on the ground, over dried leaves that crunched under its paws and dried pine needles that stuck between its toes.

Other spirits marked its passage, and then resumed tending their trees and rocks and streams. The humans didn't notice it at all. To them, it was as fast as a blur, and those who saw it thought it was a quirk of the light. Just a streak of green.

The fox spirit felt the moment that it left Aratay and ran into Chell. It hurt, as if a string were tied around its innards and pulling backward while its body plunged forward. The spirit felt yanked from within, but the queen's order permeated all, overwhelming the instinct to stay in its own land.

It sensed the other spirits, the ones linked to Chell, a mix of earth, fire, water, and wood, and saw before it the rolling fields and meadows. Golden stalks swayed in the wind. Trees, laden with fruit, crowded in pastures, and vegetables overflowed their fields.

Every inch of the land felt ripe.

The spirits of Chell worked in the fields, quietly and calmly. They didn't acknowledge the spirit of Aratay as the little fox spirit sped through their lands, but they silently passed word of its arrival—the news flickering fast across the fields, faster than the fox itself.

The news reached the fortress of the queen long before the spirit did, and when it did, she was ready. Exhausted, the fox flopped on the floor at the feet of the queen of Chell.

She bent down, her bones creaking, and untied the note from around the fox's neck. She unrolled it and read. Pursed her lips. Rolled the note back up, retied the ribbons.

"What does it say, Your Majesty?" one of her advisers asked.

"It's from the queen of Aratay, offering help with the harvest," Queen Gada lied. She would not give her adviser the excuse to send any of her heirs away. She needed them all—they were the only ones in this land she trusted.

"Ahh, curious. What will you say in response?"

Queen Gada smiled at the fox spirit. "I will accept." Carrying the fox into the Chellian Queen's Grove, the queen of Chell plunged her mind into the mind of the little creature, broke its bond with its old master, and made it hers.

THE SECOND SPIRIT FLEW TO THE NORTHEAST, TO THE ICY LAND OF Elhim. It was a water spirit with a child's body and dragonfly wings. It was entirely blue, translucent, and believed it was the loveliest being ever to grace Renthia. It enjoyed flying beyond the borders of Aratay, so others could appreciate its beauty. Over Chell, it danced with the other water spirits and caused rain to fall over several fields before it flew on to Elhim.

The air was cold the instant it crossed the border, and the ground was covered in a thick sheet of ice. The spirit liked the ice—the mirror-smooth ice reflected the spirit nicely, its beautiful blue and its lovely wings.

Deeper into Elhim, the ice changed: here were forests of ice, trees with delicate snow-leaves. And cities of ice, with sculpted towers and fortresses. The ice had been twisted into pinnacles that rose into the air then splayed out like antlers in a forest of odd shapes. In other places, it had been smoothed into vast cliffs that forced the little water spirit to fly higher and higher, up where the air was colder and colder.

As the spirit flew closer to the palace of the queen, the ice became even more beautiful, carved into sea creatures and forest animals and nameless shapes of such delicate beauty that the water spirit began to wonder if its reflection had been lovely after all.

The palace itself looked as if it were made from lace. Delicate ice strands were woven together in flowerlike patterns to create its walls. Following the command of the queen of Aratay, the water spirit flew unerringly toward the tallest tower, seeking out the queen of Elhim.

As it reached the palace, two ice spirits shot out from behind a pinnacle of blue ice. The water spirit had a chance to see itself reflected in the mirror-smooth bodies of the ice spirits and think, *Yes, I am lovely*—right before the ice spirits plunged through its heart.

The water spirit froze.

And died.

Queen Xiya of Elhim never knew it had come.

One day, her daughter would find the little spirit's body and think it was quite beautiful. She'd bring it inside to admire, and she'd discover the message. But that would not happen for an entire year.

THE THIRD SPIRIT, AN AIR SPIRIT, JOURNEYED SOUTH, TOWARD the islands of Belene.

It was shaped like a sparrow, but with knife-sharp metal feathers. It had been the hardest spirit of the three for Queen Daleina to command, but once the order was imprinted, the spirit was determined to reach the ocean queen as quickly as possible.

It flew straight south, defying the air currents, without wavering its course. When it reached the southern border of Aratay, it did not slow. It shot into the ocean air and soared high above the water.

Below, the ocean roiled as if it were fighting with itself. The sky was a bruise of swirling purple, blue, and black. The closer the spirit flew to the islands, the wilder the winds and water became. The sparrow spirit felt the spirits of Belene: wild with rage, and the spirit's own rage rose up to meet it—

But the queen of Aratay's command still rang through the little sparrow spirit.

It kept flying.

The islands lay ahead, jewels encircled by raging sea. The air spirit of Aratay saw several water spirits of Belene hurl themselves at the islands' shores. These ocean spirits were massive, with hundreds of tentacles and bodies as large as the islands. They looked like mountains rising out of the sea. Other spirits within the sea responded to them, forming axes and swords of water to pound against the monsters, keeping them back—spirits were fighting spirits.

As the air spirit flew, it saw a funnel of water rise from the middle of the chaos. The waterspout stretched and warped, and then it bore down on one of the islands.

The island was built out of the bones of spirits: a turtle shell as large as a city, a rib cage of a sea monster, a chain of vertebrae from a sea serpent. Grasses and palm trees grew on top of the bones, and between them were clusters of villages with homes decorated with shells. The streets were paved with mother-of-pearl, and the humans were screaming and running through them.

The spirit thought that was amusing.

The waterspout continued its path toward the island, and the sparrow spirit shot ahead of it, faster than the spout was. It flew through the highest window of a spiral-shaped tower, where it sensed Queen Asana of Belene stood.

She was peering through a telescope at the waterspout. Her braids were unraveled, and her crown of shells was lopsided on her head. She was bleeding from a gash on one shoulder.

The air spirit thought that after it delivered its message, perhaps it would help the waterspout and make the foreign queen bleed more.

"What's this?" Queen Asana asked. Dropping to her knees, she untied the message from around the air spirit's leg and read it. "The queen of Aratay asks for an heir, if we can spare one." She made a sound that was half like a laugh and half like a choking gasp.

The sparrow spirit didn't see the humor, though it thought if the waterspout tore through the city, that would be amusing. Straining to peer out the window, it tried to watch both the queen and the battle on the sea.

Standing, Queen Asana wrote a message on the back of the note. She finished and retied it around the air spirit's leg. "Please tell her to send *us* help," she said to the spirit.

The little spirit felt a churning inside. The call of the vengeful ocean spirits was strong and growing stronger. It tasted saliva filling its mouth, wanting blood. It stared fixedly at the gash on the queen's shoulder.

Queen Asana closed her eyes for a moment, and the spirit felt a command sink in: *Return home.* "I'm deeply sorry, but your queen is on her own."

She then released the air spirit.

With its new order, the spirit flew out the window. But the waterspout called to it, and the rage of the sea was too strong. It joined with the ocean spirits, forgetting its mission, and attacked the islands.

# CHAPTER 20

Daleina felt the loss of the three spirits. First one, then the other, then a few days later the third. She didn't know if they'd died or if her order had failed to hold them at such a distance, but each loss felt like a jab.

Somewhere in Aratay, she knew a bit of the land died.

She sent other spirits to heal it, as best they could. But they were already stretched thin. There were so many barren patches now, and her spirits were still sluggish to respond to her commands—even with Queen Naelin gone from Aratay, they hadn't yet shaken the aftereffects of her emotional hurricane.

She felt a headache form.

*I need a new idea.* Her people had to be kept safe. Presiding over the Council of Champions, she didn't tell them that she'd tried to reach out to other queens, or that she'd failed. Instead she focused on their reports on the progress of their candidates.

Champion Boden had the floor. An older man with a thick white mustache and a booming voice, he'd been droning on for a while. ". . . preparations for devastation. I'm proposing that heir training include a rotation of guard duty of the emergency winter stores. Furthermore—"

Sensing a spirit approaching, Daleina straightened and held up one hand to silence the champions. The spirit was flying fast toward the top of the tower, and she felt its urgency. News from the north? *Please let it be good!* "One moment, and then we will continue."

She crossed to the edge of the chamber, beneath an archway. Golden leaves curled around the vines above her, and she felt as if she were wearing a second crown.

The spirit came into view: a white deer with wings, one of the air spirits of Aratay. It had feathers instead of fur, and she felt the imprint of Naelin's thoughts in its mind. It *did* bear a message. She was right.

Landing, its hooves echoed on the chamber floor, and all the champions watched, tense. Daleina stroked the feathers on its neck. *You've had a long flight. Thank you for flying so far and fast. Only a strong spirit could have done that.*

It preened at the compliment.

*May I have the message?*

The white deer didn't carry any note—Naelin was powerful enough that she could imprint her message in the spirit's mind, which was incredible. It made Daleina feel weak in comparison, especially in the aftermath of losing the three spirits she'd sent. Reaching for the deer's thoughts, Daleina heard the message as if Naelin were speaking right next to her. Her voice in the deer's memory was only a little distorted, as if she were talking underwater or through a windstorm. "Queen Daleina, I have reached an agreement with Queen Merecot. I will be relinquishing control of the spirits of Aratay and tying myself to the excess spirits of Semo, then bringing them to the barren areas to bond with the land. Ambassador Hanna says to tell you it was her idea. And Ven says to tell you not to worry, I'm not stupidly reckless. His words, not mine, though I believe he's right.

"The transfer of spirits will begin in the morning. Be ready."

Daleina withdrew her hand from the deer spirit's neck. Her heart was fluttering fast, and she knew every champion was watching her to gauge her reaction. Keeping her voice calm, she said, "Thank you for delivering this message. You may leave."

Wings outstretched, the feathered deer ran across the chamber and took flight.

After its departure, Daleina turned to her champions and

wished she had a chance to process her reaction. Concisely, she summarized the content of Naelin's message, and then let the waves of shock flow over her as the champions reacted in their usual overly loud manner. After all Daleina had been through, the sound of the champions arguing didn't shake her anymore. Raising her voice over them, she cut through their debate. "Queen Naelin has chosen to protect the people of Semo *and* the people of Aratay. By committing herself to this course of action, she prevents a future invasion by Queen Merecot, thus protecting two countries at once. The canopy singers will immortalize her choice and sing of it for generations to come. In the meantime, your mandate is unchanged: continue to seek out candidates and train them as quickly and as well as you can." *In case this all fails spectacularly.* She then dismissed them. Except one. "Champion Havtru, if you please."

She waited until the others had filed out, down the winding stairs. Champion Havtru waited patiently on one knee. He then rose. "Your Majesty?"

"You haven't chosen a candidate yet."

"I, um, have been taking Champion Ven's advice, taking my time to seek out the best possible candidate. I've been looking beyond Mittriel, and . . ."

She waved his words away. "Since you aren't currently training a candidate, I have a favor to ask: would you go north and bring home Ambassador Hanna? Queen Naelin may have decided to take on this risk—and if she thinks it's the right thing to do, I'm not going to stop her." *She's going to die,* Daleina thought. *She'll be vulnerable in the moment she releases her spirits, and the spirits will kill her. Merecot won't be able to stop them . . . if she even wants to.* And then squelched the thought. Perhaps Naelin, Ven, and Hanna had reason to believe all would be well—Naelin seemed to think so, in her message. Still . . . "She has Champion Ven and Ambassador Hanna there to advise her, and if they believe this is the best course of action, then so be it. But after she has finished being noble and self-sacrificing, there will be no more purpose to Ambassador Hanna's presence in Semo. I want her safely home, before Queen Merecot invents another disaster."

"Your Majesty, her guards would be better suited . . ."

"She's going to argue, and Champion Ven will likely defend her. He likes defending people. It's his thing. So I need someone of equal rank to Ven to, well, shout him down if need be. A guard can't do that. But you can. You will need an excuse so that Queen Merecot doesn't see your arrival as an insult—I'd rather she didn't know I don't trust her—so please feel free to invent whatever lie suits you."

"Very well, Your Majesty." Havtru bowed. "I'll bring Ambassador Hanna safely home."

She laid a hand on his shoulder. "Thank you, Champion Havtru. And if you could clobber some sense into Ven and get him to come home too, ideally with Queen Naelin and her children, I'd appreciate it." She didn't have much hope of that. Knowing Naelin, she'd leave when she was ready, not before, no matter whom Daleina sent. *But I have to try.*

"You, um, forgive me, but . . . You don't approve of Queen Naelin's decision?"

Daleina sighed. It was a brilliant idea that would save both the people of Aratay and Semo—she'd meant every word when she said that. It was selfless and brave and everything that Daleina admired. But it could easily get Queen Naelin killed. "I do," she told Havtru. "It's only that I'll feel better once everyone's home."

HAVTRU WISHED HE HADN'T LIED TO THE QUEEN. BUT CHAMPION Ven had been both specific and emphatic: Havtru was to keep his candidate secret and safe. And Cajara was worth keeping safe. He'd lucked into choosing a brilliant candidate, even if she herself didn't know it yet.

Hurrying through the palace, Havtru ran through a mental checklist of what he'd need to do and bring for his trip north. Bedrolls, skillet, soldier rations, bow and arrow so he wouldn't have to eat soldier rations . . . and double everything, for Cajara. He hoped Ven would approve of the decision to bring her. It was a risk—Queen Merecot had been behind the assassination of heirs—but he also couldn't afford to delay her training, or risk leaving her in Mittriel unprotected. At least in the north, he'd be with her.

*I have to bring her.*

*It's my responsibility to make sure she doesn't die.*

Cajara trusted him, and she'd been abandoned so many times by people who were supposed to be her family that he wouldn't even consider leaving her behind. His job was to strengthen her, not break her again.

He rounded a corner and nearly plowed into a man who was waiting for him with outstretched hands. The man stumbled back but regained his balance as he cried, "Champion Havtru, a word! Please!"

Havtru paused. The man looked familiar . . . "Have we met?"

"Unlikely. I'm only a woodsman. Renet's my name. But . . . you know my wife. Former wife. Future wife again, I hope, if she'll have me. But even if she won't . . . She's the mother of my children. Please, Champion Havtru, I know you came from the Council of Champions. Has there been any word from Queen Naelin? Are my children . . . That is, I've heard rumors . . ."

*I do know him. Or who he is. Poor man.* He thought of Queen Naelin's plan to save the people of Semo and Aratay. *How do I tell him his former wife is about to risk her life?*

"You have! Is she . . ." Renet's voice cracked. He ran his fingers through his hair. He looked, Havtru thought, as if he hadn't slept in weeks.

"I'm about to leave for Semo," Havtru said. "If you'd like me to deliver a message to her, I can do that for you."

It was the least he could do.

He thought of his own wife. What he wouldn't give to send one last message to her!

"Take me with you!" Renet cried.

Havtru drew back. He couldn't do that. He had specific orders, and they didn't involve transporting civilians across the border. "I'm sorry, but—"

"The rumors say my children are there, and she's gone to save them," Renet blurted out. "But she's not going to come back. I know it. I know her. She thinks this is her final act, saving our children, and I can't . . . I can't lose her. My children can't lose her."

Havtru hadn't had children. He and his wife had talked about having them, but the time was never right. Wait a while longer, she'd say. After the next harvest, he'd say. Next season, she'd promise. One more year, he'd say. And then there was no more time. She was gone, taken from him in an instant by spirits who should never have attacked his village. He'd survived only because Champion Ven had arrived, and he'd survived after that only because Ven had given him a new purpose in life.

But he'd never forgotten his old life.

It occurred to him that regardless of the truth of any rumors, if he brought Renet, it would be a perfect excuse for his trip north. Queen Daleina didn't want it known that she didn't trust Queen Merecot, but if he was there escorting the queen's husband to see his wife . . . "All right. You can come. But we leave tonight."

Renet blubbered his thanks.

Havtru hoped he didn't regret this.

# CHAPTER 21

Ven did *not* like this plan.

He strapped his armor into position, tightening it too far and then loosening it. Glaring at himself in the mirror, he thought, *I won't be able to protect her.* No matter how many weapons he brought with him, how many blades he slid into his boots, how many bows he put in his quiver. He wasn't to be allowed into the grove.

"You're angry," Naelin said behind him.

She was already dressed: a simple white gown and the crown of Aratay on her head. A servant had braided her hair into some complex knots that made Ven wonder how many blades he could hide within it. Sure, she had her power to protect her, but Merecot was powerful too. And in the moment when Naelin abdicated her hold on the spirits of Aratay, she would be at her most vulnerable. Merecot would have full control of all the spirits of Semo, and the two women would be alone in the grove, without him.

*I hate this.*

"I'm not angry at you," he told her. "I'm angry at the spirit-damned tradition that keeps me from going in with you. You'd think in unusual circumstances tradition could be bent." If the champions had accompanied the heirs on the day Daleina had been crowned . . .

"Merecot has Erian and Llor, so she makes the rules. But in

this case, it's not just her rule. It's the spirits—they view the grove as sacred. Only the queen and her heir may enter." She held up a hand, stopping him before he could object. "I know you went with me to the Aratayian grove, but this is Semo. Different grove, different spirits. Besides, I think it's best not to agitate the spirits before I do this, don't you? They're already agitated enough." She was speaking evenly and brightly, as if he were a child about to pitch a fit.

"Stop that," he told her.

She furrowed her brow. "Stop what?" A hint of the anxiousness she had to be feeling crept into her voice. *Good*, he thought. *She shouldn't be calm about this.* Alert and afraid was the best way to be. The best way to not die.

"You can say what you want to me," Ven said. "You don't need to protect me by pretending to be all right."

Her shoulders sagged. "I love that about you." She flopped into a nearby chair, another carved stone monstrosity smothered in pillows.

*She loves me*, he thought. This was the second time she'd said the word "love." He realized he was grinning foolishly and tried to hide his smile within his beard. She'd said the words so casually, as if it were a matter of course, which made it feel even more true.

"You can still back out of this. We can find another way. Rescue Erian and Llor, and flee."

"You say that like it would be easy. We're outnumbered, on enemy territory, and Erian and Llor are guarded by her spirits—spirits I can't control, not while Queen Merecot has her fist around them. Besides, I can't abandon the people of Semo to their fate. Not to mention Aratay—if I don't help, then Queen Merecot will go back to her delightful plan of assassination and invasion."

"All the more reason for you not to be alone in the grove with her."

Naelin closed her eyes and sighed. "If I die in there, promise me you'll take Erian and Llor home. Bring them to Renet. He'll look after them—he's not as irresponsible as he used to be."

"I'll take care of them myself, if you want me to." Kneeling before her, he took her hand in his and kissed her knuckles. Her fingers curled around his.

"Marry me," she said.

He froze, mid-kiss. "Now?"

"Yes. Before I enter the grove."

"You're not going to die in there." He'd never thought about marriage before, not to anyone, but if he was to marry, of course it would be to Naelin. He never wanted to be parted from her—he'd proved that by coming here. But a wedding? Now? This wasn't a proposal; it was a pity gesture to the man she planned to leave behind with her glorious, sacrificial death.

"You just as much said you think Queen Merecot plans to murder me." Her eyes popped open. "So marry me first. It will make a better song for your sister to sing."

"That's a ridiculous reason to marry." His throat felt clogged. It was hard to force the words out and make them sound normal. He didn't know how she could talk about her own death so matter-of-factly. His hands tightened around hers.

"Then marry me because you love me." She leaned forward and looked at him with such intensity that it felt as if she were memorizing every feature of his face. He wished he had a less scruffy face to offer her.

"I do love you," he said.

Naelin smiled, and he felt as if he were looking straight into the sun. And he knew in that instant he wouldn't say no, not if this made her glow so much. "You made me feel when I didn't want to feel anything anymore," she said. "And now . . . Ven, I'm not going to die in there. You're going to marry me, I'm going to take the spirits, and we're going to bring them home with Erian and Llor."

He smiled back, even though his heart hurt. "Good plan, Your Majesty."

MERECOT RAISED HER EYEBROWS AT AMBASSADOR HANNA. "I suppose a few hundred spirits will make an adequate wedding present?" She'd chosen to meet with the ambassador in the gardens, because the sculptures reminded her of what a queen could do with her power when she wasn't worrying about volcanoes and avalanches and other spirit-born disasters.

The pebbles crunched as Hanna rolled over them. "I'm sure that would suffice, especially if a few could be wrapped in ribbons."

Her eyebrows shot higher. "Continually surprises me that you have a sense of humor."

"Mmm. Queen Naelin wished me to convey that she doesn't want to inconvenience you or your people. If you could but supply a dignitary to officiate—"

Merecot waved away her words. "Bah, we can do more than that. Semo would be delighted and honored to host such an event. In fact, the courtiers will be giddy with joy. They'll make it a night to remember." Probably drench the entire castle in diamonds in honor of the event. And the city itself would be celebrating for weeks . . . but that might be a good thing. *This will be excellent for public opinion. First, a lavish party, and then a solution to the spirit problem.* Granted, it wasn't the solution she'd planned, but she could work with it for now.

In fact, she already had several ideas. When she had time, she'd have to share them with Queen Jastra. But first, she had a wedding to plan!

As she began to make lists in her head—at least twelve musicians, an array of food including their most traditional Semoian dishes . . . oh, and they'd use the West Room of course, festooned with whatever fripperies her courtiers wanted—Merecot beamed at Hanna. "A royal wedding in Semo! Songs will be written about it. Horrible, sappy, romantic songs, but it will be a nice change from the usual ballads about death and mayhem." Perhaps she could have a portion of the evening devoted to songsmiths debuting their newest creations—*after I excuse myself for the night, so I won't have to listen to their warbling.*

"Queen Naelin and Champion Ven won't want a fuss," Hanna said.

"Then we won't tell them we're making one," Merecot said. "My people will love this!" *And they'll love me for it.* "Are you against a bit of subterfuge in keeping plans from the besotted couple?" She expected Hanna to refuse, but instead Hanna nodded seriously.

"Indeed, I would recommend it. They don't need to know the extent of the celebration until the day of." Hanna quit rolling her chair and leaned back, folding her hands in her lap. "How soon can such an event be arranged, though? I believe they want to be wed before the transfer of spirits."

"It can be done quickly." Merecot then held up one hand and touched the minds of the spirits in the garden—a trio of tiny earth spirits playing with gravel, as well as a water spirit bathing in a fountain. She viewed the garden through their eyes, checking to be sure there were no stray gardeners or courtiers to overhear her and Hanna. Once she was certain, she said to Hanna, "We can use the wedding as a distraction. While the guests are consumed with merriment, Queen Naelin and I can visit the grove."

"You don't wish to make the transfer of spirits public?" Hanna asked. "You should at least alert your chancellors and your military."

Merecot snorted. "Definitely not." People would panic. Or have opinions. Either was inconvenient. She'd rather it be a done deal and then present their success to the adoring public, or else bury their failure as quickly as possible and shift the blame elsewhere.

"Won't your people need to be prepared in the event of failure?" Hanna asked.

"Why? So they can run around in terror?" But it was a valid point. Merecot considered the matter, pacing beneath a stone sculpture of . . . *Really? A sheep dressed as a courtier?* The statue was an exquisite representation of a sheep standing on its hind feet with a chiffon puffed skirt and a surfeit of necklaces. Sometimes the garden sculptures made Merecot dream of more peaceful times, but sometimes they made her wonder about the priorities of her predecessors. *Here I am, trying to save the world, and they were carving sheep ladies.*

The statue, though, did remind her that so far, she hadn't chosen an heir from the flock of hostile Semoian candidates. *Because all of them are unworthy.* None of them had been happy about an interloper from Aratay taking the crown, and so Merecot hadn't liked any of them in return. If her failure were catastrophic, if she'd made a miscalculation and neither queen survived this attempt . . . Only she and Jastra knew how to reach the grove. And Jastra, as the former queen, would be one of the spirits' first targets.

Merecot felt a pang of guilt. In her obsession with Aratay, had she failed one of her basic duties to Semo?

Glancing at Hanna, Merecot thought of a way to sidestep the issue. *So long as Jastra and I aren't the only ones who know how to reach the grove, I don't have to choose a successor. If I die, it can be someone else's problem.* She smiled at the elderly ambassador. "You will accompany us when we leave the celebration. But you'd better prepare your guards to accept your absence—they aren't invited to the after party."

With that, Merecot pivoted and strode through the garden, fast enough that she was certain Hanna couldn't follow her, not without assistance. She didn't want to answer any questions. Besides, she had a wedding to plan.

AMBASSADOR HANNA SAT PLACIDLY IN THE CENTER OF HER chambers as a courtier held up a necklace. "The Crown was given this necklace by the stonemason Herro, on behalf of the knights of Nimoc, in gratitude for the creation of their town. Queen Rakka carved their town within a mountain—it is said to have been the grandest collection of caves ever seen, until it collapsed in the Tragedy of Enneva Falls." The necklace was an elaborate twist of gold, cradling sapphires and rubies.

"It's beautiful," Hanna said.

The courtier looked delighted at her assessment. "Wait until you see the Bracelet of Joy! It took three generations of jewelers to piece together, legend says, and the last jeweler was said to cry tears of blood as she finished, which is why the diamonds look as red as rubies."

"That sounds lovely as well."

As Hanna was dressed in even more jewels, the courtier told her a story for each, and seemed happier and happier with Hanna's responses—Hanna had the sense she didn't have an attentive audience often. When she finished, Hanna felt as if she were dressed in the history of Semo, which was nearly certainly the point. "You look beautiful!" the courtier gushed. Waving toward a servant, she had a mirror brought in front of Hanna.

*I look elegant.* Not at all like the strict headmistress of an elite academy. She looked as frivolous as any courtier. The gown was layers of blue and purple, falling over one another like petals of a just-bloomed flower. Her white hair had been twisted with so much gold that it sparkled like sunshine, and the jewels . . . It felt as if she were wearing the sky around her neck and on her arms. "Thank you."

"You're most welcome, Ambassador Hanna." The lady dropped into a curtsy.

Guards opened the bedroom door to admit Champion Ven. He'd been dressed too, albeit with far fewer jewels. He still wore his green leather armor, but it had been cleaned and mended, and he wore a stiff shirt underneath it. He tugged at the collar as if it were strangling him. His beard had also been trimmed and neatened, and his hair was smoothed. Hanna repressed a smirk. "You look very handsome, Champion Ven."

He snorted. "Let's get this over with."

She clucked her tongue. "That's not the attitude for the groom on his wedding day."

"They tried to tell me I couldn't take my weapons." He scowled at the nearest guard, as if it were his fault. The guard shrank back.

Hanna noted he still carried his sword. She supposed "tried" was the operative word. "Have you ever even been to a wedding?" she asked, torn between exasperated and amused.

"I thought we'd find a tree to stand under, say vows, and then kiss hard enough to embarrass everyone who's watching."

"You're such a romantic."

"She doesn't want romance; she wants insurance." He shook his head. "Forget I said that. Just nerves." He moved behind her chair and pushed her forward. "I'm supposed to escort you."

Hanna couldn't help being amused as she looked back and up at him. This wedding was a stroke of diplomatic brilliance, but she knew that wasn't why Naelin was doing it. "She loves you, you know."

He tugged on his collar again. "I know that. Love her too. Hate this shirt."

"Stop tugging on it. You'll stretch it out."

"That's the idea."

Flanked by guards in ceremonial armor, they processed through the castle. Queen Merecot had called on the spirits to decorate for the wedding in mere hours, and the results were spectacular: the castle looked like a cake, with ivory buntings instead of frosting and bouquets of jewels instead of fondant flowers. Hanna admired it, even as she thought it was all a bit ridiculous.

Every courtier had dressed in his or her finest as well, draped in jewels that undoubtedly all had their own stories and histories. The West Room had been chosen for the site of the wedding, but it had been transformed with lush red carpets everywhere and golden ribbons dangling from the arched ceiling. On a dais, Queen Naelin waited with her children beside her, both dressed in gold and silver. Hanna felt Ven slow, nearly forgetting to walk, much less push her, when the two queens came into view.

Queen Merecot was beautiful, of course, in a midnight-blue gown, with her hair with its white streak artfully arranged to gleam in the sunlight that poured through the high windows. But Queen Naelin had also been transformed into an elegant creature out of legend. She looked serene, dressed in an exquisite gown of pale green, the color of new leaves in the spring. She didn't wear a single Semoian jewel but instead had living vines wrapped around her bare arms. The leaves were deep green, all except for one golden leaf at the hollow of her throat.

Hanna sighed happily.

Whatever the reason, however ridiculous the extravagance, this would count as the pinnacle of her career: facilitating the wedding of the Mother of Aratay to the Hero of the Forest and cementing peaceful relations between Aratay and Semo.

She cried a few polite, happy tears, along with everyone else when the couple exchanged their vows—heartfelt declarations of love, in voices that carried through the West Room—and she cheered with everyone else when Champion Ven and Queen

Naelin kissed, elegantly, framed by the sun that poured through the windows.

Hanna was beside them with a perfect view as they turned to face the adoring crowd.

And the look on the bride's face was such a perfect mix of joy and sorrow that it nearly broke Hanna's heart. *Oh spirits*, Hanna thought as her cheers faded in her throat. *She's found her perfect happiness . . . and she's just realized that tonight, in the grove, she might lose it.*

# CHAPTER 22

E rian loved every second of the wedding:
How happy Mama looked.

How happy Ven looked.

How pretty the castle was.

How everyone cheered.

How she was asked to stand with Llor beside her mother for the ceremony. She'd been given a royal jewel to hold, the Diamond of Eternity, which was supposed to symbolize everlasting love. There was a story that went with it, about a queen who'd married a man who worked in a diamond mine. On the day he proposed, he found this stone lying next to his pickax, as if it had been left for him—he took it as a sign of their love. The courtier said that on their wedding day, it rained diamonds, which Erian thought sounded painful.

She cheered with everyone when the bride and groom kissed, and her mother kissed her forehead as Erian placed the Diamond of Eternity on a pedestal beside them.

And then she and Llor were ushered out of the West Room to the cheers and the music. *Now we'll go home, all together, and it will be perfect.* Maybe their father could live near them. She wondered if they'd still live in the palace in Mittriel, or if they'd live in the outer forest. *Mama likes the outer forest, but the palace is nice too.*

Llor clung to her hand, close by her side, as they were shooed up a tower into a room near the top, to wait for their mother and Ven. It was a nice room: two fluffy beds piled with pillows, a couch by a fireplace, a table with a tower of pastries. A wide window with a view of the mountains was open, and a sweet breeze wafted inside. Releasing Erian's hand, Llor beelined for the pastries and stuffed one in his mouth.

Then they were left alone, which was pretty much the first time they'd been alone since their arrival in Semo. Or almost alone—Erian knew there were guards just outside, several of Queen Merecot's best. She tried not to mind that they were always guarded. After all, they'd been guarded in Mittriel too. And at least these new guards were human, instead of spirit.

"I want Mama and Ven," Llor said loudly, still chewing the pastry. Crumbs dribbled down his shirt. "Why can't we stay with them?"

"Because that's not how they do weddings here."

They'd been told they couldn't stay for the entire wedding. Children weren't allowed—another Semoian tradition, like the Diamond of Eternity. She knew Mama and Ven had argued against that, but Queen Merecot had overruled them. "Her land, her traditions," Mama had told Erian. "Be a good girl and look after your brother. Try to get some sleep. We'll have a long journey tomorrow."

"But they missed us. They said so." His lower lip was quivering, still dotted with crumbs. *Oh no, tantrum coming!* Erian thought.

Crossing to him, she knelt quickly and hugged him, which was awkward in her dress. The satin creaked when she stretched her arms out. "Don't worry. After we're home, we're all going to be together forever and ever. That's what the wedding meant."

He nodded, and then his eyes widened. "Then why are *they* here?"

He pointed over her shoulder, and she turned.

Two very familiar air spirits had landed in the open window. They had leathery skin and vicious beaks, and Erian was certain these were the spirits that had ripped them from Bayn's back. She pushed Llor behind her and backed slowly toward the door.

Llor broke away from her and ran toward the door. He screamed as he tugged on it. She ran to him, helping him pull. "Help!" she yelled. "Guards, help us! Please, help!"

The door didn't open.

And no one came.

She felt talons close over her shoulders, and she was yanked backward, out the window. Llor was screaming too as he was pulled by the second spirit, also out the window. They were carried away from the castle, away from their mother and Ven, away from their perfect future.

Hand in hand with her new husband, Naelin faced the cheering crowds of Semoians and wished Erian and Llor had been permitted to stay—she'd told them it was because of tradition, because she didn't want to scare them with the truth: they were still prisoners, at least until the transfer of spirits was complete. She hated being parted from them, even if it was just for a few hours.

*Better that they don't worry*, she comforted herself.

At least they wouldn't be nearby when Naelin and Merecot went into the grove.

Queen Merecot whispered in her ear, "Well done. An Aratayian queen wedding her champion on Semoian soil is a diplomatic coup of the highest order—you've made my people feel lots of warm and fuzzy thoughts toward your wooded homeland."

"Glad to hear it."

"And I'm not planning to kill you tonight, so there's that to be happy about too. Now smile at the nice, cheering people."

Naelin didn't find that very reassuring. There were so many ways tonight could go wrong, even with the best intentions. But she plastered a smile on her face, because that's what the crowd needed to see, and she continued to smile while she watched the traditional dances performed in her and Ven's honor. Clapped when she was supposed to clap. Bowed when she was supposed to bow. And tried to appreciate it when a gold-clad woman hailed as the singer with the highest voice in the land proceeded to pierce everyone's eardrums with an absurdly shrill aria.

"Sira would have loved that," Ven murmured.

She glanced at him to see if he was joking.

He wasn't.

They smiled at each other.

Beyond him, the sun had nearly reached the western mountains. Already the sky wore a rosy tinge. She blinked from the blaze of the sun as it streamed through the wall of windows. Jewel-toned glass framed each of the windows, casting pools of colored light.

*As soon as this is over, we can all go home. Together.*

Softly, so her voice wouldn't carry, Queen Merecot said, "As the poets would say, when the mountains pierce the sun so deeply that it bleeds, we will go. Truly, you could not have picked a better distraction for my people. Everyone loves a wedding and all the implied happy-ending nonsense."

"Your soldiers will barricade the castle?" Ven asked, in an equally soft voice.

Merecot nodded. "Yes. No spirits will enter here. I've told them it's out of an overabundance of caution. Weddings are special, you know."

"This one is," Ven agreed.

The queen of Semo ignored that. "Of course, if things get truly out of hand, I can't promise my endearingly rambunctious spirits won't collapse the castle or shake down the mountain, but if it reaches that point, we'll both be dead, so what does it matter?"

"Your selflessness is indeed worthy of legends," Ven said.

Merecot smirked. "It will be."

"You have guards watching my children?" Naelin asked. "They must be kept safe, or the deal is off." She wanted to make even more threats: if any harm came to them, she'd unleash every spirit she controlled onto Semo. She'd tear this country apart rock by rock.

"I have my finest guards with them. All human guards, not spirits. Your precious darlings will be safer than anyone else in Semo. And hey, aren't *I* supposed to be using them to threaten *you*?"

"Let's just do this," Naelin said through gritted teeth.

Merecot just smiled pleasantly at her people and said to Naelin, "When the time is right."

The musicians played faster, and the Semoians flocked to the dance floor like bejeweled birds. Skirts swirling, the women danced in circles, lightly touching hands, while the men linked arms and marched first right, then left. Glasses were clinked. Laughter rose to the crystal chandeliers.

The hours passed.

On the dais, Naelin watched the sun sink. It did look as if a peak were piercing it. Tinged with blood, the sun spread as it descended into the mountains. "It's time now."

Queen Merecot nodded slightly and stepped forward. Raising her arms, she addressed the adoring crowd. With her eyes fixed on the sunset, Naelin didn't listen to Merecot's speech or pay attention to the music, dancing, and cheering that it spawned. The wedding guests tossed silver and gold ribbons into the air, and more glasses brimming with amber liquid were passed around.

As the music crescendoed, Ambassador Hanna rolled through the audience first, parting the crowd, and Naelin followed with Ven out of the West Room. Queen Merecot swept by with so much grace and elegance that a few of her subjects swooned when she passed them.

*Everyone loves a wedding,* Naelin remembered Merecot had said. It seemed she was right. The people all adored the bride and groom, their queen, and one another, at least for tonight.

Outside the West Room, Naelin released Ven so he could push Ambassador Hanna's chair through the corridors. They didn't speak as they crossed the castle. She wished she could have seen Erian and Llor after the wedding, tuck them into bed, and reassure them that all would be well.

*Let's just get this over with, and then we can all be together.*

Two hallways from the West Room, Merecot ordered her guards to stay behind. Three hallways away, Hanna signaled to her guards to leave as well.

This part of the castle was silent, except for their footsteps and the crunch of Hanna's wheels. On the walls, the tapestries were faded and frayed, and the stone behind the sconces was stained black from decades of smoke. Another corridor, and Naelin noticed the dust on the floor: there were no footprints. Cobwebs clung to the ceiling. *Strange*, Naelin thought. She knew Merecot wasn't about to clean her own castle, but she had both caretakers and spirits at her command. She wondered why this wing of the castle had been ignored.

Unwatched, the two queens, the champion, and the ambassador entered a small courtyard lit only by the rising moon, a weak crescent vulnerable to the clouds. A few stars were visible.

Naelin glanced at Hanna, but the ambassador seemed unconcerned about the fact that they were in a forgotten part of the castle without any guards. She'd been similarly unfazed by the scope of the wedding ceremony. *They've been talking behind my back*, Naelin guessed. She wondered if that was cause for alarm and decided no, she trusted Hanna. Plus it was too late for alarm. She was committed now.

The courtyard looked abandoned: shriveled weeds filled the cracks between the stones, a few arches had crumbled and the rubble had never been removed, and the center of the square was loose dirt.

"What you are about to witness is a closely guarded secret," Queen Merecot said. "The queens of Semo have traditionally hidden the location of the Semoian grove, in order to control which heir was able to replace them."

Naelin walked forward. *This can't be the grove.* It didn't have that same sacred feeling of the Queen's Grove in Aratay. She turned in a circle, looking at all the tumbled arches. *It's just a neglected, old courtyard.*

"You hide your grove?" Ven asked, disbelief and disapproval clear in his voice.

"Impractical," Ambassador Hanna said with a sniff. "Queens cannot always predict their deaths." Naelin agreed with that—history was full of examples. It was why the canopy singers were so important: their drumbeats could spread word of the queen's death before too many innocents died.

Beside her, she noticed Ven was also scanning the area, watching for threats—half his attention on Merecot and half on the courtyard. There were shadows everywhere: in the corners, behind half-dead trees, beside the rubble.

"One heir at all times must know how to reach the grove," Merecot said. "Unfortunately, at this time, I haven't chosen which heir to trust, perhaps because they all hate me. And each other too, but mostly me."

"Even more impractical," Hanna said.

Naelin agreed with her again. So many innocent people depended on the queen. To keep the location of the grove a secret was bad enough, but for Merecot to have gone this long without a successor voluntarily, while Queen Daleina sent her champions out in a desperate search for suitable candidates . . . "Impractical and irresponsible."

"I don't criticize your country," Merecot snapped. "You shouldn't criticize mine. Besides, it's because of the power struggles between the heirs that I was able to become queen, and that was the best thing for Semo."

*She doesn't lack for confidence,* Naelin thought. She wondered if they'd misread her—if everything about Merecot was a misread. This could still be a trap.

"What you're about to attempt is dangerous," Ven said. "If the spirits rebel and you are killed, and no one knows the location of the grove . . ."

"That's why I've invited Ambassador Hanna to accompany us, at least as far as this courtyard," Merecot said. "Ambassador Hanna, you will remain here as insurance against our failure."

Naelin glanced at Hanna, who raised her eyebrows and said, "I assumed I was invited to ensure neither of you dies in this endeavor."

Merecot dismissed this. "You don't have the power to ensure that. But you can watch how we access the grove, and if my spirits start slaughtering everyone, you can ensure that the death toll isn't overly catastrophic by guiding an heir here. Any of the nitwits will do. You can always poison them if they prove inept."

*She's so casual about lives,* Naelin thought. Real men, women, and children were at risk, and Merecot didn't care. She thought of Erian and Llor and hoped they had enough guards around them.

At least Merecot had promised none of the guards were spirits. However, it didn't stop her from saying, "You're sickening."

"I'm practical," Merecot said. "Vast difference. Not everyone who is born is meant to survive. I have a responsibility to my people as a collective whole, not to any particular individual. But maybe that's the difference between you and me. I value all my people equally. You cherish a few above all others. That's why I'm a better queen than you are."

*I never pretended to be a good queen*, Naelin thought. *But I'm better than Merecot.* Merecot was immature and immoral, a combination with the potential to turn deadly. *Potential? No—she's already proved deadly.* Innocent Aratayians had suffered and were still suffering from the invasion, and think of all the candidates she'd had murdered! "You only care about yourself."

"Not true. I don't care about myself at all. Everything I do is for the good of Renthia. You, on the other hand . . . Of the two of us, I think it's clear which of us is the more selfish. I care about the fate of thousands of people, yet you would have given up all your power, abdicated the throne, left Aratay in danger, for the sake of your children."

Naelin bristled. *She has no right to judge me*, she thought. "I love my children more than my own life!"

"You love your children more than anyone's life," Merecot said. "As my sister found out. But that's not the issue, and who you love is not my problem—at least, I hope it isn't. So long as you serve their needs, the excess spirits won't care where your loyalties lie, and neither will I. Let's do this, shall we?"

Naelin wanted to argue. This young girl playing at queen had no idea what it meant to be a mother. She'd never woken ten times in the night, just to check that her child was still breathing. She'd never worried about whether she was making her child too scared or not scared enough while she warned them to be careful, always careful. She'd never been aware—so aware that it made her skin prickle and her heart thump faster—of how little she could control in the world around them, of how fragile they were, and of how finite days were. "You don't—"

And then she cut herself off as Queen Merecot summoned

a massive earth spirit. Shaped like a giant slug, it burrowed up through the dirt in the courtyard. Broken flagstones spilled back from its bulbous body.

Naelin stepped back—she'd been so caught up in feeling outraged that she hadn't sensed it, but here it was, looming in her consciousness. Its hate felt hazy and distant, as if leftover from a previous emotion, and she sensed no coherent thought beyond *down, down, dig deep, dig down.*

"Creepy thing," Ven muttered, hand straying to his sword. "Naelin?"

"It's not attacking," Naelin said.

"Of course it's not attacking—I summoned it," Merecot said, exasperated, as she climbed onto its back. "The Queen's Grove of Semo is hidden within the mountains. Fastest way to reach it is to take tunnels. If the worst happens, Ambassador, this is the kind of spirit an heir must summon. It and its ilk know the way."

"And I find an heir how?" Hanna said testily. "Since you've shirked your responsibility to choose one."

"All the heirs attended the wedding. You'll find them in the West Room. Choose whomever seems least annoying." Leaning down, Merecot held out her hand to Naelin.

Naelin hesitated. *Can I trust her?*

"Not the time for second thoughts," Merecot said. "Climb on board. I've got a whole country full of people depending on me who need this to work."

She wondered if Merecot saw her people like they're her children. *Could she?* If so . . . Before Naelin could decide, Ven stepped in front of the earth spirit. "I'm coming too."

"You can't," Merecot said. "We discussed this. Unlike the spirits of Aratay, the spirits of Semo won't enter the grove if others are present. Or more accurately, they *will*, but they'll be very pissed off. Your presence will endanger our lives."

"I'll wait outside. But I will go with my wife as far as I can."

Merecot looked as if she was about to argue more, but Ambassador Hanna didn't let her. "If I must stay here, then he must go," Hanna said. "Besides, your people would be suspicious if they saw him without his bride so soon after the wedding, and I know you want this to be secret. At least until you're sure it will succeed."

The other queen scowled but agreed. "It *will* succeed. But fine. Come with us, Ven. You can't enter the grove, but you can lurk outside it in whatever threatening manner you'd like. Honestly, you champions are more stubborn than mountain goats. And believe me, Semo has more than enough of those."

Naelin climbed onto the spirit, and Ven got on behind her. The earth spirit's flesh squished beneath her. It smelled sour, like dirt with dung mixed in, after the rain. Breathing through her mouth so she wouldn't smell it, she hung on to its stiff hairs as the spirit plunged back into the hole it had made.

Inside the tunnel, the darkness was complete. She saw the same whether her eyes were open or closed, and the only sounds were their breathing, the huffing of the spirit, and the sprinkling sound of pebbles rolling downhill. It was equal parts horrifying and disgusting, but Naelin said nothing. She thought about Erian and Llor. *Once I finish this, I'll never have to be parted from them again. Assuming it works . . .*

At last, the slug spirit emerged from the tunnels. Above, the sky was dimpled with stars, and the mountains were black shadows that sliced up the night sky. She saw torches lit in a line toward slabs of stone, standing side by side in a circle.

The Queen's Grove of Semo.

All three of them slid off the spirit's back. Merecot plucked dirt off her dress and straightened her crown. "Shall we?"

Ven placed his hands on either side of Naelin's face and kissed her so deeply that she felt as if her bones were melting. She caught her breath while he turned to Merecot. "Understand that if you emerge from the grove and Naelin does not, I will kill you."

Merecot smiled frostily. "You will try."

Naelin placed a hand on Ven's chest, as if that would hold him back if he decided to attack Merecot. "Let's not threaten each other when the goal is to survive this, right?" She pleaded with her eyes, trying to make him understand that she *did* intend to survive this. She had a purpose now, and a goal. Everything had changed when she'd learned of what Queen Jastra had done. He put his hand over hers, holding it until she stepped away.

"Aw, that's sweet," Merecot said, rolling her eyes. "Come on."

The queen of Semo headed toward the circle of stones, and Naelin followed after her. Wind whistled through the canyon, and cold pricked her arms. She heard no other sound. No birds. No animals. No crickets. She felt as if the mountains were watching her.

The only light was from the line of torches and the crescent moon above. She wondered who had placed the torches here, or if they'd been lit by fire spirits. She sensed no spirits nearby—even the earth spirit who'd brought them had retreated back into the rock.

Far in the distance, south beyond the border, she felt the rest of the spirits of Aratay like a tingle. She couldn't distinguish between individual spirits, but she knew they were there, linked to her. She wondered what it would feel like when she severed her connection to them. It could hurt. Or it might feel no different from clipping off a dead fingernail.

Much closer, Naelin brushed her mind against the serpent-shaped spirit of Aratay who had carried her to Semo. She'd sent their other mount, the feathered deer, away earlier, to bring her message to Daleina, but this one was still at the castle, awaiting her orders. *Go south. Fly to Aratay.* She wanted it closer to Daleina, where the other queen could more easily reassert her power over it.

Naelin felt the spirit fly toward the border and felt a twinge of . . . *I can't be feeling sadness. I never wanted to be their queen. You can't regret what you didn't want.*

The two queens entered the stone circle.

"Careful. It's slippery," Merecot said. "I fell twice when I was crowned."

"Really?" She couldn't imagine Merecot ever doing anything that uncontrolled.

"Not really. I'm just trying to make you feel better. Did it work?"

"No." It was barren rock within, but polished until it gleamed, so smooth that Naelin had to walk gingerly to avoid slipping. *Hardly a historic moment if I fall on my butt*, she thought. On the other hand, at least there was no one here to see, except Merecot.

Still, even empty, the grove felt oddly alive. The silence was a hushed one—the silence of a person holding her breath, not the hollow silence of a vacant room. It was the same feeling as the Queen's Grove in Aratay, as if she'd walked into a place so steeped in memories and expectations that the very air remembered.

Merecot halted in the center of the circle. Turning back to Naelin, she held out her hands and waited for Naelin to pick her way over the slick stone.

Reaching her, Naelin took Merecot's hands. "All right then. I'll abdicate first, then you release your spirits, then I claim them."

Merecot swung Naelin's arms from side to side, shaking them out. She seemed far more cheerful than was appropriate. "Relax. Worst that can happen is a painful death."

"And the destruction of both Aratay and Semo, if Daleina can't control her spirits and you can't control yours." Naelin said it calmly, but it was a real possibility. As far as Naelin knew, nothing like this had ever been attempted before. What if Merecot accidentally lost control of all of them? What if Naelin wasn't able to gain control? No one had ever released a portion of their spirits before, and the Semoian spirits from the untamed lands were far wilder than any Naelin had ever encountered. *All of this has the potential to go horribly, terribly wrong.* And her husband was just outside the grove, alone and exposed.

Grinning, Merecot nodded. "End-of-the-world stakes. Yay! You go first."

"For the record, I don't like you, but I trust that you want to be a good queen and that you have the best interests of your people at heart."

"For the record, I don't care, and you can trust that I want to be a *great* queen."

Closing her eyes, Naelin concentrated. She felt for her connection to the spirits of Aratay, and to her surprise she also "saw" the connection of the spirits of Semo to Merecot. As if she were snipping threads on embroidery, she severed the threads connecting her to her spirits, careful not to touch any of the threads leading to Merecot, though she felt as if she could have. All the threads lay before her. *I release you. I abdicate. I am not your queen.*

*Not your queen.*

She heard them echo her, distantly: *Not our queen.*

*Not ours.*

*Not ours.*

*Not.*

And Naelin swayed, feeling suddenly weak, as if she were a water bucket that had been drained—the sense of the spirits of Aratay were gone, to be replaced by an awareness of the spirits of Semo: coming toward the stone grove, hating her, hating their queen, determined to destroy them both.

Or at least Naelin.

MERECOT KNEW SHE COULD KILL HER.

Right now.

Easy.

She wouldn't even have to shed a drop of blood herself. Just call on one of the earth spirits to suck Naelin down into the stone, or one of the air spirits to raise her up and drop her. She had full control over every spirit in Semo, and all of Naelin's strength couldn't compare to that.

The instant that Naelin released the spirits of Aratay, Naelin staggered back, losing her grip on Merecot's hands, and Merecot let her fall backward. The older queen slipped on the slick rock ground and sprawled out at Merecot's feet.

For that moment, Merecot looked down at Naelin and contemplated murder.

It was the original plan: kill the queens and seize the power. Queen Jastra would have been whispering at her to do it. The old queen had sworn an opportunity would present itself once the wolf protector was removed.

*This is an opportunity, but I've a far better plan,* Merecot thought. *Don't* kill Naelin. Let her take the wild spirits and go, and then visit Daleina with hands and conscience both clean—

and at full strength, without the distraction of the excess spirits. If Merecot were innocent of regicide, then Daleina might welcome her old friend with open arms.

*And then, maybe, I have a chance to fulfill my destiny.*

Kill Daleina first, take control of Aratay, and then use the combined strength of both Aratay and Semo to squash Naelin with her paltry number of excess spirits.

But first, Naelin had to live now, so she could die later.

Reaching down, she helped Naelin back onto her feet. "Ready?"

Naelin took a deep breath, and Merecot saw her brace herself. *Good.* "Better be," Merecot told her. "The spirits who aren't linked to the land are *very* strong."

"So am I," Naelin said grimly.

Merecot could admire that. Concentrating, she reached out—the spirits of Semo had already sensed that something was happening in the stone grove and were hurling themselves there as fast as they could. The wind was whipping around the grove hard, slapping at Merecot and Naelin, and the ground began to quiver under their feet.

She felt for the wild ones, the ones who weren't sunk deep into the soil of Semo, the ones who wanted to fight and wanted to flee and wanted to tear apart the world she was trying to hold together. Grabbing ahold of the invisible connection that bound her to them, she imagined she was coiling those lines around her hand, tightening them into a single rope.

And then she cut the rope.

NAELIN FELT THE SPIRITS OF SEMO SCREAM—THE WILD ONES broke free, while the others strained at their bonds. *I could take them all*, she thought. At this moment, Merecot was weak. If Naelin pushed her mind into the swirling chaos, she might be able to wrest control of all of them, the ones from the untamed lands *and* the ones native to Semo, away from Merecot. Within the grove, she could feel the threads of their connection.

*I could ensure she never invades again.*

*I could protect Queen Daleina and all my people from her and her ambition.*

*Maybe.* If Merecot didn't stop her. If the spirits didn't fight back. If Naelin even wanted this. *I . . .*

*I want Erian and Llor.*

She plunged her mind into the maelstrom of spirits.

*Choose me,* she told the wild spirits. *I will be your queen now. Choose me. Now!*

Her thoughts, her emotions, her will was battered by the howling of the spirits. They wanted to rip, destroy, break, kill. She heard a rumbling around her, and the earth bucked beneath her feet. Naelin slammed down hard on her knees. Pain shot up through her legs, but she barely felt it. It was buried in the pain all around her as the spirits' minds tore at hers.

She felt herself scream, but she couldn't hear her own voice. It was swallowed by the shrieks and cries. Her muscles felt as if they were being ripped apart, her bones felt as if they were cracking within her body, and her mind splintered.

And then she saw herself, from the outside, as if through a hundred eyes at once, multiplied and distorted. Her vision of her body twisted, as if she were being wrung like a rag, shaken and ripped into a million pieces.

She fought to pull herself back together, and it was like gathering sand in her arms. But she wasn't lying to Merecot when she said she was strong.

She *was.*

*You are mine,* she told the spirits. *I am yours.*

*I will take you home.*

A pause.

She felt her body fall forward, hard, on the ground, and she was whole again, for a moment. And then the spirits were inside her, ripping through her thoughts, holding up her memories and shattering them into fragments as if they were made of glass.

She saw herself, a child, the night her parents died.

Saw them again. Heard them scream.

Saw Renet, the moment she met him. Kissed him. Married him.

Erian, born squalling, and then suckling at her breast, living, breathing, growing, and then Llor, his tiny face screwed up in a scream. And then they grew, running into the house and throwing their arms around her, laughing and chattering.

The spirits tore through her memories until they found the moment she'd lost Erian and Llor, when they were taken from her. And then she saw the moment she found them again, when they ran into her arms with tears on their cheeks. They paused, expectant, and at first Naelin was confused.

And then she understood.

*I will hold you,* she told the spirits, *like I held them. In my heart.*

*Take us,* the spirits said.

And she did.


IN THE EMPTY COURTYARD, HANNA FELT THE MOMENT THAT CONTROL of the spirits shifted. It was a few stray seconds. Alone, she rolled across the courtyard to look out between the arches toward the mountains in the west.

She saw a peak crumble.

And then she saw a new mountain rise in its place.

*Good,* she thought. *Very good. If I've done nothing else in my life, I have done this.* Saved a kingdom. Saved a queen. *This could have been an ending. But it's a new beginning.*

# CHAPTER 23

Even though she knew it was coming, Daleina felt the recoil as if it were a punch. She slammed backward in her throne, her head smacking against the wood. She heard cries around her but didn't have time to reassure her chancellors.

Plunging into the minds of her spirits, she spread her will through them. *Calm. I am here. You are not alone. I have not abandoned you. Cling to me.*

And to her surprise, they clung.

She felt their relief like a waterfall, all their feelings rushing through her, but primarily pure relief as they were released from the conflicting tug of two queens. Daleina swaddled them in her hope and her strength.

And for the first time she realized she didn't hate the spirits. Not anymore. Everything she'd told Naelin was true: you couldn't hate them. You had to accept them, even love them. They were a part of the world, and alongside their hatred and rage, there was also beauty and the desire for life to thrive. She fed them all of her wishes and hopes and dreams for a peaceful future, and they, bereft from Naelin's abdication, lapped it up as if her thoughts were water down their thirsty throats.

Daleina opened her eyes. "She did it." Straightening in her throne, she smiled at her chancellors, feeling stronger than she had in weeks, even months. "All right, tell me everything that needs fixing. It's time to heal Aratay."

Her chancellors took her at her word, and the meeting stretched late into the night. It ended only when her seneschal insisted and shooed the chancellors out of the Sunrise Room. He scolded her about not sending them away sooner, taking on too much, and not taking care of herself. She smiled at him and laughed lightly. "Why do I have to take care of myself when I have you to take care of me for me, Belsowik?"

"You're giddy with lack of sleep, Your Majesty." He helped her off the throne. Her legs felt stiff from sitting so long, and her back ached, but she still felt better than she had this morning. It was as if the spirits were strengthening her.

"Do you know where I can find Healer Hamon?"

"I'll have him summoned to you," the seneschal said.

She waved off that suggestion. "No need to interrupt his work. I can go to him. Can you find out where he is?"

"I believe he's with his mother." The disapproval was thick in his voice. The seneschal could see through Poison-Master Garnah's bright cheeriness, and despite her work in saving Daleina from the poison, he obviously did not like her. Not much escaped the seneschal's notice, Daleina had discovered. *Good judge of character. Hope he likes me.*

"How do you even know that?" she asked. "Do you keep tabs on everyone I care about?"

He answered seriously. "Yes."

Daleina walked through the palace in such a good mood that she wanted to skip, but decided it wouldn't be majestic enough. She contented herself with smiling at everyone and was rewarded with smiles, bows, and good wishes. At the door to Garnah's rooms, she let her guard knock and announce her.

"Oh, how deliciously delightful!" Garnah said from within.

Daleina thanked her guard and entered. Lounging on a couch, Garnah was strumming on a small harp, badly, and Hamon was peering at a collection of tubes and beakers across the room. He straightened when she came into the room. "Your Majesty!"

"You seriously call her that?" Garnah asked him.

"She's the queen. She's owed respect."

"You call her that while you're, you know, with her?"

Daleina felt herself blush.

"Mother!" To Daleina, he said, "Forgive her. She suffers from a medical condition known as Horrible Personality."

Garnah laughed. "That was very nearly witty. I'm proud of you, my boy."

For Hamon's sake, Daleina tried not to smile. She knew how much of a nightmare Garnah was as a mother—she couldn't imagine the horror of growing up under the power of someone like Garnah—but the woman did have a sense of humor that Daleina found refreshing after dealing with dour chancellors and dramatic champions.

Concern in his eyes, Hamon crossed to Daleina. "Is everything all right?"

"Good news, for a change." Daleina beamed at him. "The plan worked."

"Yay!" Garnah cried. "The queen is dead!"

"She's *not* dead. I said *good* news. She abdicated control of the spirits of Aratay and assumed responsibility for the excess spirits of Semo . . ." She trailed off. At least, she was mostly sure that that's what had happened. Her sense of spirits did not extend beyond the border, but she would have felt if Naelin had died, wouldn't she have? "At least, that was the plan, and the first half went well, so I'm going to assume the second half did as well."

"Yay?" Garnah said. "The queen might not have died?"

"Hopefully no one died," Daleina said. "The only thing I'm certain of is that I'm the only queen of Aratay again."

"Without an heir," Garnah said.

"*Mother*. You aren't helping." Coming over to Daleina, Hamon put his arm around her. "It's entirely possible everything will turn out fine."

There would be issues when Naelin returned and tied her spirits to the barren areas—they'd have to figure out how the borders would work, whether Naelin would rule a separate country within Daleina's. But Daleina had confidence they could figure all of that out.

Garnah smiled brightly at them both. "In the meantime . . . I was just telling Hamon here how much I would really like grand-children. I think you should name one after me."

This time she couldn't help it: Daleina laughed out loud.

SNEAKING AWAY FROM HOME AND TRAVELING NORTH ALONE WAS not the best decision that Arin had ever made, but Queen Naelin and Champion Ven hadn't left her much choice. She'd packed what she'd been able to scrounge from her parents' kitchen: several loaves of bread and a cake, but she hadn't eaten meat in days.

On the plus side, nothing had eaten her.

*Probably because I smell bad enough to churn any predator's stomach.*

She hadn't dared descend to the forest floor to wash in any of the streams. The safest route was midforest, so that's what she'd stuck to. Now, only a few miles from the border, she wished she'd braved a stream. *The border guards are going to get one sniff of me and say, "We don't want your stench in Semo."*

For the past several miles, she had been trying to think of what to say to get past the border guards. Queen Naelin had been invited. *Me . . . not so much.*

If only they hadn't left her behind, this would have all been much easier.

*And I'd be able to protect Queen Naelin, like I promised I would.* It had been obvious to everyone that the queen and Champion Ven were waltzing into a trap, and it was obvious to Arin that she could help. *But I can't if I'm not there!*

She reached the end of a rope bridge and plopped down on the platform to rest. Above her, she heard the sweet birdlike song of a canopy singer—a wordless melody. Leaning her head back against the trunk, Arin listened as the gentle music drew closer.

And then it cut off abruptly.

She sat up straight. Had the singer fallen? Been attacked by spirits? Arin scanned the nearby branches for any movement, but saw nothing.

"Hello, young traveler!"

Arin yelped as a woman swung in front of her—she was upside down, dangling with her knees around a skinny branch. Her frizzy hair puffed down in a cloud beneath her head, and she was smiling happily, as if finding Arin had made her day.

"Um, hello." Arin bent her head to the side, trying to see the woman right side up.

"It's unusual for people as young as you to travel so close to the border by themselves. But I'm not going to ask if you're lost, because I can tell you're not."

"You can?" Arin didn't *think* she was lost, but it was difficult to be sure. "I'm traveling to Semo. I heard the passage through is north?"

"Only a mile more. But you'll want to cross at dawn. The Semoian spirits are fussy—they think everyone who crosses at night is an invader, and they tear them apart." The woman swung back and forth, and her poofy hair swung with her.

Arin wanted to reach out and grab her, but the woman didn't seem worried about falling. "Definitely don't want to be torn apart. Thanks. Are you the canopy singer I heard?"

"My name's Sira. I was preparing the trees for sunset. Everything changes for them when dusk comes. They can't drink the sunlight anymore, and different birds and creatures scurry across them. I always thought it must be scary for them, so much change every day. So I sing to comfort them."

"Yeah, night can be scary." Arin wasn't sure what else to say to such a speech. And it was true that nights alone in the forest had been terrifying. Suddenly, she didn't want Sira to leave. "Where do you go at night? Do you have an extra place to sleep?"

"There's only enough room for my mother and me, and sometimes my brother, when he comes to visit. But now he's gone to Semo. Oh! There are others on their way to Semo!" Sira smiled even brighter. "You may wish to join them. I'll take you to them!"

She scampered squirrel-like over the branches, and then swung from a rope to the next tree, laughing as she swooped through the air. Arin hurried to follow as Sira swung from rope to rope, tossing back the ropes each time. It reminded Arin of when she and Daleina were little, before Daleina went to the academy, when they'd race all around the trees. She soon found herself laughing too, until at last Sira stopped on a platform.

To the north, the vast oaks and pines switched to slender birches. In between them, not far away from Arin and Sira, campfire smoke snaked up to the sky. "Mother is with them," Sira said, "either advising them or yelling at them. Possibly both. You'll be welcome by their fire."

"You aren't coming too?" Arin didn't love the idea of approaching strangers, despite the fact that Sira had been a stranger ten minutes ago.

"My feet won't touch the forest floor until it has stories to tell me. I'm not done with the trees yet." She said it so matter-of-factly that Arin bobbed her head in agreement, as if this statement made perfect sense.

Arin glanced back at the figures around the campfire—she counted four. Three were seated and one stood, but it was impossible to see more detail than that. She turned back to ask Sira another question . . . but the canopy singer was already swinging back through the trees and then climbing, without ropes or ladders, even higher toward the precarious treetops.

*My first canopy singer,* Arin thought. *And she was just as strange as I'd always imagined.* It was known to take a special kind of person to spend their lives so high up that the branches might or might not hold your weight. *I liked her, though.*

Arin located a rope ladder descending from the platform, and she climbed down. By the time she reached the forest floor, the sun had set, and the brightest light was the campfire.

She walked toward it, telling herself to be brave like Daleina. In the distance, she thought she heard the soaring voice of the canopy singer, but the wind stole away half the melody.

By the time she reached the campfire, only three figures surrounded it: two men and a girl who looked to be Arin's age. Of the three, the girl was the only one who looked up at Arin's approach. She had blue and black hair drawn severely into multiple braids, and she wore a cloak pinned at her throat with a brooch shaped like a tree with flame-red leaves. She studied Arin with pale gray eyes. Arin stared back, not even sure why she was staring, except that no one had ever looked at Arin so intensely before. *Most times, no one notices me at all.* Except to note she was the queen's little sister.

"Hey, I know you!" one of the men said. "You dosed me with sleeping powder!"

Arin blinked, tore her gaze from the pale-eyed girl, and looked at the two men for the first time. *I know them! Both of them!* The one who had spoken was Renet, Erian and Llor's father, and the other was one of the champions. It took her a minute to remember his name: Champion Havtru. "I'm sorry about that," Arin said. "It seemed like the right thing to do at the time."

"Guess it was. But you didn't have any right to endanger my kids." He was glaring at her, which didn't seem like a good start. He looked like the kind of person who liked to yell. She wasn't overly fond of being yelled at. She much preferred it when everyone liked her.

*Maybe I should have stayed up in the trees and waited for dawn on my own.* But her gaze drifted to the campfire, where skewered meat was already beautifully browned.

The pale-eyed girl touched Champion Havtru's sleeve and spoke in his ear, too softly for Arin to hear. The champion nodded. "Join us, child," he said. "We have plenty. And tell us why you're so far north on your own."

"Queen Naelin sent me," Arin said, sitting before Renet could object. "I'm to meet her and Champion Ven in Arkon. We were traveling, then got separated. I'm to rejoin them."

Champion Havtru squinted at her. "Which is it? She sent you or you were separated? Doesn't seem like Champion Ven to lose a traveling companion." He scratched at his beard, and Arin couldn't tell if he was being curious or if she seemed suspiciously nervous.

*I'm supposed to be with them—that much is true.* Just because she very strongly suspected Daleina had convinced her champion into bringing Arin home and deliberately leaving her there . . .

The girl lifted one of the skewers off the fire and handed it to Arin.

"Thanks," Arin said. She blew on it once, then bit into it. She winced as it burned the top of her mouth but didn't stop eating. "I'm Arin."

"Cajara," the girl said softly. Her voice was light and sweet, reminding Arin of a puff pastry. *If Cajara were a food,* Arin decided, *she'd be a dessert.*

"Still don't get why you're here," Renet said.

*And Renet would be the sour lemonade, before any sugar is added.*

"She's here now," Cajara said, just as softly as before. "Can't she travel with us?"

"Renet has a point," Champion Havtru said, "or could have a point if he weren't being surly about it." He pounded Renet on the shoulder, a little too hard to be just jovial. "It's dangerous crossing into Semo these days. Are you sure that's where you're wanting to go?"

*Yes. No. Maybe it's just where I* have *to go.* "Queen Naelin and Champion Ven could be walking into a trap. I can help them."

"You going to put everyone in Semo to sleep?" Renet asked sarcastically.

It actually wasn't a terrible idea, though she didn't have that much of the sleeping powder with her. She'd mostly brought potion-laced charms to slow down spirits. She just shrugged and continued eating. *At least I'll be well fed when I sneak into Semo.* "Why are you all going?"

"To escort Ambassador Hanna home, once her work is done," Champion Havtru said, "as well as Champion Ven and Queen Naelin, if they'll come."

"She took guards, didn't she? Why does she need an escort?" Arin could guess the answer: *Because it's a trap.* So before anyone could answer, she pressed on. "Sounds like we're here for the same reason. Maybe we should travel together."

*Please say yes.*

If she traveled with them, they could get her past the border guards. Plus she'd be safer with a champion and . . . a candidate?

Was that what Cajara was? She glanced at the girl again and saw Cajara was looking at her.

Cajara blushed and looked down at her hands.

"Are you a candidate?" Arin asked her.

Cajara shook her head without looking up.

Champion Havtru answered for her. "Cajara's a family friend. She only has affinity for a couple of spirits. Came along for the experience."

*He's a terrible liar*, Arin thought. It was a flimsy excuse to bring someone across the border. "You should say she's your niece at least. Recently lost her parents to spirits, you're the only family she has left, and she refused to be left behind."

"Huh. Plausible enough."

Renet's eyes bulged. "Wait—Cajara's a candidate?"

"She's just my niece," Havtru said, trying out the lie.

Cajara glanced up, met Arin's eyes, then looked down again. *Her eyes are more lilac than gray*, Arin thought. "It's close to true," Cajara said. "Champion Havtru feels like my only family." Her voice was so light that her words were nearly lost in the night breeze.

Champion Havtru patted her shoulder. "Just call me Uncle Havtru."

"Congrats on your new family," Arin said to her.

She offered a quick, shy smile, so fast that Arin almost didn't see it in the flicker of campfire light.

Arin wanted to ask her more, not about her family—that wasn't get-to-know-you talk—but about her: what she thought about where they were and where they were going, whether she wanted to be here, whether she felt like she had to. Before she could frame any questions into words, Cajara shot to her feet.

"What is it?" Champion Havtru was on his feet only a second later, his bow in his hand. He reached for an arrow from his quiver. Renet stood more awkwardly and drew a dagger from his waist.

Pointing north, Cajara whispered, "The spirits at the border. Look."

At first Arin couldn't see anything through the birch trees.

But then her eyes picked out movement: loosely shaped like humans but vastly larger, the Semoian spirits were drawing together along the border, side by side.

"What are they doing?" Arin whispered.

From what she could tell, the giant spirits weren't doing anything but standing in a row. *Are they going to attack?* But they weren't facing Aratay. They were looking northward.

"Waiting," Cajara said softly.

"For what?" Arin asked.

Cajara was silent for a moment, with that faraway look that Arin's sister always got when she was speaking with the spirits. "For something wonderful to happen," she said. "Or something terrible."

They waited too.

The spirits didn't budge.

Night darkened around them, and the fire dwindled. Renet gave up on the vigil and tended to the fire. Champion Havtru kept his bow in his hand but didn't notch an arrow. Cajara didn't move.

While they watched the border, Arin watched her. She couldn't put her finger on why the other girl was so fascinating. It wasn't as if she'd talked much. But there was something both strong and vulnerable about her at the same time. It made Arin want to get to know her better.

*Why am I thinking about her when I should be worrying about the spirits?*

Then Cajara gasped and staggered back. Champion Havtru reached out and caught one arm, stopping her before she fell into the fire. Arin automatically braced her on her other side. She didn't let go, even when Cajara steadied herself. "Are you all right?" Arin asked.

"I . . . don't know. Yes."

"What happened?" Champion Havtru asked.

"Something. Everything. I don't know."

She wouldn't—or couldn't—explain more. A few times she started to try to put whatever she'd felt into words, and then she'd stop, fall silent, and shake her head.

Eventually, the stone giants on the border shuffled away, and the four travelers climbed into their bedrolls and stole bits of sleep until dawn crept across them. Arin dreamed of stone crushing her and of the earth gaping open beneath her feet.

When Arin opened her eyes, it took her a minute to remember where she was, who she was with, and why she was here. And it took another minute to process the fact that there was a feathered air spirit perched on Cajara's wrist.

Fully awake now, Arin bit back a shriek.

"It's delivering a message," Cajara said quietly. She seemed amused at Arin's alarm, though it was hard to read her expression. She might have been merely happy that the sky was blue.

Cajara nodded at Champion Havtru, who was reading a parchment that must have been rolled around the spirit's leg—it still had a curl to the paper from being rolled up. Going back to looking at the spirit, she stroked the feathers on its neck.

Arin watched her for a moment. "So you're just a family friend—excuse me, *niece*—with affinities for only a few spirits?"

"Yes." Meeting her eyes steady, Cajara added in her soft, sweet voice, "And the queens want you to go to Semo to help."

"That's right," Arin said.

And Cajara smiled at her—a smile so amazing, so just for her, that Arin felt herself blush. "Then I'd guess we'd better go to Semo together," Cajara said.

And Arin couldn't help but think, *I'd go with her anywhere.*

# CHAPTER 24

Ven wanted to leave without any fanfare, but Naelin said no, they couldn't sneak away like thieves. Queen Merecot's people deserved to know all was well, she argued. So Ven gritted his teeth and suffered through a ridiculous farewell ceremony that involved an endless stream of praise, platitudes, and other ridiculous nonsense.

They'd be leaving Ambassador Hanna in Semo with Queen Merecot to handle the aftermath—they'd mutually decided not to share the details of what happened in the grove until after Ven, Naelin, and the children had passed beyond the borders of Semo. After they were long gone, Hanna would support Merecot in revealing that they'd jointly solved the problem of restless spirits, with a whole bunch of vague statements. There would be a lot more celebrating. *But they'll celebrate without us*, Ven thought. *And more important, without that spirits-be-damned tight shirt.*

That thought cheered him up.

Once the official farewell was complete, Ven and Naelin mounted two flying water spirits, formerly Merecot's but now tied to Naelin—not that anyone in the crowd knew that. The spirits were shaped like winged horses but had scales like a fish. Sparkly fish scales. Ven was trying not to think about how ridiculous he looked riding one.

As the Semoians cheered, they took to the sky.

The people of Semo believed the newlyweds were on their way to celebrate their marriage, alone and far from prying eyes, per Semoian tradition. In truth, they planned to circle back to the castle, scoop up Erian and Llor, and then exit the country with a few hundred spirits in tow.

*Not as romantic, but a lot more practical.*

Airborne, he clung to his mount as Naelin led them in a circle, behind a mountain peak, and then out again on the opposite side of the castle. The children would be waiting for them in the third spire—the windows were to be left open so Naelin and Ven could fly directly inside. Erian and Llor would be waiting, ready to go, Merecot had assured them.

Ahead, Ven spotted the spire with the open window, exactly as Merecot had described. He ducked as they flew inside, even though the window was broad enough for twice his height. His spirit landed and folded its wings.

"Erian? Llor?" Naelin was calling.

"They should be right here, waiting for us." Ven dismounted. He'd been there when Merecot sent instructions to her guards, before the wedding ceremony had begun—Naelin had insisted on human guards, not spirits. She didn't trust the Semoian spirits, no matter how good Merecot claimed her control was.

Naelin's voice was tight. "They *should* be."

"But they're not."

Naelin tried not to panic. Not to think the worst.

But she'd lost them once before.

*Not again. Not twice. Not when we were so close to bringing them home!* "Merecot promised they'd be here. She promised to keep them safe, with guards. Where are their guards? *Where are my children!*"

Ven shoved at the door. Kicked it.

Solid, it didn't even creak.

Naelin felt her heart beat so fast that it hurt inside her rib cage. It was hard to swallow. "Erian! Llor!" She reached for a spirit—her mind curled around one of her new earth spirits.

Grabbing control of it wasn't as easy as with an Aratayian

spirit, but she gave it no option to squirm away. She called it to her, and she felt it scurry up the side of the tower, making holes in the rock wall with its stone fists until it clambered over the windowsill.

It was a squat, stone creature with a tortoiseshell back. It stood on its hind legs and regarded her with cold, liquid eyes. *Open that door,* Naelin commanded.

*How?* it asked. Its mental voice felt like loose gravel pouring through her mind.

*Bash it down.*

The spirit liked that order.

It rammed its body against the thick door, splintering the wood around the hinges, until it had battered through. Ven gave the wood a kick, and then he stepped through the broken frame.

Naelin heard him gasp, and she felt a surge of glee from the earth spirit. She caught a glimpse through its eyes: red, smeared on the castle walls, and knew instantly:

*The guards are dead.*

"Where are my children?" she asked again. She felt her body begin to shake. "What has Merecot done with my children?" Sending her mind out again, she grabbed the nearest Semoian spirit—it wasn't one of hers. She felt it resist her, but she forced it to come anyway.

*Tell me what happened here.*

It didn't know.

She sorted through its memories, but found nothing of Erian and Llor. Naelin reached for another spirit—it too knew nothing. "This is too slow. I need Hanna."

"I'll bring her," Ven promised.

"Hurry," she growled.

VEN RAN THROUGH THE CASTLE—HE KNEW EXACTLY WHERE TO find Ambassador Hanna, in her room with her four guards. He spoke as few words as possible: "Attack on the children. Naelin needs you." And then he and the guards were carrying Hanna and her chair back through the castle, up the spire, as quickly as possible.

A few Semoians tried to stop them and question them.

He barreled through them, not caring who they alerted, and then up the stairs, past the murdered guards.

Ven would not be stopped.

*Don't let me be too late. Don't let Naelin have done anything stupid.* If she were to confront Merecot *before* they located the children . . . They didn't know what Merecot wanted, or what she planned to do with them this time.

He heard Hanna gasp as she saw the dead guards and then swear colorfully when they barged through the door. Lowering Hanna's chair to the ground, he surged forward, ready to defend his new wife, and then stopped—

Naelin was seated cross-legged in the center of the room.

*She's fine,* he thought with relief. *But the spirits aren't.*

Dozens of tiny Semoian spirits lay strewn around her, moaning in pain.

"Teach me how to do it," Naelin commanded Hanna. "How do I winnow through all their minds to find the spirits who know what happened? Some of them must have seen. This castle and these mountains are full of spirits. At least one must know what happened to my children!"

Another fire spirit fell onto the hearth. It struggled as if against an invisible hand. Naelin held the spirit with her eyes as the spirit writhed.

Hanna did not reply. Instead, she ordered her four guards to check the bodies, to see if anyone had survived, though from the quantity of blood Ven knew that was useless. She also ordered them to watch for any rogue spirits.

"Shout if you need us, Ambassador," Evenna said. Then she and the other guards jogged back into the corridor. "Champion, we're trusting you to protect her."

Ven circled back to push Hanna's chair closer, but she held up a hand to stop him. She beckoned to him, and he leaned down. Her voice was pitched low so Naelin couldn't hear. "There's little chance the children survived an attack this violent," Hanna said heavily to Ven. "And there is a very strong chance that those Semoian spirits witnessed her children's deaths firsthand, and a strong chance those deaths were not painless. If Naelin were to see that in their memories, through their eyes, and watch her children die . . . Think about what could happen if Naelin loses herself again to rage and despair. The spirits she's linked to are barely under control. She'll fuel them, and they'll rip this land apart."

"So? Let her rip it apart!" He caught himself. "No—I don't mean that. We'll keep her from destroying the world," he tried to reassure Hanna.

"How?" Hanna asked.

"Somehow."

"'Somehow' isn't good enough."

"It has to be good enough!" He held Hanna's gaze for a long moment until she wilted. He felt an instant of guilt for that, bullying an old woman, but this was Naelin!

"If this fails, it's on you." With that, Hanna wheeled herself across the room, to where Naelin sat cross-legged, deep in concentration already.

Ven approached her as well, beside Hanna. He took Naelin's hand in his.

Naelin didn't open her eyes. "I *will* have answers."

Softly, Ven said to Hanna, "Help her. Please." He pleaded with his eyes—*Help me save her*, he thought—and at last she sighed again, this time a resigned sigh.

"Spirit memory is partially collective," Hanna said. "They share thoughts. An event like this—where a spirit tied to Semo ventured into Aratay—would have spread and been dissected. You need to chase it down to where it's brightest and strongest. I recommend focusing on a single image: the gold in the children's hair, for instance."

Ven watched as Hanna guided Naelin's mind on her search. He'd never liked this part of being a champion, when he couldn't follow his charge on her journey. He occupied himself with listening as the castle guards discovered the corpses.

Hanna's four guards had remained in the hallway, and Ven heard them explain what little they knew. He heard their voices rise, as the castle guard threatened to call for the queen.

*Not yet*, he thought. First find the children. Then deal with the queen.

"Got one," Naelin whispered.

"Draw it here," Hanna said. "It will resist, but it may also be curious."

Ven shifted his attention to the sky, and after a few minutes, he was rewarded: a familiar shape with leathery wings and a sharp beak hurtled toward the window. He didn't move as the air spirit dived straight inside, aiming for Naelin.

Closer.

Almost . . .

He then struck, leaping to intercept the spirit, drawing his sword at the same time and striking, flat of the blade first, on the spirit's neck—with the blade flat, it didn't cut but the force of the strike drove the spirit down, as Ven intended. He hurled his weight against the spirit's shoulder. In an instant, he had it down, his foot on its back, his blade pressing against its neck. He pinned it down on the stone floor.

"Search its mind," Hanna said.

They held their breaths, watching Naelin concentrate.

At last, her eyes snapped open. "Two air spirits—exactly the same kind as before, which can't be a coincidence—carried them away from the castle. Alive. Merecot did it *again*. She stole them away from me a second time, when I was so close I should have been able to stop her and save them!"

Stepping away, Ven released the spirit. With a cry, it reared back.

Naelin froze it in place with one glance.

It glared at her, murder in its eyes, but she didn't spare it a second look.

"Ask it where it took them," Ven urged. Maybe if they could follow them . . . *I'd happily fly on spirits again if it means we can catch them.* He didn't know how much of a head start the spirits had. He thought of the bodies in the hallway—if he checked how fresh they were, that would give them some kind of time frame, but he didn't want to leave Naelin.

"It doesn't know," Naelin said. "Its orders were to kill the guards."

Hanna was frowning. "Why would Merecot want to kill her own guards...?"

Naelin rose to her feet. "Let's ask her that, as well as where the spirits are taking my children, before we destroy her."

On this, Ven was in perfect agreement with his new wife.

AFTER THE FAREWELL-TO-THE-NEWLYWEDS EXTRAVAGANZA, MERE-cot gave a nicely rousing speech and then retreated inside to her chambers with Queen Jastra. For a moment, she let herself just rest, with her mind closed to the spirits and eyes closed to the world.

*It's been a ... unique week.*

She knew she'd have to prepare for the next step soon, but for now ... Naelin, Ven, and the children were on their way back to Aratay, taking the troublesome spirits with them.

Opening her mind, she reached out, intending just to check— *What ... ?*

For at that moment, Merecot felt Semoian spirits screaming and immediately jumped to her feet. *What is Naelin doing to my spirits?*

Queen Jastra laid a hand on her wrist. "Stop."

"But she's hurting them!"

"Let her." Folding her hands calmly on her lap, Jastra stud-ied the silver tray of delicacies. A sampling of desserts from the wedding had been delivered directly to Merecot's chambers, per Merecot's command. She'd planned to celebrate in the privacy of her rooms.

*I should be celebrating! It all went well! She's supposed to be gone! Why is she still here, hurting my spirits?* "Jastra ..."

"Patience, Your Majesty." Jastra selected a concoction made with salt and caramel. She popped it in her mouth and chewed with a delighted sigh. "Try one. Delicious. And trust me: Queen Naelin will come to you."

Merecot paced.

She hated doing nothing.

*No one is allowed to hurt my spirits but* me.

"At least explain why!" Merecot burst out.

"Remember how I told you an opportunity will present itself? Sometimes you have to nudge that opportunity along. Create a situation in which it will blossom."

Merecot quit pacing. She stared at Jastra. Slowly, trying to keep her voice steady and calm, she asked, enunciating each word, "What did you do?"

"It's not what I did that's important; it's what will happen next," Jastra said. "She will attack you, and you will defend yourself. You, with the power of all the spirits of Semo behind you. And her, with the power of only a few hundred, barely controlled, wild spirits that aren't tied to any land. With such a power imbalance, you'll easily defeat her."

"And why will she attack me, after I threw her a lovely wedding and gave her everything she desired?" Merecot clenched her fists then released them. She forced herself to breathe evenly and think clearly. This was *not* the plan.

"Because your spirits took her children into the untamed lands."

Merecot was at a loss for words. She looked at the ex-queen across the room. Jastra smiled triumphantly, as if she had done something immensely clever. *Instead of immensely reckless and stupid.* "By now they are already there," Jastra said.

"Then they're dead," Merecot said flatly.

"Not necessarily."

"No one survives the untamed lands. Least of all children." She thought of the boy and girl–they were just ordinary, innocent kids. Sure, she didn't like little kids much, but that didn't mean they deserved to die. Kidnap, fine, but not this. *I have* some *sense of right and wrong. And this goes too far.* "You sent *my* spirits, behind my back, to kill Queen Naelin's children?"

"Remove them, not kill," Jastra clarified, as if that made any difference when the untamed lands were involved.

Merecot shook her head. She wished she could shake this knowledge out of her mind. "You're right–she'll want revenge. You can't attack cubs without angering the mama bear."

"Yes! Precisely! She fights you, and you destroy her. You have the advantage—your spirits outnumber hers, and you have better control of them." Jastra was practically rubbing her hands together in glee. "She knows this, which is why she had to be goaded into action. It's brilliant! You'll be able to eliminate one of the Aratayian queens, as well as the problematic spirits in one fell swoop! I have turned your mistake into victory!"

*Argh!* Merecot gritted her teeth so she wouldn't scream out loud. She knew the kind of damage Naelin had done to Aratay the last time her children were endangered. It had taken serious power at the border to repel her. And now Naelin was within Semo, in Merecot's castle. *I'll win, of course. But it won't be a pretty fight.*

Perhaps worse, though, was the fact that Jastra had backed her into a corner, neatly and efficiently and without Merecot's knowledge. It made her feel powerless—and that was *not* a feeling she enjoyed one bit. She'd had a plan, and it was working. "I did *not* make a mistake. Allowing Naelin to take the excess spirits was the correct call, both for Semo and Renthia."

"In the short term, perhaps. I'm sure it seemed that way," Jastra said, her voice full of sympathy. "But in the long term? Oh my dear, I wish you had consulted me first! You followed your heart instead of your head, and in doing so, unraveled all our plans."

*Because I had a new plan! A* better *plan!* Let Naelin go, and then, under the guise of peace, visit Daleina . . . and eliminate her. And then—*and only then*—battle Naelin. But now . . .

*Daleina will never let me near her if I've just murdered Naelin!*

"You shouldn't have done this," Merecot ground out. "Especially not this way."

It was true that killing Naelin had been the original plan if the queens refused to abdicate, but even then they'd planned to make it seem like an accident. A rogue spirit. Or a fall—Naelin was older, distraught over all she'd endured. This . . . Everyone would know Merecot was responsible.

Jastra shook her head and clucked her tongue, as if that made her seem like an old wise woman. *But she's not,* Merecot thought. *She's just another person who has betrayed me.* "You hadn't the nerve for what needed to be done," Jastra said. "It's important you remember this is about *all* the children, and sacrifices must be made—"

"Yes," Merecot cut her off. "They must." She felt her shoulders sag, and then she straightened. This was not the time for weakness. *It's only that I trusted Jastra. I liked her. And now . . . she's left me with no choice.* It just galled her, because Jastra was right.

*I have to do what's best for Semo. And for Renthia.*

Looking beyond Jastra, Merecot said, "Have you heard enough, Your Majesty?"

Queen Naelin was crouched in the windowsill, several of her spirits behind her. Champion Ven was already within the room, his sword drawn. The two of them hadn't moved closer while she'd been questioning Jastra.

"This could be staged," Ven said to Naelin.

Naelin's eyes were on Merecot, and Merecot saw the rage and distrust in them. She wished there were another way. *I should have taken the time to explain to Jastra how the plan had changed.* No, she wasn't going to feel guilty about this. It wasn't her fault! *Jastra should have known I'd have a new plan. She should have trusted me!*

She wished Jastra had believed in her the way Merecot had thought she did. She wished they'd never involved children. She wished she'd left that damn wolf alone.

"You have betrayed me, Jastra," Merecot said quietly. "And you have committed an act of war against Queen Naelin of Aratay. I am sorry for what I must do, but you have left me no choice."

She meant every word.

Stepping back, Merecot withdrew her protection from the former queen of Semo. And the spirits felt it almost immediately. At first they hesitated, as if unsure what to make of this.

But then they came.

Howling, they flew through the halls of the castle, through the windows, down the stairwells, all of them converging. Fire spirits flew from the hearth, a blur of flame. Ice spirits laid frost trails across the floor. Water spirits gushed through the windows. Air spirits whipped around Jastra. Tree spirits pinned her arms together and filled her mouth with leaves, while earth spirits tore her apart.

Merecot forced herself to stand and watch.

At last, when the screaming ended, she closed her eyes and realized she was crying.

# CHAPTER 25

Carefully, as calmly as she could manage, Naelin broke the shocked silence with the most important question: "Is it true that Queen Jastra went into the untamed lands and came out again?"

"She certainly did," Merecot said in a ragged voice. "Fool that she was." The insult lacked bite, though. Her cheeks were wet with tears. But Naelin didn't have enough room in her heart and mind to worry about Merecot's feelings.

Naelin felt as if an ocean were surging inside her. *If Queen Jastra can do it, so can I. I can search for them. I can find them.* She met Ven's eyes, and knew he was thinking the same thing. Erian and Llor could still be alive! They could rescue them! If they dared. If she were strong enough. *I have to be.*

"You're thinking of doing it too, going into the untamed lands," Merecot accused. "You can't. You have to take the excess spirits to Aratay, as we agreed—they can't stay here."

She was right. The spirits couldn't stay here. Naelin felt them, clawing at the back of her mind, buzzing like a hundred mosquitoes. If she left them, they'd be essentially queenless, worse than if she'd never come at all.

"What if instead of taking the extra spirits to Aratay ..." Naelin said slowly, the idea solidifying as she spoke. "... What if ... I take them with me back to the untamed lands?"

"You'll die," Merecot said bluntly. "Jastra spent years preparing for her trip. Only a powerful and well-trained queen can leave the known world and hope to survive. You fit the first adjective; fail on the second."

"I won't be going alone." She'd have all the excess spirits with her—a veritable army. And she'd have Ven by her side. She looked at her champion.

Ven nodded. "You won't be going alone."

"Aw, how sweet," Merecot said. "You'll both die." Crossing to the door, she summoned her guards. "Please see that Queen Jastra's body is taken to the Tomb of Queens. And clean this room up." There was a tremor in her voice that she almost successfully hid—Naelin heard a hint of it as Merecot turned back to her and Ven. "You're serious about this?

"Tell us where your spirits entered the untamed lands," Ven demanded. "That will give us a starting point. Even if Queen Jastra hijacked those particular spirits, you must be able to read the minds of spirits who saw them pass."

Naelin watched as Merecot concentrated, her eyes unfocusing. For what seemed like the thousandth time, she thought, *Can we trust her?* She kidnapped Erian and Llor once; she could still be behind the second kidnapping. She could be manipulating them as some part of a broader, more elaborate plot to rule Semo and Aratay.

Her shock, though, had seemed genuine.

*And there isn't time for second-guessing. Every minute we waste is a minute too long.*

At last, Merecot shook herself. "Stupid creatures returned to the only part of the border they knew: in Aratay, near the village of Redleaf, where they lost the Protector of Queens. I suppose that was the simplest order for Jastra to give them."

If they'd flown that far, then maybe there was still a chance to catch them. "Please explain everything to Ambassador Hanna," she said to Merecot. "And send word to Queen Daleina—she'll need to know I won't be bringing the spirits to the barren lands."

Merecot's eyebrows shot up. *She spends most of her time looking at me as if I'm crazy,* Naelin thought, *when she's the one who set all this in motion.*

"You know Daleina won't trust what I say," Merecot said.

"Frankly, it doesn't matter. She'll feel it when we cross the border." Naelin tried to think through if there was anything else she could do to prepare, anything else that would tip the odds from "impossible" to "merely difficult," but everything inside her was screaming, *Go, go, go!*

WITH WIND IN THEIR FACES, THEY SOARED ABOVE THE MOUNtains. It was just past dawn, and the sun was behind them, shedding light on all the rocks beneath them. *Ought to make it across Semo into Aratay by tonight*, Ven thought. *The spirits would have flown straight. So can we.*

It helped if he thought of this as an ordinary hunt. Follow the trail, find the prey.

*Maybe we can make up time.*

*We have to.*

As they crossed another mountain, he heard a *whoosh* and then the sky was filled with spirits: hundreds of them, rising up from the canyons and valleys. Beside him, with her arms spread wide, Naelin had her eyes closed and was arched back. Wind streamed her hair backward, and the spirits flew all around her. Below, more ran across the ridges and peaks of the mountains—streaks of gold and red and black.

*The spirits without a land*, he thought. Her *spirits*.

Some of them flew closer, and he saw their eyes, filled with fire or darker than night. One hissed, showing three rows of wolflike teeth. Another spat crimson spittle into the air. It seared onto the back of another, and the injured spirit howled, whipping around to strike at the spitting spirit with talons as long as swords.

*Oh, great.*

He'd never hunted with an army before. Especially one that had zero discipline and even less loyalty, to either their Queen or each other.

*This is going to be interesting.*

WITH HER NEW SPIRITS, NAELIN FLEW ACROSS SEMO. SHE FELT their minds pressing in on hers, as if they wanted to swallow her whole—thoughts, memories, feelings. Over and over again, she saw the moments that shaped her: the day her family died, the day she married Renet, the day Erian was born and the day Llor was born, the day she met Ven, the day she lost her children, the day she found them . . . but the spirits always wanted more. They rummaged through her mind, exposing little memories: the croon of a lullaby sung by her mother, the sound of sizzling eggs, the taste of fresh berries, the smell of fresh laundry in the spring breeze, the feel of Ven's lips on hers, the way her body shook when she laughed hard enough, the sensation of brushing her hair . . . so many little details at once that she felt bombarded.

She didn't feel the wind rushing on her face or see the snow-capped peaks below them, as her mind was plunged from memory to memory, and she was only vaguely aware when they crossed from Semo into Aratay. She didn't notice when the sun blazed brilliant red on the horizon and the forest below sank into shadows, a vast dark sea of branches and dying leaves. She didn't feel the night chill, and when, well after midnight, Ven called to her that they needed to stop, she needed to rest, she didn't hear him until her spirit shrieked and jerked backward.

An arrow had flown by its face.

Ven was holding his bow.

With a pleasant smile on his face, he said, "Stop for the night?"

She didn't want to. "Erian and Llor . . ."

"We can't help them if we're drained of all strength," Ven said.

She knew he was right. And she felt the exhaustion in the smaller spirits. A few had flagged behind, far behind, and she knew she couldn't leave them. She'd taken on this responsibility, and she couldn't leave them queenless in Aratay, to kill and destroy.

Yet it meant her children were alone. And in danger. And maybe hurt, and certainly scared, and surely . . .

The grief hit her like a blow to the gut, and she almost collapsed into a heap as both the emotions and exhaustion swept through her. She needed to rest, but she didn't dare rest. She needed to do her duty, and yet the only duty that mattered was to her family.

*How can I possibly do this?*

She looked over and saw Ven watching her. And while there was concern in his eyes, it wasn't patronizing. It wasn't *pity*. His eyes simply said, *You can't help anyone if you're dead.* In a way, it was a bit brutal. *He knows how much this devastates me.* Yet, that was almost certainly what he was trying to convey: empathy *and* commitment to her oaths. Brutal, yes. But necessary.

It was exactly what she needed.

*Besides, I'll need all the help I can get in the untamed lands.* Fighting through the chaotic swirl of thoughts, she projected a command: *Down. Rest.*

And the spirits obeyed easily, as if they'd always obeyed her, though she thought it was more likely they obeyed because they wanted to rest than because they respected her authority. They plunged down through the trees, knocking off the last of the golden leaves. Several lit on branches in the canopy, while others plunged deep in between the trees. She felt them infiltrate the forest—and as her spirit landed on a branch beside Ven's, she felt a wave of uneasiness.

She stayed mounted on her spirit while Ven climbed off and began setting up camp, stringing hammocks between the branches.

"The trees don't want us here," she said suddenly.

*No, that's not right. Trees don't feel.*

But she felt watched . . .

No, worse than watched. Hated. Feared.

Around her, the ex-Semoian spirits were filling the trees. The feeling wasn't coming from them. She tried to pinpoint the source of *wrongness* that pervaded the air. Around her, the spirits chattered and chittered and chirped as they burrowed into the ground, grew new branches onto the trees, and dusted the leaves with frost.

Then it dawned on her. What she felt was the spirits of Aratay pouring toward them. Agitated. Angry.

"We can't stay here," Naelin said, louder.

Ven stopped.

Her spirits noticed the Aratayian spirits surrounding them. She felt her spirits press closer to her, felt their anger shift outward, and felt them begin to sink into the land beneath them. Quickly, Ven unhooked the hammocks and tossed the supplies onto the nearest spirit that could fly—a black serpent with iridescent dragonfly wings. Naelin climbed onto a water spirit shaped like a swan.

*Keep moving*, Naelin ordered the spirits.

The spirits resisted—they liked this land, they wanted to stay, reshape the earth, grow the trees, play in the breeze. *Not yours*, she told them firmly. *We can't stay.*

It was worse than dragging reluctant children on a walk, because the spirits itched to fight. She felt them snap quickly from exhaustion to rage, and they wanted to tear, rip, rend, destroy. *No. Come. Fly, run, crawl.*

*Follow me.*

She felt the haze of all the memories burn away, like fog in the sun, and she focused on the single command, guiding her spirit up higher and higher above the canopy.

Naelin drove them across Aratay as the spirits of the forest pursued them. When one of her spirits stopped to snap at a tree spirit, she wrapped her mind around it and propelled it forward. She felt sweat dampen her back and her hands as she clutched the feathers in her spirit's neck. It bucked beneath her—it too wanted to spin around and *fight, fight, fight.*

*Come*, she told it. And while it obeyed, the command seemed to drain her. She was pushing the spirits—and herself—too hard. Already, lights began dancing in front of her eyes . . .

"We won't make it!" Ven shouted. His spirit was weakening beneath him. She felt it as it struggled to keep pumping its wings. She tried to will it to stay aloft, but even if she weren't completely wiped, she couldn't make a spirit suddenly find strength it didn't have. "It's too far to the untamed lands! Naelin, we'll have to stop!"

But if they stopped, the spirits would fight, and she couldn't let them tear apart Aratay. She *wouldn't.* Which meant they needed someplace safe to stop. Somewhere the spirits wouldn't attack those of Aratay. Somewhere they could rest. Somewhere . . .

And then she remembered the whole reason these spirits followed her in the first place: the barren patches. Her little army could rest safely within one of the dead zones.

She reached with her mind and, instead of looking for spirits, looked for the *absence* of spirits. She felt one, not far, a small circle of emptiness within the trees.

*There*, she told the spirits.

They streamed toward it.

She felt the spirits funnel into the barren circle, and she guided her swan in, diving through a swarm of spirits. She saw the dark forest ringing them, hazy through the bodies of so many spirits. She felt them continue to pour into the tiny space.

The swan landed on the ground, and she slid off it. Her knees buckled and she sank to the ground. Her palms touched the earth. The soil felt strange, dry and dead, and the air too tasted almost metallic. Her wild earth spirits burrowed happily into the earth, and her sense of it began to change as they filled it, bringing it back to life, bonding with it—

*No, it is not yours*, she cut them off sharply.

Confused, they halted.

The spirits couldn't bond to this land—she'd never be able to bring them out of Renthia into the untamed lands if they did. And besides, there were too many of them for such a constricted space.

*Only tonight*, she told them. *Not ours.*

"Can we stay here?" Ven asked.

"I don't know," Naelin said. "Yes. But we can't stay long. The spirits . . . they want . . ." She lost track of the rest of the sentence as the thoughts of the spirits pulled her into their minds again.

They wanted to stay.

They wanted land.

They wanted sky.

They wanted fire, ice, water . . . Flames skirted the edge of the barren circle, and little sprouts burst from the dry earth, to be tinged with frost then frozen. A sheet of rain swept through, and the earth spirits pushed from deep within, shaping the ground up—

*Stop. Not ours.*

They whispered back: *Ours. Now, ours.*

*Not yet. You're going home.* She pictured the untamed lands, the shifting haze, and she pushed the image out.

They recoiled.

*Here. Now. Home,* they told her.

But they were fighting with one another. It was only a bit of land, a small circle, not nearly enough for the hundreds of spirits she'd brought with her. Barely enough for them to squeeze into for the night.

She felt a hand touch her arm, and she jumped.

"You need to eat," Ven told her.

"They're . . ." Words failed her, and Naelin waved her hand at the spirits clustered around them.

"And you need to sleep. I'll keep you safe." Ven met Naelin's eyes.

She couldn't sleep, not with so many spirits pressing around her, wanting to fight one another. It wouldn't take much for them to launch into one another, and the two humans in the middle . . . She had to keep control of them. "They want to bond with the land," Naelin told Ven.

"You can't let them," Ven said.

"I'm aware of that."

He was silent for a moment. "How can I help you?"

She loved him for that question. As before, it was exactly what she needed to hear. Naelin let herself sag against him and felt his arm around her—one hand because the other held his sword. "Just be with me."

She pushed her tired mind out into the sea of spirits. *Rest. Sleep. Rest, sleep.* She repeated the order over and over until she felt the spirits sink and sag. They were exhausted too, after being severed from a queen and bonding with a new one, after traveling across Semo and into Aratay. She felt the flurry of thoughts and emotions around her begin to slow and then dissipate. *Sleep.*

*Sleep.*

*Sleep.*

The spirits slept.

Curling up against Ven, she closed her eyes. She didn't think she slept, but morning came faster than she expected, so perhaps she did. Awake, the spirits began again, trying to bond with the barren patch and clashing with one another over the same scrap of lifeless dirt.

*Onward*, she told them. *Toward home.*

They questioned her: *Home?*

On the back of a feathered deer spirit—this one with silver and black feathers—she drove them out of the barren circle and up above the forest canopy. She felt the spirits of Aratay following, watching, hating, and hoped Queen Daleina had a tight grip on them. *She must feel this*, Naelin thought. Every hedgewitch with a shred of power had to feel it as her spirits swept through the forests.

She showed the spirits the image of the untamed lands again, and she felt their resistance. They didn't want that. Now that they'd seen Aratay, they wanted to stay in a land that had already been shaped and solidified. She pressed the image harder into them. *Home.*

*Not home*, they replied, and they threw images back at her: the towering mountains of Semo, the wide fields of what she thought was Chell, the glaciers of Elhim, the seas around Belene. *We want our own home.*

*You'll have one, in the untamed lands*, she told them. *You can be happy there. No queen. No orders. No commands. Once I find my children, I'll abdicate and leave, and you can live your lives without any of the humans you hate so much.*

*Unfinished.* She felt the word as a feeling more than a word. The others echoed it around her, and she felt their sadness.

*Unfinished. Undone. Interrupted. Humans . . . Cannot return to the untamed lands. Cannot be without a queen. Don't want to. Don't leave us. Can't. Can't. Don't make us. Unmake. Undone.*

And then a soft, quiet: *Please.*

She followed the thought into the mass of spirits. It was from a little air spirit with a thin humanlike body and delicate wings. Feeling the touch of Naelin's mind, it flew closer and alit on the deer's head. It held on, wrapping its long fingers around a feather.

*Why?* Naelin asked. Aloud, she said, "You hate queens. In the untamed lands, you'll be free. No humans. No queens."

The little spirit shuddered. "Stupid human, you don't understand." Her voice was as shrill as a whistle in the wind. "Beyond the borders of Renthia lies the chaos of the world beginning, unfinished. Do not send us back to the beginning."

"But you can't stay here," Naelin said. "You need your own home."

"Not home," the spirit said. "Never became home. Long, long ago, it began."

All around, the other spirits echoed her: *Long, long ago.*

*Long ago, longer ago, still longer ago, back, beginning, before beginning. Yes, before the beginning...* "Before the beginning, we were called by the Great Mother of Spirits to shape this world, seed this world, breathe this world to life."

*We came. We shaped. We breathed.*

*We did not finish.*

"We did not finish. We should have shaped this world to perfection, given it form, given it life, given it all, but before we were done, *your* kind came."

*Humans.*

*Scourge.*

*Born too soon.*

"You were not to be here yet. We were not ready."

*Not time.*

*Not your time.*

*Not our time.*

"The world wasn't finished, but you were here, and we did not know what to do. We were afraid. We were angry."

*We hated you.*

*Hate.*

*Still hate.*

*It was not your time.*

*You were not to be born yet. Not yet. We were not done. We were not gone.*

"We found you," the little spirit said. "And we killed . . ."

*You killed.*

*We killed.*

*All of us killed.*

"And the Great Mother tried to stop our fight. But she died in the battle. She was not supposed to die. But she did, and the world was unfinished, and we were still here and you were here, and this was never supposed to be. We were supposed to finish and change, become the world's protectors, but we did not, this was not to be, because *you* came. And you were not enough. You are not enough. But you are something. With you, we make something out of nothing. But it is your fault there is not more, your fault so much is undone, and we will never forgive you."

Naelin tried to make sense of the story. She never knew the spirits had their own story of how it all began, of where their hatred came from. She only knew the spirits needed queens and yet hated them. "You were supposed to make the world . . . and then leave?"

"Not leave," the little spirit said. "*Change.* We would have become what we were meant to be. But we lost our fate. It died that day, with Her." And the sadness rose in waves from the little spirit and permeated the others. It swamped them, and they did not speak again as they kept flying westward as the sun trekked above them.

At nightfall, Naelin found another barren circle and fought them again as they tried to bond with it, harder this time.

"What's going on?" Ven asked her quietly.

"They don't want to go back," Naelin said.

"Can't blame them," Ven said.

"But they're spirits. They hate us. I thought . . ." She'd thought the spirits in the untamed lands were free, the way they wanted to be, but she'd been wrong. "They told me their creation story. It's different from any I've heard." She told him what the spirits had told her.

When she finished, Ven said, "Wish my sister were here to hear that."

"They think it's true." She'd never felt sorry for spirits before, but when she'd told them about the untamed lands and about her plan to leave them there, she'd felt their fear. Like children, afraid of being abandoned by their parents.

They'd lost their Great Mother.

The queens, they'd said, were poor substitutes.

*But we're all they have.*

Reaching out, she sent them a thought: *I won't abandon you there.*

The spirits paused. As if all of them were holding their breath at once, she felt them listening to her. *Is that what you're afraid of? Being without a queen in the untamed lands?*

Yes. Yes, it was.

*I'm going with you.* She pushed them the memory of Erian and Llor. *I need to find them. Help me, and I won't leave you alone. We'll go into the untamed lands together, and I promise I won't leave you behind. We'll come back, and we'll find you a true home.*

A ripple went through the spirits. It was a mixture of fear and something Naelin had never felt in them before.

Hope.

The spirits agreed.

BRACED BETWEEN TWO PILLARS, DALEINA STOOD AT THE TOP OF the Queen's Tower and tried to ignore Hamon and his mother bickering behind her.

"If she really wants to talk to me, she shouldn't make me climb so many stairs," Garnah was griping. "Also, she should provide a lounge chair at least. I don't sit on floors."

"This is the most secure place in Mittriel," Hamon said.

"Pfft. Not so secure. Chop a few support branches, and we'll all plummet to our deaths on the forest floor. Boom! Splat!" Garnah made a variety of squishing noises.

"Secure from spies, Mother."

Daleina heard shuffling and the crinkling of fabric behind her, then a theatrical sigh before Garnah said, "Most likely, we'd be impaled on one of the lower towers long before we hit the forest floor."

"Mother. Enough. Daleina didn't call you here to murder you."

"Delightful news," Garnah drawled. "But I'd prefer to hear such assurances from Her Majesty."

That was her cue to turn around and reassure Garnah, but instead Daleina sank her mind into the forest, reaching out to the spirits, soothing them. *Safe. You're safe. They won't hurt you. Don't hurt them. They'll be gone soon.* She felt the spirits twist and squirm—they wanted to hide or attack or chase or flee. *Calm. You're safe.*

She couldn't keep her spirits from following the swath of foreign spirits that clung to Queen Naelin. They hovered around their camp, watching the intruders' every move. Ripples of unease spread across Aratay, from spirit to spirit. She couldn't stop it, or even slow it. All she could do was try to keep it from building into anything more.

*Do no harm.*

*Leave them be.*

*Watch, if you must. But just watch.*

She couldn't reach far enough to see through their eyes at such a distance, the way that Queen Naelin could, but she could sense them congregating in a squirming, squalling mass outside of the village of Redleaf. Naelin had made it that far at least. Another night, and she and all her spirits should be across the border into the untamed lands.

Daleina had never wished for anyone to go into the untamed lands before, but once Naelin crossed, the spirits of Aratay should relax again and resume paying attention to the land. There was still so much to heal! Winter was coming fast.

Confident her spirits were heeding her for the moment, she finally addressed the others in the room. "I've received a message from Queen Merecot, confirmed by Ambassador Hanna," Daleina reported. Hamon already knew this, but the information was new to Garnah. "Queen Naelin is bringing the excess spirits into the untamed lands. She's nearly there." The spirits had congregated around a strip of barren land—that part of Aratay had the most barren patches, thanks to Naelin forcing so many spirits to die fighting the Semoian spirits when her children were taken. Keeping a hand on the pillar, Daleina turned to face Garnah and Hamon.

Hamon smiled at her, and she let the warmth of his smile wash over her. It was the one steadying force in her always-tilting world. She could trust his love. *I can't trust Naelin's grip on her spirits and, if I'm being honest with myself, I can't trust my own grip to ensure Aratay's spirits do not attack.* The very truth of the situation was enough to drive a weaker person to tears, but Daleina was by no means weak. And with Hamon by her side, his quiet strength adding to her own power, she had a confidence she hadn't experienced in quite some time.

"Then it's almost done," Hamon said.

She nodded. "Nearly, but I'm not lowering my guard until it is."

His smile shifted into a frown. "You'll need to sleep at some point. You've barely gotten any rest. You won't be any good to Aratay if you collapse."

Garnah was staring at her son. "You are such a mother hen."

"I'm her healer, Mother. It's my job."

"You're a nag, that's what you are. She's a grown woman who can take care of herself. Let her sleep when she wants to sleep." Garnah then frowned at Daleina as well. "That said, you should sleep more. You have vicious circles under your eyes. People will think the spirits have been punching you."

"Figuratively speaking, they have. But they'll be calmer once Queen Naelin has crossed the border." She quickly explained what occurred in Semo, and Naelin's solution.

Garnah absorbed the news without changing expression. "She does have style."

Daleina felt her lips quirk into a smile, and then she felt a jolt of rage from the west—she quickly shouted with her mind, *Calm! Peace! Do no harm!*

The spirits snarled, but subsided. Her hands had tightened into fists as her previous confidence dissipated. It was going to take constant vigilance until she felt secure about the fate of her people. She uncurled her hands and massaged them. Her nails had dug half-moons into the flesh of her palms. Crossing to her, Hamon took her hands in his and rubbed them.

"Suffice it to say, this information is not to be shared," Daleina said, "at least until she's left Renthia. After that, I'll issue an explanation—I'm sure her spirits have been seen, and people must have questions."

"Sounds as though you have it figured out," Garnah said. "So how do I fit in?"

"Once the spirits are in the untamed lands, it should be over. Semo should be safe. Aratay should be safe. Queen Merecot should have gotten everything she wanted and have no more reason to threaten Aratay."

Cocking her head, Garnah narrowed her eyes. "But you don't think it's over. Again, though, is there a reason I had to climb all those stairs?"

"Because she asked you to, Mother."

Cutting off whatever clever retort Garnah had, Daleina said, "Because I need to be sure, for my people's sake. I am inviting Queen Merecot to Mittriel for a peace summit. If all goes well, we'll sign treaties ensuring there aren't any more invasions or murder attempts."

"And you want me to . . ."

"Make sure there aren't any murder attempts." Holding up one finger, Daleina sent her mind spinning west to slap down another earth spirit who was trying to burrow beneath a foreign spirit. *Leave them alone.* She then drew her attention back to Garnah. "Hamon was right: I'd like you to be my adviser for Queen Merecot's visit."

"You mean your poison tester," Garnah corrected. "The new title is appreciated, but—"

"I mean adviser," Daleina said. "If I may be blunt—"

"Oh yes, I love blunt!"

"You and Merecot share a lack of morality. You may be able to read her better than I can. Predict her next move. If she comes, she'll have ulterior motives—I want to know what they are, and whether they pose a threat to Aratay or to me."

Garnah blinked. "You have style too, Your Majesty."

THE QUEEN OF SORROW

Hamon began to speak. "Daleina, my mother can't be trusted—"

"You love me," Daleina said to Hamon.

"Of course."

"Well, as much as you hate it, Garnah loves you, in her own way. If I die under her watch, you won't forgive her. She wants—spirits, *needs*—your forgiveness. I can trust her in this."

Hamon nodded. She could tell he wanted to argue with her, but she could see he also knew she was right. "I'll never trust her. But I trust *you*."

Gifting him with a smile, Daleina turned back to Garnah. "I'll expect you to be at my call throughout the entire visit. You may use whatever means you wish to observe."

"You want me to spy on her?" Garnah said, delight in her voice. "Your childhood friend? A neighboring monarch with whom you're trying to forge an alliance based on mutual trust? Oh my dear, has the crown corrupted your sunny optimism at last?"

Daleina elected to let the "sunny optimism" comment lie. "She is my friend. And I do love her and will always love her. But I don't trust her."

"Wise," Garnah said. "Those we love can betray us the most."

Hamon murmured, "You'd know all about that."

"That hurts," Garnah said, her voice barely registering she knew what the word "hurts" meant.

Daleina squeezed Hamon's hand to silence him. She knew it was asking a lot of him, to allow his mother so close to her. But she also didn't need the two of them to bicker about this. She respected that he disagreed, but now wasn't the moment. Now she just needed everyone to do their jobs, and his job was to support her, plain and simple.

Not that it wasn't a risk, of course—the Queen's Poisoner could have her own agenda—but Daleina felt certain she was reading the woman right. Garnah was unscrupulous, but she also loved Hamon, in her own way, and she was desperate for Hamon to see that. Daleina was offering her a chance to prove herself. "Will you accept?"

"Is there a catch?" Garnah asked.

"My word is final in any decision." To be as clear as possible, she added: "That means no murder unless I say it's necessary."

Garnah nodded as if this were a normal request. "Always good to include an 'unless.' Exactly when do you expect Queen Merecot to arrive?"

"I have already sent a message to Champion Havtru with instructions to deliver the invite in person with all the appropriate pomp and circumstance so that it's clear it's an official invitation," Daleina said. "Of course, Merecot may fear a trap and say no."

"That would be sensible," Garnah agreed. "Is Queen Merecot sensible?"

"Not in the slightest," Daleina said. "She'll come."

Garnah grinned wolfishly. "Then I accept."

Daleina held out her hand, and Garnah knelt on one knee and kissed Daleina's knuckles. If Merecot came with death in her heart, Garnah would ferret it out. Daleina was certain of it. *And if she comes with hope instead . . . I'll greet her with open arms.*

Standing, Garnah dusted off her skirts and adjusted the feathers on her hat. "Oh, this is so exciting! And here I thought all royalty was noble and boring. I am so very pleased with my Hamon's choice. Hamon, you should marry her before she discovers how noble and boring *you* are."

"Thank you for your advice, Mother," Hamon said stiffly.

"May I be excused to prepare?" Garnah asked Daleina. She looked as giddy as a child who'd been presented with a three-tier cake.

"Of course, and thank you," Daleina said. She was silent as Garnah retreated from the tower and began to huff and puff as she descended the many stairs. "Hamon . . ." Turning to him, she saw a strange expression in his eyes—a bit of shyness.

"I *do* want to marry you," Hamon said, "if you'll have me. I had thought . . . there was your coronation, then the poisoning, then the invasion . . . I didn't think you wanted the extra stress of a wedding, but if you do . . ."

Leaning forward, Daleina kissed his cheek. "That's the most unromantic proposal I've ever heard. And you are right—I don't have time for a royal wedding now. But I *do* have time to make love to you." She kissed his neck and unbuttoned his collar.

"Here?"

"Like you said, it's the most secure place in Mittriel," Daleina said, and then drew him to her against a pillar. Far to the west, the spirits of Aratay felt a wave of joy splash over them, calming their fear and distracting them, as Daleina very deliberately did not block them out.

# CHAPTER 26

Every Renthian knew that to enter the untamed lands meant certain death, which was why Ven decided he should sharpen his sword. Sitting on a branch at the border, he methodically ran the edge over his whetstone and tried to avoid pessimistic thoughts. Or really any thoughts at all.

Beside him, Naelin was looking out into the haze. She jumped as a rock punched upward in the middle of the untamed lands. Mist swirled around the rock, and it didn't move again. The only sound was the wind between the trees of Aratay behind them and the *shick-shick* whisper of Ven's blade on the stone.

"Is this a profoundly stupid idea?" Naelin asked.

"Not profoundly," he said lightly, trying to make her smile— and failing. "Worst case, my sister will get a great song out of this."

"Your sister will never forgive me if you die."

"She forgives easily." Ven inspected his sword, tilting the blade so that it caught the sunlight. "But I don't plan to die today." He jumped to his feet.

"Me neither."

"Glad we're agreed on that." He hooked Naelin's hand with his and drew her in to kiss her. "If they're still alive in there, we'll find them. I promise."

She smiled, though it was a shaky smile. "You're very good

at being heroic." She drew in a deep breath, and Ven could tell she was about to say something difficult for her. *She's going to tell me not to come*, he thought. Sure enough, she said, "But you don't have to be. You should stay in Aratay. Return to being a champion."

*Knew it.* He considered arguing with her, convincing her that his love was true and he'd follow her literally beyond the ends of the earth, but instead he leapt off the branch and skidded down the curved trunk of the tree as he called, "Last one in cooks dinner for a week!"

He heard her surprised laugh behind him, and he slowed so she could catch up with him—and then he saw her shooting past him, on the back of a tree spirit with mossy skin and six-prong antlers. She plunged into the mist, and the wild spirits streamed around her. Sword drawn, Ven ran in with them.

All laughter died.

Whiteness curled around him. He squinted into the haze, but all he saw was the shifting shadows, different degrees of whiteness, swirling and spinning around him—it was like the fog that builds when fire meets ice. "Naelin?" he called, and his voice came out as a combination of a whisper, a squeak, a growl, and an echo.

The ground felt spongy as he walked forward. Sword raised, he twisted his head in all directions, walking forward, then sideways, then backward, trying to see everywhere at once, but there was nothing to see.

A whistle of wind rushed past him. He readied his sword.

A cackle, high, unearthly.

The palms of his hands were sweaty, and he cursed himself for not holding on to Naelin as they entered. He didn't think the haze would be as thick as this. "Naelin, answer me!"

He heard his own fear, tasted it, as thick as mucus coating the back of his throat. He gripped his sword tighter, then swept it through the mist. Bits of whiteness clung to it, like cobweb strands. He began slashing in front of him as he strode forward.

*They're here.*

He felt spirits all around him, brushing past his legs, around his sword, and he heard them laughing at him. He couldn't tell if they were Naelin's spirits or other, wilder spirits from the untamed lands, and at that moment, he didn't care. They were between him and Naelin.

He charged forward, clearing the haze out of the way with his sword—and as if his sword were the wind, the haze cleared for him, and he realized the mist wasn't empty air at all.

It was full of spirits.

All around him, the world was choked with spirits.

"Ven!"

He ran toward her voice.

From his left: "Ven!"

His right: "Ven!" Higher pitched. A mad giggle.

It wasn't Naelin.

He halted.

He couldn't be certain *any* of those voices were her. The mist curled closer to him. He felt a long finger stroke his arm. Steadying himself, he lifted his sword eye level. The spirits pressed in, murmuring and crooning and cackling.

He waited, counting his breaths.

He felt prickles on the back of his neck. A spirit was there, breathing close to him. Closing his eyes, Ven drew in air.

And then he exploded into movement.

The spirits who had drawn close weren't fast enough to evade him—he'd switched so suddenly from stillness to motion that they were caught off-guard. His blade slid through them. He felt them die.

Swing right.

Drop down.

Kick and jab. Elbow back. Palm upward, slamming into the face of a spirit, and then he stabbed, felt it slide in, heard the cry, pulled back, and twisted to slice at the whisper of wind behind him. An ice spirit shrieked as his sword bit into it. He drew back then struck again, a whirl of motion.

And the untamed spirits retreated, as if unused to anyone fighting back. He heard them rustling, and he opened his eyes to see he stood in a clearing of gray stone. Pale-blue sky was visible overhead, and the whiteness had retreated.

At the edge of the haze, he saw a flash of color: Naelin.

He ran toward her with his sword ready. Around him, in the mist, he saw light flash—lightning strikes within the clouds. Beneath his feet, the earth shifted. He didn't let any of it distract him and ran across moving ground, his feet landing lightly, knees bent deep, never depending on the earth to hold him as he sprang across the clearing.

Midair, he swung his sword, and he felt it impact. A spirit reared back in pain, and as he landed, he saw it tower above him: an earth spirit with a stone face and a body of brambles. It clawed at him, and he dodged in a roll, blade protected against him.

And then he was at Naelin's side.

Her eyes were closed, and her arms were spread wide, fingers splayed. Positioning himself at her back, he fended away spirits that dove for her.

The ground rumbled beneath them, and he felt it rising up higher and higher. He crouched for balance, but Naelin stood straight and tall. The earth rose up and up until they towered above the swarm of whiteness.

Lowering her arms, Naelin looked back at him. "The spirits of the untamed lands don't want us here."

"Yeah, noticed that. Where are *your* spirits?"

"Coming," she said, and then hundreds of spirits circled them, on the ground around them and in the air above them, driving back the whiteness.

NAELIN FELT THE VASTNESS: HUNDREDS OF THOUSANDS OF SPIR-its, stretching out toward the horizon—if there even was a horizon in this place. It felt endless. She drew her own spirits closer, in a tight circle around her and Ven. They felt pitifully few.

*I never thought I'd come to the point where I felt safer* with *spirits.*

But these were *her* spirits. And even though they had come from the untamed lands originally, they were bonded to her now, and that made them instantly different from the unleashed spirits who roamed this land. Her spirits knew what it was like to have a queen, to be controlled and have control, to be able to create and destroy but with restraint. Unlike the ones here . . .

*How can Erian and Llor be here? How can they* survive *here? And how can I find them either way?* She felt like a single leaf in an overwhelmingly massive forest. She'd thought she was strong, but this place . . . From their vantage point on top of the rock, she surveyed the untamed lands in all directions.

The forests of Aratay were no longer visible, though she could feel the border to the east, a sharp cutoff to the sense of wall-to-wall spirits.

*They're not wall-to-wall,* Naelin told herself. It only seemed that way because there were so many, and they flitted so quickly that many were almost indistinguishable from the gauzy fog. She felt the attention of the spirits shift away now that she and Ven were motionless. *They have the attention span of children.*

"Which way?" Ven asked.

She studied the sea of mist. It all looked the same—except no, it didn't. Squinting, she saw a flash of blue in the distance, far to the southwest. It widened, and the mist shifted away from it. A river? A lake? Perhaps an ocean.

Ven pointed north. "Mountains."

She saw gray peaks above the clouds. She could have sworn they hadn't been there before, but they must have been hidden by the mist. Even unleashed spirits couldn't form mountains that quickly. Smoke curled from the peak of one of the mountains, and it was ringed with blackness. She thought she saw a streak of red, like a bloody tear on the side of the peak.

"Northwest," she decided, between the sea and the volcano.

He nodded. "It's the clearest path. A sensible choice."

*Nothing about this place feels "sensible."*

It felt as foggy as a dream. Summoning a spirit with leathery bat wings and a cat body, Naelin climbed on its back, with Ven behind her. He kept his sword unsheathed and held her waist with only one arm. The spirit kicked off the rock and flew westward.

As they flew farther in, the mist became more wisplike, and

she saw it wasn't all blankness like it seemed from outside. There were colors here.

Red. Fire that danced across stone.

Blue. A snake of a river that shifted and then tumbled into a waterfall.

Gold. Lightning that chased from the sky but never hit the earth.

Black. A crevasse in the earth that was so deep it was only darkness.

They flew over a canyon that looked as if a great hand had scraped it from the earth, and they flew over a single tree whose branches snaked in twisting braids for miles. In the north, the volcanoes bubbled and boiled. In the south, the seashore seemed to shift and undulate.

Stones molded themselves out of the earth into towers that then tumbled into dust. Naelin and Ven flew between them. A field of ice erupted into frozen shards.

All of it was ever-changing. The more she saw, the more she felt the hope inside her wither. *No one could survive in a land like this*, she thought. The spirits recarved the landscape every moment: a canyon became a lake became a field of ice became a cliff became a waterfall. *Down*, Naelin ordered the spirit. "There." She guided them to a circle of brilliant green. Flowers were blossoming throughout the field, a riot of colors on plants from spring, fall, and autumn all at once, cycling through the seasons right before her eyes.

She spotted the spirit in the center of it. The earth spirit looked like a green-skinned man with black antlers. His eyes were black as well; even the whites of his eyes glistened black.

She thrust an image of Erian and Llor at the spirit. *We seek a boy and a girl.*

She felt its confusion.

She couldn't read it as well as the spirits she'd bonded to, but she could sense it, the same as she could before she became queen. It was agitated. It hadn't expected them to come to it. It didn't like them here. It wanted to be left alone, yet it also yearned—for what, she couldn't sense, but she felt it reach achingly toward them.

*Humans*, she pressed. *Have you seen any? Have you seen a wolf? A great gray wolf?*

Instead of answering, it turned and galloped away. The flowers withered in its wake. The air smelled sour from the dying flowers. Naelin wrapped her mind around her own wild spirits—she felt them, frightened. They huddled together.

*How do I find them? Help me find them!*

"Protect me while I search," Naelin told Ven.

"Always." He stood beside her, sword raised, while she sent her mind with the spirits, spreading out through the untamed lands. Split into hundreds of eyes, she swept across the constantly shifting landscape. She touched the minds of other spirits, briefly, felt their shock, their confusion, their anger, their hope.

*Hope?*

It reminded her of what she had felt from her own spirits, but she didn't have time to consider it. She focused as her spirits searched the land. Dimly, beside her, she heard cries and shrieks and knew that Ven was fighting, but she kept pressing onward, searching, searching . . .

She felt only spirits. Saw only the wildness.

At last, she drew back, and she fell onto her knees, crushing the dead flowers. Beside her, Ven lowered his sword, and she saw a circle of spirits withdraw as her wild spirits flew back toward her.

As the spirits of the untamed lands withdrew, she tried to think how next to search. She'd have to compel the spirits from here to help her, search their memories. It wouldn't be easy, but . . .

"Naelin." Ven's voice was soft, insistent.

She looked up.

Across the field of dead flowers stood a ragged child. Human, not spirit. A boy younger than Llor, with dirt smudging his cheeks and clothes that dangled around him. He stared at them for a moment, and then he ran.

# CHAPTER 27

Hanna folded the paper and let her hands rest on her lap. She didn't know how Merecot was going to react to this invitation. *With suspicion, of course.* The untrustworthy always saw deceit in others. *Knowing Daleina, the offer is likely genuine. And will likely get her killed.* Hanna didn't know how Daleina had suffered through so much and still kept her idealism intact.

*Damn inconvenient.*

They'd managed the extraordinary here: siphoning away the excess spirits. Best to leave well enough alone and not invite trouble onto your doorstep. Hanna had already had the servants pack for her and her guards, and had been anticipating a pleasant trip home, without any more excitement.

Briefly, Hanna considered pretending she hadn't received the note. But that would be cowardly, and, more important, impossible, with Champion Havtru so proud that he'd been able to deliver it in person. He'd arrived shortly after dawn, with a man, a girl, and Queen Daleina's sister.

Staring out the window at the mountains, Hanna tented her fingers under her chin. It was a hostile kind of beautiful here, with mountains cutting the sky in every direction. The morning sky looked under attack by the peaks, and that thrilled her just a bit.

"Ambassador Hanna?" Champion Havtru asked from behind her.

He was a good boy. Earnest. Worked hard. He'd also, she realized, arrived here very quickly, if Daleina had indeed waited to send her message until after Queen Naelin had left. "You traveled here on foot, Champion Havtru?"

"Yes, Madame Ambassador."

*Interesting.* "On foot from Mittriel? With the queen's message?"

"A spirit delivered it to me at the border, and then we hurried the rest of the way."

Aha, then he had been sent for another purpose. *Maybe Daleina has a plan after all.* Certainly she wouldn't have risked her sister without a good reason. Hanna crooked her finger at him, to indicate he should come closer.

He bent down.

"Tell me your true purpose," Hanna whispered.

He whispered back, "To bring you home."

That was it? She didn't know what she'd expected, but an escort was not it, considering she already had her guards. She wished Daleina were a better strategist, but Hanna had the strong sense that the crux of the queen's plan was: invite Merecot and make friends again. "And you brought your candidate to assist?" She waved her hand at the young girl who stood a few paces behind him, next to a man dressed in brown who looked like he'd be more comfortable chopping wood than standing in a palace. The girl appeared to be about fourteen, no more than fifteen, with braided black hair and pale gray eyes. She hadn't spoken since she'd arrived. The queen's sister, Arin, stood protectively next to her.

"Oh, Cajara is not my candidate," Champion Havtru said.

*Of course she's not*, Hanna thought, resisting an eye roll. But if he wanted to pretend that the girl was just a family friend or a stray relative who fancied a trip to Semo, then she had no interest in arguing with him. She made a mental note not to trust Havtru with any stealth missions. "How about him? Is he just a friend as well?"

The man in brown stepped forward and bowed awkwardly. "Madam Ambassador, ma'am, my name is Renet. From East Everdale. And I'm here to see my wife, Naelin. Queen Naelin. My former wife. That is, I'd like to speak with her, if I may. And our children?"

*Oh, poor man.*

"I've, uh, heard some rumors since we came to Semo." He twisted his hands together, fidgeting like a child. "Guards at the border. People in the city. In the palace. They're all talking. They say Naelin . . . Queen Naelin . . . They say she . . . She's gone to the untamed lands? But that's impossible."

He was looking at her with pleading eyes, as if begging for her to laugh and say it wasn't true. She couldn't say that. Hanna gestured toward the cushioned chairs. "You might want to sit." She didn't know what rumors he'd heard, but she did have news she thought he'd welcome. "She's not planning on dying. She believes . . ." It was difficult to say the next part exactly right. She didn't want to either crush him or raise his hopes unrealistically. "She's gone to rescue your children. We have reason to believe they're in the untamed lands."

Arin gasped. "But no one—" With a glance at Renet, she bit off the rest of what she was going to say. Cajara reached over and took Arin's hand.

"The untamed . . . How? Why?" Renet stammered. "They're supposed to be in Semo! Everyone said . . . That's why Naelin . . . Not the untamed lands!" He'd gone pale and started to shake. She was glad she'd told him to sit. He didn't look as if he'd be able to stand. Havtru looked stunned as well. Surprisingly, the girl Cajara's expression didn't change. Her face was as placid as it had been since she'd arrived. *A nice change from all the histrionics of Queen Merecot and the emotional hurricane of Queen Naelin,* Hanna thought. *If this is Havtru's candidate, I approve.*

"I must go with her!" Renet cried.

"You can't," Hanna said, this time barely able to suppress her eye roll. *As if this man could do anything there.* "She's already gone. But don't worry. Champion Ven is with her. He'll protect her, and if your children are alive, they'll find them and bring them safely home."

"I should be with her. They're my children. And she's my wife."

He swallowed hard, and his throat bobbed. "That is . . . There was another rumor . . ." He faltered, as if he couldn't even put it into words.

"She's Champion Ven's wife now," she said as gently as possible. "But they will find your children, if they can."

He deflated like a wilted flower on the couch. Sinking his face into his hands, he moaned. At last, he said, "I wasn't worthy of her. Or them. Erian and Llor. Never was. But I will be. When they return to Aratay . . . they'll see I have changed. I *will* change!"

Hanna gave him an encouraging smile. "Excellent!" And that was all the energy she wanted to spare on a stranger's emotional needs. She turned to Havtru. "We'll begin preparations for our return to Aratay. I'll tell my guards after we meet with Queen Merecot."

Havtru's face relaxed into a smile, as if he'd been expecting her to argue with him about leaving Semo. *I'm ornery,* Hanna thought, *not stupid. Of course I'll go back. Someone has to keep an eye on Merecot.* "You three rest and recover from your journey," she said to Arin, Cajara, and Renet. "Champion Havtru and I must go deliver an invitation."

Oh, sweet, naïve Daleina. Merecot had to work hard to keep a triumphant grin off her face. "What a delightful and unexpected invitation," she said to Ambassador Hanna and Champion Havtru.

"I know what you're thinking—you suspect a trap—but I believe it's sincerely meant," Hanna said, a hint of weariness in her voice that made Merecot think she was genuine. She clearly believed that Daleina's motives were innocent, and if Merecot was reading the ambassador correctly, she didn't approve. That was almost amusing. "Queen Daleina wants to establish a permanent peace."

*Of course it's not a trap. Daleina won't kill me. She doesn't have it in her.* "Don't we all want that? And how nice that she sent a champion to deliver her invitation. Makes it all formal and official."

Champion Havtru bowed.

The last person she wanted to see in Semo, aside from her old headmistress, was another reminder of the life she'd set aside: a champion. Merecot hadn't lasted at Northeast Academy long enough for one of Aratay's much-lauded champions to choose her. And he hadn't come alone, she knew. A man and two girls had accompanied him, though they'd stayed behind for this meeting. She had spies watching them, of course; she'd know who they were and why they'd come in short order. *Not that it matters.* She had what she wanted.

*Best not to look too eager.*

Narrowing her eyes at Hanna and Havtru, Merecot drummed her fingers on the armrest of her throne. "This is a time of change for my country. My people need me here . . . Yet this is a historic opportunity. Few queens visit their neighbors."

She didn't mention her last "visit," and they, politely, didn't either.

"We would be honored to escort Your Majesty to Mittriel," Champion Havtru said with another bow. He then fiddled with the collar of his shirt. He seemed uncomfortable in her presence, which was also amusing. She had to work again to keep from smiling.

Merecot waved away his offer. "I don't need an escort." She silently ordered one of the smaller spirits to blow open one of the large windows, and then summoned her favorite mount: an air spirit with golden feathers, an eagle body, and a man's head. He swooped into the throne room and circled the chandeliers. "As you can see, I have my own transportation. You are, of course, welcome to enjoy the hospitality of my castle."

She had no intention of letting them slow her down. Not when victory was so close.

"But Your Majesty, it would be our privilege to . . ." Hanna began.

Merecot let out a little laugh. "Oh, there's no need to trouble yourselves. I know the way." She thought of Queen Jastra and wished she could have said "I told you so." *See, I did have a plan, and it's happening even more quickly than I'd imagined. If only you'd believed in me more . . .* One queen gone, and an open invitation to visit the other. Access to Daleina, near the Aratay-ian Grove. It was like Daleina was giving Merecot everything they'd wanted, wrapped in a pretty bow. *If I'd killed Naelin, this wouldn't have happened.*

She tried not to picture Jastra in her last moments. *I can't be missing her. She betrayed me.* But she couldn't help wishing things had turned out differently. It would have been nice to have someone on her side, advising her, rooting for her.

Hanna was frowning. She had a formidable frown that still made Merecot wonder if she'd finished her homework. "Queen Merecot, as official ambassador to Semo, I should accompany you. I believe I may be able to aid . . ."

Merecot smiled merrily, hoping it wasn't obvious that she was delighted to soon be free of her old headmistress. "Oh, you've done quite enough. Why not rest here while I pay a visit on my dear old friend? We can chat again after I return."

Indeed, there was a lovely secondary benefit to leaving them here, under the protection of Merecot's guards: they'd be assur-ances against Daleina's good behavior. *After all, Daleina's and my last meeting was . . . dramatic.* Having her beloved headmis-tress as well as one of her brave champions—not to mention the potential assassins and the palace guards who'd accompanied Hanna—would make nice leverage if Merecot needed it. *At the very least, it will ensure Daleina plays nice.*

Both the champion and ambassador began to protest, but Merecot cut them off. "You'd only slow me down. If I fly fast enough, I can reach Mittriel before nightfall. I do love to make a dramatic entrance." She paused, reaching with her mind to touch the gold eagle spirit. "And a dramatic exit."

The enormous eagle with a man's head dove from the chande-lier, and she leapt from the throne onto its back and flew out the window. Tapestries fluttered in her wake, and she reveled in the feeling of near-victory.

WHILE THE QUEEN OF SEMO FLEW SOUTH, DALEINA REHEARSED her welcome speech for her former-friend Queen Merecot in the mirror. She had two options: the let-us-have-peace speech and the you-are-irredeemably-evil speech.

Lounging on a couch behind her, Garnah said, "I like the second one."

Daleina didn't turn around. "Your opinion on this is not required."

"Remind me again why Mother is here," Hamon said. "There's been no word from the north that Queen Merecot even received your message, much less accepted your invitation."

Squaring her shoulders, Daleina studied her own face in the reflection. She'd dusted pale powder under her eyes but it only made her look ghoulish, not less tired. She rubbed her cheeks hard until they pinkened. *There, I look a little more alive now.* "She's already coming. She'll be here shortly."

Behind her, she heard Hamon jump to his feet, knocking over a small table. A vase crashed onto the floor. He was scooping up shards of pottery when she turned around. "You should have told us," he said. "The guards . . ."

"I'll need you to leave, Hamon."

He stopped.

"You can't be here when she comes," Daleina said as gently as she could.

"I'm not leaving you alone with that woman," Hamon sputtered. "She had you poisoned!"

"Your mother will watch for that." Reaching out with her mind, Daleina felt the spirits only a few miles outside Mittriel react as the other queen flew through the trees. Through their eyes, she saw Merecot as a golden blur.

"You can't trust her either," Hamon said.

"Hamon!" Garnah said in feigned shock.

Ignoring his mother, Hamon crossed to Daleina and took her hands. His hands felt dry and soft in hers. "You know I would give my life to keep you safe." Earnest, devoted Hamon. She nearly smiled, but she didn't want him to think she was mocking him. He meant every word, and she treasured that—he was one of the few people in the palace who she knew had no ulterior motive.

She knew how rare and lucky it was for a queen to have someone she could trust so absolutely.

"I know, and we must assume Merecot knows this too, which is why I need you elsewhere, ready with antidotes if I need them." She didn't want to tell Hamon that while she trusted him with her own life, she didn't trust him with Merecot's. He'd made his opinion on the poisoning abundantly clear, and she didn't want him to do anything rash in the name of defending his queen. *Just because I know he loves me, it doesn't mean I know he'll behave the way I need him to.* "Trust me, Hamon. Please leave."

He wasn't happy with her. She hadn't expected him to be.

Leaning forward, she kissed him. "Please, Hamon." Placing her hands on either side of his face, she gazed at him, trying to put all her love and trust into her eyes. *You are my safety*, she thought. *The one rock that won't move, the one tree that won't fall, the river that will carry me and never drown me.* "Leave. For me."

He left, still unhappy, and Garnah chuckled. "You know my son's weaknesses. *You.* You give him exactly the kind of love and trust a boy like Hamon needs." Shuffling over to a side table, Garnah poured herself a crystal goblet full of spiced pear juice. She popped a chocolate into her mouth. Daleina didn't know how she could eat at a time like this. She felt jittery inside and out.

"Do you know what he was like as a child?" Garnah didn't wait for Daleina to answer. She talked as if she were conversing only with herself. "Pleasant. You've never had children, so you don't know how unusual that is. Children can be charming or intelligent or imaginative or destructive balls of chaotic fury. But they're rarely 'pleasant.' Our neighbors would coo over him and tell me how lucky I was to have such a well-behaved son. And Hamon would go on pleasing them, being unfailingly polite and kind. For many years, I assumed he was deliberately manipulating all those fools."

Daleina pictured Hamon as a child, bright-eyed and eager to please—and how impossible it must have been for someone as empathetic as he was to have a mother who casually murdered people, including her own husband, Hamon's father. *It's a wonder that Hamon came out of his childhood whole.*

"It wasn't until long after he left me that I realized the silly boy was sincere. He has a towering need to love and be loved. He truly cared about the well-being of all those ridiculous people. The only one he never found room in his heart for was me. Do you know how it feels to have your own child deny you?"

Daleina was saved from having to reply by the shriek of a tree spirit.

*She's here.*

Striding across the room to the balcony, Daleina called to the spirits in Mittriel, felt their agitation, drew them closer to the blur of gold that crossed into the city. She asked the spirits to flank the queen, like an escort—they already wanted to watch her, so it was easy to coax them into the trees and the air. At Daleina's direction, the spirits of Aratay funneled the queen of Semo toward the palace, where Daleina waited, her heart pounding in her throat.

Garnah joined her on the balcony. "I admit, I am looking forward to meeting her."

"Wait within," Daleina ordered. "I greet her alone."

A massive golden eagle with a human face burst through the branches. It shook the trees, and red leaves swirled in its wake, falling in spirals. Daleina heard Garnah retreat behind her, for once not making any witty comment or arguing. With her eyes glued on the eagle spirit, she kept her mind open to the spirits of Aratay. She wouldn't put it past Merecot to try to seize control of them, or attack them, or . . .

*I don't know what to expect from Merecot, which is the problem.*

So she waited.

SHE'S STILL WEAK, MERECOT THOUGHT AS SHE FLEW TOWARD THE palace, flanked by the spirits of Aratay. She could sense the spirits' curiosity mixed with hostility, and she knew Daleina was prodding and coaxing them to follow her. Even with the power of a queen, though, Daleina didn't have the kind of control Merecot did. Merecot owned the will of the spirit she rode. If she'd brought her invading army of spirits with her, she could have easily overwhelmed Daleina's spirits, assuming she didn't have another irritatingly powerful heir like Naelin up her sleeves.

Merecot circled the palace, looking down on the Chamber of the Queen's Champions and the Queen's Tower. *This should have been my palace.* She'd been born in Aratay and always expected she'd be queen of her homeland. As a child, she'd spent hours imagining herself living in the white trees of the palace, climbing the famous stairs to the Council of Champions, holding the fate of the forests in her hands . . . She remembered playacting with Alet, quietly so their parents wouldn't hear—both sisters dreaming of a life different from the one they had at home.

In their games, they'd always been the heroes.

And they'd always won.

*I'll win for you, Alet.* She was so close now. Just one more hurdle.

Clearly anxious, the spirits of Aratay circled with her, and Merecot wondered if she sensed their own nervousness or Daleina's.

*It has to be one of those, though, because* I'm *not afraid*, Merecot told herself. *And I'll prove it.*

As the eagle soared high above the queen of Aratay, Merecot leapt from its back. *If you mean peace, Daleina, catch me. If not . . .* If not, Merecot could recall her spirit to catch her before she splatted un-royally on the ground or impaled herself on a spire.

*This is your test, Daleina. Are we going to fight, or talk?*

Wind roared in her ears.

*Catch me!*

An ermine-like spirit with bat wings caught her and then dumped her onto the balcony. Merecot sprang to her feet as if her entrance had been just as graceful and dramatic as she'd planned. The problem was, she wasn't certain whether it was her command or Daleina's that had sent the spirit. Smoothing her skirt, she wished she hadn't panicked right there at the end. She hoped Daleina hadn't noticed. Calmly, with as much dignity as she could muster, Merecot said, "You invited me, and I have come."

"Welcome to Aratay," Daleina said.

Daleina, somewhat to Merecot's surprise, looked queenly. She was dressed in a silver gown that pooled around her feet like melted moonlight. Her red, brown, and gold streaked hair was loose, and she wore a circlet of woven ivy. *Nice effect,* Merecot thought. "Royalty becomes you."

"Thank you," Daleina said. "You look well also."

*Okay, so we're going to be stiff and formal. Too bad I don't do stiff and formal.* "It's the lack of sleep and the constant stress. Really does wonders on the complexion."

Daleina didn't crack a smile. "I hadn't heard that."

Both queens stared at each other. "So . . . Ambassador Hanna was worried I'd think this was a trap. Is it?" Merecot asked in a falsely bright voice. "Did you invite me here to kill me?"

No change in expression. "I did not."

She was certain Daleina didn't have it in her, but if she did . . . *Let me see if I can prod her into revealing anything.* "Last time I saw you, you'd had my sister killed. It's logical to assume I'm next."

"I think you misremember your history. Your sister was my dear friend," Daleina said, "and she died in an assassination attempt that you ordered. But is this truly what you wish to discuss? It's certainly not why I called you here."

"Invited me," Merecot corrected.

Daleina inclined her head. "Invited."

"I'll bite," Merecot said. "Why am I here?" She braced herself for a litany of demands. They'd need to negotiate a peace treaty, and Daleina would surely expect to have the upper hand, given that she'd sacrificed her co-queen to aid Semo. It was possible she'd want to reexamine the border between their countries, or set laws in place that would ensure the protection of those borders. Frankly, Merecot didn't care if—

"I wanted to see if we're still friends," Daleina said.

Merecot stared.

She blinked.

She cleaned out one ear.

Then the other, deliberately and sarcastically slowly.

"Really?" Merecot asked.

If her theatrics affected the other queen, Daleina didn't show it. She just nodded and held out her hand, infuriatingly serene.

"Truly. We were friends once, remember? I want to be friends again, somehow, if we can rebuild whatever trust and affection we once had—"

"I can't decide if you're naïve or stupid."

Daleina's hand didn't waver, and she was looking at Merecot as intently as Merecot looked at a spirit she wanted to subdue, as if her eyes could bore directly into her brain. "Maybe both. But either way, for the sake of both of our people, I want your friendship back."

*By the spirits, I think she's serious.* That was . . . unexpected. "So I take your hand, and then what? We swap stories late in the night? Sneak into the palace kitchen for a snack? Giggle? Because I don't giggle."

"We secure the safety of both of our peoples." Hand still out. Eyes still earnest. Still ignoring Merecot's attempts at humor.

"You're absurd," Merecot said.

"Perhaps. But I was once your friend," Daleina said. "I want to be again."

Merecot stepped backward, and her back bumped into the rail of the balcony. There had to be a trick here, some kind of ploy to get Merecot to lower her guard. Merecot wasn't naïve enough to believe Daleina meant it. Queens didn't have friendships, least of all with each other. And who talked like this anyway? You didn't ask someone "be my friend" unless you were six years old. You became friends in a natural progression that didn't involve grandiose statements on a palace balcony. "That's . . . nice?"

"Merecot."

"Daleina?"

Daleina lowered her hand.

"You're withdrawing the offer of friendship?" Merecot asked.

"I'm resting my arm," Daleina said. She lifted her hand again, held it out toward Merecot, and waited, a completely placid expression on her face as if she intended to keep this up as long as it took. *Maybe she did.* Daleina was known to have a stubborn streak.

"I tried to kill you," Merecot said, trying to shock Daleina out of this exasperating serenity. She didn't mention she'd come with that purpose again.

"All friendships have bumps."

Still the hand. Still the stare. It was beginning to get more than a little unsettling. Merecot didn't like feeling that she wasn't in control of the conversation.

"I also invaded your country," Merecot pointed out.

"I am prepared to forgive you."

"Aha, so you haven't forgiven me yet! You don't really trust me. If I said, 'Yes, let's be buddies right now,' you'd have me spied on. You'd wait until I lowered my guard, and then you'd . . . do whatever you plan to do. What do you plan to do, Daleina?" She hadn't intended to ask her right out, but this conversation wasn't going the way she'd expected it to anyway. Besides, she preferred being direct.

She just didn't expect Daleina to be so . . . she couldn't even come up with a word to describe how Aratay's queen was acting.

"I plan to protect my people," Daleina said, "until the day I die, at what will hopefully be a very old age. And I plan to live in peace with my neighbors, from this day forward. We share a common enemy, Merecot. We don't have to be enemies with each other."

Merecot felt a twinge of something. *Hope*, she thought. *Or indigestion.*

"That common enemy is exactly why I did all I did," Merecot said. "I want a better life for *all* Renthians." She studied Daleina's hand once more. Over and over in her head, she could hear Jastra's voice saying, *It's a trick!* Except Daleina had never been tricky. Stubborn, yes. Naïve, yes. Weak, yes. But not sneaky. Despite being the bottom of the class with spirits, Daleina never cheated. She just worked harder. *That could be what she's doing now. Working harder, to become my friend again, for the sake of her people.* It was kind of admirable. *She must hate me, deep inside. I'd hate me.* "What exactly does a friendship between two queens entail? I suppose you'll want me to swear to never attempt to murder you again."

"I want you to swear to talk first, *before* you try to kill me," Daleina said.

"So you're not ruling out the killing part if it's necessary?" Not that Merecot *wanted* to kill Daleina. In fact, standing with her now, she couldn't quite believe what she'd almost done and what she'd come here to do. Daleina seemed so *alive*. So . . . *Oh, spirits, do I actually admire her? Weak, untalented, overtrusting, naïve, idealistic Daleina?*

She heard a muffled snort from inside the chambers, almost a laugh.

"You have someone spying on us? Right now, when you're asking me for a leap of faith? Bit cynical of you, isn't it?" *So much for trust and friendship.* Merecot plunged her mind into the palace, searching for a spirit in order to look through its eyes, but there were no spirits within.

"Of course," Daleina said. "I'm hopeful, not stupid." Her hand still was held out.

"Then you *have* changed." Merecot paused. "I didn't actually mean that. It was just such a good setup for the insult, I couldn't resist."

"I understand," Daleina said gravely, but Merecot thought she saw a flicker of an almost-smile. She wished she could see what Daleina was thinking.

*If I could penetrate the minds of the spirits who were linked to her . . .* Quickly, in the pause in the conversation, Merecot slammed her mind into the thoughts of the spirits that hovered around the palace. She'd never tried to "read" anyone's mind this way, but the theory was sound. She could see the memories of spirits, so if they held the memory of Daleina's thoughts and plans . . . Sifting through the spirits' minds, she found . . .

Nothing.

They knew nothing.

Daleina didn't share her thoughts with them. She was linked to them, yes, but it was a softer link than either Merecot or Naelin had. *Clever,* Merecot thought. Daleina must keep herself shielded from them. Or else she isn't strong enough to forge a more in-depth connection. Either way, it meant Merecot couldn't access any memories the spirits had of her thoughts. Once more, she was at a disadvantage ... and that bothered her a great deal.

"Say I say yes, I want to be friends again. What happens next?"

"You'll be offered the hospitality of the palace, shown to a room, led to the baths, and invited to dine with me here in my rooms. Then we talk."

Merecot held up one finger. "I already stated no giggling."

"There will be no giggling," Daleina agreed.

*I came all this way. May as well see where this goes. I can always kill her later,* Merecot thought. She was closer to the grove than she'd ever been. She could kill Daleina, race to the Aratayian grove, and seize the crown. Right now, with whatever army of spies was listening, Merecot knew she'd be foolish to try. Queen Jastra would have told her to do it anyway—use her strength and control of the spirits, use Daleina's hopefulness against her to surprise her. *But I'm not Jastra, and I have other cards to play.* "You haven't asked me about Ambassador Hanna or Champion Havtru. I gathered you've noticed I returned without them."

"You won't harm them," Daleina said, certainty in her voice.

"Oh? You're sure of that?"

"You won't need to," Daleina said. "I've invited you here in peace."

Again, the naïveté amused her, but at the same time, it irked her. Because there was no way Daleina didn't know its effect on her. *She's ... toying with me.* Yet it still wasn't quite clear how. *I should be the one controlling the conversation. I'm supposed to be outsmarting her!*

Merecot tried hard to keep her expression as bland as possible. *I underestimated her. She knows I left them behind as hostages.* Daleina kept surprising her. *This may be a more interesting visit than I thought. I wonder ... if she'd listen.* She'd come here planning to take the crown by force, but if she could convince Daleina to abdicate willingly instead ... ?

Was it possible? Was Daleina smart enough, wise enough, *queen* enough, to understand *why* Merecot had to be queen of both Semo and Aratay? She'd never planned to explain herself, but if there was a chance that Daleina would listen and believe ...

*I could try.*

For a moment, she felt breathless, nearly light-headed. She couldn't put a name on the feeling that rushed through her, but she thought maybe it was hope.

"In that case, I'd be delighted to accept the hospitality of your palace." Merecot held out her hand, and Daleina clasped it.

Daleina instructed Belsowik to escort Queen Merecot to the guest chambers, and she ordered spirits to prepare it in advance, stealing finery from other rooms of the palace to drape Merecot's rooms in as much splendor as possible. Judging by the number of jewels draped over Merecot, she associated finery with being queen. *Might as well oblige her.* She didn't know if any queen of Aratay had ever hosted a queen of another country, voluntarily or not. Few queens were powerful enough to keep their spirits under control from a distance. *We tend to stay put, and not try to invade one another. One country's spirits are bad enough—no one wants more. Except Merecot.*

After Merecot had been swept away, she located Garnah, who had wisely retreated to Daleina's inner bedroom and hidden. Daleina made a mental note to have Hamon check the room for any stray potions or powders before she slept. "I assume you heard all that?"

"She's absolutely charming," Garnah said, climbing out from behind a chest and smoothing the wrinkles in her skirt. She straightened the feathers in her hair. "I adore her."

"Can I trust her?" Daleina asked.

"Yes. Decidedly yes." She held up one finger. "Once you determine what she wants. She's the kind who will be steadfast in her pursuit of her goal."

"She wanted to be rid of the excess spirits in Semo," Daleina said.

"Ah, but why?"

"Because they were tearing apart the fabric of her country."

"Why should she care?"

"Because people were losing their homes and dying, and it's a queen's responsibility—"

Garnah pursed her lips and made a rude noise. "You think Merecot cares for that?"

*What a ridiculous question*, she thought. *Every queen cares about her people!* Daleina began to reconsider her idea of including Garnah in these meetings. She had very little understanding of human emotion—Hamon would have said it was because she'd never experienced it. But before Daleina replied, she forced herself to truly consider the question. She had asked for Garnah's opinion expressly because of her lack of compassion. *Is it true* every *queen cares? What about Queen Fara?* "Merecot has wanted to be a queen for as long as I've known her. She believes it's her destiny."

Garnah pressed again. "Why?"

"Because the world needs—"

"Don't project your own nobility onto others. It's not a weight we want to carry." Garnah waved her hand in the air as if shooing away flies. "You need to discover *why* she wanted to be queen so badly that she left her school, her home, her family, her everything. Why she was willing to kill for a land that's not her own. And more important, why she's come here now, at risk to herself, even though she should have everything she wants. You need to know what she truly wants."

*She's right*, Daleina thought. *Merecot doesn't think like I do.* That was why she wanted Garnah listening to these meetings in the first place. "What do *you* want?"

Garnah smiled. "All I want is my son's love."

Though rationally she knew she shouldn't, though Hamon would have cautioned her not to, though Garnah had been a terrible mother, Daleina believed her. "Then we continue."

# CHAPTER 28

Daleina wished Arin were here. She'd have created miraculously extravagant confections in the kitchen that would have distracted from the awkwardness of entertaining Daleina's would-be murderer. *On the other hand, it's better that Arin's safe at home. I can handle a little awkwardness.* After all, the entire reason Daleina was doing any of this was to keep Arin and people like her safe.

Merecot slurped her soup, then dabbed the corner of her lips with a napkin.

Daleina didn't know how she was supposed to convince Merecot to reveal her true motivations. She could ask point-blank and hope that Merecot was in the mood to monologue. Or she could be patient and hope Merecot revealed herself on her own. *As Garnah said, she's here, so she clearly wants something. But what?* Maybe if she just got Merecot talking, tried to get her to open up . . .

"Tell me about your sister," Daleina offered.

Merecot stiffened. She laid her soup spoon down and folded her hands on her lap, white-knuckled. "You knew her. You claimed to be her friend."

"I was *her* friend. And I think, for a moment, at least, she was mine. But I only know what she let me see. And I know some of it was true and some wasn't." Maybe Alet wasn't the best choice of topics. She hadn't meant to open a wound.

*But here we are. And the wounds ran both ways.*

"Occurs to me that you don't have the best track record with friends. All of them seem to die around you. Maybe I'm better off not being your friend."

That felt like a knife in the gut. She thought of Mari and Linna and the others. Most days she was able to make it through several hours without thinking of them. Maybe someday she'd even be able to think of them without picturing them lifeless and blood-soaked in the grove, but not yet and not today. "Maybe Alet was better off not being your sister," Daleina snapped, and then she sucked in air, trying to steady herself again. She could *not* afford to lose control, not with Merecot.

"Ouch," Merecot said. "So the queen does have teeth."

*Be calm*, she ordered herself. *Think of Aratay. We need this peace.* "Were you close to your sister?" She wanted to sound kind and gentle, but the best she could manage was calm and polite.

"You want the sad, terrible story of Alet and my childhood?" Merecot asked.

"You never talked about her, or about your family at all."

"It wasn't a pleasant topic. Parents who didn't want us, and poverty that nearly killed us. Escaped all that as soon as I could. How about you? You never talked much about the formative event of your childhood, the tragedy that set you on your path to your destiny."

Daleina looked down at her soup and realized she hadn't even tasted it. Everyone knew her tragedy: Greytree. But few knew she still dreamed about her cousin Rosari, telling her stories until she fell asleep. Few knew she still saw the faces of her childhood friends, mixed with her classmates who had died on Coronation Day, as if death erased the time between them. She wished she could remember what they looked like alive better than she could picture what they looked like dead. *Isn't time supposed to fix that?* "It wasn't a pleasant topic either. What was the moment you knew that you wanted to be a queen?"

Merecot picked up her spoon and ate more, as if she weren't as uncomfortable with this as Daleina was. *She must be*, Daleina thought. But Merecot answered conversationally, as if this were just a pleasant chat between casual acquaintances, "I always knew. It was my destiny."

"I don't believe in destiny." She couldn't believe in it. Daleina didn't want to ever think her friends had been *destined* to die. It was a terrible thing that shouldn't have happened.

*And it was because of me, not fate, that it wasn't worse. I couldn't save them, but I did the best I could, both in Greytree and in the grove, and prevented tragedy from becoming a pure disaster.* She was proud of that. And she wasn't going to foist either credit or blame onto some nebulous "destiny." Even more firmly, Daleina said, "No—destiny has nothing to do with it. We shape our own future."

"If things continue as they have, we shape a bleak future, then. One day, the spirits' more violent nature will win out, and they will destroy every human in Renthia. One day, the queens won't be able to stand against them. One day, they will win and lose at the same time, and all this will end." Gesturing as if she could encompass the entire world, Merecot swept her arms out and knocked over a decanter. It crashed to the ground, and wine seeped out into the carpet. "Wait—don't call a servant to clean that."

"*You* intend to clean it?" Standing, Daleina scooped up an embroidered napkin, intending to sop up the wine. It was ruby red, made from grapes from the Southern Citadel, a rare vintage according to her seneschal. She'd chosen it as a peace offering, as well as the soup made from rare white truffles. *I don't even like mushrooms.*

Merecot caught her wrist. She no longer seemed casual or even calm. "I'm trying to tell you something important, Daleina." She hesitated, as if warring with herself. "The spirits are plotting our destruction!"

Daleina twisted her arm, pulling out of Merecot's grip. She wasn't sure what had prompted this change in tone. Merecot sounded almost desperate. "The spirits are always plotting our destruction, Merecot," Daleina said patiently. "That's what they do, and that's why we're here—to hold them back."

"What if we're not enough?"

"We have to be enough," Daleina said. "We're all there is."

She didn't understand why Merecot was looking so feverishly intense. She felt prickles on her skin and glanced toward the door, where she knew Garnah was listening. Garnah had been here when the food was served, to check it all for poison, but then Daleina had dismissed her out of sight. She wondered if it would have been smarter to keep her in the room, as well as a few heavily armed guards. "Is it fear? Is that why you're queen? Are you afraid of the spirits? I'm trying to understand you, Merecot. I really am. Help me understand. Why did you try to kill me?"

"For my people. You know that."

"You could have come to me and asked for help."

"If I'd asked, you could have said no."

"So you went with murder as your first-choice option! Why?" She realized she was shouting but couldn't stop. All the old anger felt like it was pounding inside of her, wanting to burst out of her. She wanted to scream at Merecot, to shake her, to rage like the spirits. "There were other ways! Queen Naelin found another way. You could have too! Was it a failure of imagination, or is there something else you want? Do you hate me so much? Is it greed? Ambition? You want to be queen of the world?"

Merecot smirked. "Queen of the world. I like the sound of it. Yes, since you mention it, I do want to be queen of the world."

*There it is. Greed and ambition.* Daleina puffed her breath out, feeling strangely disappointed. It was such a small, petty reason to do what Merecot had done. She felt herself deflate, her anger dribbling out, replaced by a kind of pity. "I expected more from you."

"More than queen of the world?"

"*Better* from you." She studied her old friend sadly. Merecot was thinner than she should be, her cheeks sunken beneath her prominent cheekbones, as if she hadn't been eating, and she had shadows under her eyes, as if she hadn't been sleeping. Her black hair was pinned harshly back, the white streak as visible as a bolt of lightning. Her jeweled crown was tight around her fore-head, tight enough to leave a mark. "You were the best. Every-one thought so. Even Headmistress Hanna believed it. You could have—"

Dropping back into her chair, Merecot slammed her palms on the table, knocking her spoon to the floor. "By the spirits, you are so sanctimonious! You think you're better than me, that your purpose is more noble than mine. And what is this grand pur-pose of yours? To survive? To eke out another day for the people of Renthia? Another day where they all live in fear, never know-ing if it's their last day, never knowing if they're going to be torn to bits while their family watches, helpless. It's a pathetic life you want for our people. I want more! I want an end to fear! I want the world to be the way it should be, for our people to live their lives as they choose, to trust that they will have a future to live."

Daleina had never seen Merecot so serious or so passionate. She stopped scrubbing the spilled wine. "Merecot, what are you saying?"

Lowering her voice to a whisper, Merecot leaned down and said, "I want to destroy the spirits. All of them. And I know how to do it."

MERECOT SPREAD HER NAPKIN OVER THE WINE STAIN ON THE carpet. Clutching one already-stained napkin as if it were a se-curity blanket, Daleina was staring at her with a shocked expres-sion. Merecot resisted rolling her eyes. *You'd think after being queen, she'd have learned to hide her emotions.* She'd expected her words to have an impressive effect, but Daleina was silent. *A queen shouldn't ever be struck dumb.*

That said, it *had* been a dramatic statement. One she hadn't planned to share before coming here. And as expressive as Da-leina's face was, Merecot still wished she could read her thoughts. "Come on, Daleina. Look lively. You have to admit it has appeal."

"You can't destroy them," Daleina sputtered. "Destroying the sprits would destroy Renthia."

"I can prevent that."

"You can't!" She was shaking her head. "The land will *die*. You've seen the barren areas in Aratay—you caused plenty of them. You'd turn all of Renthia into a wasteland."

"Don't be silly, Daleina. You think I'd suggest this if I hadn't thought it through?" No one else had enough power to conceive of the possibilities. But she knew it was possible. *And so had Jastra.* If she could make Daleina see even a hint of the beautiful future Merecot could imagine . . . *Then maybe I won't have to kill her. Please, Daleina, be willing to listen!* "You want to save people, right? That's your thing."

"I . . ." Daleina stopped, studying her. "Yes?"

"You're a hero." *Surprisingly difficult to say that without sounding sarcastic,* Merecot thought. But she meant it. Daleina was a hero, like out of one of those piercing canopy-singer ballads, annoyingly consistently noble.

"I just want to keep people safe."

Merecot believed her. That had always been true. *I was a fool to not take it into account.* She blamed Jastra—the older queen had been convinced that none of the other queens would understand, that they all valued their power too much, and that they'd be unwilling to give it up even for the good of the world. But Daleina . . . she was honorable and self-sacrificing and all the goody-goody characteristics that made a person heroic.

"I'm sorry I tried to have you killed," Merecot said.

She meant it. She should have talked to Daleina. Not about the excess spirits, but about all of it. Daleina was just heroic enough to agree.

*And if she says no, killing her is still on the table.*

*Jastra would have loved that.*

Merecot wasn't worried about the guards that she knew were posted outside the door. If she killed Daleina, she'd do it fast this time, and no one would dare attack her after—with Queen Naelin gone and no heir available, they'd need her to stop the spirits of Aratay from killing everyone. She would be the only one in all of Aratay with the power to seize the crown.

*I can't lose. Either way, yes or no, I move forward.*

*But if Daleina says yes . . . It would be nice if I could avoid murdering the one person alive in the world who ever wanted to be my friend.*

*Not essential . . . but nice.*

It occurred to her that Daleina hadn't responded to her apology. "I don't want to kill you anymore," Merecot pushed.

"Happy to hear that," Daleina said, no emotion in her voice.

*I can't quite blame her for not believing that.* Merecot smirked, then sobered. "So we're clear, I will if I have to. But you're wrong about why. I don't want to be queen of the world because of the power. I want it because it's my destiny, because I am the strongest queen who has ever lived, and that means I am the one who can save Renthia. I can destroy the spirits once and for all." She gripped the table as she stood. "You invited me here to see what I have up my sleeve. This is it. I want to save the world. The question is:

"Will you save it with me?"

Daleina folded the napkin she'd been clutching, laid it on the table, and excused herself. *I'm not fleeing*, she told herself. *I'm taking a moment to gain perspective.*

*Just keep telling yourself that.*

She heard Merecot call after her, "I'm telling the truth! We have the same purpose. My vision is just grander than yours, because I'm more powerful. I've always been more powerful. That's why I'm the only one who can do this, and that's why you need to abdicate and let me do what I'm destined to do!"

Daleina stepped through the door to the side of the chamber, between the tapestries, and shut it behind her. "Is she telling the truth?" she asked Garnah.

Garnah barked a laugh. "She thinks she is."

Daleina began to pace, trying to sort out her thoughts and separate reason from wild hope. "I've never heard Merecot talk like this. She seems to believe everything she's saying."

"And why shouldn't she? Yet ask yourself this: Does it make it *true*? Do you believe she knows how to destroy the spirits? It would be an impressive feat that no queen has achieved in the history of Renthia." She looked at Daleina shrewdly. "But you didn't come out here to ask for my opinion."

"You're right." Daleina knew her own past experience with Merecot was coloring her impression of her words. She *wanted* to believe that Merecot spoke the truth. If she truly had a way to destroy the spirits, it would explain so much of what Merecot had done. *And it would be incredible. Life-changing for everyone. An end to the pain, the death, the fear! Peace, like no one in Renthia has ever known!* It seemed to be both too much to hope for and everything she'd ever dreamed of. "I want you to talk to her. Pretend to be a servant sent to clean up the wine spill and distract her. See what she reveals to you."

Perhaps surprisingly, Garnah once again didn't argue, let alone bristle at being asked to be a servant. Daleina didn't have time to worry about that, though, as the poison master bustled through the door to distract Merecot. While that was happening, Daleina reached out to brush the minds of the spirits in Mittriel and outside the city. There were hundreds, under the earth, in the trees, in the air, small and large, burrowing and flying and slithering and crawling, breathing life into the land and then choking it.

One by one, Daleina sent them away from Mittriel. She drew them out of the city, sending them toward the empty swaths of forest where there were few if any to harm. She persuaded the Aratayian spirits who surrounded Merecot's eagle spirit from Semo to bring that spirit with them, and they were only too happy to oblige.

In short order, the capital city was empty of all spirits.

Fires fizzled, though they didn't die. The breeze slowed until there was stillness in the air. If anyone had measured such a thing, they would have seen that the plants were growing slower, and that the water in the streams far below had slowed to a trickle. The spirits weren't dead, merely absent, and it would only be for a time.

Just long enough for Daleina to convince Merecot to tell her her whole plan, without a single spirit overhearing.

Merecot paced as an old servant woman bustled into the room and began sprinkling a powder on the wine stain. *I shouldn't have spoken*, Merecot thought. *I scared her off. Daleina won't understand. She can't comprehend having the kind of power to do what needs to be done.* Daleina didn't know what it was like to have complete control over thousands of spirits, to hold their minds inside hers and know she could snuff them out in a moment. *It can be done! I only need to be a little stronger . . .*

If Merecot could hold both Semo and Aratay, she should be strong enough.

And then once the other countries saw her success, they'd agree to let her save them as well. All she needed to do was get Daleina to abdicate.

*Or kill her.*

*But I'd prefer if she were willing.* Jastra had never considered that possibility, but then the old queen had never met a queen as idealistic as Daleina.

She told herself to be patient.

*I hate being patient.*

Merecot smelled a lemony spice that made her nose wrinkle and looked over to see the powder had eaten through the rug and was working on dissolving the wood floor. She marched over. "What are you doing?"

"I've never been very good at housecleaning." Standing, the servant dusted her knees off and smiled at Merecot. It was a predatory kind of smile that made Merecot think of the mountain cats that hunted on the slopes of Semo. Instinctively, she recoiled.

"You're not a servant."

"Very observant, Your Majesty. I'm here to watch you while Queen Daleina composes herself in the washroom. Whatever you two were talking about shook her up. Were you threatening to poison her again? Incidentally, I wanted to ask you, where did you obtain such a fascinating poison? I'd never seen its equal. Brilliant use of extract of wheat viper venom. And it must have been combined at extraordinary temperatures to activate the linseed."

"Who are you?" Merecot asked.

"Master Garnah, the Queen's Poisoner, at your service," the

woman said with a bow. "Actually, that's a lie. I'm not in your service in the slightest. I serve Queen Daleina, at least for as long as it suits me. But I do admire your style."

Merecot eyed the powder that had bored a shallow divot in the floor. "Thank you? Um, do you plan to do something about that before it creates a hole?"

The woman pulled a vial out of a pocket in her skirt and poured a few drops onto the powder. It sizzled and steamed, and then the powder shriveled into a ball of gray dust.

Merecot decided this "Poison-Master Garnah" was the most interesting person she'd met in a long while. "Are you the one who fashioned the antidote to the poison used on Queen Daleina?"

"I may have been involved. Who concocted it?"

"It was a gift," Merecot said.

Garnah leaned forward eagerly. "From whom?"

Merecot debated herself for a brief moment, then decided to tell the truth. "I found it in the royal treasury, shortly after I claimed the throne. It was labeled as a coronation gift from the former queen of Belene to my predecessor, Queen Jastra, decades ago."

"Fascinating. And how did you know it was a poison and what it did?"

"It came with a detailed letter. Apparently, the queen of Belene was looking for allies outside the islands—the coronation process in Belene is rather brutal." Mcrecot hadn't really dug much deeper than that—she wasn't all that interested in the politics of Belene, at least not yet. *One country at a time.*

"Really? I live in the wrong place. They use poison?"

"So it seems. For whatever reason, Queen Whatever-Her-Name-Was thought Jastra would appreciate the gift. She didn't have a use for it before she abdicated, but I did."

"Intriguing," Garnah said.

"Are you close to Queen Daleina?" Merecot asked. She wondered why Daleina would send her pet poison maker to talk. Was it to intimidate Merecot? To threaten her? *What is Daleina up to now?* "Can you tell me how she feels about being queen?"

"Mostly exhausted," Garnah said. "She's had more than her share of challenges."

*True enough.* "And if I were to offer to relieve her of her challenges, how do you think she'd react?" Merecot knew how she'd react if anyone offered to "relieve" her. The offerer would find her head being tossed back and forth by the nearest spirits. Reflexively reaching out, Merecot tried to brush the minds of the nearby spirits—

And found none.

She reached out farther . . . and still found nothing. It was as if she were cut off from the thing that made her *her.*

She hated the feeling.

*Daleina, what did you do?*

Merecot spun, her skirts swirling around her, to face the door that Daleina had exited through. "So she just went to the washroom?" she snarled. More like she was setting a trap. Merecot suddenly realized she'd turned her back on a woman who had powder that could eat through the floor and the skills to undo the Belenian poison. Moving quickly, she darted behind a couch and watched Garnah.

Garnah merely smiled at her, and the woman's amusement made Merecot even angrier . . . and a bit more frightened.

And Daleina came back through the door.

Daleina had cut off both her weapons and her escape route. Granted, Daleina didn't have any spirits to call as weapons of her own either, but with Garnah, it was two against one . . .

*It* is *a trap! I knew it! How could I be so foolish?*

"What did you do?" Merecot barked at her.

"I bought us some privacy," Daleina said. "Poison-Master Garnah, thank you for entertaining our guest. If you would please excuse us?"

Garnah beamed at both of them. "Delightful chatting with you. And thank you for the idea for where to retire in my dotage." Bowing, she scooted out the door and shut it behind her. Merecot didn't doubt that she'd remained, listening.

Scowling at her, Merecot saw Daleina's eyes light on the divot in the floor. "What did she . . . Never mind. As you've clearly noticed, there are no spirits left within Mittriel, either yours or mine, to overhear us. So explain everything. How do you plan to destroy them?"

*It's . . . not a trap?*

DALEINA LISTENED AS MERECOT TALKED:

"The key is that I need to be strong enough for it to work. Obviously, I started out powerful. And the more powerful you are to begin with, the more powerful you are as a queen. Hence the difference between you and me." She paused, then added, "No offense meant."

With a tight smile, Daleina said, "None taken."

*I know she's more powerful than I am. That's obvious.* Daleina wasn't offended by the truth. She *was* offended by the invasion and the attempted assassination, but for the sake of Aratay, she was setting aside her anger and anguish. Or trying to.

Merecot continued. "When you become queen, your power—however much it is—is amplified. The spirits share their power when they choose you. This is why a queen has the strength to keep her spirits from slaughtering her people. Mostly."

Every child knew that. It was the reason Renthia needed queens. But Daleina was determined to be patient. She folded her hands on her lap and tried to pretend she was listening to Headmistress Hanna lecture, instead of Merecot. "Go on."

"So here's my revelation: even a powerful queen can be made stronger. Okay, so it's not much of a 'revelation,' really. It's logic. You must have noticed that when a spirit dies, you feel weaker. Well, the reverse is true, too: if an additional spirit chooses to share its power with you, then you become stronger. So if you—and by 'you' I mean me, of course—can become queen of enough spirits, then you can become strong enough to issue a command that would destroy them!"

*And destroy Renthia in the process.* Daleina tried not to interrupt, though she badly wanted to. She'd seen firsthand what happened when spirits died. All around Aratay was the proof: the barren lands, the destroyed homes, the ruined harvest. But Daleina kept quiet, with effort, wanting Merecot to finish first before she began berating her for abject stupidity. *And for raising my hopes.*

"Queen Jastra realized this years ago and tried to do it by capturing more spirits in the untamed lands, thinking they would bolster her power. But without land, the spirits were uncontrollable, and she spent all of her extra energy keeping them from ripping Semo to shreds." Merecot paused as a flicker of pain flashed across her face, then was gone—so fast that Daleina thought she'd imagined it. "Overall, it was a bad idea. What she should have done is conquer a second kingdom, thereby doubling her power with nice, stable spirits, who aren't busy fighting one another over a mountain or two."

"And that's why you had me poisoned and my heirs killed?" Daleina kept her voice flat, but her hands were squeezing together so tightly that her nails dug into her skin. *This is a terrible idea, pursued by terrible people.*

"Precisely." She said it so casually, Daleina almost flinched. *Why, exactly, do I want to be friends with her?* She answered herself: *Because a friendship with Merecot would mean peace for my people.*

*Unless Merecot destroys the world first.*

Merecot continued. "I thought that if I could conquer Aratay, then with the combined strength of Aratay and Semo, I'd have enough power to issue a command that will change the fate of Renthia. You can't do it—even as queen, you don't have the power. But I do. That's why it has to be me."

Holding up a hand, Daleina stopped her. Even if she accepted that Merecot could become powerful enough to do it, why would she ever want her to? She pictured the barren lands, the lost homes, the lost lives. "You said you wanted to destroy the spirits. How would you do that without destroying everything and everyone we know in the process?" She tried to keep her voice even and calm, but it was difficult. This was madness. She couldn't believe she was having a conversation about why her friend had tried to kill her and had had so many others killed. Still, if this—an end to spirits—was what Merecot truly wanted,

Daleina at least had to give it to her: she couldn't say the goal wasn't grand.

*She doesn't think small, that's for certain.*

Daleina didn't know whether she wanted to scream, cry, or laugh. *Maybe all three. And then shake Merecot until she sees sense.*

Merecot waved her hand dismissively. "I was being dramatic. Destroying the spirits would of course destroy the land. No, I don't want to kill them. I want to *change* them! I want to order them to evolve. I want to force them to . . . well, *become* the land. I suppose that's the best way to put it. Instead of nature spirits, we'd merely have nature, the way it's supposed to be."

As she said this, Merecot was watching her reaction. And Daleina couldn't help but react. Her mouth fell open. That was . . .

Bold.

And also brilliant.

If the spirits were changed, if they could be altered en masse in a fundamental way . . . Carefully, not wanting to hope, Daleina asked, "What exactly do you mean?"

"The spirits weren't meant to be like this, continually torn between shaping the world and dismantling it. They were supposed to finish creating this world and then change to become a passive part of it." Merecot gestured at the windows, the ceiling, the wall, as if they represented the world. "You've heard our versions of the creation story. Here's theirs: they were supposed to evolve into a new kind of spirit, but they didn't. They couldn't."

Despite herself, Daleina began to feel drawn in. She thought of the gratitude story her parents always told before every meal, and the ballads that the canopy singers sang. "Because the Great Mother died."

"Yes! After her, no one had enough power to change them."

Could it be true? Were the spirits supposed to have evolved?

"For generations, queens have kept the peace with relative degrees of success in their own lands. They gained enough power through the spirits they controlled to keep the status quo, but not enough to truly influence the spirits, to force them to finish their evolution. But if a queen were to have *more* power . . ." Merecot trailed off as if the conclusion were obvious.

Daleina stared at her. She couldn't believe she was hearing this. She couldn't believe she was *considering* this. But if it were possible . . .

It wouldn't just change the spirits.

It would change the world.

Merecot sighed dramatically. "Really, Daleina? I paused so you could jump in with your own 'aha!' revelation. You were supposed to use your towering intellect to fill in the blanks."

"Fill it in for me." She refused to leap to conclusions, though she was pretty sure she knew exactly where Merecot was going. She wanted Merecot to say it, all of it. Out loud.

"Fine. Once I'm strong enough, once I can draw strength from the spirits of both Semo and Aratay, I'll finish what the Great Mother couldn't. I'll order the spirits to change." Her face was flushed, and her hands were shaking. Merecot obviously believed every word she was saying.

And Daleina couldn't help but believe her too. Or at least, couldn't help but *want* to believe. She knew how powerful Merecot was, and the spirits of Aratay, combined with the spirits of Semo, would make her even more powerful. *Powerful enough?* she wondered. "You think this is a thing that can be done?"

"I think this is a thing that was *supposed* to have happened long ago, before humans ever walked the lands of Renthia, before Renthia even existed. Something went wrong long ago, and I want to make it right. Help me make it right, Daleina."

It was an amazing thought. If it was truly possible . . . *It would be a miracle.* In a hushed voice, as if Merecot had uttered a spell she was afraid to break, Daleina asked, "What are you asking me to do?"

She knew the answer before Merecot said it.

This was what Merecot had been leading to. This was why she'd come. She'd already said it multiple times, in fact, she just hadn't said *why* until now.

"Abdicate," Merecot answered. "Let me take control of the spirits of Aratay. With them and with the strength of Semo, I can do this. It requires someone with enough strength giving the right command." She leaned forward, intense. "I know the right command, and I am the right someone."

"And you didn't want to tell me any of this before now?" Daleina felt outrage build—Queen Jastra and Merecot had the solution to the problem that had plagued Renthia since the beginning of history, and they were just . . . keeping it secret?

"I didn't think you'd understand, or agree," Merecot said. "So that's why the poisoning. But given a choice, I'd rather work with you than against you. We used to be friends. It would be nice if we could be again."

Daleina did not change her expression. She held herself very still. Merecot may be ambitious and ruthless and many other things, but she'd never been a liar.

*If it's possible . . .*

*If there's even a* chance *that it's possible . . .*

An end to the spirits, to the deaths, to the fear.

She thought of Arin's boyfriend, Josei, of her own lost friends, of her childhood home of Greytree, of the fallen champions and the ordinary people of Aratay who had suffered at the hands and claws of spirits. If the spirits were to "evolve" . . .

*No one else would have to die.*

She would be fulfilling her ultimate duty as queen: to protect her people.

Merecot had talked about destiny, and Daleina had rejected it. But if she was to choose a destiny, it would be to do all she could to save all she could. And now Merecot was offering her a way to do exactly that. *If it works.* "You believe this. Do you have any proof that the command will work? Proof that the spirits *can* be changed?"

"Bayn. Your wolf. He's an evolved spirit."

"And now he's dead because your spirits drove him into the untamed lands. Do you have any other proof? Any *living* proof?"

"Call back a spirit or two," Merecot said. "Ask them to tell you their story. Ask them about their lost destiny. Ask about who or what they were supposed to be. In truth, I'm only planning to do what the spirits themselves want."

Daleina shook her head. "But they–"

"Just listen to them. Please, Daleina. And then give me your answer, whether you want to save the world or . . ." Merecot trailed off.

"Or?" Daleina prompted.

"Or die, so I can."

# CHAPTER 29

There was a child in the untamed lands.

Not *her* child, but as Naelin stared at the space where the ragged child had stood, she felt hope stir within her, so hot and fierce that it felt as if her veins were filled with boiling water. "Ven, was that—"

"Yes, I saw him too." Ven bounded across the rocks as they undulated beneath his feet, rising and falling in response to an earth spirit burrowing beneath them. Naelin felt it slither past, deep within the ground, a massive bulbous worm with sluggish thoughts of destruction. She called to one of her own spirits, an earth spirit that looked like a horse made of smooth black stone, and climbed onto its back.

*Follow the child*, she ordered her spirits. *Do no harm.*

Swarming around her, the spirits changed course. They poured in a river over the rocks and into the crevasses. She rode with them, the horse's stone hooves striking the backs of other spirits and then they in turn clawing past the horse spirit, a writhing stream of bodies.

"You'll scare him, Naelin! Hold back!" Ven called.

"You're the one with the sword!" Naelin called to him. But she reined in her spirits, letting them swirl around her. Absently, she stroked the back of a winged ermine spirit who flew beside her.

It hissed through its fangs. *Shh, I will stay with you,* she soothed the spirits.

She felt their agitation through her bond with them, vibrating like a plucked string, and she blanketed them with calming thoughts. It only partially worked. Her own thoughts were nowhere near calm. *If a child could survive here, then maybe* my children could have.

It was common knowledge that no one survived the untamed lands.

But common knowledge could be wrong.

She pushed her mind toward the spirits on the edges of her swarm, watching Ven through their eyes. He climbed over the rocks, batting away an ice spirit that tried to sink its icicle claws into his arm. His mouth was moving—he was calling to the child. Naelin pushed herself deeper into the spirits, listening.

"WE SWEAR WE WON'T HURT YOU!" VEN CALLED. "COME BACK! We're looking for someone! We need help. Please!" He was aware he didn't present the least-threatening sight, with his green leather armor, scarred and bearded face, sword in his hand, and bow and arrows on his back. He also had spare knives in his boots and an extra in his front pocket. But he had to be less alarming than Naelin, with her spirits.

Frankly, he found her intimidating like this.

Not that he'd admit that.

He scrambled over the rocks, which would not stay still. *Gah! This place is a nightmare!* As he climbed a boulder, the rocks rumbled again, split, and a spurt of fire shot up from the crevasse. "Naelin, can you do something about this?"

Two ice spirits, laughing, shot past him. He rubbed his ear as the cold stung and watched as they dove into the fiery crevasse, filling it with ice crystals that crinkled and crackled until they solidified into a solid blue sheet. The ice spirits danced beneath the ice, spreading flowerlike patterns from below. Ven jumped off the boulder and, crouching, slid down the new ice river.

"Boy! We need your help! Come back!"

Seeing the end of the ice river, Ven leapt to the side. He held still, listening. The mist coiled and curled around him, and he heard a crack of thunder. Rain began to fall, smacking his cheeks and seeping beneath his armor, soaking his shirt underneath.

Just as suddenly, the rain stopped. Sun beamed down for a moment and then was swallowed. *I lost him.* Straightening, he turned to trudge back to Naelin.

And there before him was the boy.

Ven did not move. "We're looking for someone. Two someones, a boy and a girl named Llor and Erian." He thought about asking about Bayn as well. *It's too much to hope for that he's survived. Protector of Queens or not.* Bayn had been in the untamed lands for far longer than Erian and Llor. *Then again . . . this boy survives here . . .* "Can you help us find them? And a wolf? We call him Bayn." He kept his voice soft and gentle, sheathed his sword, and spread his hands in front of him to show he meant no harm.

The boy did not speak.

But then the boy beckoned to Ven and began walking, jumping from rock to rock, using his hands for balance, as if he were a squirrel in a tree. Ven didn't hesitate, keeping his eye on the boy as he followed. He trusted that Naelin would be behind him, keeping the spirits in check.

The land around them continued to change: toward the north, a mountain spewed flames on one side of its face while it wept waterfalls on the other. Ice crystals shaped like trees sprouted into a forest farther to the west, only for wind to blow them apart. *Unnatural place,* he thought. And yet, what the spirits did here was nothing compared to what he saw next. Because when he crossed the latest ridge, he halted, shocked.

It was a village. Of sorts.

A collection of huts made from uneven planks of wood lashed together and leaning up against boulders, the town—*More like a camp,* he thought—was smushed close, as if the buildings themselves were huddled together, afraid of the outside world. *Which,* he supposed, *is exactly what they are afraid of.* He saw fire pits between them, a few lit with pots hanging on spits, and laundry was strung between windows. Perhaps more than anything, it was the laundry that disturbed him. It was such an easy sign of domesticity that would get overlooked elsewhere, but here, it drove home just how out of place all this was in the untamed lands.

A few people came out of the huts as they approached: men, women, children, all of them as dirty and underfed as the boy. Ven raised his hand in a wave. "We mean no harm!"

One of the women scurried forward and pulled him down from the rocks. "Quickly, quickly," she muttered, "before the spirits see you." As soon as he passed the first hut, the people all surrounded him, pressing close, patting his arms, his hair, his pack, and murmuring at him.

"I'm looking for a girl and a boy named Erian and Llor"—and then, because this was all impossible anyway, he added, "as well as a wolf named Bayn. Have you seen them?" He pushed away the fingers of a young girl who was probing his front pocket. "What is this place? Who are you all?"

The woman who had brought him in stepped forward to answer, and then she whitened and shrieked. Others began to run. The children were herded together. Curiously, after the initial shriek, there were no more screams, just a grim determination to flee. *They've done this before*, he thought. Whipping out his sword, Ven turned, ready, and saw Naelin riding in on a wave of spirits. Her hair streaming behind her and her expression fierce, she looked almost like a spirit herself.

He lowered his sword. "It's all right! She's a friend! She won't hurt you! A friend!"

"She brings the spirits!" a man cried.

"She controls them," Ven said. "She's a queen!"

Clustered together, they stopped running. But they clung to one another as the spirits whipped between their huts and around him.

"Call them off, Naelin!" he shouted.

And the spirits retreated. Small and large, they huddled in a ring around the village, perched on the rocks and hovering in the air. Naelin dismounted and hurried forward. "Erian? Llor? Are you here? It's me! Please be here!"

"We're looking for her children," Ven explained. "They were brought into the untamed lands by two spirits."

"You said you also seek the wolf, the Protector," an old woman said.

*They knew Bayn?* "Yes," Ven said. "Is he here?"

"And my children?" Naelin added. "Have you seen them? Are they alive? Are they all right? Where are they?" She grabbed the old woman by the shoulders.

Gently, Ven pried her hands off the woman. "You're scaring them," he said to Naelin. He knew what she was feeling . . . No, he didn't know, but he could imagine it and he could see it, reflected in the agitation of the spirits. "Clamp it down. You're spilling."

She glanced up at the spirits, who were hissing and spitting and growling. She closed her eyes for an instant, and the spirits calmed minutely. "I'm sorry." He saw her take a deep breath, and he wanted to put his arms around her and hold her close. *This has to be agony for her.* But answers would come only if they didn't drive them away.

"You must mean the children at the grave," a woman said.

Naelin staggered backward.

"Grave?" Ven repeated. *Not dead. Please, don't let them be dead.*

"The Grave of the Great Mother," the woman said—this one appeared to be a mother herself. She had two boys clinging to her legs, and she was cuddling them closer to her as if her arms could protect them from the spirits, if they decided to attack. *How had these people survived here?* Ven wondered. The woman continued, "They came recently, with two spirits, nasty creatures. The Protector chased away the spirits, but kept the children. Those are their names: Erian and Llor."

*Bayn did that? He's here, and he saved them?*

"Alive?" Naelin breathed.

"Yes, Your Majesty."

NAELIN FELT . . .

There were no words for what she felt.

But there were colors: sun-gold yellow and deep summer green and clear blue, the colors of growth and wellness and *life*. And the spirits absorbed the burst of her emotions, and around them the wind spirits whipped into dust devils, the ice spirits shed fireworks of snow, the earth spirits exploded from the ground in a shower of dirt and pebbles that rained down.

"Scary again," Ven murmured to her.

She tried to pull back on the vicious hope, but only just a bit. She didn't care if she was scaring these people. *My children are alive!* "I need to see them. Take me to them."

The woman cowered away from her. "Only the Protector can approach the grave." Stepping forward, a little girl piped up, "We don't know the way!"

"Come," an older man said. "Let us show the hospitality of our village. You must be tired from your journey here. Rest yourselves. Share a meal with us. Please, what are your names?"

"Naelin."

"Queen Naelin, formerly of Aratay," Ven put in. "And I am Champion Ven."

The older man's hand shook, and there were gasps from the people crowded around them. Hushed whispers: "A miracle! I never thought I'd see the day." And then the boy they'd followed: "Have you come to save us?"

*I've come for my children*, Naelin thought. But Ven was already answering, kneeling on one knee to be at an even height with the boy, "What do you need saving from? You've survived here, in this hostile land. How have you done it?"

A woman answered, "We move when we must. Harvest when we can."

"But the spirits," Ven said. "You're outnumbered, vastly. Without a queen to control them—how do you stay alive?" *Stop asking questions*, Naelin wanted to say to him. *First Erian and Llor, then you can ask anything you want.* But she was afraid if she spoke, the villagers would retreat again.

The woman shrugged. "Not so many of us to threaten them." She gestured at the few dozen people that huddled close. "Plus they don't like to come here, so near the grave."

"Then it's near?" Naelin pounced. The idea of her children being alive, being near, but her not being able to touch them, to hold them, ate at her until she wanted to claw at her own skin. *I need to see them!*

"Are there others like you? Humans, in the untamed lands?" Ven asked.

Naelin wanted to scream at him. *Erian and Llor! Ask about them!*

"Yes, we've seen a few other groups. We keep our distance, for the most part. Safer in smaller numbers, and easier to find food if we're spread out too."

"Fascinating," Ven said.

Naelin shot him a look.

"Well, it is," Ven defended himself. "Miraculous, really. We always believed entering the untamed lands was a death sentence, but you're here thriving."

A man snorted. "'Thriving,' he says. Each year more of us die than are born. Some days there's no food for any of us. Some days it's all saltwater for miles around. Some days we wake to fire and ash. Some days we wake to cold so deep that some of us don't wake at all."

"We need a queen," another said, "and here you are, an answer to a prayer." And a few pressed closer again, stroking Naelin's arm, and it was if she were seeing them for the first time. How dirty and tired and hungry and *scared* they looked. And . . . how hopeful too. Strangely, it reminded her of the spirits now surrounding them, the ones that called her queen. How they too had felt hope. It confused her, yet she couldn't shake it. She patted their hands, unsure what else she could possibly do. She'd thought life in the outer forest was difficult, but these people . . . They were living lives of unimaginable hardship. Naelin looked at them, really looked at them, and saw the hope in their faces shining broader and brighter with each passing minute.

She didn't know how to tell him she'd only come for her children.

Thankfully, she didn't have to.

Before she could decide how to respond to them, she heard a howl, and Ven cried, "Bayn!"

The wolf ran out of the haze, between her spirits, toward them, and Naelin let herself feel a little more hope herself.

# CHAPTER 30

Ven knelt and threw his arms around Bayn's neck. The wolf panted onto his shoulder and leaned against him heavily, as if he were hugging the man back. "Never thought I'd see you again, my friend."

The wolf licked his cheek.

"Uh, thanks? You missed me too?"

Naelin crouched beside them. "Bayn, are my children all right? Can you take us to them? Please?"

Bayn looked at her with such intelligence in his eyes—pity, understanding—that Ven was embarrassed he'd ever thought Bayn was an ordinary beast. *Clearly, he's extraordinary.* "You survived," Ven said. "I didn't know. I would've come sooner, if I'd known. Why didn't you come back to us?"

An old woman, one who had spoken before, said, "He belongs to this place. He cannot leave it, not without a queen to help him cross. One helped him cross long ago, or so the stories say. We have awaited his return—and the coming of a queen—for many lifetimes."

Ven wanted to ask more questions. Had Merecot been right? Was Bayn some kind of "evolved spirit"? How long ago had he crossed? And what queen had helped him? He was certain it hadn't been Daleina or Fara. *I would've known if either had ever left Renthia.* Exactly how old was Bayn? Was "lifetimes" literal or hyperbole? *And why were they waiting for him? And for a queen?* There were no queens in the untamed lands—that was part of the very definition. *If they wanted a queen, they should have come to Renthia.*

He wished Bayn could speak.

"Please," Naelin said. "My children."

Bayn trotted away from them, looking back once, and then breaking into a loping run. Ven and Naelin ran after him. From behind them, he heard the people calling, "Don't leave!" "Help us!" "We need you!" And: "Come back for us! Don't forget us!" And also: "We hope you find your children! Good luck!"

He waved once to show he'd heard them, and then all his focus was on chasing Bayn across the uneven landscape. Thunder crackled in the sky above them as blue and purple clouds mixed. Rain spattered his face.

Naelin's spirits flowed around them, smoothing the way—stifling a fire, diverting a river, filing a chasm—as they followed Bayn. Ahead, through the rain, Ven saw a cave leading into a gray rock that loomed out of the haze. Running faster, Naelin scrambled over the rocks calling, "Erian! Llor!"

And they came. Erian and Llor, out of the cave, across the rocks, and throwing themselves into Naelin's arms. Laughing. Crying.

Alive.

*MY CHILDREN!*

Dropping to her knees, Naelin held out her arms, and her children ran into them. She felt their warm bodies impact against her. She stroked their hair. Breathed them in, sweat and smoke and the sweetest smell that only came from the two lives she'd brought into the world. Rain fell around them, and she wasn't even sure any of it hit them . . . or if she cared that it did. "You're alive," she whispered into their hair. "You're here."

Llor sniffled into her neck, and Erian was clinging to her so tightly that Naelin felt her fingers pressing deep into her skin, bruising her, but she didn't care. She held her close.

"Mama, you came for us!" Erian said.

"I knew you'd come!" Llor said. "I said so!"

"I didn't believe it," Erian declared. "I thought you wouldn't come to look for us, because you'd think we were dead. No one survives the untamed lands. Everyone knows that. I thought we'd be trapped here forever, until we *did* die."

Llor buried his face against her again. "Bayn wouldn't bring us home."

Naelin held them close. "I came. I'm here. We'll never be apart again." She felt relief and joy—pure joy—spilling out of her, flooding the spirits, and felt it mirrored back. Around her, the earth exploded in life: flowers blossoming over the face of the rocks, trees bursting between the crevasses thickening as they shot toward the sky. She heard the rushing of water and felt sunlight flood their faces as her spirits drove back the haze and filled the land in a ring around them with life, teeming with a riot of colors.

Beyond it, she felt the spirits of the untamed lands drawing closer. She felt their hostility, scratching at the edges of their circle of overabundant life, and she shuddered and hugged her children and Ven closer. *No.* The outside world couldn't intrude yet. This was her moment of joy, a moment she'd never thought she'd have. She didn't want it to end.

"The villagers said Bayn *couldn't* bring you home—he couldn't cross the border," Ven said, laying one hand on Erian's shoulder and another on Llor's. "But we can. And we will."

Naelin turned to Bayn. "Thank you for saving them."

The wolf sat, with his tail curled beside him, watching them with his yellow eyes. He made a doglike whining noise.

"What is it?" Ven asked, as if he expected Bayn to answer.

At his question, the wolf rose and trotted into the cave.

"What's in there?" Naelin asked Erian and Llor.

"A dead body," Llor said. "It's kind of neat."

That was not an appropriate thing to say about a dead body. And why were her children staying in a cave with a corpse anyway? "I'm a terrible mother," Naelin murmured.

"You came," Erian said simply, hugging her waist as she stood.

Ven drew his sword.

"You won't need that," Llor said. "She's already dead. Come on, we'll show you." He scrambled ahead of them, over the rocks.

Naelin felt as if a coat had been ripped away from her on a winter day—suddenly cold, a little bereft, the moment that she was no longer touching both her children. Following Llor and holding on to Erian, who didn't seem to want to let go of her hand either, Naelin climbed over the rocks up to the opening of the cave. Together, they entered.

Shadows enveloped them, and Naelin called on two small fire spirits to light the way—but her fire spirits balked at the entrance, their glow only shedding a faint light into the darkness.

It didn't matter, though, because ahead a light bobbed as Llor came trotting back to them, carrying a torch.

"Careful with that," she admonished as the flame dipped back and forth.

"I can carry it," Llor said. "I'm careful."

"He burned himself this morning," Erian reported.

"Be *more* careful," Naelin said.

Excitedly, Llor grabbed Ven's hand and pulled him deeper into the cave. Naelin and Erian followed. She felt a breath of wind in her face, and the cave opened onto a chamber of glittering white—smooth quartz that sparkled from the light of seven torches plus Llor's. Llor placed his into a holder on the wall.

In the center of the room was a raised black stone pallet, and on it lay moss, curved in the shape of an unusually tall and large woman. Tiny white flowers grew on her body from the moss. Naelin took a step forward. The enormous woman's eyes were closed with black stones over each one, and her hands were folded on her stomach.

Naelin shivered. There was an oddly familiar feel to this place. She thought of the Queen's Grove in Aratay. Rock surrounded them, not trees, but there was something about it that felt similar. It had a sense of heavy silence.

"Who is it?" Ven asked.

"The Great Mother of Spirits," Erian said.

Both Naelin and Ven stared at Erian, then at the mossy body.

*This* was the being who had created them all? *No wonder the cave feels like a grove,* Naelin thought. It was a sacred place . . . *the* sacred place.

Naelin instinctively pulled her children closer to her. She reached out with her mind and touched her spirits, but they were distracted: the spirits of the untamed lands surrounded them, pressing closer, squeezing them up against the rock of the cave.

"The villagers want a queen, and Bayn was supposed to find one," Llor said, piping up from within the circle of her arms. "At least, that's what they said when Bayn brought us here."

"They said we have to stay with the Protector," Erian said, "until a queen comes."

"And they said Bayn was gone for a hundred years!" Llor threw his hands out wide when he said the word "hundred."

"Two hundred," Erian corrected.

"Three hundred!" Llor shouted. "Four hundred!"

"Anyway, it didn't sound very likely," Erian said to Naelin and Ven.

Out of the corner of her eye, Naelin saw Ven shift onto the balls of his feet. He looked ready to fight. But who would he fight? Bayn, who had saved Erian and Llor from Queen Jastra's spirits? Softly, Naelin asked, "Bayn, is it true? Are you from here? Did you come to Renthia to find . . . me? Or someone like me?"

Bayn trotted over to the bier and sat beside it.

Maybe that was his answer. *But I'm not sure what it means.* "The people in the village," Naelin pressed. "Did they send you into Aratay?"

The wolf tilted his head.

"Did you send yourself?" Ven asked.

Bayn looked deliberately into Ven's eyes and nodded, humanlike, as if he'd understood every word. He then laid his head on the mossy hand and let out a puppylike whimper.

Ven's voice was flat. Naelin wondered what he was thinking. "You went to find a queen—the villagers said they'd been awaiting your return *with* a queen," he said. "Like Naelin. But then you were chased back here . . . and you couldn't return?"

"Bayn saved us," Llor said.

"I know, sweetie," Naelin said.

"Then why does Ven look so mad?"

He was right—Ven had half drawn his sword, though Bayn had not twitched a muscle other than to move his head. In the glow from the torches, the wolf's eyes flickered yellow.

"Because Bayn had other reasons for being with us and being nice," Erian said. "He wanted Mama. Because the people in the village wanted her. Or someone like her."

Llor frowned. "The people are nice. They gave us food."

"I came here for my children, that's all," Naelin said to Bayn. She was grateful they were alive and had been taken care of. It was more than she'd ever dreamed possible. But this little adventure was over. "And now that I've found them, it's time to go home."

*Please, let us go.*

Ven slid between her and the wolf. They began to back out of the cave.

Bayn darted across the cave, past them, and then stopped in front of them, filling the entrance to the cave. He crouched, his legs tense. Naelin corralled Erian and Llor behind Ven. Sword raised defensively in front of them, Ven advanced. "I don't want to hurt you, old friend. And I know you don't want to hurt us. All we want is to get these children safely home."

For one terrible moment, Naclin thought they'd fight.

But then Bayn bowed his head. Dropping to the cave floor, he rolled and exposed his throat. "Thank you, my friend," Ven said. He sheathed his sword, and Naelin followed him with the children past the wolf.

Once they were past, Bayn got to his feet and let out a mournful howl.

With a cry, Llor broke from of Naelin's grip and ran back to Bayn. "Llor, no!" Naelin cried. She grabbed for him, but he was too quick.

Launching himself forward, Llor threw his arms around Bayn's neck. "Come with us! Please! We love you! You're our friend!"

The wolf lowered his head, cheek pressing against the boy's cheek. Naelin surged forward and then stopped—the spirits, her spirits, were howling in her head. She grabbed on to Ven's arm as their pain shot through her and her knees buckled under her.

"Mama!" she heard Erian, distant.

Her vision swam, and instead she saw through a hundred eyes as the untamed spirits tore into her spirits. "Ven, they're attacking!"

She felt him twist from her, his sword raised, looking toward the sky.

"They're attacking my spirits!" And she threw her mind into theirs, strengthening them, fighting with them as thousands of untamed spirits converged, united by a single thought so loud that she could feel it reverberating across the untamed lands:

*Destroy!*

# CHAPTER 31

Daleina listened to the spirits' story, of the Great Mother who died and, with her, the intended destiny of spirits, humans, and the world. She saw it all unfold around her as the spirits flooded her mind with images and their sorrow and anger at the loss that had happened so very long ago. When the spirits withdrew, she was left gasping, her cheeks wet with tears, and her throat raw, though she hadn't felt as if she'd been screaming.

"Intense, isn't it?" Merecot hadn't moved from her chair across the dinner table in the center of Daleina's outer chamber.

Gripping the arms of her chair, Daleina forced herself to breathe deeply and evenly until the room around her quit wobbling. "How many queens do you think have heard that?"

Merecot shrugged. "How many queens do you think would ask? Or listen?"

She was right. Certainly Daleina had never asked them before.

In a quiet voice, with a hint of awe, Merecot said, "The spirits are the 'builders' of the world, and their work was interrupted before anyone could say, 'You're done.' Someone needs to tell them 'You're done,' and then all of this will stop. The killing. The hatred. The anger. The fear."

Standing, she crossed to the window and looked at the twinkle of lights cradled in the branches of the trees of Mittriel. She tried to imagine what life would be like if people didn't have to fear the spirits. She thought again of Greytree and her childhood friends, of her classmates who had died in the grove, of Queen Fara, and of Naelin, who'd never wanted to be queen. "You believe you're strong enough?"

"I am the strongest queen who has ever lived." Matter-of-fact.

"Naelin's strong too," Daleina pointed out. "Why couldn't she have done this? Or any of the queens who came before? Fara was strong. Countless others have been strong. And yet no one has ever succeeded in stopping the spirits altogether."

"We've always been separated into different countries. Just weak enough that we'd never think to try this. But if I controlled both Semo and Aratay . . . I can do this, Daleina. I know I can. It's what I was meant to do!"

*I believe her*, Daleina thought.

She couldn't pass up this chance to save the world. It would be the culmination of everything she and every queen before her had ever strived for, the fulfillment of every dream of peace. It was more than she'd dared hoped to ever achieve.

Daleina looked out again at her capital city, full of men, women, and children with hopes, fears, and dreams. *Given this chance . . . how can I refuse to even try, for their sakes?*

But she'd need to be certain her people would be safe, if she and Merecot failed. She'd need to ensure the champions and their candidates were prepared to protect Aratay, and she'd need a way to wrest power back from Merecot, if it proved necessary. She'd talk to the Council of Champions about the first. And she'd talk to Garnah about the second. "I will speak with the champions at dawn."

Merecot rose too. "Daleina . . ."

"Finish your meal and sleep well."

"And tomorrow? Will you help me change the world?"

Daleina hesitated, wondering if she should say the truth: Yes, she would help her, but if Merecot failed, if anything went wrong, if the people of Aratay were put in any danger . . . *I'll have to do what Merecot said she would do to me.*

*I'll have to kill her.*

But Daleina didn't say that. Instead, she smiled and said, "Yes, Merecot. I will."

MERECOT ABANDONED ANY PRETENSE OF EATING AND INSTEAD paced back and forth, across Daleina's chamber, out onto the balcony, back inside. She felt the spirits far in the distance, like an itch in her head, but she didn't try to draw them back. It was too sensitive a time.

*She believes me*, Merecot thought.

And then: *She believes in me.*

It was extraordinary.

*And to think I tried to have her killed.*

She'd never regretted anything so badly in her life. Actually, she didn't think she'd regretted *anything* in her life, and it bothered her more than she cared to admit. She'd underestimated Daleina—or at least she thought she did. It all depended on whether Daleina went through with it and actually abdicated in favor of Merecot. *She could still chicken out. I might still need to kill her.*

And now that thought made her sick.

Her hands felt sweaty, and she wiped her palms on the skirt of her gown as she paced. If she'd had her spirits, she would have called them to listen in on the council with the champions. They weren't going to like this. Not one bit. If they talked Daleina out of it . . .

"You'll still have to kill her, if things go sour," the poisoner woman—Poison-Master Garnah—said, coming into the room. It was as if she knew Merecot's thoughts, and that made the queen angry. If Garnah noticed, she didn't let on, instead continuing, "Or try to. We won't let you, of course. It will be a whole messy thing with plenty of collateral damage, but that doesn't concern you, does it?"

"For a spy, you aren't very stealthy," Merecot observed. "This is the second conversation we've had. Isn't that breaking spy protocol?" *Daleina must have spoken to her when she left.* She wished she'd thought to eavesdrop.

"I'm a terrible spy," Garnah agreed, "but a formidable enemy. You don't want me for yours."

"I'm not already?" Merecot studied the other woman, careful to keep a distance between them and at least one bulky item of furniture. She didn't come as far as she had by being careless, and now would be a terrible time to drop her guard, when she was on the verge of achieving everything she ever wanted.

"Of course not! I think you're delightful." Garnah beamed at her. "I just want to make sure we're clear: I will be accompanying you into the grove, with Queen Daleina's blessing. Don't tell me it's not done. I excel at things that aren't done, as do you. Besides, the spirits of Aratay are used to crowds of heirs in their grove—they won't mind one silly old woman."

"You're no match for angry spirits," Merecot said.

Garnah's smile widened until she was baring all her teeth. "Hah! We'll see tomorrow, won't we?"

DALEINA SAW THREE POSSIBLE OUTCOMES:

One was success. She didn't need to plan for that.

Another was betrayal. She'd spoken with Garnah after leaving Merecot—the Queen's Poisoner would accompany them into the grove, bringing her various potions. At the first sign of deceit, she'd use them on Merecot.

And third was failure. The spirits could kill both queens, leaving Aratay queen-less at a time when the country lacked heirs.

Striding through the palace, Daleina asked Belsowik to summon the champions to the Chamber of the Queen's Champions at dawn. She then shut herself in her chambers and began composing letters.

First, she wrote to the headmistresses of every academy in Aratay, advising them to instruct their teachers and students to be prepared to issue the "choose" command at midday, should the worst-case scenario occur. Then she wrote to Hanna, laying bare Merecot's plan and requesting that Hanna select one of the Semoian heirs—if she and Merecot both died, then the headmistresses and their students could suspend the spirits with the "choose" command until Hanna arrived with an heir. She sent the message with her fastest spirit, directly to the mountain castle.

It would be the champions' job to prevent casualties until the command took effect. *If all girls and women with power are standing ready . . . and if the champions are prepared . . . then it shouldn't be like it was when Queen Fara died. Her death took Aratay by surprise. I won't let that happen again.*

At the first light of dawn, she climbed the stairs to the Chamber of the Queen's Champions. She hadn't slept, of course. Instead she'd spent the night replaying the spirits' story in her mind, and trying to think of anything else to prepare. Now she felt calm.

Stiff back and folded hands, she sat motionless on the white wood throne to wait for her champions. The air was still, and the autumn leaves looked gilded against the arches. *They're not going to like this*, she thought, but they had to be warned. If things went badly . . . *I need them ready to defend Aratay.*

Last time a queen died, there was chaos, and many innocents died. With an abdication, it should be a smooth transfer of power. *But I'm not preparing for best case; I'm preparing for worst.*

The champions filed in and took their seats.

Too many chairs were empty. She let her eyes linger on them, and she thought of Champion Ambir, Champion Piriandra . . . Her eyes landed on Champion Ven's chair. For all she knew, he was dead now as well, killed as soon as he entered the untamed lands. It was too much to hope for that he and Queen Naelin had survived.

*I'm alone*, she thought.

Except that even as she thought this, she knew she wasn't. She had Hamon, and her beloved seneschal, Belsowik, was as devoted as always. Even the champions were now on her side. Since she'd repelled the invasion, there had been no more talk about her being unsuited to rule. She was now their beloved queen.

Daleina drummed her fingers on the armrest of her throne and then stopped herself. She wanted to appear calm and in control, not like the nervous mess she felt inside. *We'll see how "beloved" I am after this.* Raising her voice, she said, "Welcome, my champions. I will ask you to hear me out before you begin your objections. I also ask you to recognize that I am aware there is significant risk. But the reward to us, to all of Renthia, is, I believe, worth the risk. I hope you will agree with me."

Straightening in their seats, the champions listened.

And then, of course, they objected.

But at last the talk shifted: if she was to attempt this, how could they best protect the people? Their candidates would be ready to issue the "choose" command, in concert with all the girls and women in the academies, and the champions would be prepared to lead Aratay's soldiers to defend the people until that command took effect. Daleina would also send the spirits to the least populated areas of Aratay in advance, to buy them all extra time.

By midday, they had a plan for how to disperse the spirits and how to deploy the champions, guards, and soldiers that Daleina was happy with.

Or not precisely "happy" with. *If we need this plan . . . I'll be dead.*

DALEINA DID NOT DRESS FOR DEATH. SHE KNEW THE ODDS OF HER surviving abdication and knew that her survival would depend on how well Merecot controlled the spirits and how much she cared about protecting her old friend. Given their history . . . Daleina knew she couldn't depend on her. Still, she dressed as a queen prepared for a ceremony, with layers of silk that fluttered behind her like wings and a silver crown shaped like tiny flowers.

While she prepared, she felt Hamon watching her. He hadn't tried to talk her out of it, which surprised her. Nor had he said anything at all. He'd only watched her, as if he were trying to memorize her every move. It was hard to stay optimistic when he was looking at her like that. "If you have something to say, say it."

"I'm not saying goodbye," he said.

"Good. Because this isn't goodbye."

"It's not," he agreed. "I'm coming with you."

Sweet but impractical. "You aren't. This is between Merecot and me."

"And all of Aratay," Hamon said. "But all of Aratay can't fit into the grove, so you'll need to be content with me and my mother."

"You know I asked your mother to come?"

"She told me."

"And you aren't going to try to talk me out of it?"

"She can defend you. And I can heal you, if need be. I'd insist on all the champions too, but you already sent them out across Aratay." He said this as if it were a gross miscalculation, rather than a thoroughly discussed decision.

"The people need to be defended, in case anything goes wrong," Daleina said. "I've deployed all the champions, as well as the city guards, to protect the innocent."

"*You* need to be defended, in case anything goes wrong." He was standing, and she'd never seen such a fierce look in his eyes. "Let me help. Please, Daleina."

She thought for a moment about ordering him to stay behind. She could do it. She may have sent the spirits deep into the forest, as far from the bulk of the population of Aratay as possible, but she still had command of all the palace guards.

But did she really want to?

*No, I don't.*

"All right," Daleina said.

Hamon blinked. "Did you just agree? I'd prepared a list of points as to why including me makes sense."

Daleina held up her hand. "I don't need to hear it. But I do want to know, outside of your worries for me, if you think this is a mistake. Do you think Merecot's plan will work?" *Please say yes.* She'd wrung agreement from all the champions, and had even received a letter, via spirit, from Ambassador Hanna, but still, she wanted to hear it from Hamon's lips.

Hamon opened his mouth, shut it, and then opened it again to say slowly, "It sounds possible. But no one has ever tried before. At least, not that I know of."

"Which is something I keep wondering: *Why* hasn't anyone ever tried this? Spirits have plagued Renthians for generations. Surely someone at some point must have had this idea," Daleina said. "Has there never been a queen like Merecot before?" She'd heard of plenty of powerful queens in the history books and songs, and she'd felt the incredible reach of Naelin's power. She found it hard to believe there hadn't been others equal to Merecot.

Hamon took her hands and raised them to her lips. "Of course there have been powerful queens before, happy to seize whatever power they could in the name of protecting their people."

*He means Fara*, Daleina thought.

"But as I understand it, for this to work it requires more than one powerful queen. It requires two: one to take power and one to give it. If this is to succeed, it won't be because there's never been another queen like Merecot. It will be because there's never been a queen like *you*."

# CHAPTER 32

Daleina hadn't been back to the Queen's Grove since the day she was crowned and buried her friends. She hadn't wanted to ever see the place again. Every step into the grove came with another memory, and when she saw that even in autumn, the ground was still blanketed in green with white flowers, the tiny blossoms looking like freshly fallen snowflakes, she wanted to turn and run.

But Daleina didn't run away. She never did.

She walked to the center of the grove, between the graves, and faced Merecot.

"I used to dream of being crowned here." Smiling, Merecot held out her hands toward Daleina, waiting for her to take them. "You don't know how much this means to me."

"Tell me this isn't just ambition," Daleina said, not moving.

"Ambition isn't bad when you're trying to change the world."

Hamon spoke up. "You need to keep Daleina from being killed. You know what the spirits will do the second she abdicates." He'd dressed in healer's robes, and Daleina had watched him cram his bag full of every medicine he had. Garnah carried no bag, but her skirts were full of pockets with powders and potions. Several pouches hung from her belt.

Merecot waved her hand. "You forget—I've done this before.

With Queen Naelin. And I kept Queen Jastra alive for years, didn't I? Even though thousands of spirits despised her?"

Garnah snorted. "At least until you had her killed."

"Yes. Until then."

If Daleina hadn't been watching her face so closely, she might not have seen it: a shadow of a frown that looked like regret. *She has emotions*, Daleina thought. *She hides them, but she's not like Garnah. She's capable of guilt, regret, mercy, love.* "I trust you," Daleina said.

"And I'm showing my trust in you, by allowing your people here with us," Merecot said.

Hamon began to object, but Daleina cut him off. "You don't 'allow' me anything. I am queen here, at least for a few minutes more. And this is my choice." She said it as much for her companions' benefit as for Merecot's. "All right, Merecot, my friend. Let's save the world."

Closing her eyes, Daleina reached out with her mind and felt the threads that linked her with the spirits of Aratay. She held them gently for a while, feeling the swirling emotions and desires of the spirits, the way they loved the earth and the sky, letting that connection flow through her until she felt as if she were Aratay, within the soil and the wind.

And then she severed the connections, one by one.

Like a scissor cutting a string.

With each, she felt the recoil. Merecot held her hands and did not let go.

Daleina thought she heard words around her, in the grove, but they were distant, as if underwater, and she couldn't make sense of them. She felt so very alone. She reached out with her mind—but nothing was there.

She didn't remember feeling this weak before. Or this empty.

Distantly, she heard howls, but not with her ears—they were the howls of the spirits, now free, streaming across Aratay toward the grove, coming for her.

"Tell them to choose," she heard.

She grabbed on to those words and pushed them outward.

*Choose.*

*Choose!*

And then she heard Merecot's voice, reverberating inside her, "Choose me!"

MERECOT FELT AS IF LIGHTNING SKITTERED BENEATH HER SKIN AS the spirits flooded into her mind. *Yes!* She stretched, her mind expanding, to hold all the new wants and needs that tugged on her. She could sense the trees around her, tall and deep, and the wind that chased between them. She felt the water in the air and the hint of ice in the sky above.

This was what she needed.

This was power!

She laughed from the sheer magnitude of it. She'd held nearly as many spirits in her mind when the wild spirits were in Semo, but the feel of spirits who were tied to the land was entirely different. She felt the strength of their connection to Renthia, and she made it hers.

*I can do this.*

All her planning and all her dreams . . . felt only a finger-touch away. Casually, as if she weren't about to change the world, she projected one thought: *You are done.*

It was simple, but wrapped in that one sentence was all that it implied: you have completed your destiny, and then now you may rest. You have finished. You can move on and evolve and cease to plague this world. Your hatred and anger are obsolete, for you have completed the task for which you were created.

The Great Mother of Spirits is pleased with you.

I speak for her.

*Change.*

And the spirits heard her words. Across Aratay and Semo, her words sank into the minds and hearts and into the very essence of the spirits. She felt them grow limp and sink down from the sky, from the trees.

*It's working!*

Merecot pushed harder, boring down on them.

*Let go.*
*Be free.*
*Be gone.*

Watching Merecot, Daleina could not hear her commands. She saw the threads, connecting them to Merecot, not to her, not anymore. She couldn't hear the spirits, except as a distant haze that made her head ache if she reached for them.

But she felt the moment that the trees began to die.

Creeping around her, the air tasted stale and sour. She heard a cracking sound, as if a piece of paper were being crumpled over and over. Or as if winter ice were breaking in a stream. Looking up, Daleina saw the golden leaves, once glorious in their autumn brilliance, shrivel into brown and begin to fall.

All the leaves, falling around the grove, in a shushing sound as they drifted down through the still air. *It's not working*, she thought. "Merecot? Merecot, you have to stop! The land is dying! Merecot, stop!" Grabbing Merecot's shoulders, Daleina shook her.

But Merecot did not respond.

She did not stop.

West of Aratay, beyond the borders of Renthia, Ven knew the spirits of the untamed lands were in a killing frenzy, attacking Naelin's spirits. He couldn't feel them the way that Naelin could, but after so many years fighting spirits, he didn't need to. *Besides, the tornadoes kind of give it away*, he thought.

Just beyond the ridge of rocks, three funnels of wind rose toward the sky. They looked like dark undulating snakes, defying gravity to stand upright, swaying. Between them, fires burned bright. Shielding his eyes, Ven tried to see into the battle.

"Take the children," Naelin ordered him. "Get them across the border. I'll hold the untamed spirits back and then meet you in Redleaf."

"Not leaving you," Ven said as both Erian and Llor clung to their mother, crying and screaming at her to not make them leave her.

She hugged them, clearly not hearing what he'd said. "You

must go with Champion Ven. I'll rejoin you. I promise. But as soon as I leave here, the spirits will follow me—and their attackers will follow them. You need to get across the border."

Lightning branched across the sky, struck the earth, and a water spirit burst out from between two rocks. It rose higher and higher, the watery shape of a serpent with wings. A water dragon. As it reared, it knocked boulders from the top of the ridge, and water gushed over the edges. "One of yours?" Ven asked.

Naelin didn't answer—she was concentrating.

He saw ice spirits dart at the water dragon, and ice crystallized along its wings. Howling, it stretched, and the ice shattered. He heard the cracks from where he stood. The dragon spirit lunged forward, and water gushed over the ridge. And then Ven realized something else: the camp of humans was in the water spirit's path.

"Naelin, the children are safest with you," Ven said. "There's something I have to do." He adjusted his grip on the handle of his sword. He bent his knees, trying to convince himself he was still good for one more outnumbered, terrible-odds fight.

"No, Ven! There are too many. I won't let you!"

"Not your job to protect me." He kissed her quickly on the cheek.

"You know I can stop you if you make me."

"There's a camp full of people down there," Ven said. "And this time, I'm not too late to save them. I've been too late so many times, Naelin. Let me at least try."

Naelin's hands were in the air, sketching patterns, and her spirits were obeying her, flying the patterns she sketched, holding back the air and fire spirits. "Fine. Stubborn idiot. I can keep a path clear for a little while, but you have to move fast."

He didn't wait to discuss it any further. He leapt forward, bounding across the rocks that shifted beneath him. Slicing his sword at spirits that whisked over him, he ducked, dodged, and ran toward the camp where they'd left the people.

He found it besieged: men, women, and children were running through knee-high water, trying to find a safe path out. "To me!" he called. He sheathed his sword and unhooked his bow.

Notching an arrow, he aimed it at a fire spirit that was diving toward an older man. He shot it through the forehead, and the arrow incinerated, but not before the fire spirit reared back.

Ven leapt down into the valley, splashing into the icy water. "Come on, this way, follow the rocks up!" He guided the people into a line. A stream of fire shot over them, and he charged forward, firing another arrow into the cometlike core of light.

Above, the water dragon screamed. It clashed with a host of fire spirits that flew at it. Steam billowed from its body, and Ven lost sight of it. The mist rolled across the camp. "Grab hands!" Ven ordered.

His command was repeated by the people, and he hoped they were obeying—those nearest him were clutching one another, at least. "Follow me!" he called, and he hurried to the front of the line. "Toward the cave! Head for the grave!"

He pointed them in the right direction and then hurried down the line, ensuring there were no stragglers. As he did, an earth spirit burst from the rocks beneath him and grabbed his ankle. Other earth spirits, made of rocks and shaped like small men, burst through the rocks, seizing the legs of people, yanking them down. He drove the butt of his bow into the face of one, knocking it back, and then he leapt between people, whacking spirits with his bow as if it were a staff. As soon as he caught his breath, he reached for his sword. As he sliced, he heard the sound of pebbles, and then a louder rumbling.

"Avalanche!" one of the women cried.

And then it got worse.

Water slammed into them, waist-deep, and people screamed. They grabbed the children, who were crying and shrieking, and lifted them out of the water.

He'd never fought so many on such unstable terrain—the air, the earth, the sky, it was all his enemy. But he wasn't going to fail these people.

*Never again.*

NAELIN FELT AS IF HER MIND WERE FRACTURING. SHE KNEW what she had to do: keep a channel clear until Ven returned with the villagers, and then escape, all together, to Aratay. Her spirits could hold off the untamed spirits long enough . . . Couldn't they?

*They'll die*, she thought.

She squashed the thought as quickly as she could.

But she was so closely linked to the spirits that they felt her think it. Despair rippled through them, flowing back to her. *Don't leave us*, they whispered back to her. *Please, don't leave us to die.*

It disturbed her, hearing their pleas. They were killers. Their kind hunted humans. Hated humans. Wanted everyone dead and gone, so they could have their world back the way it was before the Great Mother of Sprits died, before the humans came too soon. *Why should I save them?*

Spirits like these had killed her parents while she'd huddled, hidden. She'd lived in fear for so many years—

Through her bond, Naelin felt a spirit torn in half, its limbs ripped apart, by an untamed earth spirit, and her knees buckled. She looked up, and there was no more thought about helping the spirits. *Her* spirits.

Remembering how she'd practiced with the spirits before she left for Semo, she pushed her mind out, forcing them to work together, guiding the ice spirits to freeze the wings of a water dragon. She sent her fire spirits skittering over the ice crystals of ice spirits. Her wind spirits whipped faster, creating a wall of wind on either side of Ven and the people. They were making their way toward her, step by step. She couldn't tell if he had them all and couldn't spare the attention to look. An untamed fire spirit was clinging to one of her tree spirits, and she felt its pain as the flames scaled his barklike skin. She directed a water spirit to douse it, freeing it, and she felt a shiver of gratitude as the wounded tree spirit scuttled away as fast as it could.

There were too many of them, though.

*Don't let us die*, the spirits whispered.

But Ven hadn't reached her yet, and they were all still deep within the untamed lands, backed against the cave. Bayn positioned himself in front of Erian and Llor, protecting them, and she let him guard her children as she focused on the spirits, driving them back but losing ground.

*Hurry, Ven.*

The circle around them tightened as the untamed spirits advanced, and despite all her strength, her spirits began to die.

It felt like part of her was dying with them.

# CHAPTER 33

Daleina kept screaming at Merecot. "Stop! Merecot, you have to stop!"

Around them she heard the trees creak and crack. Leaves were falling faster, like rain, and coating the grove in a thick blanket of gold. Every breath felt wrong, and the air tasted sour. She couldn't reach far enough to feel the damage throughout Aratay, but if it was here, it was everywhere—the spirits touched every piece of her land. *And Semo.*

"You're killing both our countries!" Daleina shouted. "Stop! It's not working!"

But Merecot's eyes were vague, and her lips were curled into a smile. She was elsewhere, deep within the spirits. *Why can't she feel them dying?* Even Daleina could sense it—the threads that linked Merecot to them were gray and frayed.

Daleina felt herself shoved aside. She stumbled, and Hamon caught her as she fell into the leaves. Dust billowed up from the too-dry earth beneath the leaves, and the leaves crinkled as they shriveled. Garnah had pushed past her and was kneeling beside Merecot. Reaching into her robes, she pulled out a vial and held it up to the light, checking its contents. It was thick and ruby-red, the viscous fluid clinging to the glass of the vial.

Yanking away from Hamon, Daleina lunged forward. "No!"

Garnah shook the vial, mixing the liquid until bubbles formed.

"She must be stopped. You have to see that. This is the only way. This is why you asked me to come!"

She'd asked her in case Merecot betrayed her. But this wasn't betrayal!

"I can't watch another friend die," Daleina cried. She'd lost so many. Linna, Mari, Revi, Iondra . . . all of them had died, so many of them here in this very grove. Their bodies were deep in the earth beneath the leaves. She couldn't add another to their number. "There has to be another way!"

"Daleina." Hamon's voice was soft, gentle, a healer's voice, her lover's voice. "You have to let her go. With her death, the spirits will be released. Aratay will be saved."

"And Semo," Garnah added. "You're letting two countries die out of sentiment." She spat into the leaves and unstoppered the vial. "It will be quick, I promise you that."

*The spirits will be released . . .*

"Thank you," she said to Hamon, and she knocked the vial out of Garnah's hand. Both mother and son watched, startled, as the vial shattered on the ground, and the poison spread into a puddle—Garnah would have more, but Daleina didn't give her a chance to reach for it. She shoved her mind at the frayed threads connecting Merecot to the spirits.

And she severed them.

Thousands of spirits, unleashed at once.

Merecot hissed out air, and her eyes focused on Daleina. "What have you done?"

Around them, the spirits flew into the grove. They tunneled through the earth. Out of the corner of her eye, Daleina saw Garnah reach into her robe, pull out a new vial, and hurl it at the spirits. It exploded into sparks.

Hamon rushed to Daleina's side, but was knocked back as an earth spirit burst through the ground in front of him. Daleina reached for the spirit's mind to stop it, hold it—and Merecot slammed into her.

"You took them!" Merecot screamed, clawing at her.

"I saved you!" Daleina yelled back. She pushed against Merecot.

Merecot drew a dagger from within her robes. Daleina tried

to send the command *Choose* ... But Merecot was striking at her, filled with as much fury as a spirit. "Listen to me!" Daleina cried, dodging. "The land was dying! Your plan was failing!"

Merecot was beyond listening. She was as consumed with the same rage as a spirit. As she hacked at Daleina, Daleina dodged as well as she could even as she reached for her own knife, the one that Ven always insisted she carry.

She fought back.

Merecot was swinging wildly—she was untrained. But Daleina had been trained by the best champion alive. Kicking, dodging, twisting, and striking, she used what Ven had taught her as both Merecot and the spirits attacked her.

*Choose*, she thought at the spirits. But she couldn't hold on to the thought, not with Merecot striking at her and the spirits diving for her. Caught in the swirl of spirits, she couldn't see Hamon and Garnah.

"Merecot, stop!" She struck hard, knocking Merecot backward.

A spirit wrapped its vinelike arms around Merecot.

Across the grove, Daleina heard Hamon scream, and she ran for him—in time to see a fire spirit drive its fist through his shoulder.

She ran faster and knew she'd be too late. And knew without a doubt that spirits everywhere were attacking across both Aratay and Semo, and people in both lands were dying. "Hamon!" she screamed. And a thought flashed through her mind: of Arin and her parents, who should have been safe, but now weren't, because of what she and Merecot had done.

*We failed* ...

In Semo, people were dying.

The earth spirits shook the mountains, and the water spirits overflowed the rivers. Entire towns slid down the slopes in rivers of water, fire, mud, ice, as air spirits plucked men, women, and children from the rocks as they tried to flee.

Inside the castle, Ambassador Hanna wheeled through the corridors while her four guards fended off earth spirits who were tunneling through the floor both behind and in front of them.

Evenna was in the lead, with Serk behind Hanna and the other two on either side of her. Their swords were sticky with blood, sap, and dirt. They fought well, but they were tiring too. She could see it. And yet, what really worried her was *why* they were fighting in the first place.

*What, by all the spirits, has Merecot done?*

She'd received Queen Daleina's letter, and she'd been impressed with the audacity of the plan. For Merecot to believe she could do what the Great Mother, the creator of all, could not . . . The arrogance was mind-boggling, but the theory had been sound. She'd told Daleina that in her reply. She'd also told her that the most probable outcome was Daleina's death, with Merecot left as queen of both countries and the spirits unchanged.

Still, though, Hanna had honored Daleina's request. In fact, she'd just come from identifying several possible successors, before earth spirits caused half the castle to slide down the mountain. She didn't know if the heirs had survived.

Hanna called the command as loudly as she could, *Choose!* and hoped that the heirs and other women of power were doing the same—and hoped there were enough of them to be heard. She didn't want to think about what would happen if there weren't. "Get to the other Aratayians," Hanna ordered her guards.

Jogging ahead, Evenna yanked open one of the doors, then another.

Champion Havtru, Cajara, and Arin burst out into the corridor. Havtru's sword was drawn. "It's happening again," Arin said, her voice shrill, near panic. "Like before. When Daleina . . ." Her eyes were bright, as if she were on the verge of tears, but she blinked them back.

"Not Daleina," Hanna corrected. *These are Semoian spirits.* "Merecot."

"We have to get somewhere safe, the heart of the castle," Havtru said. He issued orders to Hanna's four guards, directing Coren to scout ahead and Serk to watch their backs.

Arin ran to Hanna's chair and began pushing her faster through the corridor. Havtru and Cajara ran on beside her. Folding her hands on her lap with her knives, Hanna concentrated

on projecting the command. *Choose, choose, choose! Please . . .
choose.*

A fire spirit raced through the hall toward them. Shaped like a
dog, it was made of pure flame. It slammed into Evenna, and Tipi
yanked her back, smothering the flames. Howling, the spirit flew
toward Hanna. Havtru leapt in front of her, his sword drawn, but
his sword sliced harmlessly through the fire.

"Cajara!" Arin cried. "Stop the spirit! You can do it!"

Spreading her hands in front of her, Cajara concentrated—and
the fire dog yelped and pivoted, racing in the opposite direction.

"Brilliant!" Arin cheered. She hugged Cajara.

Cajara looked startled, then pleased—a small smile touched
her lips.

*I was right,* Hanna thought. *She* does *have power.* And an idea
occurred to her. Either a terrible idea, or a brilliant one. "Wheel
me around," Hanna ordered. "We have to go out."

All her guards protested.

Hanna overrode them. "Candidate Cajara, you have affinity
for all types of spirits, yes?"

"Yes." Her voice was so soft that Hanna could barely hear her
over the shrieks of the palace people and the rage-filled cries of
the spirits.

*That shyness could be a problem,* Hanna thought. The girl
would need strength and confidence, in addition to power. "Tell
me about yourself, girl."

Havtru broke in. "Ambassador Hanna, I don't think this is the
time—"

"I am not speaking to you, Champion Havtru," Hanna said in
the same voice she would use to berate a first year trying to make
an excuse for not turning in their homework. No, she didn't have
time for anyone else's nonsense—at this moment, the only thing
that mattered was Cajara. As she focused on the girl, she also
continued to issue the "choose" command to the spirits. At some
point, her command would converge with others, and it would
be multiplied until it impacted into the consciousness of the raging spirits. Until then, they had to survive. "There's an air spirit
up ahead. Do something about that, Champion."

"Cajara isn't . . ." he began.

"Cajara is not your concern right now. That spirit is."

Arin sprinted ahead. "I'll get it!" As she ran toward the air spirit, she drew a charm out of her pocket and threw it at a flicker of light. It caught the spirit square in the forehead. The air spirit squealed, then dropped to the floor.

"Help her," Hanna ordered Havtru.

With one more glance at his candidate, Havtru sprinted ahead. Before them, Hanna saw a body in Aratayian colors, slumped on the floor: the young guard Coren. It was a sharp pain, seeing him dead, but she kept her focus on Cajara. *If I don't find a way to end this, he won't be the only one to die.*

"Answer me, girl! Why do you want to be queen?" Hanna was aware she was yelling, but she could feel air spirits closing in around them. She knew there must be others. Just because she lacked the affinity to sense them, it didn't mean they weren't there. Aiming one of her knives, Hanna threw it at a torch on the wall—a fire spirit squealed.

Staring at the wounded fire spirit, the girl didn't answer at first, and Hanna was about to bark at her again. Then at last she said, "I love the forest."

"Yes. And?"

"My family . . . we lived on the forest floor. Berry-pickers. That is how we knew Champion Havtru. Or knew of him, I mean."

Hanna was aware of the champion's past. He'd been a berry-picker, though he'd lived midforest, before his wife was killed by spirits and Ven recruited him. She readied another knife. "You said 'lived.' Past tense. Family dead?"

"Oh, no, Ambassador. They're well. But the forest . . . It died around us. I felt it die. I knew the spirit who was tied to our land. I used to play . . ." She trailed off.

"You befriended a spirit?" This didn't bode well. Or did it? "And the spirit never tried to harm you or your family?"

"I never let it, even though they . . . I never let it hurt them, no matter what," Cajara said. "And when she died . . . I went to Champion Havtru and told him I wanted to be his candidate."

Hanna noticed instantly that Cajara said "she" instead of "it" for the spirit, which told her more than any of her other words what she needed to hear—and it wasn't good. Or, it wasn't what she knew to be good. Hanna trained her students to hold the spirits apart, to remember they weren't human, to remember their instincts were fundamentally opposed to human life. But something about the way Cajara spoke . . . it intrigued her. She had to be sure, though . . .

"Queens don't befriend spirits."

"But they do save them, when they can," Cajara said.

It was a good enough answer.

Hanna barked directions as Renet ran toward them. He had a woodsman's knife in one hand and a bow and quiver of arrows on his back. He was panting. "The spirits are attacking!" he cried. "And your guard—"

"Yes, we are aware, Woodsman Renet," Hanna said crisply. *What did Naelin ever see in this idiot?* Beyond them, Havtru, Evenna, Serk, and Tipi were fighting the spirits off, and Arin was lobbing vials and charm bundles at them. Her potions were at least as effective as Havtru's sword—any spirit splashed by one of her liquids or pelted with one of her herb bundles either froze, burned, dropped, or ran.

"Queen Merecot is dead?" Renet asked.

"Apparently," Hanna said.

Arin, puffing, ran back to them, excitement in her voice. "Then Daleina won?"

Knowing Daleina, she'd never call it winning. "I'd thank you not to say that while we are the only Aratayians within the Semo castle." *Merecot was my student too. I failed her.* She hadn't expected Daleina to resort to this. She'd trusted that Daleina meant peace when she said peace. *Perhaps she changed.* She had suffered at the hands of Merecot. *Perhaps I misjudged her.*

*Perhaps, though, none of this matters right now. What matters is that we keep moving.*

Hanna guided them through the halls as Havtru, Renet, and her guards fought off the spirits with their weapons, Arin battled them with her potions, and Cajara deflected them with her mind. The spirits were swarming the corridor—pebble-like earth spirits were burrowing through the floor and crawling over the walls and ceiling. An ice spirit, shaped like a snake with wings, slithered through the air, only to meet one of Arin's potions. Hanna threw two more of her knives, and Havtru retrieved them for her.

At last, they reached the courtyard . . . the old, neglected one with the weeds and the broken flagstones. *And the way to the grove*, Hanna thought.

"You say you love the forest," Hanna said to Cajara. "Can you learn to love the mountains?" Beside her, Renet was fending off a tiny earth spirit that had latched onto his ankle. Bounding over to him, Havtru pried it off and flung it against a pillar.

"Aratay is my home," Cajara said.

"All of Renthia is your home," Hanna said. She reached for another knife—she didn't find one. She'd used them all. "And Renthia needs you. Will you answer her call?"

"I don't understand," Cajara said.

Arin grasped her hands. "She wants you to be queen, Cajara."

"But I can't—"

"You can! If you won't believe in yourself, then I'll believe in you for you. That's what I did for Daleina. I always knew she could do it. And I know you can too."

Hanna wheeled forward. "Summon an earth spirit, a large one from beneath this courtyard. You, my dear, must be the new queen of Semo, as soon as we can reach the grove." She expected Cajara to protest more—she wasn't ready. Hanna knew it, Havtru knew it, Cajara knew it. She couldn't have been training for more than a few months, with less raw power at her disposal than Naelin. But Hanna did not know how to reach the true heirs of Semo within the damaged castle—Cajara was here, and Hanna was the only one who knew how to find the grove.

She spared a brief thought to wonder if Merecot had intended this outcome, as a backup, but then dismissed it. Merecot was too arrogant to conceive of defeat, and too selfish to consider the fates of the Semoian people if she should fall.

Regardless, Hanna didn't have time to waste thoughts on Merecot, because the earth spirit burst through the courtyard. "Control it," Hanna ordered.

"It's strong!" Cajara yelled. *Yet she isn't backing down,* Hannah thought. *She* can *do this.*

Sweat beaded on Cajara's forehead as she fought to control the monstrous spirit. From above, other spirits swarmed toward them, drawn by the battle of wills between the candidate and the spirit.

Arin had positioned herself at Cajara's back and was throwing powders and potions with deadly aim at the spirits, keeping them from Cajara, while the candidate focused on the earth spirit.

"We must ride it!" Hanna shouted. "Guards, defend us. Havtru, help me." Hurrying to her, Havtru scooped her out of her chair. He carried her, running toward the spirit as Cajara fought to master it.

Hanna saw Serk fall, an ice spirit slicing him down the sternum. Shrieking, Tipi leapt forward, hacking at the spirit, shattering it beneath her blade.

Cajara was speaking out loud, soothing the bulbous earth spirit, and at last it bent its head down. Havtru tossed Hanna onto its back and climbed on behind her.

More spirits rushed into the courtyard. Larger spirits: stone monsters that looked like half bears and half men, a bull-like beast with a snake's tongue and fangs, and three serpents with diamond scales.

*We aren't going to make it,* Hanna thought.

Cajara climbed onto the earth spirit's back, behind Havtru and Hanna. She held her hand out, and grabbing it, Arin scrambled up.

"Evenna! Tipi! Fall back!" Hanna ordered. But she could already see they were too far away, enmeshed in their own battles. Both were wounded—Evenna's shoulder was charred and blackened, and Tipi had streaks of blood like tears on her cheeks.

"Go, we'll hold them!" Evenna ordered.

Hanna wanted to close her eyes. She'd seen this too many times before. But this felt worse, because they weren't just dying— *they're dying for me.*

*I can't waste their sacrifice.*

"Renet, hurry!" Havtru called.

"I'll hold them back too!" Renet said. "Go!" Charging forward to join the two remaining Aratayian guards, he fought the spirits, hacking at them as if they were trees he was trying to fell, buying them precious time. "Tell my children to be proud of me! I've finally done something useful!" And then a spirit stabbed with its claws hand through Renet's stomach. He doubled over.

He'd been a fool . . . but he was a brave one. *I'll tell them*, she thought. *He will be honored. If we survive.*

"Tell the spirit to go," Hanna ordered. "Now."

Carrying them, the earth spirit dove deep into the ground.

IN THE QUEEN'S GROVE IN ARATAY, HAMON FELT SEARING AGONY as a fire spirit's fist slammed into his shoulder. He heard himself scream, but the sound was lost in the cries of dozens of spirits all around them. His eyes locked onto Daleina's for a brief moment before she was swept away, fighting both Merecot and the spirits.

He fell to his knees. They hit hard, but he barely felt it.

His hearing felt muffled, as if cotton were shoved into his ears. He felt pain rippling across his body, and he waited, unable to flee, for the final strike.

It didn't come.

Instead the fire spirit dissolved in front of him, compressing into ash. His mother slapped a cool mass of leaves over her shoulder. "Hold that there," she instructed.

His hands, shaking, held the poultice. It was radiating coolness through his body. It chilled his fingers as he touched it. His thoughts were swimming, connecting slowly together, as his mother stood in front of him, legs straddled wide, with charms in each hand. She was screaming insults at the spirits as she hurled charms at them.

The charms exploded all around them, circling her and Hamon.

"See, my boy," Garnah cried, laughing, "I'll keep you safe! Mother's job, they say. Mother's joy. To protect my little boy. That's all I ever wanted. Just didn't know how. Never knew how. Instead I scared you away. But I get why. Because I'm scary. Hah! Want to see how scary I can be? Come at me, spirits!"

As Hamon struggled to rise, his mother hurled charm after

charm at the spirits that surrounded them, driving them back with deadly accuracy. He reached shakily into his pocket and pulled out an herb, stuffed it into his mouth and held it inside his cheek—the pain receded, and he drew his knife. He stabbed at every shadow, every wisp, everything that moved in front and beside him, while his mother stood at his back, hurling charms.

"We've got them, my boy! Keep it up! Don't—" Her voice broke off, and he felt her crumple at his back. He turned, in time to catch her as she fell, slumped against him. He felt blood on his fingers, hot and wet, on her side.

"Mother?"

"Well, this wasn't supposed to happen," she whispered. He lowered her down. She'd been sliced in the side, deep. Her breathing was fast, hitched. "Looks like you're getting what you wanted."

Around him, the spirits swirled.

# CHAPTER 34

Daleina kicked hard against Merecot's knee, then jammed her fist into Merecot's side. Her friend huffed as the air was knocked out of her. Spinning away, Daleina struck upward with her knife and jabbed into the slippery thigh of a water spirit. "Enough!" she yelled at the spirits. "Choose! Choose, damn you!"

"Choose," she heard Merecot say, panting on the ground, looking up at the sky. Daleina looked up too. It was filled with swirling spirits, clogging the air between the trees, blocking out the sun.

*Choose! Choose!*

And the spirits stopped.

Hanging in the air, they at last drifted between the trees. On the ground, the earth spirits slumped down or milled listlessly around the roots and rocks. Fire spirits dampened their flames. Daleina sank to her knees beside Merecot. She kept her eyes on the other queen. *No—not* other. *I'm not a queen anymore.*

"I can't feel them," Merecot said.

"What?" Her legs? Her arms? *How badly did I hurt her?* Ven hadn't taught her to fight cautiously. He'd assumed her enemies would be spirits. He'd taught her to fight hard to save her life, and that's what she'd done. Daleina realized she ached everywhere, in places where spirits had burned and froze and jabbed her. She touched her cheek and felt wetness. Drawing her fingers back, she saw the tips were red. While she'd fought Merecot, the spirits had attacked both of them. She was amazed she was still whole. *I wish I could thank Ven.*

Collapsed on the golden leaves, Merecot was wounded in a dozen different places. Blood spread through her silk sleeve, and a darkening bruise colored her cheek. But none of her injuries looked deep enough to be fatal. "The spirits," she wheezed. "They're gone. I can see them, but only with my eyes. I can't *feel* them! What did you do to me?"

Daleina shook her head. She'd severed the links. The severing must have been more serious than she'd realized. But she couldn't spare the energy to speak. Instead she reached out to the spirits in the grove and beyond.

*Choose me.*

*Once again, let me be your queen.*

She touched the spirits of Aratay, and she felt them respond, linking to her, accepting her, loathing her and loving her. She tried to reach farther—but her power was never as vast as Merecot's. She couldn't reach beyond the northernmost birch trees.

She felt a handful of tiny spirits curling above her, crafting a crown of leaves to lay on her head once again, and she thought of Naelin, far beyond the borders of Aratay.

"You truly can't sense them?" Daleina asked.

Merecot gave her a withering look. "I wouldn't lie about this."

If it was true, then it meant she'd discovered a way to remove the affinity for spirits—the thing that Naelin had wished for so desperately. *If I'd known this sooner, I could have granted her wish.* Naelin could have returned to her forest village with her children and never known any of the power or the pain of being queen. She wouldn't have had to give up her home. Her children would never have been in danger. *If she ever returns from the untamed lands, I can tell her . . .* But she wouldn't, Daleina knew. The untamed lands were death. Both Naelin and Ven would have perished soon after crossing the border. *I failed them.*

"Semo?" Merecot asked.

Daleina shook her head. *I failed to save them too.*

"And so my people die, because you aren't strong enough."

"No, they died because you thought you were strong enough," Daleina shot back. "But you weren't."

Merecot fell silent.

Around her, Daleina felt life return to Aratay once more. The wind blew, the trees swayed, and the forest went on. It was all she could do.

She hoped it was enough.

MERECOT LAY ON THE GOLDEN LEAVES IN THE CENTER OF THE grove and stared up at the swirling spirits. She'd never felt so alone. "You should have killed me."

"I couldn't lose another friend," Daleina said.

Turning her head, Merecot looked at her, saw the spirits crowning her, and closed her eyes. "I will hate you always." She meant every word.

"That doesn't matter," Daleina said infuriatingly. "I made my choice."

ON THE OTHER SIDE OF THE GROVE, HAMON KNELT BY HIS mother. "You deserve to die," he told her. "You've killed so many people, and you haven't cared."

"Ah, but I saved you," Garnah said. "In the end, at least I did that. I can die contented."

"I'm not giving you that kind of peace," Hamon said, and he opened his healer's bag. For the first time since he'd entered the grove, his hands were steady as he began to sew his mother's wounds.

TO THE NORTH, IN SEMO, ARIN READIED ANOTHER PACKET OF herbs. She'd laced this charm with poisonous bark mixed with pepper dust. She didn't know why the spirits hadn't calmed yet—the Semoian hedgewitches had to be trying the "choose" command. *Maybe the spirits here are just too strong.*

Arin glanced over her shoulder at Havtru and Hanna—they were fending off an air spirit that looked like a bat made of glass.

She then looked at the circle of stones in front of them, the grove. "You have to do it," she told Cajara. "Go!"

Cajara seemed as stuck as those stones.

*She can do this. I know she can. And I can help her.* Daleina always said she became queen because of Arin—to protect Arin. *I was Daleina's motivation. I can be Cajara's too.*

"You don't have to stop them," Arin said to Cajara. "All you have to do is keep me safe."

And then, before she could lose her nerve, she ran into the grove.

She heard Cajara call her name, but she didn't stop until she was within the circle of stones. Unlike the Aratayian grove, the grove in Semo was a bowl of smooth, black stone. Granite pillars lined it, and the mountains towered above.

Looking up, Arin saw hundreds of spirits.

One of them saw her and shrieked, "Intruder!" Others took up the cry. "Traitor! Defiler!" They whipped faster in a circle, and the air around the stone circle cyloned. Pebbles were lifted into the air. Arin blocked her face with her hands as dust and gravel pelted her.

*Maybe this was a bad idea.* "Cajara?"

"There are so many," Cajara said. Standing in the center of the stone circle, untouched by the cyclone, she looked so lost. "And they . . . I can hear them . . . They don't want you here. You're not an heir. They . . ."

Pushing against the dust-choked wind, Arin crossed to her. She took Cajara's hands in hers. "Don't think about them. Look at me. Focus on me."

Lowering her gaze from the spirits, Cajara met her eyes.

"Good." Arin shuddered as an ice spirit grazed her arm, the cold shooting down to her fingertips. She kept her voice calm, as if this were a pleasant summer day. Behind Cajara, she saw an earth spirit, a stone giant, rise out of the ground. It held boulders in its fists. "Now all you have to do is tell them to choose you."

Cajara shook her head. "I'm no one. Why would they choose me?"

"*I* choose you," Arin said, and then she leaned forward and kissed Cajara. Cajara's lips tasted sweet, like strawberries just ripened in the summer heat. She pulled back, but not too far.

Foreheads touching, she whispered, "Tell the spirits to choose you too."

Cajara's eyelids fluttered closed. Still holding on to one of Cajara's hands, Arin reached into her pocket for another potion-laced charm . . . and felt nothing. Her supplies were gone. She looked up at the sea of spirits filling the sky, and at the stone monsters closing in on them.

"I choose you," Arin repeated.

Far to the west, in the untamed lands, Ven hacked his way through the wild spirits. There were so many of them, diving, charging, tunneling, biting, fighting, in a whirlwind of talons and claws. He was bleeding from dozens of wounds.

*I will not fail*, he promised himself. He kept the people clumped tightly together as they moved forward, bit by bit. He couldn't see the cave or even the rock formation where it was, but he knew it was ahead.

Naelin was clearing a path for them—a narrow one, but he could thread it. He ran up and down the line, protecting the children, the men, the women, the old and the young. He didn't see the faces. But he did see the eyes, full of fear. And full of trust.

He fought for them, widening the tunnel through the mist as they pressed on toward the cave where the body of the Great Mother of Spirits lay. Inch by inch, he won ground. Until at last he reached them: Naelin with Bayn and the children, outside the mouth of the grave.

"In," he ordered the people.

They touched him as they passed—his face, his hand, his arm, as if they were blessing him or seeking his blessing. He kept his eyes trained on the spirits, but he felt them.

"Can you clear a path to Aratay?" he asked Naelin.

"I can try," she said. "But . . ."

"But what?"

"My spirits will die."

Naelin felt the spirits suffering.

*Don't leave us*, the spirits whispered. *Don't let us die.*

The untamed spirits were pressing in, gaining ground with every strike. All she had to do was call enough spirits to carry her, Ven, her children, and the villagers, as well as Bayn if he wished to come. They could fly for the border of Aratay on the backs of a handful of spirits while the rest of her spirits defended their retreat. Her spirits were strong enough to keep the untamed spirits at bay for at least a while. *Long enough for us to escape.*

The people would live.

But her spirits would die.

*I don't care*, she told herself.

But she did care. Yes, she hated spirits as much as they hated her. Yes, they filled the world with fear. They forced all of humanity to lead brief, frightened lives, always expecting an arbitrary death at the whim of a spirit. Bridges snapped. Ladders broke. Trees fell. Winds blew hard at the wrong moment. Fires broke out while people slept. And then there were the direct attacks, from spirits who dared.

But they also felt fear. They felt hope and anger and joy. They felt, therefore they were worthy of care. She didn't have to love them. She didn't have to stop being scared of them herself. But she *did* have to protect them. Serve them, as they served her. Because she had promised them. If they helped her find her children, she'd said, she wouldn't leave them.

While Ven herded the people inside to the relative safety of the cave, Naelin looked at Erian and Llor. They were her primary responsibility. Her children.

*We are yours too*, the spirits whispered. *And you are ours. Our destinies are linked.*

*The Great Mother is dead*, she thought back. *There are no destinies. There are only choices.*

Erian's face was streaked with tears. Llor wiped his cheek and nose with the back of his hands. Naelin drew her children close to her as she kept her mind within the swirl of spirits. Beside her, the wolf watched her with yellow eyes.

"I know what you want me to do," she said to Bayn.

He, as always, said nothing.

It was her choice. It had to be. And it *was* a choice. She could escape, return to life in Aratay. She could shed the remaining spirits at the border and become what she was before: a woods-woman, with children. She could begin a new life, perhaps in Redleaf. Ven would return to the capital—he had duties, and she knew him better than to think he'd forsake them, even for her—but he'd return when he could. She had no doubt of that. He loved her, and he loved Erian and Llor. He'd come here, risked himself, for the three of them.

*Because you risk yourself for those you love*, she thought. *You* choose *to do it*.

Standing, she wrapped her arms around her children and led them into the cave. The people buzzed around her, talking and whispering, but she didn't speak to them. She walked straight be-tween them to the mossy body of the Great Mother—they parted to let her through.

She didn't know what had happened long ago, whether the Great Mother was murdered, died by accident, or died by sacri-fice. It didn't matter. What mattered was what they did now, the humans and the spirits.

*We live. Together.*

"We aren't leaving," she said.

And then she sent her thought outward: *Live. With me. I am your queen, you are my spirits, and this is our land.* She plunged her mind into her own spirits and then into the land, tying them to it with threads that she saw as glowing lines. Eagerly they dug in, thanking her in their own way, even as they started to shape the land around them.

Then she reached out farther into the tangle of untamed spirits.

She claimed them, as many as she could. And she claimed the land.

Knowing there was another way, knowing she could have saved herself, knowing she could have returned to Aratay and lived happily ever after with her family around her—if only she had been willing to let the spirits die—Naelin chose to become queen of the untamed lands, as far as her mind could reach.

# CHAPTER 35

In Semo, outside the grove, Hanna closed Champion Havtru's sightless eyes. "You were an excellent champion," she told him. "Greet your wife with pride."

She sat slumped beside his body for a long while, before she found the strength to drag herself to the earth spirit. It hadn't moved since Arin and Cajara had entered the grove, and Hanna doubted she had the ability to control it. Her affinity was for air. But she rested her tired body against the spirit anyway, willing it to stay while she watched the stone circle of the Semoian grove.

At last, she saw two figures walk out, hand in hand: Arin and Cajara... *Queen* Cajara, with a crown of diamonds and other precious jewels dug from the mountains of Semo. The girl was stumbling as she walked, weaving between the stones in the path, but seemed unhurt. Arin was helping her, keeping her from falling. Hanna wished she could go to them but could only wait until the two girls reached her.

"Your Majesty," Hanna said.

"They want..."

"I know," Hanna said as kindly as she could. This had to be a shock to the poor girl. "You must control them. It's on you now. Tell them do no harm."

"That's all?"

"For now, it's enough."

Cajara closed her eyes.

Hanna wasn't powerful enough to sense how far the new queen could reach, but Cajara's expression eased, and she opened her eyes.

"They hate me," the girl reported.

"Of course they do. They hate us all."

"But they want me too."

"You're bound, for better and for worse," Hanna said. "Think of it as a marriage." *An unhealthy marriage in which you're only staying together for the kids.*

Arin grimaced. "Or not."

Cajara let out a little chirp of a laugh, frowned, as if surprised to be laughing, then laughed again. She sobered quickly, though. "I wasn't ready."

"No one ever is, when the future comes." Hanna held her arms up, hating that she needed to ask for help. A world filled with so much power, and she couldn't stand. *Stop it,* she told herself. *You're alive. That's power enough.* "Help me mount? We can't stay here. The Semoians must meet their new queen."

Over her shoulder, Cajara asked, "Champion Havtru, can you—" and saw her champion's lifeless body.

*Poor girl. First to lose her homeland, then her mentor.* Hanna spoke gently. "He kept them from the grove until you could claim the crown. And he kept me alive." She wondered if the girl had seen death up close before. There were few in Renthia who hadn't. Still, it was a shock if the death was someone who was supposed to keep you alive. She braced herself—this shock piled on top of all the others of the day could prove to be too much for the young queen.

But Cajara simply said, "We can't leave him here. Not like this." There were tears on her cheeks, but she was a quiet crier. And more important, she didn't collapse in despair or fall apart in panic. *Perhaps she will handle the crown just fine,* Hanna thought.

"You have the power," Arin said. She was holding Cajara's hand again. Hanna approved—the new queen of Semo was going to need as much support as she could get. "He can be buried here."

Cajara shook her head. "No, he'd want to be home."

"Then send him there," Hanna suggested. "As far as the border. From there, the Aratayian border guards will take care of him. And when we've left here, perhaps you could send my four guards as well. And the woodsman Renet to his family. They all deserve to be buried with honor, at home." Searching through her skirts, Hanna located a piece of parchment. She'd kept it for her next message to Daleina, but it would be better used for this. While she wrote a note to the border guards of Aratay, explaining who he was and how he died and to expect five more bodies to follow, an air spirit spiraled down from between the stone peaks. It was a bird-shaped spirit with a body as soft as clouds. A tree spirit scurried down from the tree and lifted Havtru's body onto the spirit, nestled on the bird's back. Hanna handed the note to Cajara, who affixed it onto Havtru's leather armor, threading it onto the straps. She then crossed his arms over his chest and whispered to him.

Hanna couldn't hear her words, but she didn't need to. She bowed her head in respect until the air spirit lifted off, carrying Havtru skyward. They watched him until the bird spirit was indistinguishable from the clouds.

For several minutes, there was silence. Then Cajara spoke again. "I don't know this land. I don't know these people. What if the Semoians don't like having another Aratayian as their queen?" Hanna heard the quaver in her soft voice. Fear.

Hanna smiled. "We'll make them like it." Now, *that* sounded like a challenge worthy of her skills. She hadn't had a challenge like this in . . . well, not since she'd taken over at Northeast Academy.

"You'll stay with me?" Cajara said, her young eyes brightening.

"Of course we will," Arin said firmly.

"But what about your family, your home, your bakery . . . your dreams! And you, Ambassador Hanna, your academy—it's your life's work!"

Arin shrugged, as if this were a minor decision. "I'm allowed to have new dreams."

"And making queens *is* my life work," Hanna said to her. "We will both stay."

Naelin buried Renet in the untamed lands, beside the cave of the Great Mother. Quietly, the villagers helped her dig—they'd lost two of their own as well in the spirit attack, and they lined all three graves in a row.

On either side of her, Erian and Llor clung to her hands. Both of them were silent.

Ven handed out shovels, rotating them among those who wanted to dig. He then came to stand beside Naelin and the children. Releasing her, Llor flung his arms around Ven and buried his face in Ven's stomach. Ven stroked his hair.

Softly, Ven said, "They never had graves before. Not that stayed."

She nodded. Others in the village had told her that. They'd tried to bury their dead with honor and dignity, but the markers would be swallowed by the earth. Or the hill they'd chosen would be transformed into a lake. "These will stay," Naelin promised. "And we will stay."

*Bring me stones*, she asked the earth spirits. *As beautiful as you can find.*

She felt the spirits burrow deep into the soil and within the rock of the mountains as she watched the villagers lower the three bodies, wrapped in white cloth, into the fresh graves. She could have had the spirits also refill the dirt, but she didn't—the people wanted to do it themselves. *Not "want,"* she corrected herself. *Need.*

As the first shovelful of dirt landed softly in the hole, Erian turned away. Naelin knelt and wrapped her in her arms. Erian began to cry into her shoulder.

Pressing her lips against Erian's hair, Naelin wished with all her heart that she could take the pain away. She felt spirits cluster around her. Rain began to softly fall, and she didn't try to stop it. Air spirits thickened around them—she felt their curiosity, as well as a mirror of her sadness.

Like with the rain, she knew she could control it now—if she wanted to, she could block that sadness away, keep it from spilling onto the spirits, but she didn't. *Not today. Today we all mourn.*

*For those who died. For those who are left behind. For futures we could have had.*

As the final shovelful was added to the graves, Naelin felt the earth spirits return. She called to them, and the earth disgorged jewels:

Opals that glittered with a hundred colors.

Rubies with fire-red hearts.

Diamonds, cloudy and rough.

Also, beautiful shards of tiger-striped stones, pink-laced granite, pure white marble, and mica-flecked basalt. Swarming, the earth spirits laid the gems and rocks over the three graves.

"Will you make the white flowers bloom?" Erian asked, muffled against her shoulder. "Like in the forest?"

"Yes," Naelin said, stroking her hair again. "And I can make them bloom again every time you miss him."

"I'll always miss him," Erian said.

"Then they'll always bloom," she promised.

She then called to the tree spirits, and white flowers spread over the graves and over the Great Mother's cave. They bloomed all around the feet of Naelin, her family, and the villagers.

WITHIN THE PALACE IN MITTRIEL, HAMON CHANGED HIS MOTHER's bandages. These had less blood on them, which was a nice improvement. She was beginning to heal. Her hand closed on his wrist.

"You won't look at me, Hamon. Why not?"

He looked at her, then looked away, fixing his eyes on the rolls of bandages and tubs of ointment. He'd saved her. His tormentor. The murderer. She'd be free and healthy and ready to hurt more innocent people whenever the whim struck her. "I want you to leave, when you're well enough."

He expected her to argue, to say he was her beloved son and of course she had to stay by him and make up for the time they'd lost, or some other nonsense that he'd never believed. She hadn't stayed for him; she'd come and she'd stayed only for herself.

But she didn't argue, which was a minor miracle. "I have been thinking that a journey would be nice. See the world while I still can, after your wedding, of course. Perhaps Semo, the land I've heard so much about. Or Belene. There are some fascinating potions that I'm told come from the islands."

He did look at her now, fully, to see if she was lying. It would be like her to raise his hopes then laugh when she dashed them, but she had a contemplative look on her face. *Perhaps the brush with death has changed her.* Then he dismissed that as impossible. His mother would never change.

She patted his hand. "It's enough that I know you do love me after all."

"I don't," he said.

"You saved my life, after I saved yours."

"It was only right," Hamon said. "And I am a healer. It's my sworn duty."

"No one would have known. And if they had, they wouldn't have blamed you. Queen Daleina wouldn't have, and I know that's what you care most about. Don't worry, Hamon. I won't speak of it again. It's enough to know that deep down, you do love your mother."

He was going to protest again, but she had closed her eyes and begun to snore.

And . . . he wasn't sure she was completely wrong.

MERECOT SIPPED THE PINE-NEEDLE TEA AND WAS SURPRISED THAT it had honey in it, not poison. In Daleina's shoes, she wasn't sure that she'd be so gracious. "I apologize for trying to kill you again. I was upset." The words felt awkward in her mouth, like pebbles stuffed in her cheeks. And "upset" didn't begin to cover it.

Daleina didn't say anything, and Merecot couldn't be sure that Daleina had even heard. She had that distant look of talking with spirits. *I used to wear that look.*

"I appreciate that you haven't put me in prison," Merecot continued. She didn't really understand why she had her freedom. She may not have power, but she should still be considered dangerous. *Daleina is entirely too trusting. Or maybe she simply knows she's the more powerful one now.* "I'll be returning to Semo, I guess."

"You don't have to," Daleina said, stirring her tea. She had circles under her eyes but was still sitting as stiff and proper as Headmistress Hanna always did. "Queen Cajara is adjusting, I'm told. You could stay in Aratay. It was once your home."

"Definitely can't do that." She'd never be able to bear the constant reminder of what she'd lost. And of what she'd nearly done. Putting down her teacup, Merecot crossed to the open window. A light breeze blew in, tinged with a hint of chill, a harbinger of the coming winter snows. "I truly thought it would work."

"So did I. We share the blame."

Merecot rolled her eyes. "I think I deserve more of the blame. Let me carry the guilt, Daleina. You've taken everything else from me."

She heard Daleina sigh behind her. "That wasn't my intent."

"Intent or not, it happened, and now I have to live with it." *But live how?* She'd always had her power. It had made her who she was. It had shaped every choice she'd ever made. Now when she reached for it, it felt like reaching for a ghost. It slipped through her fingers and faded into memory. It was even hard to recapture the feeling of *how* she'd done it, pushing her thoughts out, sending others. Now when she pushed . . . she felt only silence, as if she were pushing into a dense down pillow.

Leaning against the window, Merecot viewed the city that she'd nearly ruled—she wondered if any of them knew the details of what had happened in the grove, and how much they'd hate her if they knew.

*They probably already hate me*, she thought. *I did try to kill their queen—twice. And kidnapped their other queen's children. And invaded, causing much of their forest to die. And, failing to control the spirits, let many others die . . .*

She almost laughed at the thought. *Of* course *they hate me.* What she truly wondered was if they hated her as much as she hated herself.

Daleina was silent behind her, and Merecot felt an itch on the back of her neck, as if she were being stared at by dozens of bumblebees. It was annoying. "What?"

"I didn't speak."

"But you want to. Go on, say whatever you want to say."

"Your affinity for spirits might not be gone forever. Your power could still return."

It might, or it might not. Merecot wasn't in the mood for Daleina's unbridled optimism. *Doesn't she ever get tired of being perky and positive?*

"But if it doesn't . . . You could seek out a new path, one that has nothing to do with spirits at all. Your life isn't over, which means you still have choices, whether you see them yet or not."

Merecot grunted. It was as much of a reply as she could manage, and as much as that gooey mushiness deserved. She heard a shift of fabric behind her and knew that Daleina had stood up.

"Good luck, Merecot. You've been a terrible friend, but I am still glad I saved you."

She didn't know what to say to that either. She listened without turning around to Daleina's footsteps as they receded, and the door opened and closed. Still looking out the window, she saw an ermine-shaped spirit with wings like a bat fly between the branches and then up into the blue sky above.

"Maybe someday I'll be glad too," Merecot said, though Daleina was already gone.

DALEINA DIDN'T WANT A FEAST FOR HER WEDDING—SHE DID NOT want to waste even a bit of food that could be saved for her people. Though she had the spirits working hard to repair the orchards, nut trees, and berry bushes, the stores were still low, and the winter months would be lean for many across the land. So it seemed wrong to celebrate her and Hamon's wedding with any kind of extravagant banquet.

She did, though, want music. And dancing.

It was Belsowik who spread the word, and when she woke on her wedding day, she heard music: singing from the treetops, drums and horns from the branches, and what sounded like a thousand bells.

Sitting up, she saw Hamon was already awake and standing by the balcony. Smiling, she crossed to him and wrapped her arms around his waist. "They're singing for you," Hamon said.

"For us," she corrected.

"And themselves. They're happy to be alive, thanks to you."

Out in the trees, she saw the people of Mittriel were already celebrating: on the bridges, men and women were dancing. Children were racing over the branches, pulling ribbons behind them. Already brilliant-colored ribbons were tangled in the trees, looking like nests made of rainbows, and she saw spirits plucking them off and playing with them in the air.

She walked out farther onto the balcony, and the music wrapped around her. It soared—sopranos mixing with baritones in a glorious chorus that rose above the laughing children and the dancers' drums. And then she saw them: the canopy singers, hundreds of them, perched at the very top of her city.

*They must have all come.* Or at least more than she'd ever seen. Most canopy singers were loners. She'd never heard of them gathering like this.

One of the singers, a woman with hair that floated around her face like dandelion fluff, rode a zipline toward the palace. She waved to the queen and shouted words that Daleina couldn't quite hear. Quickly, Daleina signaled to her guards to let her come. And then she reached out to an ermine air spirit to carry her from the zipline to Daleina's balcony.

*I hope this doesn't scare her. But she seems to want to talk to me.*

The singer was laughing as the spirit deposited her on the balcony. Her cheeks were flushed. "And now I've met a second queen!" she said happily.

"Thank you for the beautiful music," Daleina said, wondering whom she'd met before. Naelin? Fara?

"Oh, we had to sing for you. So you'll have happiness!" She beamed at Daleina. "My brother chose well twice! Ven's my brother. I came to ask you: The singers have heard rumors, they're composing songs . . . Are they true? Did he go into the untamed lands? And did he live?"

This was Ven's sister! Daleina had forgotten she was a canopy singer, if she'd even known that. Ven didn't talk much about family or his childhood. "I'm so pleased to meet you." She wanted to ask her a hundred questions about Ven: what was he like as a child, did she know any embarrassing stories about him, had he been born with a sword in his hand? But the singer's questions were more important. "Yes, he did. And yes, he lives with Queen Naelin in the untamed lands . . . which I suppose we can't call 'untamed' anymore, at least not their part of it." Vast stretches of untamed lands still existed, of course—no one knew how far they stretched—but Renthia itself had grown.

Ven's sister clapped her hands. "Oh, the stories he must have for me! Thank you!" She then stepped forward with arms out, as if to hug Daleina, then suddenly remembered this was the queen and dropped into a curtsy.

Laughing, Daleina hugged her anyway.

She then called to the air spirit to carry Ven's sister back to the treetops. Daleina heard her singing as she flew. "It's nice to have good news to share," Daleina said to Hamon.

Hamon held out his hand. "Shall we give them all more good news? Are you ready to marry?"

Looking down at her nightgown, Daleina laughed again. "Not quite." She then shooed him out of the room and called to the palace caretakers to help her prepare.

She wore a dress of silken lace that felt as if she were wearing clouds, and for jewelry, she asked the spirits to decorate her in flowers. Vines wreathed her arms, with just-bloomed sprays of pink blossoms on her wrists. Around her throat, she wore the necklace her family had given her when she became queen: wood carved in the shape of leaves. Her crown was woven branches with white flowers, in remembrance of those lost.

Once she was dressed, Belsowik opened her chamber doors, and her parents and her sister rushed in. She embraced all three of them. "Oh, my baby girl," her father said. "You grew up."

"We're so proud of you," her mother said. She kissed Daleina on each cheek.

"Are you ready?" Daddy asked.

*Am I?*

Daleina remembered she'd once asked Queen Fara if she'd been ready when she became queen. But how could anyone be truly ready, when you never knew what path your life would take? "I'm happy," she told him.

It wasn't an answer to his question, but was perhaps even better.

She then looped her arm around Arin's and followed her parents and Belsowik out the door of her chambers. "Are *you* happy?" Daleina asked Arin as they walked toward the Sunrise Room.

"Yes, I think I am," Arin said, a faint blush staining her cheeks. "You'll have to come visit as soon as you can. Mama and Daddy will be coming back with me after your wedding. They want to meet Cajara. And I want to show them Semo."

"You should ask them to move there with you so you won't be alone," Daleina encouraged. She knew her parents would visit Aratay, and Arin needed them more.

Arin smiled. "I'm not alone. But I think . . . maybe I will."

And then they reached the Sunrise Room, and the palace guards flung the doors open. Morning sun streamed through the windows, lighting the room so that it glowed amber. Hamon waited for her by the open window.

The wedding itself was only for family . . . but all of Aratay bore witness.

Outside, the people of Aratay were crowded onto the branches, as many as could fit, overflowing the trees. The song of the canopy singers flowed inside with the sweet autumn breeze. Daleina's parents and sister escorted her to Hamon, and Daleina and Hamon stood facing each other, by the window so all could see.

Looking into Hamon's eyes, Daleina thought she'd never been happier.

And when they sealed their vows with a kiss, all of Aratay rejoiced with them.

NAELIN HAD TOLD THEM ALL NO CASTLE. "IT'S FRIVOLOUS," SHE'D said everyone who asked—and everyone *did* ask. Her new people had waited so long for a queen that they wanted all the trappings: a gleaming city of splendors. Naelin gave them all the same answer: no, no, and no. She wanted only a simple house, built only a walk from the cave of the Great Mother, no larger than the houses of anyone else in her new land.

It was harder, though, to say no to the spirits. They *wanted* to build. Out in the untamed lands, everything they'd created had been so quickly destroyed that now they yearned to create something that would last. She felt that yearning like an itch until at last, she gave in.

She gathered Erian and Llor to her. "Tell me: what should we make?"

"Trees," Erian said promptly. "Like home."

"Mud castles," Llor said. "Like these." And he plopped into a mud puddle, with mud splashing in a wave around him and spattering his pants. Naelin winced but said nothing as he scooped up fistfuls of muck and dribbled it to make towers.

"Llor, you're all dirty now," Erian informed him.

"If you sit, you can be dirty too." He patted the puddle next to him. "Mama's going to make me take a bath anyway." He shot Naelin a look that clearly conveyed what he thought of that idea. "Bayn never makes us take baths."

"That's because Bayn lacks hands to wash you," Naelin said. "He'll be happy when you smell better. Wolves have an excellent sense of smell." She knew she should scold Llor for drenching himself in muck, but a smile kept tugging on her lips. Kneeling, she scooped up a handful of mud and squeezed it, dribbling out a tower of dirt. "All right, but we'll make the towers out of rocks so it's less messy to live in, and we'll grow trees around it."

Llor cheered, clapping and spattering mud on Naelin and Erian.

"Mama!" Erian squealed.

Naelin met Erian's eyes. She wiggled her eyebrows, then shot a significant look at the puddle and at Llor.

"Really?" Erian asked.

Grinning, Naelin nodded.

Whooping, Erian scooped up mud and flung it at her brother. He squealed and threw mud back at her. Then Naelin joined in, tossing mud at both of them, until they ganged up on her, spattering her from hair to feet.

Laughing, they collapsed in a heap in the puddle, and Naelin reached her mind out and touched the spirits. She etched in her mind an image of towers made of rocks, and the earth began to bubble, as did the spirits' excitement. Earth spirits scurried over the land and within it, pushing upward, and Naelin felt the ground shake as stone burst from the dirt: black-streaked red stone twisting into spirals that jutted up toward the sky. Calling for the tree spirits, she released them to grow a forest around it. One muddy child on either side of her, she watched as trees sprouted and thickened.

Under her command, the water spirits corralled rivers and guided them into a lake that spread across a patch of desert. She instructed other earth spirits to create cliffs, and the water spirits joyfully led the water to cascade in thundering waterfalls.

"Oh, Mama, it's beautiful!" Erian cried.

The fire spirits were fidgeting anxiously in her mind, and she sent them in: lighting fires in hearths in the homes of all her new people. Careful, controlled fires, but plentiful so that the new palace towers and all the stone homes blazed with light.

Reaching out to the ice spirits, she let them have a turn: freezing one of the waterfalls. It crackled as it crystallized, each torrent of water solidifying in midair. Glistening in the sun, it looked like a work of art.

As the others worked, she sent the air spirits out across her country and beyond the borders of her land, into the far wilds that were still untamed, to bring seeds of flowers from everywhere they could reach. They swept the seeds across the land, and she guided the tree spirits to plant them and the water spirits to help, until a riot of flowers blossomed at once for miles in every direction: reds, purples, blues, yellows, and the land was bathed in color.

With her arms around Erian and Llor, Naelin watched as her spirits danced across the land, drenching it in beauty. She decided she'd let them continue creating once they finished, but she'd send them beyond the capital, pushing them outward so the people could live their lives while the spirits lived theirs.

*It might not be peace, but it's close.*

"I think I'll like it here," Erian said.

Kissing her mud-spattered hair, Naelin said, "Me too."

Her children curled against her, watching as the land was re-born.

Ven kept his sword sharp and his bow ready—there were always spirits who didn't want to be tamed, who wanted to destroy more than they wanted to create, who tested the limits of Naelin's control. Queen Naelin had a simple and elegant solution to such rogue spirits: sever their connection to her and expel them from her country, exiling them into the vast expense of still-untamed lands that lay beyond her borders. But sometimes she missed one or two. Sometimes she was busy with other problems. Or asleep. Even queens needed to sleep. So Ven had claimed the responsibility of leading the guards who watched for occasional rogues.

It was rather enjoyable. And it had the added benefit of keeping the land safe.

He'd told Naelin he wouldn't be her champion. Another would have to play the role of training her successor. He was committed to keeping her on the throne for as long as she wanted it. Frankly, he was surprised she hadn't argued with him, but he wasn't going to complain.

One afternoon, after he'd chased an ice spirit away from the lake, Ven was whistling to himself as he sharpened his sword, when a barefoot boy ran onto the training field. "Visitor to see you, sir! From Aratay!"

He sheathed the sword and stood. *Who would visit me?*

New arrivals were unusual enough that half the village was gawking out their windows or coming outside to gawk directly as Ven trotted between the houses to greet his visitor. She was walking toward him and singing—the singing part wasn't surprising, given who it was, but the walking was. "Sira!" he called. "You're on the ground!"

"Yes," his sister replied, breaking off her song. "I always said I'd walk on the ground again, once it had an interesting story to sing."

He hurried to embrace her. "But how did you get here?"

"Aren't you happy to see me? I'm happy to see you!"

"Of course I'm happy," he told her. "I'm just also surprised." Sira wasn't the type to trek across all of Aratay, braving its dangers. She'd been content in her canopy, singing in the dawn. "Is Mother okay?" Mother would never have let Sira wander on her own. *She's dead*, he thought, and he tried to control his reaction and keep his breath even, his heart from clenching in his chest, his hands from shaking. *I should have known.* With the dribs and drabs of news that had trickled in from Aratay . . .

"She's fine. Grumpy, though."

He exhaled, feeling as if he could breathe again. "Then why . . ."

"Because Queen Daleina told me you lived. And that the songs were true! They said you were prince of a new land, and I knew you wouldn't have any singers to welcome the dawn or say good night to the sun and so I came, because I knew you'd need me."

He smirked. "Prince?"

"Prince Ven! It rhymes well with many lyrics."

"You came all this way on your own? On foot?"

Beaming at him, Sira nodded, then shook her head. "She wanted to surprise you."

He looked up over Sira's shoulder to see his mother tromping across the flower-filled fields. She had a sword in each hand, unsheathed, and was glaring at him as if this were all somehow his fault. Briefly, he wished he'd stayed in the training yard. "Mother? This *is* a surprise."

His mother reached him, sheathed both swords, and hugged him. "You married a queen, founded a nation, and didn't invite us to any of it."

"Well, um, you were busy." He hugged her awkwardly, her hard leather armor pushing against his, causing his chest piece to dig painfully into his skin. He smothered a wince as she released him.

"And what are you doing? Are you champion to your new queen? Where's your candidate?" She peered over his shoulder as if expecting one to trot into view. Ven glanced beside them and saw several of the village's children were clumped together, whispering, and a few of the adults were watching while pretending to go about their daily tasks. Two new arrivals was exciting news.

"I'm head of her guard."

She snorted. "Do you even *have* champions? Heirs? Have you done anything right here?"

"I didn't die," he pointed out. "And neither did Queen Naelin."

She dismissed that with another snort.

"Mother, you need to tell him how proud you are," Sira said. "She told me. And she's happy to see you." Mother shot her a glare, crossed her arms, then transferred her glare to Ven. Ven wondered which part of everything he'd done she was most upset about, and then he decided it didn't matter.

"Yes, I can tell." To Mother, he said, "Would a blanket apology work?"

Mother snorted again. "You didn't answer my question: does your queen have any champions?"

"Not yet." He ran his fingers through his hair. "Honestly, there have been a few details to work out. Housing people. Feeding people. Building cool castles."

Sira looked admiringly at the odd red-rock towers that framed the view. "I like them."

"Then I'm her first champion," Mother said decidedly. "You were right, Sira. He does need us. Come on, boy, show us to our quarters. Your queen did make guest quarters, didn't she? She can make us a permanent home later. There's work to be done first."

Ven didn't have any answer to any of that, except to nod.

"And, Ven."

"Yes, Mother?"

"I am proud."

ON HER RETURN TO SEMO, ARIN WENT STRAIGHT TO THE THRONE room. She was announced, and the castle guards opened the great doors for her, then shut them behind her.

"Your Majesty," Arin said.

Queen Cajara smiled. "I was afraid you wouldn't come back."

Arin grinned at her, basking in her smile. "Like you could keep me away." She crossed the throne room at a half-run. Laughing, Cajara jumped out of her throne and hugged her.

"Guess what? My parents came with me!" Arin said. "They're settling into their rooms now, but they want to meet you."

She saw Cajara's pale eyes cloud with worry.

"They'll love you," Arin reassured her.

"The Semoians don't love me," Cajara said, pulling back and sinking into the throne again. She looked small in it. Carved from marble, it could have easily fit two or three queens. Checking to be sure there were no fussy courtiers lurking in any corners, Arin plopped onto the throne next to her. Together, they fit nicely.

"Tell me everything," Arin said.

Cajara made a face. "It's the dukes. Or barons. Or I don't know. I can't tell which is which, and I think the castle seneschal has been lying to me about who's who because she wants me to embarrass myself."

"So we'll find a new seneschal," Arin said. "What does Ambassador Hanna say?"

"She says give it time." Cajara sighed. "But I don't think time will help. I can't do this, Arin! They look at me, and they see a little girl. Worse, a little Aratayian girl who doesn't know their land, their people, or their customs."

It was the longest speech Arin had ever heard Cajara say, which said a lot for how worried the new queen was. She squeezed Cajara's hand. "Then we change their customs. Start with this: you don't need them to love you. You don't even need them to like you. You just need to be their queen, and that means keeping them safe from spirits, right?"

Cajara nodded slowly.

"So you take care of the spirits. Let Ambassador Hanna deal with the dukes and barons and so forth. You don't need to meet with everyone all the time. Ask her to help."

"Do you . . . do you think she will?"

"I think—"

But Arin didn't get a chance to finish her thought. The throne-room doors slammed open, and Arin leapt off the throne. She scooted to the side as Cajara sat up stiffly—Arin quickly reached over and straightened Cajara's crown, which had slipped askew.

A guard boomed, "The duke of Pellian!"

A man in a fur-trimmed robe stomped into the throne room. "Your Majesty, I demand to know why your spirits didn't fix the North Bridge before beginning on the Southern Crossroad. It's inexcusable that the bridge to *my* region should be neglected when trade from the Pellian Mountains comprises half of all trade in Arkon, a fact that you should know by now, if you cared at all about our country—"

As Cajara shrank back farther and farther into her throne, Arin wanted to yell at the man to make him stop shouting at her. But then she had a better idea.

Reaching into her pocket, Arin stepped forward. And blew a puff of powder in his face.

He collapsed to the floor, asleep.

"Arin!" Cajara half yelped, half whispered.

"Tell the spirits to fix the bridge," Arin suggested. "We'll wake him when it's done." She crossed the throne room and poked her head out the door. "Could you please ask Ambassador Hanna to come to the throne room? And don't admit anyone else, especially the seneschal, per order of your queen." She then returned to Cajara, who looked as if she couldn't decide whether to wring her hands or burst out laughing.

"If all it will take is time," Arin said firmly, in a tone she'd learned from Daleina, "then we'll buy time."

Cajara settled on laughing, quietly, with tears pricking her eyes. Looking at the snoring man flopped on the very ornate mosaic throne-room floor, Arin started laughing too.

They were still giggling when Ambassador Hanna rolled into the throne room. She stopped just shy of the sleeping duke's feet. "Do I even want to know?" she asked mildly.

Cajara swallowed her laughter and wiped her eyes. "Arin was just reminding me that I'm here to be queen." She began to look pale and frightened again as worry crept into her voice, and Arin reached out and took her hand. "Have I . . . Do you think we made things worse?"

Hanna snorted, then peered down at the man. "He's the one who's been going on and on to everyone about how you haven't fixed the North Bridge, isn't he? I assume he came in here ranting and raving?"

Cajara nodded.

"Serves him right then," Hanna said. "He should have asked nicely. Only fools insult queens, even new queens."

Beside her, Arin felt Cajara relax. She squeezed Cajara's hand again, encouraging her. "When he wakes," Cajara asked tentatively, "could you tell him that the North Bridge is fixed?"

"Will it be?"

"The spirits are there now."

A smile spread across Hanna's face. "Clever, girls. Very clever. When he wakes, I'll tell him his queen works miracles. Let him spread that story instead. Perhaps I'll also mention that he should work on his courtly manners."

"Will you . . . will you meet with people like him, for me? Find out what they need?" Cajara asked, her voice still shaky and thin.

"Good idea. There's no need for all your time to be swallowed in meetings," Hanna approved. "I'd be happy to be your go-between."

"And I want to replace the seneschal," Cajara said, sounding braver.

"Excellent." Hanna sounded satisfied. "Never liked her. She let too many people pester you. This is a step forward. You don't need to tolerate people who don't respect you. And you don't need to speak with everyone who has a grievance. You aren't Queen Daleina. You're Queen Cajara, and you'll do things your way."

Glancing at the duke, Hanna added in a pained voice, "Except maybe try *not* to put everyone to sleep."

Arin and Cajara exchanged glances and, heroically, managed not to laugh.

ACROSS RENTHIA, IN THE ICY KINGDOM OF ELHIM, FIRST WHISPERS then rumors trickled in: the queens of Aratay and Semo had tried and failed to kill their spirits, and a new queen, called the

Mother of the Wild, had tamed a piece of the wilderness that lay beyond the borders of the world.

Queen Xiya of Elhim listened to it all, with her beloved daughter beside her.

"Mother, is it possible? Can the untameable be tamed?" her daughter asked.

"Of course not, Kaeda. It's only a story, a fable to instruct or entertain. You must concentrate on your studies and not be distracted by nonsense." She then smiled at her daughter. "Now, show me what you've made."

Cupping her hands together, Kaeda held up a rose made of ice.

Caught in its heart was a tiny spirit.

"Very nice," Xiya approved.

As Kaeda beamed at her creation, she seemed to have forgotten all about the nonsensical rumors. But Xiya couldn't forget. She woke in the night, wondering at what the truth was.

Rising, the queen of Elhim wrapped a robe around her shoulders and crossed to a bay of windows. Looking out the frost-laced windows of her ice palace, she wondered what lay beyond *her* borders, beyond the glaciers. She wondered if perhaps she should find out.

In Chell, Queen Gada heard the rumors and believed them, especially the part about the queen of Aratay and the queen of Semo joining forces, however briefly. *That* was the kind of rumor she worried about.

As she dismissed the anxious messenger, she weighed her options:

Do nothing.

Send an envoy.

Send an army.

*Or perhaps a little of all three.* Gada prepared envoys to congratulate the current queen of Aratay on retaining her throne, the new queen of Semo on gaining her throne, and the new queen of . . . whatever the new land was called . . . on whatever it was she did.

She then quietly readied her army.

Just in case.

And then she waited.

WORD DID NOT REACH THE ISLANDS OF BELENE AT ALL.

And it wouldn't, until Garnah reached those storm-battered shores. But that would not be for many months, and Garnah would be careful whom she told.

PANTING, WITH HER SKIRT HITCHED UP, DALEINA CLIMBED THE stairs to the Chamber of the Queen's Champions. She stopped at the top, smoothed her skirt, and made a mental note to make a second chamber of champions much lower down in the palace, as soon as all the vital repairs elsewhere in Aratay were done. *Which may be never*, Daleina thought cheerfully. There was always another bridge that needed to be fixed, school that had to be built, and village that wanted to expand—and that in and of itself was amazing.

It was nice to be needed for tasks that didn't involve preventing imminent death.

Given all that had happened, it was extraordinary that there were people in Aratay left to want bridges and schools and villages, and spirits left to built them. *It could have so easily happened differently*, she thought. She could have failed to stop Merecot, and everyone down to the very last man, woman, and child could have died. She could have been the last queen of Aratay, and her home could have ceased to exist.

Daleina wasn't going to forget how close she'd come to the death of everything. Lifting her face, she felt the breeze and inhaled the sharp bite of coming cold. It would be winter soon, and she'd had the spirits whipped into a frenzy, growing berries and nuts for the people to store, building warmer shelters for everyone who had lost theirs. She'd kept them so busy that they hadn't had a moment to dwell on their usual anger and hatred. *We survived, spirits and humans, and that is extraordinary.*

She'd spent time after she and Merecot had left the grove wallowing in guilt—she'd been the one to agree to Merecot's plan. She'd abdicated and placed the future of her people at risk. The deaths that had occurred before she'd been able to claim the crown again were on her head, and before she'd wed, she'd led a funeral service in honor of all who had fallen.

But sorrow was an old friend by now, and she welcomed it in, embraced it, and then moved on to the business of being both freshly married and queen. Whatever mistakes she'd made, Aratay still needed her. *Life goes on, and we live with our choices,* she thought, and then smiled at herself, wondering when she'd become sanctimonious inside her own head. *Maybe for my next feat, I'll become a* wise *queen.*

She sat in her throne and waited while her champions huffed up the stairs and filed in to claim their seats in a semicircle around the chamber. Several of them had left behind their armor and wore silver silk that clashed with their scarred faces and muscled arms, but it was nice to see them less battle-weary. All of them still carried weapons, of course—feeling safe didn't mean being foolish. "My champions," she addressed them when they'd all arrived, "please update me on your progress with my future heirs."

Leaning back in her throne, she listened as one by one they made their reports. Several candidates sounded promising, and she asked to meet with them—Belsowik would set up audiences with them in between her other engagements. When they'd finished their reports, the champions went on to discuss the state of Aratay and the spirits, what they'd observed and what they thought the people needed. She listened carefully to all of it, nodding where appropriate, and thanking them all.

*After everything, they still trust me,* Daleina thought.

Unbidden, the old child's chant came into her mind:

*Don't trust the fire, for it will burn you.*
*Don't trust the ice, for it will freeze you.*
*Don't trust the water, for it will drown you.*
*Don't trust the air, for it will choke you.*
*Don't trust the earth, for it will bury you.*
*Don't trust the trees, for they will rip you,*
*rend you, tear you, kill you dead.*

*But they trust me*, Daleina thought. *Both the spirits and the humans. I am still their queen. And I'm not dead yet.*

Queen Daleina of Aratay smiled at her champions and, reaching out to touch the minds of her spirits, allowed the first snow of winter to fall.

THE WOLF HEARD THE HUMANS TALKING AND THOUGHT THEY WERE being silly. They wanted a name for Naelin's new country, and everyone seemed to like the name that the boy Llor had suggested: Renetayn, a mushing together of Bayn's name and Llor's father's.

It wasn't that Bayn was particularly possessive of his name. It was more that the idea of naming a land as if it were your pup was ridiculous. He preferred to think of it merely as *home*. He supposed he'd never fully understand humans.

Trotting away from the thriving new village, Bayn climbed the rocky path to the cave of the Great Mother. He went inside.

The villagers kept the torches lit, but he could have found his way in the dark. He trotted through the tunnel until he reached the chamber with the bier. He sat beside the mossy body. He didn't dwell on memories often—wolves existed in the moment, and he was more wolf now than anything he was before, whatever that was. But he did remember when the Great Mother died. He'd protected her until the end. Just as he'd then protected the young girls who grew to be the first queens. Just as he'd protect the new queen Naelin.

He was aware he was unusually old for a wolf. He was also aware that he'd done well. Contentedly, he curled himself beside the mossy body of his dead goddess.

*She would have been pleased*, he thought.

Even without her, her world lived on.

# Acknowledgments

Being a writer means you spend your days falling in love with imaginary people. (And wolves. Or one wolf in particular. Love you, Bayn.) And then when you finish a book, you have to say goodbye to these people (and wolves) who have lived inside your soul for months.

Saying goodbye is triply hard with a trilogy.

Three* things make this farewell okay:

1. Non-imaginary family and friends who love you.
2. Lots of chocolate.
3. Readers who welcome your characters into their hearts, minds, and souls.

So I'd like to say thank you to my family and friends who put up with my disappearing into other worlds. And thank you to my wonderful readers (you!) for coming into these worlds with me.

The chocolate doesn't need a thank-you. I already ate it.

But there are more people whom I *do* want to thank: my incredible agent, Andrea Somberg; my fantastic editor, David Pomerico; and my amazing publicist, Caro Perny, as well as Jennifer Brehl, Priyanka Krishnan, Pam Jaffee, Angela Craft, Shawn Nicholls, Amanda Rountree, Virginia Stanley, Chris Connolly, and all the other phenomenal people at HarperCollins who helped bring Renthia to life.

And thank you to my husband and my children. You make this world magical. I love you.

\* Actually, there's a fourth thing, which is to not say goodbye at all! As soon as I finish typing this, I'll be diving back into Renthia to write a stand-alone novel set on the islands of Belene! Sorry, family, but you're going to need to get me more chocolate . . .

# About the Author

S arah Beth Durst is the award-winning author of sixteen fantasy books for adults, teens, and kids, including the Queens of Renthia series; *Drink, Slay, Love*; and *The Stone Girl's Story*. She won an ALA Alex Award and a Mythopoeic Fantasy Award, and has been a finalist for SFWA's Andre Norton Award three times. She is a graduate of Princeton University, where she spent four years studying English, writing about dragons, and wondering what the campus gargoyles would say if they could talk. She lives in Stony Brook, New York, with her husband, her children, and her ill-mannered cat. Visit her at www.sarahbethdurst.com.